Dear Gem

Hope you enjoy
reading it, and thank you
for all the support

Love Adam

Adam Shaw
So, Your Girlfriend's a Vegetarian?

A cooking diary on surviving a year with fussy eaters

Published by

LANTERN TOWER

An Imprint of Melrose Press Limited
St Thomas Place, Ely
Cambridgeshire
CB7 4GG, UK
www.melrosebooks.com

FIRST EDITION

ISBN 978 1 906561 90 1

FSC
Mixed Sources
Product group from well-managed
forests and other controlled sources

Cert no. SGS-COC-2953
www.fsc.org
© 1996 Forest Stewardship Council

Printed and bound in Great Britain by:
CPI Antony Rowe, Chippenham, Wiltshire

Dedications

THIS BOOK WAS BORN on a beach in Brazil. Over the last four years there are several people who have walked that beach with me, and this book is for them.

Above all this book is dedicated to my family. To my mother Mo, who would listen to me and encourage me like no other as I read to her chapter after chapter over the phone at night; to my brother Daniel and to my father Harry; thank you for showing me the joy of writing. I love you all fiercely.

To my army of readers and proofers, thank you for carrying around hundreds of pages of A4 on tubes, buses, subtes, metros, trains and planes and for being honest with what you read. Thank you Kate Macdonald, Siobhan Bright, Coco Maclehose, Avivite Speyer, Martin Brown, Victoria Smalley, Katy Read, Felicia Craddock, Nick Telson and Issie Farmer, also known as KtK, Bb, Whumpy, Koallita, Muffchini, Llita, Read, Fuggie, Telse and Farms.

Finally this book is dedicated to those in my life that inspire me so much but don't quite realise it. Your beauty is the desire you bring out in people to push themselves further than they ever thought possible and your greatness is that you will never fully understand how unique and special you are.

Adam Shaw, London, Summer 2009

JANUARY

Chapter One
January 1st 2008

WHERE THE HELL AM I?

No seriously, where am I?

I turned to my left and let my arm drop to my side and point its way accusingly at the sliver of light making its way through the curtain. You, you're the reason I'm awake. Bastard.

I'm home. How did I get home?

I turned back and lay flat on the bed, the sudden movement causing my hangover to announce itself to the world. 'Good Morning J!' it drummed on my forehead. 'Happy Goddamn New Year, now get up and get me a pint of coffee.' I closed my eyes as if to summon some inner anti-hangover strength and sat up, ready to start the day and the year. Turning to my alarm clock I …

THERE'S A GIRL IN MY BED!!!

WOOOOOOOOOOOOOOOOOOOOOOOOOOOOOOOOOOOOOOOO OOOOOOOOOOOOOOOOOOOOOOOOOOOOOOOOOOOHOOOOOO OOOOOOOOOOOOOOOOOOOOOOOO, A PROPER, REAL LIFE, ACTUAL BREATHING GIRL IN MY BED AND SHE'S hang on, YUP, SHE'S NAKED!!!!!!!!!!!!!!!!!!!!!!!!!

Shit, there's a naked girl in my bed and I have absolutely no idea who she is or how she got here. Did she fall? Is she real?

'Oww!'

Yeah she's real.

'Did you just pinch me?'

I looked away embarrassed. 'Hi, er no, must've been a bad dream.'

Shit shit shit, what do I do, how can I not remember any of this?

1

Typical, I get to have sex and I can't even remember it. What do I say?

'Happy New Year!'

Good one dickwad.

She gathered the duvet around her and half smiled, 'Happy New Year too J.'

She knows my name. Crap. Ok J, you're not this guy. You don't have one night stands with women whose name you don't know. Well, you'd like to have one night stands with women you don't know but you don't. As I said, you're not that guy. C'mon be honest here, maybe she'll find it endearing.

I grimaced and took a deep breath, 'Look, I'm gonna sound like a real shit here, and please believe me when I say I don't normally do this, but what happened? I can't remember a thing, did we … y'know?'

She looked at me face-on and started to laugh, 'Ha, do you really think you were in any state to do anything last night?! No we didn't have sex.'

'Oh ok, that's good' I lied. 'And so you are …?'

She shook her head disapprovingly, 'Jasmine, friend of Mel's. Anything coming back?'

I shook my head, extended my hand and smiled, 'No, but really nice to meet you Jasmine. I think you're the first person I've shaken hands with in my bedroom.'

'Hmm, well do you mind turning around, I'd quite like to get some clothes on.'

'Oh sure.' I turned around and looked at the bald and slightly deflated tree outside of my window. It looked so cold. 'There's a spare dressing-gown on the back of the door if you don't want to put on your clothes from last night. So, what happened and how did we end up in bed together naked?'

I heard her get out of bed and walk softly over to my door. 'You really don't remember, do you? I bumped into Mel in Fabric last night. I must've lost my keys in the club and, you can turn round by

2

the way, I was gutted; I was locked out of my flat, so Mel said I could sleep here as a locksmith would've cost a fortune on New Year's Eve.' I heard her smile, 'Besides, I paid fifty quid for that Soulwax ticket, I love those guys, I didn't want to waste it! Anyway ...' she paused to drink some water from my bedside table, putting the half-full pint glass down on the table with a deep thud '... when I met you and ...' she paused and began nibbling on her fingernail '... what's your other housemate called?'

'Tim.'

'Yeah Tim,' she smiled. 'Anyway you volunteered to give me your bed and sleep on the couch. I would've thought you were being a gentleman but you were so smashed I don't think you knew what you were saying.'

I paused, 'Yeah that sounds like me, but that still doesn't explain what we're both doing here now, naked.'

She looked down at me on the bed, 'Speaking of which, are you not going to put any clothes on? Well, I got under the covers, was really hot so took my clothes off and then you burst in a few hours ago naked, and collapsed on the bed. I tried rolling you off,' she chuckled, 'I tried for quite a while actually but you wouldn't budge so I thought fuck it, I was still hot and I thought you'd be out for ages so I decided to sleep here then just get up before you and go, leave you to it.' She looked at my clock and rolled her eyes. With a glint shining through she added, 'I just didn't think you'd be awake so early.'

She turned round and looked out of the window as I hopped across my room and grabbed the other dressing-gown off of the peg. The grey gown clung to Jasmine's every curve; hell, even hung-over in a man's dressing-gown she was stunning.

'Yeah sorry, I never sleep late when I'm drunk, it's a curse. Mel and Tim can sleep till midday but for me I'm lucky if I make it past nine; it gets pretty dull sometimes.' I reached for the water, 'I'm sorry about walking in here like that Jasmine, I must've gone to the toilet then got confused. I feel really embarrassed now; you've seen me at pretty much my worst.'

She grinned, 'Well then it only gets better; why don't we have some breakfast and start over? What's your cooking like?'

And that's how it all started. We headed into the kitchen in our matching dressing-gowns, I put on a vat of coffee and we didn't stop talking for the next three hours. Now, I'm not one to make quick rash judgments or anything but there's something different about this girl. You'd think some girls wouldn't really want to talk to a guy who was probably still a little bit drunk and had burst in on her naked a few hours earlier but here she was at ease, sitting in a stranger's kitchen, in a stranger's dressing-gown on only a bit of sleep, acting as if she'd been here all her life. I made her Eggy Mash Tatoe, my foolproof hangover cure.

Eggy Mash Tatoe

Ingredients

- Three large King Edward potatoes peeled and cut into very very small pieces
- Four eggs
- Four pork sausages
- Four rashers bacon
- One onion
- Tablespoonful of butter
- Two splashes of milk
- Black pepper

Method

- Boil the potatoes in boiling water for around ten minutes, add a pinch of salt.
- Around the same time put the sausages on to grill and remember to turn them every few minutes.
- When the potatoes are soft to the touch, drain and mash in a pan with a bit of milk, spoonful of butter and a bit of black pepper.
- Cut the bacon into small pieces and fry up with diced onion.
- When the sausages are done, cut up and add to the bacon and

then add the mash.

- Fry the eggs in a little butter and cook sunny side up but only for a few minutes, you want them nice and runny.

- Spoon the mixture onto a plate, place the fried eggs on top and break the yolks so the yolks run all over the potatoes and sausages.

- Serve with fresh coffee and orange juice.

Now, mashed potato at half past nine in the morning doesn't sound like the best hangover cure ever; it sounds like it would make you worse or possibly even kill you but it really works. I felt great after the food, two pints of coffee and a carton of orange juice. I was feeling wide awake but looking back I think that I was either still drunk or it was Jasmine's effect, for we sat chatting away for a couple of hours whilst the rest of my flat slept on and it was the best start to the year I've had in ages. You know how when you wake up on January the first and it's grey and raining, it's cold, you're broke as you spent all your money the night before and it was anticlimactic, again, and you get that awful feeling where you think, God, January first, we've got to start all over again. All I've got to look forward to is at least four months of rain and grey, as if whilst we were asleep someone slipped grey filters over our eyes? Well I didn't have that feeling; I walked out of that kitchen excited to start the year because who knows what could happen, and with whom.

I left Jasmine in the kitchen chatting to Mel and had a shower. Maybe this year will be different because I have started this one with a phone number and caught up in those eleven little digits is a whole world, and a world I want to get to know.

Chapter Two
January 5th 2008

THE DAY AFTER NEW Year's Day I texted Jazz, wondering if she wanted to meet up with me during the week and I guess whatever Mel said did the trick because she agreed and the next day we met for a drink. We had an awesome time and it showed me that New Year's Day wasn't a fluke because once again there was no awkwardness or long pauses or anything, and we just talked on and on until closing time.

The girl is beautiful. She's pretty petite, but with this amazing mane of black curly hair running down her back. It's all I can do not to just reach out and run my fingers through it ...

Her hair matches her eyes, these deep dark brown pools full of light. Some people have quite dead eyes as if there's nothing behind them, but with some other people it's as if in their eyes there's a little man with a flashlight and a big grin, and whenever that person looks at you the flashlights shine.

I think I need to tread carefully though; I mean she is Mel's best friend so it kinda puts pressure on it from the start, whatever may happen. I already sat Mel down and asked her if she'd be ok with me dating Jasmine and she instantly dismissed it and said it was fine, but went kind of quiet. I left her alone for a bit but later that evening she came into my room, flopped on my bed and said, 'To be honest with you I'd love it if the two of you got together, you're both two of my favourite people and if you think there's something there then go for it, you have to, you can't wonder "what if?", and I don't want to be the cause of either of you wondering "what if ...?"' She paused. 'So yes, I'd find it weird if say one of you told me something you didn't want the other to know or needed advice on something, but I'll get over it.'

She shrugged, 'Hurt her and I'll nail your balls to the wall, but then again I'd say the same thing to her.'

I frowned, 'She has balls?'

Mel hit my arm, 'You know what I mean.'

I nodded, 'I promise I won't, and I'll use Tim for my advice; he's a guy anyway, he knows where I'm coming from.'

'Tim!' Mel snorted. 'He's even worse than you! He'd find it easier to wrestle a horse than even talk to a girl!'

I heard a chair scrape from next door as Tim protested, 'I can actually hear you Mel, the door's wide open! Anyway who says I'm no good with advice; I've had my fair share of relationships.'

'No you haven't!' I choked out as Tim came in to sit on my bed. 'Apart from Sarah, have you ever been out with someone for more than two weeks?'

He folded his arms in defence, 'Well, for a start I went out with Sarah for three years so that kinda counts for something and yes, of course I have! What kind of a question is that?'

'Who else have you been out with Tim?'

'Charlotte.'

'Who?' we chorused.

'Charlotte! You know Charlotte J, we went to school with her and we took the same bus every morning. We were together for like eight months at least ... Two weeks, honestly guys.'

I reached across my desk and threw a pen at him, 'You went out with Charlotte when you were eleven. It doesn't count.'

He slammed my duvet in frustration, 'We were very much in love!'

'You weren't in love! It took you two months to hold her goddamn hand! You never went on a single date in eight months and besides, you were eleven, it doesn't count! Did you even kiss her?'

'Of course I kissed her!' He retorted.

'How many times?'

'I don't know,' he said, scrunching his brow. 'Do you always count how many times you kiss a girl?'

'How many times Tim?'

'Twice.'

'You kissed her twice in eight months?'

'Yeah, first time was horrible. Like someone shoving a raw vibrating chicken breast in my mouth. Second time wasn't much better; it was in Chris Wood's cupboard playing spin the bottle. All I can remember was that I couldn't get my arms all the way around her. Still, nice girl.'

'Wow. So what happened to Charlotte?'

Tim turned to Mel, 'She dumped me on the last day of school; part of me always wondered if her friends dared her to go out with me till the last day of term.'

'And this, my dear friend,' Mel asked, her face full of disbelief, 'this fountain of knowledge about my sex, is who you turn to in times of need?"

'Wouldn't have it any other way.'

My flatmates wanted to know everything about my evening with Jazz and so I sat there, with this stupid grin on my face telling them about this great evening, and how I can't stop thinking about her and all of that soppy crap you get at the start of something when you think you're the only person who's ever felt what you're feeling and so on.

'OK, so help me out here, what do I do next? I want to see her tomorrow but that's too soon isn't it? I don't want to do what I normally do and rush in and put her off.'

'Right,' says Tim, clearing his throat and preparing himself to impart some words of wisdom. 'How many times have you seen her?'

'Once, well twice if you include New Year's.'

'So next time you see her is the third time?'

'Mmhhmm.'

'And the third date is normally the time when things move on a bit don't they?'

I shrugged, 'So what are you thinking?'

'Invite her over, cook her dinner.'

'You think? It's not too soon for that?'

'Dude, no offence but your cooking skills are pretty much all you've got going for you; you've already cooked her that mushy crap you always make me eat when I'm hung-over and that stayed down so why not show your cards, cook her something special.'

I turned to Mel, 'What do you think?'

She tilted her head towards Tim, 'Well for once fattie lover's got a point, go for it. Wait a day or two before suggesting it but yeah why not? As Tim said, your cooking's pretty much the only interesting thing about you, so do it soon, before she realises you have no other strings to your bow.'

As usual, all advice from my friends is wrapped up in layer upon layer of piss-taking but they have got a point. I am a pretty good cook but then again I'm passionate about food, and I think the whole reason you have a passion for something is that you're pretty good at it. I love getting stuck in, getting your hands messy and making huge portions of food that use every single frying pan. Put me in a kitchen and I'm like a pig wallowing in mud, chucking burning hot pans into the sink or wielding a knife like some kind of psychotic samurai. I'd love to be a chef but I was a bit too lazy for that. I graduated from uni and in my mind I thought that to be a chef I'd have to peel potatoes for twelve pence an hour for five years, and to be honest I really couldn't be bothered so I went off to an events management company, got on a graduate programme and six months later I'm still there. It's a pretty good job, a lot of fun and I love all that behind the scenes at parties, seeing and chatting to famous people stuff but I just can't see myself doing it in ten years' time. Maybe that's when I should try to run my own restaurant. So, I am pretty passionate about food and Tim's idea of cooking for Jazz was actually a pretty good one. I just hope she goes for it.

Chapter Three
January 7th 2008

I'M STRESSED. JAZZ LOVED the idea but now she's almost here and I've got shed loads to do. Mel and Tim have gone out so I can have the place to myself but, (and I know for a fact Tim did this), they seem to have made as much of a mess of the flat as possible before they left, just to piss me off in their own funny way, cheers guys.

Now, living in London on a graduate wage my flat is about the same size as Tim's interest in feminism, i.e. pretty small. My room is decent, then the kitchen is quite spacious but our lounge is a joke. There are two sofas and a tiny coffee table and that's it, no dining table or anything and no space for one. Herein lies the problem. Do I a) serve dinner in the kitchen which is a bit scabby, not very atmospheric but has a table, or b) serve in the lounge, where we'd have to sit on the couch and have plates on our laps but it's a nicer room, with a CD player and comfortable couches etc., or do I c) serve in my bedroom, where I have a small table and there's a good amount of space but it might seem a bit weird if she turns up and I'm like 'Hey I know this is the third time I've ever seen you but come into my bedroom, wow there's my bed, let me just put these candles on and play some music?'

The sound of the doorbell reverberated around the flat. Wiping my hands on a dishcloth I lit a few candles, put on a CD and opened the door. She looked … Well there are no words, she just looked incredible. Her long black coat was wrapped tightly around her body, accentuating her curves. She smiled at me as the warmth of my flat rushed out to envelop her and I leant in to kiss her cheek.

'Hello you.'

'Hello you.'

She smiled at me again, a big full-frontal smile. One of her front teeth, which is a tiny bit crooked, peered through her full lips. This always happened when she smiled, and I loved it, it was like some sort of prize that I get to see when I make her smile.

She stepped in and followed me up the stairs to the kitchen.

'Erm I'm still cooking,' I turned back towards her, 'you're not hungry just yet are you?' We made our way down the corridor.

'No no, had a late lunch so I'm good to wait a bit.' Walking past my room she noticed the table and two chairs and said, 'Ha, are we eating in your bedroom J?! That's a little presumptuous dontcha think?' as she raised an eyebrow inquisitively at me.

I turned back to her, 'Yeah well it's either there or on our knees in the lounge, and it's pretty hard to rip apart a crab on your knees.'

Jazz paused and turned towards me, 'Crab?'

I raised my eyebrows, 'Huh?'

'We're having crab for dinner?'

'Yup, and I can't find the tools you use to crack them, so we'll just have to use our hands and teeth, that's fine right?'

'Erm.'

'They should be fine, I mean I haven't started cooking them yet, they're still alive in the kitchen.'

'I er,' she stammered, 'yeah ok, well I've never really eaten crab before except in a restaurant, I'm not totally sure what to do.'

'It's easy.' I took her hand, 'Come pick which one you want.'

She swallowed. 'Right.'

I grinned, 'Jazz I'm fucking with you!'

'You're such a little shit!' she screamed as she picked up a pillow and launched it at my head, 'I was thinking I'd have to gnaw at a crab politely for an hour and a half!'

'Yeah, cause it's really easy to nibble on a crab politely,' I laughed as I threw the pillow back.

'I would've done it! And made it look good!'

I pulled her down onto the couch so we were sitting next to each other, I turned towards her and we kissed hard, passionately. Then we kissed again and again and again. Separating from me she flashed the tooth, 'So what are we having then if it's not crab?'

Honey Glazed Figs Wrapped in Prosciutto on a Bed of Rocket and Spinach Leaves

Ingredients
- Six figs
- Six slices of prosciutto
- Six cocktail sticks
- Clear blossom honey
- One handful of spinach leaves
- One handful of rocket leaves
- Balsamic vinegar and olive oil

Method
- Put a few big spoonfuls of honey in a frying pan and cook on a very low heat. Stir it constantly so it doesn't boil or stick to the pan.

- When the honey's hot, put the figs in the pan and just keep rolling them round for a few minutes so that the figs get warm and softish and the honey covers the figs and forms a second skin. Probably take two to three mins.

- Whilst you're doing that mix the spinach and rocket together and put a handful of each on each plate. By adding spinach you play down the taste of the rocket which can get a bit overpowering.

- Mix together the olive oil and balsamic vinegar for the salad dressing, roughly one part balsamic to four parts olive oil.

- Take the figs out, but keep the heat going on the pan. Wrap each fig individually in a slice of prosciutto, and keep it together with a cocktail stick through the middle. Add a bit more honey to the pan and whack the figs back in but only for around twenty seconds each side, you don't want the ham to cook and turn into bacon, you only want it hot.

- Remove the cocktail sticks and place three figs on each plate on top of the leaves, arranged all on top of each other like a triangle; it looks good.

- Decorate the outside of the plate with a spoonful of salad dressing all the way round the rim then serve immediately for the figs get cold quickly.

Griddled Salmon with Chilli, Ginger, Coconut and Lime on Rice Noodles

Ingredients

- Two salmon fillets
- One diced large red onion
- Four diced small spring onions
- One small green chilli, deseeded and diced
- One square inch of raw ginger, peeled and diced
- Either a can of coconut milk or a block of creamed coconut. Milk is better
- Handful of diced mushrooms
- Two limes
- Splash of soy sauce
- A splash of fish sauce
- Two portions rice noodles
- Coriander to garnish

Method

- This one looks and tastes complicated but is ridiculously easy.

- If you have time to do a marinade, do it. Mix up a bit of soy, ginger, chilli and a splash of coconut and pour over the salmon, wrap it in cling film and leave it in the fridge for an hour or so.

- Slice up the ginger, chilli, spring onions and onion and fry in a wok with a bit of soy sauce, juice of half a lime, teaspoon of fish sauce, a spoonful of sugar and some black pepper.

- Wait about five minutes then add the mushrooms.

- Boil up some water in a pan and add the rice noodles, they take about two minutes to cook.

- Now depends on how you like your salmon, but put the fillet in the pan, add some coconut milk, the juice of the rest of the lime and

13

pile all the other ingredients in the pan on top of the salmon, let all the flavours mix.

- I only cook my salmon for about a minute on each side as I like it rare, but if you want to cook it for longer, do, but never for more than five minutes and remember to turn it once.

- Put the cooked rice noodles on the plate, arrange the vegetables on top, then place the salmon on the vegetables. Garnish with half a lime and some chopped coriander, very easy.

We'd already sunk a bottle by the time we finished our salmon. I looked up and noticed that Jazz was twirling the noodles around and around her plate, her brow furrowed.

'You OK?'

'Can I ask you a pretty big favour?' she said nervously.

'Shoot.'

She took a deep breath, 'Well, I know this is kinda sudden and everything and I'd completely understand it if you were to say no, but an old friend of mine is getting married in two weeks and it's at this big castle in the country and I was wondering if you had nothing else to do if you wanted to come with me?' The words were sprinting and leaping out of her mouth by now as she twirled the noodles quicker. 'I'm not going to know many people there and it's gonna be quite posh and "English" and I've lost touch with a lot of the people and I don't think his parents are too keen on me and I don't really know the bride and … Oh God, forget it, it sounds like a nightmare, no I'll go on my own, forget it. This salmon's lovely, really how di—'

I lightly put my hand on hers 'Chill, I'd love to come.'

'Seriously? You'd come? I mean, you wouldn't be bored?'

'Course not, I'd get to spend the day with you, eat and drink for free at a posh wedding and get to show you off; it'll be fun. Plus it'd be cool to meet your friends.'

She looked down, 'Well, they're not really my friends anymore, we all haven't seen each other in a few years and it was a bit of a shock to get the invitation to be honest with you. I guess I'm just worked up as Julian's the first person I know to get married, just a bit weird y'know?'

I nodded, 'Yeah, none of my lot are married yet, although I think a few are getting there. Three or four of my uni mates have been with someone for about four or five years now and I guess you get to the point where you start thinking about it.'

'I think we're far too young to think about it. I mean we're still changing so much, the people we are now is different to the people we were five years ago and the people we will be in five years. How do you know that the person you become or that your partner becomes will still be as lovable?'

I shrugged, 'I guess you don't, that's the gamble you take.'

'But how can you gamble on something like that? I mean how can you agree to spend the rest of your life with someone when you don't know what they're gonna become, or how kids will change them, or if they'll have a mid-life crisis or an affair? How do you know? That's why I'm just a bit freaked out about Julian's wedding.'

I paused. 'My brother came within six months of being married y'know.'

Her eyes widened, 'Really?! What happened? How old was he?'

I rested my elbow on the table, 'Well it's a really long story so I'll save it for another time, but he was with this girl for seven years or so, since his second year of uni. Anyway they got engaged, we all got really excited about the wedding, my brother asked me to be one of the best men …'

'He made you best man? That's sweet.'

'Yeah, anyway, about six months before the date, it all came to a head and they both realised that they'd become friends instead of anything else, and that if after everything they'd been through they were only just friends, was there much point in getting married?'

'Shit, so they called it off?'

'Yeah, had to cancel everything …' I tailed off.

Jazz twirled up the last of her noodles and pushed her fork towards my mouth. 'Are they still friends?'

I nodded through the noodles, 'In principle yeah, I guess. They chat every once in a while but she couldn't really hack the London lifestyle, like she used to get the odd panic attack and stuff so she's moved to Leeds and works in a small office and is pretty happy. Thing is she's with someone, they live together, and my brother's been on his own since it happened about eighteen months ago, so I think it's pretty tough on him.'

'He's called Matt right?'

I nodded, 'Yeah, we're close but he's just not really the kinda person who opens up to many people. He's a very logical, straightforward person; Jess is out of his life so there's no point talking about it but it must still hurt I guess ...'

A brief pause flooded the table as we both felt a tinge of awkwardness.

Jazz broke the silence, 'So, do you think that the first time I come over we end up talking about break-ups and the fear of marriage is a good sign for me and you?!'

I laughed, 'I feel like I've known you for longer than eleven days though! It's weird how we're both so close with Mel but never met previously. I mean I lived with her at uni for three years and never heard you mentioned once. You never came to visit did you?'

'Well Bristol is a bit of a trek to Nottingham.'

'No it's not,' I protested, 'I used to go there for weekends, it's only a few hours!'

'Well, I had a bit of an interesting uni experience. It got pretty intense for me and I didn't really leave, it became my world. Mel and I just saw each other in the holidays.'

'How'd you mean intense?'

'Well I was with this guy for a few years and we had a few problems and it ended quite messily.' She studied her fingers before looking up at me, the flicker of the candles danced in her eyes. 'I kind of alienated myself from home people as I was in Bristol all the time which meant that when it ended I didn't really have any real friends to turn to as a lot of uni people sided with him. I think that's why me and Mel are so close; when I came back to London I got back in touch with a lot of school friends as I didn't really have any others, to be honest. How sad do I sound?'

I nodded my head sarcastically, 'Yeah, real pathetic. I can't imagine you not really having friends. How come it ended then?'

She grimaced, 'Can I save that for another day? I don't want it to ruin tonight.'

'Course.' I held my hands up, 'You don't have to tell me at all if you don't want to. I have a habit of just asking questions until somebody asks me to stop.'

She smiled and got to her feet, 'Shall we go sit in the lounge? I'm tired of sitting on these chairs, they're pretty hard.'

I downed the remnants of my glass, 'Sure, I'll go open another bottle; I'm pretty full so shall we hold on dessert?'

'God yeah, I'm stuffed.'

Sexual tension is such a strange thing. One moment, one look or little smile and the whole atmosphere changes. The air feels heavy, like you could almost reach out and pluck at it and all these background noises appear, or maybe that's just the blood rushing around your head and your heart beating quicker. But, as soon as I walked back into that lounge and saw Jazz sat on the couch everything changed.

I put the wine on the table, not even bothering to pour out two glasses. I crossed over to where she was sitting, knelt down on the carpet and kissed her. A long deep kiss full of thick red wine and the promise of the night that lay before us. She arched her neck to me to kiss me deeper, putting her arms around my neck, letting a small moan escape her lips.

I think my favourite thing about the first time you're with someone, is the way that it all takes such a long time, how it's all such a discovery. We're all guilty of it when you've been with someone for a long time; you're lying in bed, start kissing, hands reach for the usual places, you both undress and before long you're having sex and it's not satisfying. But for me, the build-up is what really matters. You've just been given this completely new body to explore, so why dive straight into the sex? It's so much fun to spend ages just kissing, keeping clothes on for a while, removing them slowly bit by bit.

So that's just what we did; for hours it seemed like we were kissing, biting, touching lips, necks, backs, keeping most of our clothes on. Then she began to undo my shirt, sliding her fingers across my stomach, making it spasm as I tucked my left hand around her back and undid her bra.

She pulled away. 'Did you just do that with one hand?'

'Maybe.'

'Impressive! Did you used to practise with your Mum's bras around a chair when you were a kid? Every boy did that right?'

I pushed her lightly, 'Jazz! I'm not answering that question! Come here.'

'Nup, you did didn't you, you're blushing!'

'I'm not answering that question!' I protested. 'Come on, come back.'

'Not until you admit to practising taking your Mum's bras off chairs! I hope you were a gentleman and at least bought the chair dinner. So, did you?'

She began pinching my chest.

'Stop it, stop it, yes I did ok! And it wasn't a chair anyway.'

'What was it, a teddy bear?'

I looked down at the carpet sheepishly.

'You dressed your teddy in a bra and practised taking it off! That's so adorable, if a little weird. Did you ever get caught?'

I pushed her back gently, 'Jazz, talking about my Mum's bras and what I got up to as a kid is kinda killing the mood y'know? Besides it was a big panda, not some sort of little teddy bear.'

Her eyes widened, 'Your first sexual experience was with a big panda, wow. Were they double or triple clasps?'

'Jazz!'

'Soooo sensitive aren't we! Girls used to practise with rulers y'know?'

I raised an eyebrow, 'What?'

'Doesn't matter.'

We kissed again and again and started peeling off each other's clothes until soon enough we were in our underwear.

'You are so beautiful, do you know that?'

She kissed my nose and gave a little laugh, 'Thanks hun, but from the looks of things I don't think your brain is in control of your thoughts right now so I'll take that with a pinch of salt!'

I gave her a little shove, 'Jazz I mean it, really.'

'I know you do; sorry I'm just being annoying and making silly jokes. Sorry, maybe I'm nervous, I dunno.'

We were now completely naked, a mix of intertwined limbs moving together, hands roaming. I moved on top of her and began to kiss my way down her body and work myself towards her inner thigh. Jazz closed her eyes and pushed her head back into the couch's armrest as she began her slow journey towards climax. I reached up to hold her hand and she gripped it tightly, moving it to cover her breast as she reached down with her other hand and started toying with my hair, gently pushing down on my head. After a while, following her lead I began to move quicker as Jazz began to moan. Her body shuddered as she was hit by wave after wave until finally she looked at me and smiled, her eyes all glazed.

'Mmmm, ok I'm gonna go to sleep now I think.'

I lightly bit on the soft skin of her inner thigh, 'No you're damn well not!'

'Yeah I think so.' She pushed me away with her feet, 'You should probably get on with that washing up anyway.'

I grabbed her ankles, 'So this early on in our relationship and I'm your bitch already, great.'

'Yeah you are, I've always wanted a boyfriend for a bitch, I think it'd be fun.'

I stopped and looked up at her, 'You just called me your boyfriend.'

She paused and smiled, 'I guess I did. It felt good.'

'Yeah?'

'Yeah, J.'

'Mm?'

She extended her hand towards me, 'We're nowhere near done.'

'No we're not, not by a long way.'

I moved on top of Jazz, gripping onto the couch and began to kiss her. She wrapped her legs tightly around me, pulling me closer as she dug her nails into my back.

'Are. You sure. That Mel and Tim. Won't be home soon?'

'Positive, they've gone to the cinema, an hour more at least.'

'Good. Could be. Quite awkward. With Mel.'

Legs and hands flew as we moved together on the couch. I pressed down hard on her and kissed her deeply, her hands reaching for mine and squeezing them hard. We swapped and Jazz climbed on top of me, pushing her hands down on my chest and bringing her lips hard down on mine. Moving to a new rhythm she twisted her hips and moved from side to side, quicker and quicker. As we both came together she bit my lower lip hard before collapsing limply on top of me.

For a few minutes neither of us spoke. We just lay in silence, getting our breath back and feeling each other's hearts beating against skin.

I don't know why but I suddenly started to laugh, which made Jazz laugh.

'Stop it, you're gonna make me cry! Stop!' She started pinching my sides again which only made me laugh more as I'm VERY ticklish there, which made her laugh more.

I pushed her shoulder gently, 'OK, where are you ticklish?'

'Aahh that'll be telling, you'll just have to find it.'

I started running my fingers over her skin and she remained tight-lipped.

'Nup. Not even close, soooo cold. Speaking of which, I'm freezing, can we get into bed?'

'Yeah sure, you go on in, I've got an idea.' I kissed her lightly and walked off butt-naked into my kitchen.

Tiramisu

Ingredients

- 200g mascarpone cheese
- 200g crème fraiche
- Two egg yolks
- Four tablespoons sugar
- Half a pint of very strong freshly brewed coffee
- Two shots minimum of dark rum (more if you want to make it stronger)
- One pack sponge fingers
- A few drops of vanilla essence
- Cocoa powder to dust

Method

- Mix the crème fraiche with the sugar, mascarpone cheese, vanilla essence and egg yolks until it's mixed to a smooth consistency.

- Arrange the sponge fingers end to end in the base of a big salad bowl.

- Mix the hot coffee with the rum and pour half over the sponge fingers in the bowl, ensuring all the fingers are touched by the liquor.

- Spoon out half the creamy mixture over the sponge fingers so that all the fingers are equally coated.

- Sprinkle with cocoa powder.

- Place the remaining sponge fingers on top of the mixture, creating a two tier effect.

- Cover with the last of the coffee and cream mixture.

- Sprinkle with cocoa powder, cover with clingfilm and refrigerate for at least two hours.

Jazz was already in bed when I walked in with the bowl of tiramisu, two spoons and the bottle of wine.

'You read my mind! I'm hungry all of a sudden!'

I opened the bottle and poured out two glasses, 'Yeah me too, odd that.'

Jazz and I had sex twice more that night, in between polishing off another bottle of wine and a bowl of tiramisu. When sleep came it was one of the most contented I've had in a long time.

Chapter Four
January 8th 2008

I AWOKE THE NEXT morning feeling pretty happy. Looking across I saw that Jazz was still fast asleep, with the duvet wrapped tightly round her and nestling under her chin. I lay there for a while, just thinking things through and letting some of the stuff we'd been talking about and doing sink in. I think there's a hell of a lot to Jazz that I've got no idea about. She really intrigues me; I want to know everything about her. I found myself wondering about what it was she didn't want to talk about last night. What was this intense time at university?

I love where this could be heading. I haven't met anyone I've been so into in a while now. I'm quite a picky person when it comes to women, which I know is also a defence for not getting much action but Jazz is pretty much ticking all my boxes right now. My last serious relationship ended a few months ago and nothing really that special has happened in between. I was single during my last year at uni, which was something I think I really needed to do for myself as I'd been in relationships on and off since I was fifteen. When I left uni and started work I met Charlie, who worked in PR in an office opposite from me. We lived really close and would always end up on the same train to work, walking down the same streets to almost the same places. We got chatting, got on, went out for a drink and it all happened from there. It lasted for about three months before I broke it off. We were practically living together all of a sudden, working next door to each other, spending lunch hours together etc., and in the end I just found it too suffocating. I find in relationships that I really need my own space otherwise I feel like I'm shut in a cage and I get very moody. I wasn't getting space with Charlie and I'd begin snapping when she hadn't done anything wrong. Neither of us was having any fun and so after a week of constant fighting I called it off, and I think she was quite relieved too.

Jazz seems different. I can't quite explain what it is yet but there's something definitely different about her. It sounds really corny to say it's the fire in her eyes but I think it may be something like that. I get the impression that if you hurt Jazz you're screwed, maybe never forgiven. If she lets you in then I think there's this passionate desire to be with you. I don't mean that just sexually, I mean I think she doesn't trust people easily so if she does, she wants you to know that you're one of the special people. That's why I think she's not that forgiving as it's a big thing for her to let someone in; if they abuse that trust they're done for.

I glanced over again; she seemed to be in a pretty deep sleep. I pulled out a few strands of hair that had got caught in her mouth and eased my way gently out of bed. I could hear my housemates making noise in the kitchen and the smell of freshly brewed coffee was wafting under my door.

'Morning.'

'You little shit, you had sex on our couch last night, that's rude!' exclaimed Mel as she put down a mug of coffee heavily in front of me, spilling some of it onto the wooden table.

'No I didn't!' I protested. 'We stayed in my room all evening.'

'Tim?' Mel raised her eyebrow at Tim who turned from the stove where he was frying an egg.

'OK, we put it to you, Mr Jonathan Camfield, that on the evening of January 7th you and Miss Jasmine … erm, Jasmine …'

'Loyland'

'Jasmine Loyland, did consummate your relationship on our sacred couch, part of this family since the great Ikea sale of 2005. How do you plead?'

'Not guilty of course.'

'You little fibber Camfield,' hissed Mel.

'Quiet in the court. Would the defendant please acknowledge exhibit A.'

Tim gestured through the door towards the couch where two red pillows lay exhausted on the floor.

'We had a pillow fight.'

'Sure.'

'We did!'

'Will the defendant please acknowledge exhibit B, two recently lit burnt-down candles. I thought you said you stayed in your room?'

'We did, well for most the night. We came in the lounge for dessert; no sex was involved I promise.'

Tim gestured back towards the couch, 'Will the defendant please acknowledge the final exhibit?'

Jasmine's tiny black thong lay rolled up on the floor by the armrest.

I sighed, 'Ah.'

'Not only did you have sex on our couch, you then lied about it! How am I supposed to sit on that couch tonight, knowing what two of my friends did on it the night before?!'

'Sorry Mel, I guess we just got a bit carried away ...'

Mel turned away in mock anger.

'So, evening went well I take it?' Tim looked over from the stove and winked.

'I had a fantastic evening. I'm completely crazy about her,' I grinned.

I saw a smile pass between Tim and Mel.

'That's great, really great.'

'Thanks for clearing out last night; what film did you see?'

'Ah it was amaaaaazing, we went to see "Made of Honour", it was really really good wasn't it?' Mel grinned and looked up at Tim.

Tim shot me an evil look behind Mel's back, 'Sure was, and only over two hours long! I just didn't want it to end!' Tim muttered something under his breath and turned back to his egg.

'Well I'm glad you had a good time too.'

He spun back around and shook his head, 'Good time? I'd rather nail my hand to the wall than sit through a film like that again.' He pointed the spatula towards me threateningly, 'You owe me bud, big time.'

'Tim!' Mel squeaked. 'You said you liked it!'

'Only because you did, I didn't want to upset you. Although the amount of times you cried during the film I don't think you could have got more upset.'

I sat at the table and sipped from my coffee. 'What was so bad about it?'

Tim was really angry now. 'What was so bad about it? What was so bad about it? I don't know, maybe the mind-numbingly dull plot and dialogue. Ooh here's a girl and here's a guy, they love each other but she loves someone else, then they hate each other, but now they love each other, but oh no wait now they hate each other again before finally loving each other again. Quelle fucking surprise. Jeez, an autistic prawn could've written a more challenging plot. Sorry Mel, but that was the biggest chick flick I've ever seen.'

Mel smiled to the ceiling, 'It was beautiful I thought, the way he won't give up on her and tries to win her back when he's done wrong, so romantic.'

I looked to Tim, 'Oh God, I'm sorry dude, I'll make it up to you, how about a pint tonight?'

He shook his head, 'Make it tomorrow, I'm working late. Shit, my eggs.'

I bent down and was just getting stuff out of the fridge to make a killer fry-up for me and Jazz when I felt her hands round my waist.

'Morning.'

'Morning.'

I turned round and kissed her on the lips. She was wearing my dressing-gown, her eyelids still puffy from sleep. 'Sleep ok?'

'Mmmmm great, you?'

'Yeah, really, really well. Do you want some breakfast? How about a fry-up?'

She smiled, 'Sounds perfect.'

So whilst Mel, Tim and Jazz sat at the table I made a fry-up for the two of us.

Breakfast – Fry-Up

Ingredients

- Four eggs
- Four rashers of bacon
- Four sausages
- One tomato
- Ten to twelve mushrooms
- As much bread/toast as you want, at least two slices per person
- A splash of milk
- Oregano/Salt/Black pepper to season
- A splash of soy sauce

Method

- Put the sausages under the grill as they take the longest. Remember to turn them every few minutes.

- When the sausages are about halfway done, probably after about seven to eight minutes, cook up the bacon with a splash of soy sauce. Cut a tomato in half and put it in the pan too.

- Crack the eggs and fry them, seasoning with black pepper and a sprinkling of oregano.

- Remove the bacon and tomato and put in the mushrooms, adding a generous amount of milk to the pan. The effect this has is that it makes the mushrooms really nice and creamy. The mixture also combines with the leftover juices from the bacon and the soy sauce, turning the creamy mushrooms into a woody brown colour.

- Serve the eggs on a piece of bread each, and layer bacon and sausages on top of the eggs or on its side. Top with the creamy mushrooms.

Chapter Five
January 23rd 2008

THE WEDDING IS IN a few days …

The last few weeks have been good, really good and Jazz and I seem to be getting closer all the time but there's one thing I can't quite shake, one little thing that is just kicking around at the back of my head. I get the impression that there's all this stuff that Jazz just isn't telling me and not knowing it is driving me crazy. For example when we're doing the whole lying in bed talking about deep stuff, she just seems to clam up and immediately turns it round and asks me questions. I think she knows pretty much all there is to know about me, yet I still feel like I'm stumbling in the dark with her. She never tells me about any stupid drunken uni stories, or holidays she's been on; she only ever really talks about her childhood, school or her job. It's like university never happened for her. And now we're about to go to a wedding and she's going to see all her old friends, and I think it's just going to be embarrassing for me that I won't have even heard of a single one of them.

I felt bad about Tim having to go with Mel to see that shitty film a few days ago, so I thought I'd make him some food and we'd go to the pub and catch up, have a bit of man time. He's also having a pretty tough time at work at the moment, not that I understand what he does at all. He works in the city, doing something involving equity and shares. He always tries to explain to me what he does but I just switch off and stare at some spot above his eyes, normally his eyebrows, and nod every few seconds and say stuff like 'Oh right' and 'Ah ok, I get it now'. But there's something about a merger, or a takeover going on at his company and I think Tim has basically got to prove to his new boss that he deserves to stay and shouldn't be fired, so he's quite stressed.

Portabello Mushroom and Stilton Beef Burgers with Caramelised Onions and Salad

Ingredients, makes four burgers. You need to make the burgers at least an hour or so before you want to cook them, to give them a chance to firm up in the fridge.

- 250 grams mince, good stuff, not the twelve pence supermarket brand which has a kilo of fat in it

- One large red onion (only use a quarter or so for the burgers, use the rest for caramelising)

- Two cloves of garlic, diced

- One Portabello mushroom, diced

- Cheese, cut into cubes, about a handful I reckon. Use stilton or if you don't want anything that strong, cheddar will do

- Two egg yolks

- Few sprigs of coriander, diced

- Half a green chilli, diced

- Loads of salt and pepper

- Burger buns

For the onions and salad;

- Rest of the onion

- Couple of teaspoons of sugar

- Couple of handfuls of rocket

- Vine tomatoes

- Avocado

- Cucumber

Burgers take around twenty minutes to grill

Method

- In a big bowl and using your hands mix up the mince, diced onions, cheese, chilli, coriander, mushrooms, egg yolks and salt and pepper until it's all a big mush.

- Pick up a handful and mould it into a hamburger shape. Try and

29

make sure no onion, cheese or mushroom is poking out of the surface, as it'll burn when you cook them.

- Make sure the mixture is compressed and reasonably solid; you don't want it falling apart when you're cooking them. The reason you put the egg yolks in is to hold the mixture together, so if the mixture feels too dry, put another egg yolk in.

- Individually wrap the burgers tightly in clingfilm so they keep their shape, and refrigerate for an hour at least.

- When you want to cook them, grill for around twenty minutes, turning once. If you've made fat burgers, cook for longer until nice and brown.

- Chop up the onions into thin strips, heat with a little oil and the sugar. Keep cooking them for slightly longer than you normally would, about three to four minutes on a very high heat. The sugar will melt and caramelise the onions.

- Mix up the salad and add whichever salad dressing you want. I'd go for a weak one as the burgers are going to be full of flavour. Maybe just a basic olive oil and balsamic dressing.

- Put the burgers in a bun with the onions or you may want to leave the buns out completely, I normally do.

- Serve with a pint.

N.B. These burgers are awesome on a BBQ.

Tim pushed the kitchen door open and slung his suit jacket over the chair. 'Dude, legend. I've had an awful day.' He pulled out a chair, sat and rested his elbows on the table. Picking up the pint he took a long sip. He looked exhausted, poor guy. 'The merger's going ahead and we've just been told that we have to reapply for our jobs. It's fucking ridiculous.'

'What do you mean reapply? What about your contract?'

'No good.' He took off his tie, loosened his collar and leant back in the chair until it was resting on its rear legs. 'The thing is, if we get taken over all contracts have to be redrawn by the new parent company, and before they do that they want to make sure we're worth the paltry money they pay us. It's a big fat mess.'

The burgers were cooking nicely so I poured myself a drink and joined him at the table. 'So what are you actually going to have to do?'

'Work my arse off basically. I've got to show them what I've done for the company over the last eighteen months, how much money I've brought in and how many clients I've attracted. And I've got a fortnight to do it in. It's a huge job.' He ran his fingers through his hair. 'Fuck.'

'You'll be OK though, right? You've brought in your fair share of revenue haven't you?'

'Well, I like to think so but who knows? And I met the new Managing Director today; seems like a complete jackass.'

I shrugged, 'Well maybe this is a sign.'

'Huh?'

'You hate your job, it'll be even worse for you if you have to work for someone you hate, and let's be honest they'll probably catch you pissing in their coffee or something and sack you soon. The effort to reapply probably isn't more than the effort to find a new job. I bet there are loads of banks that need … people of your expertise'.

The burgers were done so I served up and opened another beer for us each.

'I don't work in a bank, I never have. I don't have the relevant qualifications to do so. I work in mergers and acquisitions.'

'Oh right. I get it.' I smiled supportively.

'What did I just say?'

'Erm, something about mergers? Is that the same as a hedge fund?' I paused, 'What is a hedge fund?'

He shook his head, 'Forget it, I'll call you next time I need to organise a dinner party or a trip to the park or something.'

'Hey, I do much more than that!'

Tim almost gagged on his beer. 'No you don't! I've been to one of your events before. All you do is walk around with an earpiece telling people to do what they were already doing! You're a glorified waiter!'

The pub beckoned us after dinner so we packed our darts and headed out the door. Our favourite, "The Freemasons Arms," is about a fifteen minute walk through Chalk Farm and Hampstead and down to the Heath. Being England and being January obviously it was freezing so we both wrapped our trench coats around ourselves, driving our hands into our pockets, pressing them against our bodies, conserving heat. No heat was to be lost through talking either. Tim and I have that kind of male relationship where silence is preferred to random chitchat. We had the whole evening to talk to each other so why bother now?

I'm always impressed at how winter evenings feel. As I said, it was freezing but clear, no chance of rain. Looking up at the sky the stars seemed so much further away than usual, and the enormous full moon projected an almost day-like light onto the frosted-over cars that we walked past. Our breath came out in big handfuls of smoke that were ungraciously parted by our faces walking forward. The feeling of stillness and calmness pervaded, as if under such a sky, under such a moon, all were equal, man, fox, car, building, all were touched by the same air, all treated the same. Even car engines seemed quiet tonight as if the cars themselves were contemplative.

Even though that was the aim of the evening, I felt a slight twinge of disappointment as we pushed open the door and became engulfed by lights, noise, smoke and laughter. The "Freemasons" is one of those arty Gastro pubs that have swept the capital in recent years. An enormous three-sided bar dominates, backed by a huge mirror against which every spirit imaginable is housed. Pisco from Peru, Cachaça from Brazil, Raki from Greece all stand in unopened bottles, a fine layer of dust covers the shoulders of the bottles betraying their infrequent use. A large restaurant covers over half the inside in which plates are precariously balanced on tables due to excessive table decorations and four different types of ground pepper. Through the restaurant lies an enormous three-tier garden littered with benches and shadows in the dark. Giant outside silver heaters stand guard over benches, glowing with pride as customers frequently eye the warm inside, waiting for a space on the sparse couches.

Indoors was full and the dartboard in use so Tim and I found a bench outside on level two, sliding into it with difficulty and instinctively trying to pull the bench towards us as we sat, as if it was a chair.

'Why don't they just put more couches inside, or tables, chairs and stools, there's acres of space in there?' Tim muttered as he lifted the collar of his trenchcoat and sunk his chin down into it.

'Because that's the minimalist fashion Tim, the people on the couches feel all the more important for being on them and we, the plebs out here, want to be like them so we may have the honour of having a couch bestowed on us.'

'But if they packed the inside they'd probably sell more, closer to the bar and everything.'

'I gu—'

'And why have these heaters on? It's fucking January, we shouldn't be sitting outside anyway. If we get used to it now what's the fun of sitting outside in July?'

'So what do you want to do? Go inside and stand?'

'No! I don't want to have to watch those chumps playing darts, I think they're still on the same game they started last week. Couldn't hit a treble twenty if their livers depended on it.'

'What's up Tim?'

He sighed, 'Nothing's up, I just want to throw some arrows. Why do we come here anyway J, it's as pretentious as fuck. I mean look at that guy.'

I half turned round; there was a guy on his own dressed in black staring intently at a group next to him. In his hand was a pencil and on the bench lay a thick pad of ruffled yellowed paper covered in sketches.

I turned back, 'He's always here. So he draws people, so what?'

'Well why does he have to do it here when people just want a drink, and why does he have to dress like a middle-aged Goth just to do it? What does he expect, one of the people he's drawing to suddenly turn round and offer him a hundred thousand pounds for their portrait?'

'Well I don't see the harm, he's got just as much right to be here as—'

'And why the fuck are you choosing some phoney artist over your best mate, why can't you just agree and let it go for once? Jesus.'

I didn't say anything, but looked away from Tim at a group of students sitting in a big circle, engrossed in a dozen different conversations.

'Look I'm sorry J, I'm just not feeling myself lately.'

I grimaced, 'No worries. What's up?'

He half shrugged. 'I don't know, something though.'

'Is it work?'

Tim shook his head, 'Fuck no, you were right, maybe it's a sign anyway. I've got some holiday stored up so I may take it and do some looking around. No, work is a pretty insignificant part of life for me.'

I opened the crisps and laid them out in front of us, 'So what's up?'

He sighed, 'I don't know, I'm just not happy with anything. I feel like I'm going through the motions and I can't see the point of anything. I work to earn money which I spend, and then I come home, hang out with the same people, take two weeks' holiday on a beach somewhere where fat Englishmen get drunk and fight each other, come home and do it all over again for another year. What's the point in it all? Even this, why are we here? We're friends, that's not going to change so why do we need to sit here to prove that? In a few hours we're both going to go back to our own lives and nothing will have changed. I just don't see the fucking point in anything anymore.'

I nodded, recognising my own discontent in Tim. 'How long you been feeling like this?'

'Dunno,' he waved his hands at me, dismissing his moment of openness. 'You know I hate winter, think it's a warmth thing. I'll be fine by spring.'

'Well that's months away, you can't go on feeling like this until then. Is there anything me and Mel can do? You want to go out after work for a few drinks Friday, get everyone together?'

He shook his head and leant in towards me. 'That's the point; I feel like I'm abnormal for not wanting to get hammered every Friday and Saturday. You say to someone you're happy/depressed/bored/ whatever and the reply is always the same, "get pissed mate". Why? Nothing's going to change.'

'It's not the getting drunk though is it? It's meeting new people, making new connections, doing new things; are you saying that doesn't interest you no more? Look at New Year's for example; if we wouldn't have gone out I'd never have met Jazz, would I?'

He smiled, momentarily lifting his mood. 'That was random though, she passed out in your bed and you "supposedly forgot" she was there.' Tim raised his two index fingers as he said the phrase, harking back to his idea that I knew exactly what I was doing on New Year's Eve when I burst in on Jazz. 'Normally, we go out with the same people, have the same chat then go home; it's boring.'

I disagreed. 'But that randomness is what makes life so exciting don't you think? Yeah we went out to do the same thing as we always do, but chance had it I met Jazz and who knows what the consequences of that chance will be? Mate, you take the chance factor out of life and you might as well never get out of bed again.'

'OK but what if it doesn't work out with Jazz, then you're straight back to square one.'

'So what?' I shrugged. 'If it doesn't work out it doesn't work out, but we tried so there's nothing to regret. There's a chance it could work out so I want to see where that leads. If it leads to a brick wall at least we'll both know.'

Tim downed the remnants of his pint and got to his feet. 'I'll snap out of it, don't worry. Same again?'

He left to get another round, leaving me to think about what he'd said. Was he depressed as in properly depressed, not just a bit low? He seemed willing to give up, just collapse in a heap and wait to see if anyone cared enough to pick him up. Mel was a trainee doctor;

maybe I should ask her for advice or maybe she knew someone he could talk to. Thing is, if he is depressed what can we do? My Mum was depressed a lot when I was a kid and it's the hardest thing to take, because all you want to do is take them by the shoulders and shake them and shout, 'C'mon snap out of it, there's a whole world out there.' But they don't respond to that, it's like they're wearing blinkers and all they can see is their depression which just makes them worse and worse. I used to come home from school and find my Mum still in bed, just unable to get up, open the curtains, do anything at all even though it was a beautiful day and there was so much to do. Yet if you just leave them, (a) they don't get any better and (b) you grow to resent them.

'Camfield! Get here now.' Tim's voice boomed into the garden. Seeing the dartboard was free I picked up our darts and moved inside.

'They didn't have any lime left and seeing as you're a Mexico lover I didn't think you'd still want a Corona so I got you a Stella.' Tim smiled and ruffled my hair, code for whatever we'd spoken about should be left outside and not mentioned again unless by him. He's so goddamn frustrating.

We hit a few warm-up shots before diddling to see who throws first. The conversation became stagnated as we took it in turns to throw our darts, drink our beer and chat.

'So tell me about this wedding next weekend. Who does she know, bride or groom?'

'Groom' I replied, 'she's never met the bride before.'

'Really? And she's going to their wedding?'

Tim left the unspoken hanging in the air.

'I know it's weird. The guy is from uni and she hasn't seen him or the rest of her mates in a while.'

'Think he's an ex?'

I nodded, 'There's something there.'

'You OK 'bout that?'

I nodded, 'Yeah. Well, I'm not sure he's an ex, I haven't asked.

She's just so unforthcoming about that point in her life.'

'But what if he is? You're going to his wedding with his ex-girl-friend, and it's not as if you know her that well.'

'Yeah it'll be weird, but you should have seen her when she asked me. She got so nervous and flustered that I had to say yes; I'd never seen her like that before. Besides, if she got that worked up she's obviously nervous so shouldn't I help her? Be someone who she can turn to or whatever if it gets too much? Or maybe she wants to show him that she can move on too? I dunno, I just think I have to go. Why,' I asked him, 'would you not?'

Tim put down his dart and took a sip of his bitter. 'No, I think you're doing the right thing, just be wary OK? A lot of people there might not like you just because you're the new boyfriend and you can't handle it if you think people don't like you. Remember, you don't know why they broke up, she might have been the one at fault, so just be careful.'

Chapter Six
January 31st 2008

'Is Julian your ex?'

We were speeding down the M4 and getting ever closer to Bristol. The traffic had been pretty shitty but we were now making good time. Jazz had been quiet and gazing out of the window for most of the journey, occasionally humming along to the radio.

'No,' she murmured to the hard shoulder.

'No? Oh.' Thank God for that I thought.

'Why did you say oh?' she asked.

I flicked my windscreen wipers to clear my screen. 'I just thought he was. You've seemed nervous about this weekend ever since you first asked me to come a few weeks ago.'

'We went through that. I just don't like weddings.' She turned her head back to the window and started looking at the people in the cars on the inside lane.

'So who is he?'

'A friend.'

'Jazz.'

'What?' she snapped.

'C'mon, help me out here. If I get separated from you, I want to know a bit about the people I'm speaking to.'

'Well we won't get separated will we? There's no-one I really want to talk to anyway.'

'Really? So why are we here?'

She sighed and shifted in her seat to face me. 'Fine, I lived next door to Julian in halls, then in a house in the second year. His best mate Andy and I had a fling in freshers' week but it was nothing, totally irrelevant so don't get all alpha male about it. Andy is going out with Laura and has been since final year. We used to be close at uni but haven't seen each other in ages but we do still occasionally email. Apart from that you've got James, Louise, Si, Becca, Claire and Alice; we were all in the same block together.'

'So your ex isn't here?'

'Jesus J, no he isn't.' She turned from the window. 'Can you drop it now? If I want to talk about something I will; I know what you're trying to do.'

'Fine.'

We didn't speak for the next twenty minutes and then only to check on the directions. Jazz ate the sandwiches I'd made the night before for the journey, a simple chicken sandwich with a Moroccan twist.

Lime Marinated Spiced Chicken and Hummus Sandwiches

Ingredients

- Two chicken breasts
- Two limes
- Half a tablespoon each of garam masala, cumin, coriander and turmeric
- One pot of hummus
- Paprika
- Few long lettuce leaves: hearts of romaine or cos
- Couple of inches of cucumber

Method

- Squeeze both limes into a pan and heat gently on their own, i.e. no oil or butter.
- Dice the chicken then cook in the lime on a high heat for a few minutes, add the spices.
- Get your bread out, roll, bap, baguette, whatever you want and instead of butter, smear both sides with a load of hummus. Generously sprinkle loads of paprika over the hummus.

- Place the lettuce and cucumber on top of the hummus then share out the chicken onto the bread, draining any excess juice.

- Eat or allow to cool and refrigerate, but because of the hummus eat within 24 hours.

The castle was enormous, absolutely enormous and rose atop a small hill. The driveway leading up to the castle took about an hour to cross and the building which was recently cleaned by the looks of it, shone brightly in the winter sun. In the breeze the castle flag fluttered strongly. We got out of the car, I locked up and went round to Jasmine's side and rested an arm on her waist. She turned to me.

'I'm sorry, really. I've never snapped at you before and I feel guilty.'

I reached down and gently kissed her cheek. 'Don't worry about it. Let's forget it.'

'K. Oh I know, tell you what, I'll find us some numbers for hotels in town for tonight, don't worry I'll sort it.'

I smiled. 'I've already booked us a place Jazz, a little surprise.'

'Where?!'

I turned towards the castle and smiled. Her eyes widened.

'No!'

'Yeah, we have the whole of the upper west wing to ourselves tonight my lady.'

Jazz squealed and gave a little jump. 'Oh how cool!' She started kissing me. 'Can't we go see the room now …?' She pushed me against the door and kissed me again.

'Well we are early …'

I took Jasmine's hand and we walked towards the entrance, clumsily kissing whilst walking.

'Jasmine? Is that you dear? Jasmine?'

A woman wearing what can only be described as an electric pink coloured snowball came out of the entrance and squinted her eyes up at us. 'Oh Jasmine it is you! Come here dear. Graham!' She turned to her left and shouted. 'Graham, GRAHAM, look who's here.'

Jazz squeezed my hand as if she was in labour then let it drop to her side. 'Mrs Van Cryder, how lovely to see you again! Mr Van Cryder, hello. How are you both? You look lovely Mrs Van Cryder.' By now we had been joined by a man who looked about as healthy as a week-old pint of milk and about as tough. He followed the invisible lead his wife tugged on and came forward, smiling.

'Jasmine, lovely to see you again. How are you?'

'Well thank you Graham, and you? You look very well, really.'

A brief silenced passed over us as we all looked expectantly towards Jasmine.

'Sorry, where are my manners? J this is Mr and Mrs Van Cryder, Julian's parents. This is Jonathan Camfield.'

'Hello,' I extended my hand and cheek, 'Pleasure to meet you both and congratulations!'

'Have you come far Mr Camfield?' Mrs Van Cryder's voice boomed out at a space six inches to the left of my left shoulder.

'Yes well, London. I don't really know if that's far or not. We thought we'd get stuck in traffic but ...'

'Darling you must come and have a coffee with us.' Mrs Van Cryder linked her arm in Jazz's and began walking inside. 'We have so much to catch up on and I'm sure Julian wants to see you.'

'I'll just unpack the car then,' I said to their retreating backs. 'Maybe join you in a minute, where are you going to be?'

No-one answered. The old couple each had an arm around Jasmine's shoulders making it impossible for her to look around. Her left hand hung by her side, clenching and unclenching slowly.

'Ok then!' I shouted after them as I turned back towards my car. This was going to be a long day.

I unloaded the car and headed up to our room, or should I say flat. We were nestled at the top of the west turret, about three floors up a wide, winding staircase carpeted with thick red velvet. We had a lounge with couches and a dining table and the biggest four-poster bed I'd ever seen which burst forth from the wall covering over half the length of the bedroom. The bed was west facing so we wouldn't get woken by the sun, not that that was a factor as the curtains were about as thick as my leg and once shut didn't allow a molecule of light in. There wasn't a checkout time tomorrow as no-one else was booked into the room, so once the wedding was over tonight me and Jazz could shut the door and the curtains to the world and not come out till the following evening. I felt like wearing nothing but a thick white dressing gown for the whole weekend, only leaving the bed to open the door to room service, bringing us champagne and smoked salmon. God I wished she was here right now. I didn't think I could wait till this evening.

I sat on the bed for a few minutes, absently flicking through the twenty or so channels on the TV. I wondered if I should try and go find that awful couple who had abducted my girlfriend. Time was beginning to get tight and I hadn't changed into my suit yet, Jazz wasn't even ready and that was going to take a while. She was doing something weird with her hair, one of those things where they plait it, then spin it round their head twelve times and it miraculously defies gravity and stays in place without so much as a whimper. She's tried to explain it to me, but like when Tim talks about work I try to understand, I really do but I just phase out. Maybe there are things men just shouldn't know, so we're continually amazed at these tricks girls are taught from birth. It's like that magic trick they do with towels when they come out of the shower. Head down, towel round it et voilà, they lift their heads with this complex Egyptian headdress arranged precariously on their heads.

My left leg was vibrating, it was a text from Jazz. *'Hiding in the toilets, I can't get away! Get ready and meet me in recep. In 30mins, sorry! xx hows the bed ;-) xx'*.

Half an hour and I was leaning against the desk in reception, looking at their room service menu. Jazz came bounding over, grabbing me by my lapels and kissing me before I could say anything. 'Look at you!' Her eyes travelled up and down my charcoal suit and lilac shirt.

'Do I look ok?'

'More, much more than ok J. Spin for me.'

I turned on the spot, shaking my hips from side to side. 'So, what's the plan? How was coffee?'

'Awful, I hate that woman I really do, and her husband's just a weak pathetic little man. Eugh.' She shivered at the memory.

'They seem to love you though?!'

She paused for a second to think about her answer, 'Yeah, well they used to visit Jules a lot at uni and I was always hanging around. I guess I was never shy and actually spoke to them so they remember me. Right,' she changed the subject, 'the ceremony is in half an hour; I've got so much to do and you need to move your car to the car park on the other side of the castle and sign it in and everything. I'll meet you outside the entrance to the chapel in twenty-five minutes?'

'So I can't help you get ready or anything? I could scrub your back?'

She kissed my nose. 'Sorry but we have got all weekend, now go.' She slapped my arse.

I put on my whiny voice, 'But Jaaaaaaaaaazz, there's a four-poster bed and eeeeeeverything.'

'And there will be later too. And J if you ever want to see me naked again you'll never use that voice. It doesn't work for you, trust me.'

She winked and turned towards the stairs, 'See you in a bit.'

Y'know, maybe the wedding wasn't going to be that bad. Free food and wine, my beautiful girlfriend in a beautiful dress and magic hair and the promise of an entire weekend of hedonism. Even if she hated Julian's parents Jazz seemed to be in such a better mood now compared to how she'd been in the car. I reparked and spent some time wandering around the grounds, feeling the refreshing crunch of gravel underneath my shoes. Forty minutes had passed and still Jazz hadn't come, but then again nor had the bride so I guess it didn't matter that she was late. The ushers kept asking me to take my seat but there was no way I was going in without her; hell I hadn't even met the groom yet.

Suddenly I saw Jazz rushing out of the castle, trying to run in her heels. She half smiled and took my hand, dragging me into the chapel. 'C'mon, let's find our seats.'

Something was up. 'You ok?'

'Mmhmm. Here we are.'

She wasn't meeting my eye.

The chapel was rammed and we had to edge past a dozen or so people as we made our way to the seats a few rows from the back on the groom's side. No sooner had we sat than we were on our feet again welcoming in the bride. A pageboy came first, aged only about six or seven, dressed in a navy suit and carrying a bunch of purple flowers. The bride followed and as she made her way down the aisle her eyes, already moist with tears, never left the eyes of Julian. The groom stood facing his wife to be, beaming with pride. He was about six feet tall, well built with light straight hair and with a jaw chiselled enough to sharpen a knife on. They took each other's hands and looked at each other full on, their smiles spreading over their faces. I turned to smile at Jazz and take her hand; she shrugged my hand off.

The ceremony started with a few songs and prayers and then the clergyman addressed the congregation. 'Before we move to the official part of the ceremony, Julian has something he would like to say. Julian.' The priest motioned towards Julian who took Hannah's hand in his, and took out a crumpled piece of paper from his pocket with his other hand.

'Ok I'm going to try and do this from memory, but just in case I need a safety net as I'm a little nervous!' The congregation laughed politely.

'Hannah, I just wanted to tell you why I want to spend the rest of my life with you.' He cleared his throat.

I love you,
Not only for what you are,
But for what I am
When I am with you.

So, Your Girlfriend's a Vegetarian?

I love you,
Not only for what
You have made of yourself,
But for what
You are making of me.

I love you
For the part of me
That you bring out;
I love you
For putting your hand
Into my heaped up heart
And passing over
All the foolish, weak things
That you can't help
Dimly seeing there,
And for drawing out
Into the light
All the beautiful belongings
That no-one else had looked
Quite far enough to find.

I love you because you
Are helping me to make
Of the lumber of my life
Not a tavern
But a temple;
Out of the works
Of my every day
Not a reproach
But a song.

I love you
Because you have done
More than any creed
Could have done
To make me good,
And more than any fate
Could have done
To make me happy.

You have done it
Without a touch
Without a word
Without a sign.
You have done it
By being yourself.

There wasn't a dry eye in the house.

I touched Jazz on the small of her back as we made our way out of the chapel. She had been crying non-stop throughout the entire ceremony and still hadn't even really looked at me. It was like we were two strangers randomly sitting next to each other. 'Jazz, you want a tissue?'

She turned to look at me and she held my gaze for several seconds as if looking at me for the first time, her lips slightly parted and her eyes moist with tears.

'I want you to hold me.'

I put my arm around her waist and pulled her close. 'No problem.'

She shrugged my arm off. 'No J, I want you to hold me, I want to feel you, I want to feel how you feel about me.' She took my hand and pulled me outside the chapel.

'What about the reception? Don't you want to say hi to a few people?' She was holding my hand hard, pulling me towards the maze behind the castle. She didn't answer. As soon as we entered the maze and were out of sight from the rest of the guests she began kissing me, hitching her skirt up and reaching for my trousers.

'Whoa Jazz, slow down a minute hun.'

She looked at me with a look I'd never seen before. A look of such intensity that if I'm honest, it intimidated me a little bit.

'Fuck me. Now.'

She unzipped my flies, pulling trousers and boxers to the floor in one swift movement. Jazz put her arms round my neck and lifted herself up and onto me. She closed her eyes and gripped my neck tightly, rapidly rocking herself back and forth and almost pushing us both back into the hedge. I reached around, gripped her arse tightly, feeling her soft skin stretch tight between my fingers and pulled her down hard on to me. She pressed her lips onto mine, biting my lips and forcing her tongue into my mouth as her breathing became quicker. Tightening her arms around my shoulders she moved quicker and quicker and bit my shoulder hard through my shirt. She came quickly, within a few minutes and then abruptly stopped as if it had never happened. I tried to carry on but she moved her hips away from mine. 'We should go back in,' she whispered into my neck.

'What? Not yet. I haven't come.'

'We should go back in.' She lifted herself off of me and pulled her skirt back down. 'C'mon, they'll be sitting down to dinner.' She wandered out of the maze and started heading towards the castle. I pulled up my trousers and ran after her, confused. She turned towards me and smiled. 'So, there's lots of people for you to meet so be on your best behaviour. I saw everyone from a distance but haven't spoken to them yet, quite looking forward to it actually.'

What the fuck was that all about? She'd just gone back to how she'd been acting after her coffee with Julian's parents. As if the last hour just hadn't happened. You know what? I couldn't be bothered to find out why her moods were changing so rapidly. It wasn't the time to start a conversation like that anyway.

As we thought, we were put on a table with the whole of Jazz's friends from Uni. There were ten of us in total, Andy and Laura,

James and Louise, both couples, then Si, Claire, Becca and Alice. They were already seated as we walked over and all gave a collective shout as we came into view.

We made our way round the table, Jazz hugging everyone and me hanging back a bit sheepishly, shaking hands when introduced.

'Jazz where the hell have you been for the last two years? You barely keep in touch with us!' Andy said, putting his arm round her neck and pulling her hard towards him.

'I know, I know, I'm shit. It's really nothing personal y'know, I just … I dunno. Anyway, can we forget about how I'm such a bad person for the evening? How have you been? Both of you?'

Jazz didn't stop talking and laughing for the next three hours and I started to have a really good time too. They were a really good bunch of people and I just enjoyed listening to them reminisce about uni. Jazz seemed back to normal which was cool; she kept catching my eye and smiling or giving my knee a squeeze under the table. I loved seeing her with her friends, laughing about the old times and smiling about what they'd shared. I don't think you can ever really know someone until you see them with their friends. See how they interact and perhaps more importantly, see how their friends care for them.

The conversation turned to us quite a few times, the group hungry for gossip.

'So,' Si, a city trader boomed across the table, 'how long have you guys been together?'

We looked at each other and grimaced slightly, 'Erm, about three weeks!'

'Nothing wrong with that!' Claire chipped in 'How did you meet?'

I half laughed into my champagne and Jazz looked down towards her lap.

'Well, it's a funny story isn't it J?' she turned to me, tilted her head and smiled, indicating I was to be the one to tell it.

'Well, basically we woke up in bed together on January first. I didn't know her name but she seemed nice enough so we gave it a shot.'

Silence reigned at the table. I carried on eating my lamb shanks. 'I'd never met her before but she was locked out of her flat so I guess just needed a bed for the night. You know how she is.'

'You little shit!' Jasmine smacked my upper arm with the back of her hand. 'Make me sound like a hussy, why don't you?! Guys, he's only joking, he's got a pretty weird sense of humour, haven't you?' She turned towards me and ruffled my hair. 'No, basically he lives with a friend from school, we all went out together on New Year's Eve and I needed a place to stay so J offered his bed and slept on the couch. Next thing I know he's getting into bed with me, completely naked and completely unaware I'm even there!'

I nodded, 'It's true, got the best shock of my life when I woke up the next morning to find a naked Jasmine in my bed!'

Andy winked at me, 'Did you peek under the covers?'

'Course he didn't!' Jazz interrupted, 'J's a good guy. You didn't, did you?' She turned to me.

'Course not.' I nodded at Andy behind Jazz's back and we air high-fived.

'Well it may not be the most romantic story but I think it's worthy of a toast.' Claire stood up, 'To J and Jazz, may they be happy together and may we actually see Jazz more than once every few years!'

'Cheers,' chorused the table. Jazz smiled at me and reached for my hand, resting hers loosely on top of mine. I squeezed it gently.

After dessert and speeches and feeling quite drunk, I reached for Jasmine's hand and took her to the dance floor. If you don't include New Year's, when apparently we tried our hand at sambaing, it was the first time Jazz and I had danced together. As we moved together she leant her head against my shoulder; looking down I could see the tiny tooth poking out through her lips.

'How am I doing J? I felt so nervous seeing them all again. I thought they'd hate me.'

I held her close to me, 'You are doing amazingly, you didn't look nervous at all.' I looked down at her. 'They love you, it's obvious they do, I think maybe they just didn't understand why you don't keep in touch. They probably thought it was you that hated them.'

'I'm so glad I came, I feel like after tonight I can call or see them without any grief or anything. Thank you for being here with me, I feel pretty lucky right now.' She leaned up to kiss me and this time we kissed gently, lightly, such a difference from the maze.

'Lucky? Jazz, I'm the lucky one. I'm having a great time and you know what?'

'What?'

I whispered in her ear, 'I'm dancing with the most beautiful woman here and soon enough I'm going to lock her away in a room with me and do all kinds of naughty things to her.'

She pushed me lightly, 'Don't be silly, I look like an idiot with this hair.'

I spun her to the music again, 'Don't be ridiculous, every man on this dance floor is looking at me right now, wishing he was in my place.'

'What about the bride, do you think she's attractive?'

God, why do women ask us these questions?

'Well she's a bride, so she's obviously going to look good on her wedding day, but she's nothing on you. Besides she's blonde, does absolutely nothing for me!'

She grinned, 'Good answer. So those naughty things you mentioned. Feel like making a start quite soon? After the maze I guess you're pretty erm, pent up?' She pressed herself against me, 'Sorry about that by the way!'

'Pent up?! Jazz I'm having problems walking let alone dancing. No, the maze was cool don't get me wrong, I'm all up for sex in random places, I love it, it's just next time can we please finish?!'

'Hey kids do you mind if we cut in …?' Andy and Laura came towards us.

'Hey, no not at all.' I let go of Jasmine's hand and took Laura's, as Jazz did the same with Andy's. She mouthed 'five minutes' at me and turned towards Andy.

So, Your Girlfriend's a Vegetarian?

Laura was an appalling dancer. No really, she was one of those people that confuse dancing with jogging on the spot. I mean really what are we, twenty-four, twenty-five? That's about twelve years' dancing experience; you've got to be able to at least move a little bit in rhythm. I tried to work with it for a few minutes but after two successive elbows in the face I suggested going back to sit down to have another glass of champagne. We made our way back to our table and pulled up two chairs.

'So you and Andy look pretty happy, how long have you been together?'

'Since our final year at uni, just before Christmas, so it's getting on for a couple of years now. We're looking for our first flat together, it's pretty exciting!'

'Any sounds of wedding bells in the distance then?'

She went all coy, 'Well one day I'd like to, let's just see.'

I searched for another question to keep the conversation going. 'So, is Julian the first of you lot to get married then?'

'Yeah, he is, second time around hey! Oh God, shit I'm sorry that sounded so crude.' She lifted her hands to her face, looked away and took a sip of Champagne.

'What do you mean crude?'

She paused and turned back, 'Well it's obvious you're ok with it otherwise you wouldn't be here, I just maybe shouldn't have made a joke out of it. Look J,' she put her hand on my elbow, was she drunk? 'I just want to say, well, from all of us as we were discussing it when you and Jasmine were dancing, we really respect you coming; it can't have been easy, not with Jazz and Jules' past, and that we really hope it works out. She looks so happy with you.'

Big fat alarm bells began ringing in my head. What the hell is she talking about?

'Jazz and Jules' past? What do you mean? I know they were close friends but I'm not the over-protective kinda guy.'

Laura screwed up her face in confusion, 'Oh my actual God. You don't know do you? Oh shit, oh shit shit shit, I thought you did.' She raised her hands to her mouth, 'Look J, forget I said anything.' She got up to leave, her face bright red. I reached up and held her arm, pulling her down into the chair.

'You can't do that Laura; what happened between them?'

'Really J, it's not my place.'

'Laura. Please.'

She took a deep breath. 'Ok. Julian and Jasmine used to date.'

'What?!'

'Yeah, they got together during second year and stayed together for a bit after we graduated.'

'What?! That's like two years! They were together for two years? She lied, she told me he was just a good friend. Why did she lie?' My heart was speeding now. I poured myself some water.

'Yeah, they were together for two years. I thought, well we thought she told you. Are you ok?'

'Well it's a bit of a shock!' I paused. 'But, but y'know what, it doesn't matter does it? It was all before we met and she hasn't seen Julian in a while so ok yeah, she shouldn't have lied but maybe she had her reasons. It explains why she's been so weird today.'

Laura nodded and studied the tablecloth.

'So how did they break up?'

Laura shook her head, 'No really, this isn't my place to say.'

I gripped her hand again as she tried to stand, 'Laura, what happened?'

She sighed, 'Well, towards the end of uni Julian proposed to Jazz.'

I spat my water all over the table. 'What?! Is that why they broke up? How did he take it?'

'Erm …' Laura shifted from side to side and wrung her hands.

'SHE SAID YES?!!!'

'Yeah, she said yes.'

'Oh my God.' I paused. 'Ok, then what happened?'

'Are you sure you want to hear this?'

'Everything Laura.'

She took a deep breath, 'Well, Julian was besotted with her, really really was but you always got the feeling he cared a little more for her than she did for him. Jazz had almost no family, no money and here was Jules offering her a life where she'd be mostly happy and never worry about money again. We all thought that was why she accepted. Anyway, they arranged to be married the Christmas after we graduated. Everything was going well but the day of the wedding arrived and Jazz just bottled it. She got halfway down the aisle, Andy was walking her down as her dad wasn't there obviously and she suddenly stopped, looked at Jules and just said, "I can't do this," turned round and ran out of the chapel, out of the castle, everything.'

'The castle? The wedding was HERE?'

Laura nodded, 'Yeah, and that's the last we saw of her. Julian was a mess, absolutely destroyed for months. It took him ages to get over her. I still don't know if he really has actually, she was the one for him.'

I felt sick, utterly utterly sick. I looked at Laura, her concern for me showing in her eyes.

'I'm sorry you had to find out like this. But what we were saying was that Jazz looks happier with you than we ever thought she did with Jules. Really.' She squeezed my hand.

'Laura, could you give me some time alone to think. And don't tell Jazz you told me; I want to talk to her first.'

'Sure. Sorry again.' Laura pushed back her chair and walked back to our dinner table where Si and James had just lit some cigars.

Fuck.

Fuuuuuuuuuuuuuck.

What the hell do I do?

Why did she not tell me? How could she think it OK to bring me to this wedding and not tell me that if it wasn't for a few seconds she would have been the one to get married here?

I bent my head to the table and ran my fingers through my hair. What the hell do I do? Do I confront her now? Make a scene, help her to ruin a second wedding for Julian? I needed a drink and I needed to be outside alone with my thoughts. I got up, grabbed a half-full bottle of wine from the table next to me and headed for the door.

Obviously I bumped into them.

'Here she is J, all back in good condition.' Andy winked, patted my shoulder and headed off.

'So,' Jazz purred. 'How about checking out the upper west wing?' She reached for my hand. I withdrew it quickly, making her stumble backwards.

'Don't you dare come anywhere near me! Laura told me everything! How could you not tell me Jazz? You lied, you looked me in my eyes and lied. Just, just leave me alone.' I turned and walked outside.

'J wait, WAIT, please.' Jazz was trying to keep up with me but failing. 'I couldn't do it, I tried, really, I just couldn't.'

'I don't want to hear it Jazz. Don't touch me.' I shrugged her hand off, 'I said don't fucking touch me.' She sank to the ground before me as I turned and walked outside.

I opened the door to our suite an hour later. Jazz must've got a key from reception as she was lying face down on the bed when I walked in. She lifted her head to look at me, tear-ridden make-up stained her face. 'J,' she murmured weakly. 'Please, let's not fight.'

I shook my head, 'You invite me to a wedding of a man you were inches away from marrying, don't tell me, actively lie about it, make me sit through an evening with your friends and now you think that because you've been crying and smeared your make-up a bit, it's all ok? No Jazz, it doesn't work that way.'

I sat on the couch in the lounge and poured myself a whisky. She came in and sat on the opposite couch, crying silently. How many more tears did she have to cry?

'I would never have married him.'

'I don't care Jazz.'

'I said yes because I thought it was what I wanted. I knew within a few days that it wasn't and it all just snowballed and I couldn't stop it. I just couldn't.' Her face crumpled and she dissolved into sobs.

'Why didn't you tell me? You didn't tell me anything. When we had dinner and you asked me about coming, when we were driving down this morning. Jazz, you full-out lied to me in the car. Did you really think we'd get through the whole day without me finding out?! Really?'

She shook her head. 'No. But it was easier than telling it to your face.'

I stood up. 'Wait, you actually wanted me to find out this way? From a woman I've never met before drunkenly shouting it into my ear at a wedding? How could you think like that? How can you have such little respect for me?' I walked behind the couch and rested my hands on its back. 'All of them Jazz, every single person there today on Julian's side would have been laughing at me. The next guy, dragged unwittingly to the scene of the crime.'

Her head snapped up. 'And what about me huh? It's not just about you, how do you think I felt today knowing the last time I saw all these people I was in a fucking wedding dress? How do you think I felt seeing his parents this afternoon? Do you think I had fun?'

I moved from the couch and knelt in front of her, taking her shoulders in my hands, 'So why didn't you tell me? If you would've told me this when you first asked me, it would've been a shock but I would've got over it; we all have our pasts and I would've been behind you even more than I was today. I was so proud of you today.' Our eyes held each others, 'But now ...' I stood up. 'I dunno, you lied and I can't get over that.'

She got to her feet so that she was facing me, 'I wanted to show to myself that it meant nothing, that he meant nothing, and that what happened was in the past. If I told you it would've been made into a big deal, when I thought it wasn't.'

'MADE into a big deal, of course I would've MADE it into a big deal, it IS a big deal. You were going to be married here to the guy who just got married!'

She reached over to me and started kissing my face. 'Darling I'm sorry, I didn't want to upset you. I couldn't tell you, it was all too soon. I didn't want to hurt you, please kiss me back, come to bed.'

I felt myself kissing her back, hard, passionately, pushing her up against the wall as she grabbed a chunk of my hair and pulled it hard. We stumbled into the bedroom and fell onto the bed. I pushed her legs open with my hand and she reached for my belt. I stopped.

'Hang on, you said you wanted to prove to yourself he meant nothing. That means … that means he does mean something to you. Part of you still loves him don't you?'

I got up off of the bed and started doing up my shirt.

'No! J, can't we talk about this in the morning? Please!'

'That's why you were so upset during the ceremony wasn't it? You were imagining yourself marrying him weren't you? You were picturing yourself saying those words, imagining yourself embarking on a life with him, probably imagining yourself fucking him right now in the honeymoon suite.'

'J …'

'You were, weren't you? That's why you wanted to have sex straight after the ceremony, isn't it? You didn't care who it was with did you? Anyone would've done, I just so happened to be sitting next to you. Turn you on, did it? Imagining yourself getting married in this castle and never having to work another day in your goddamned life?'

She slapped me hard round the face and pushed my shoulders. 'Don't you ever speak to me like that again! Who do you think you are, who the fuck do you think you are? You've known me for three weeks; you think you have a right to know everything about me and then to talk to me like that as if you know what I'm feeling? You have no fucking idea how hard it's been for me and when you've struggled, if someone offers you an easy way out yes, you consider it sometimes. I wanted you after that ceremony because for the first time since Julian I'm beginning to feel close to someone. I saw how happy he and Hannah are and ok I admit it, I did wonder what things would be like if it was me up there but J, I realised that I would have rather been sitting with you than up there. If I wanted to know what the rest of my life would be like I'd be Mrs Van Cryder, but I'm not. After that ceremony I wanted to be as close to you as I possibly could, to show you how close I feel to you. Sex isn't just always about sex J, but if you're so pigheaded about it then fuck it. Leave.'

She went into the bathroom and I heard the sounds of a bath running. I was so angry, furious. All I could see was her in a wedding dress fucking Julian. I picked up a blanket and pillow, slammed the connecting door and made myself a bed on the couch.

The next morning I awoke to an empty room.

Jazz left me a note saying she'd got a lift into Bristol and was getting a train back to London.

I drove home alone and miserable.

That was two days ago; I haven't heard from Jazz since that night, nor have I tried to get in touch with her.

FEBRUARY

Chapter Seven
February 2nd 2008

'J, THIS WAS JUST what you'd promised never to do, then all of a sudden four weeks later you're doing just that. I feel completely stuck in the middle.'

Mel and I were sitting around the kitchen table, on the Thursday after the wedding, and since our argument on Saturday I hadn't heard a peep out of Jasmine. I'd finally cracked and offered Mel a trade-off between food and advice.

'I know, I know, but I don't know what else to do. Has she been in touch with you this week?'

'Why should it matter if she's been in touch with me? It's between you and her. We've been friends for over ten years; some argument she has with you is not going to stop us talking.'

'So that's a yes then.'

She smiled sarcastically, 'Yes, that's a yes.'

I got up to stir the risotto and turned to face Mel, resting my back against the kitchen work surface. 'I'm sorry, I really am, I hate having to do this to you, I was just so completely shocked by it y'know, and you're the only one that knows her or knew her a few years ago.'

Mel nodded, 'Look, for all her bravado Jazz doesn't do very well with confrontations.' She softened. 'Her instinct is to run away and hide, that's why she left you on Sunday morning. So right now she's scared, upset with herself, upset with you and not sure what to do. I don't want to talk about if what she did was right or wrong, because I really can see it from both sides, especially knowing so much about Jazz as I do, but what I will tell you is that if this is going to go forward, be resolved, whatever, it has to come from you.' She pointed her fingers in my direction. 'She's too scared to get in touch with you as she thinks you'll get angry again and that you've had enough. So, my only advice is if you think that this is worth it, call her; if you don't think it is, don't, but stop checking your phone all the time because I can promise you she isn't going to call you.'

That made sense. 'I guess you're right, I just need to work out what I want to do, and how to do it.'

'Exactly; now hurry up, I'm starving.'

I turned back to the risotto and ladled some more stock in. Mel is a vegetarian so we were having king prawn risotto, a meal that doesn't have too many ingredients as the risotto is quite heavy and creamy and you don't want to overpower it with lots of different tastes and spices.

King Prawn Risotto

Ingredients
- 200g king prawns, de-shelled and washed
- One small red onion, finely chopped
- One bunch of spring onions, cut half into small pieces
- Handful of mushrooms
- One centimetre cubed of creamed coconut
- Three fish stock cubes
- 200g Risotto rice, preferably Arborio
- One green chilli, diced

Method
- Boil up the three fish stocks in about a pint and a half of water and keep the pan simmering throughout.
- Fry the onions, green chilli and half the spring onions in a little butter for a few minutes.
- Add the rice and add a bit more butter, cook for one minute or so, stirring and making sure the rice gets coated in butter.
- Add a ladleful of stock to the pan and stir continuously.
- As the liquid begins to get absorbed add ladle after ladle, stirring constantly.

- After ten minutes or so add the mushrooms.

- Put the piece of creamed coconut into the remnants of the stocks, stir till it dissolves then add ladle by ladle to the mixture.

- After about twenty minutes taste the rice; it should be soft yet slightly chewy. If it isn't done yet, keep adding stock as you don't want it to dry out.

- When you think it's ready add the prawns and stir for a further minute then divide onto two plates.

- Slice lengthways the remainder of the spring onions and arrange on top of the risotto.

I served up and opened some Viognier white wine. As I turned my back Mel dug her fork into my plate, spearing two prawns and eating them in one.

'Oi!'

'Yum yum yum. So what you gonna do, Romeo?'

I resisted the urge to start a food fight. 'I do want to see what happens next.'

Mel smiled. 'Good. Right answer. So get in touch with Jazz. Maybe she should've told you, maybe she shouldn't have,' she shrugged. 'It's the past, move on.'

'At least that way I can stop talking about it all the time, I've been moping around all week talking about her; you must be so bored.'

'We are J,' Tim walked into the kitchen and took my plate and began helping himself to the risotto, 'but that's more because of your general chat, not just this week.'

'It's his face I'm bored with,' chimed in Mel, 'like a hot water bottle full of lumpy custard.'

'Very funny. Tim, I've decided I'm going to get in touch with Jazz.'

'Good, what with that one pissing off home this weekend,' he pointed at Mel with a forked prawn, 'I was getting worried about the man chats you might have wanted to have.'

'That's true.' I turned to Mel. 'Why are you going home again?'

'Parents' anniversary, big family lunch on Saturday. Oooooooooooooooooh, idea …'

'What?'

'Why don't you both come?! Some crazy family time and long walks in the Peak District; perfect!'

Tim and I exchanged looks. 'OK.'

'Buuuuut there are two conditions, J. One, you get in touch with Jazz before we leave, and two, you don't moan about her all weekend.'

'Deal.'

'Gmwan thm.' Tim started gesturing with his hands.

'What are you talking about?'

He swallowed the risotto. 'Ah, hot hot hot!' Tim made a lunge for my beer and drank deeply before running over to the sink and spitting the risotto and beer out.

'Tim, how are you still single?'

'Beer and risotto doesn't work, FYI. Anyway what I wanted to say was, go on then.'

I put on my exasperated voice. 'What?'

'No time like the present; get in touch with Jazz, then you can stop moping and we can start planning an awesome weekend. I'll go pack the powersling.' He ran off down the hall giggling like a schoolgirl.

'What's the powersling?' Mel asked inquisitively.

'Mel! How can you not know what the powersling is? Y'know, the yellow catapult I had at uni …?'

'Oh God,' she pointed towards me, 'if that goes anywhere near my family I will cause you so much pain. I'm a doctor, I know how to hurt you, always remember that.'

Ladies and Gentlemen, what an advert for our new generation of doctors. The catapult was perhaps the best birthday present I have ever received. It was a twenty-first present from my mates at uni and is basically the biggest catapult in the world; it takes three people to hold it and pull it back and when you fire it, it throws whatever's in it about a hundred metres. We used to spend endless summers at university firing water ballons into the park opposite our house.

I calmed Mel down. 'No no no, we'll use it for firing stuff down valleys or into rivers, no people I promise. One or two cows maybe but no people.'

'So you texted her yet?' Tim came back in the kitchen with the powersling slung over his shoulder. He headed over to the sink. *'Just give the little girl a clean.'*

'What are you going to say?' Mel looked at me. 'Be gentle yeah?' I nodded and headed off to the lounge. I flopped on the couch and thought. What do I say? Something light where I say I want to meet up and forget this ever happened …? I'm shit at texts, I really am. There's this whole code that everybody seems to know except me, and no matter what I do I always get it wrong. Like, if I'm not doing anything and I get a text I text back straight away, so I expect the same in return. I hate it when someone takes hours to reply to a text just because it's 'not cool' to reply straight away or in case it shows the other person you've got nothing to do. Why pretend?

Hey Jazz, hope you got back to London OK, be good to meet up if you're around? x

No. something tells me referring to the morning she walked out on me is not a good opening.

Jazz! I've missed you, let's meet up if you still want to? x

Great, a girl with commitment issues and you gush how you've missed her.

Jazz, I'm sorry, let's start over and meet up. x

Whoa there, remember she's more in the wrong than you. Hmmm.

Jazz, I don't want this to be it, let's meet and chat, no arguments. What do you think? x

Perfect. And send.

Chapter Eight
February 4th 2008

TWO DAYS LATER AND we're bombing up the M1 to Buxton, right on the edge of the Peak District and the home of Mel's parents and half-sister Alexia. Tim had called shotgun in Mel's Peugeot so I was sprawled out in the back, dozing off and on, the seat belt my temporary pillow cutting into my face and leaving a line of red across my left cheek.

'Camfield? You nice and warm?' came a voice from the front.

'Mmmmmm.' I nodded and delved deeper into the seat belt.

'OK, go!'

All of a sudden Tim and Mel both began to unwind their windows as Mel inched her right foot down on the accelerator and crept up towards ninety. The freezing February wind slammed into me, knocking all the breath out of my body and pushing me back.

'Noooo!' I shouted. 'Not again! It's freezing, do the windows up!!!'

Mel looked at me in the mirror, 'What's that, J? Can't hear a thing!'

'It's sooooooooooooo cold!'

That lasted for a few minutes before they got tired and wound the windows back up, high fiving with their free hands. Arseholes. Tim turned his iPod back on and connected it to the radio and Big Phil started blaring out of the four speakers.

Now I know this may be a controversial opinion, but the genius that is Phil Collins is fantastic music for road trips. Every song is a hit, every song a singalong from Disney classics to the earlier

Genesis stuff. 'In The Air Tonight' has to be the best though, especially if you're not driving and therefore have your hands free for air guitar and drumming. Tim knew what I was thinking and put the track on, turning the volume up so that the roar of the motorway was drowned away. I waited a few minutes until the drums came in before I started drumming furiously on the back of the passenger seat as he played air guitar and Mel sang.

And I've been waiting for this moment, for aaaaaaaall my liiiife, oh loord, oh lord.

We settled into an easy silence as Big Phil drifted over us. Familiar scenery flew by and I started drifting off, thinking about the dozens of times I'd made the same journey in my car on the M1 between London and Nottingham.

So Jazz texted me back later that night and I think it's all good. She said she didn't want that to be it either and she apologised for running off like that but just needed a bit of space. She's coming over on Sunday night when I'm back and I'm glad it looks like it will be sorted, plus it means I can chill out and enjoy the weekend. Mel's family are great and we all get on really well; her Dad is a retired doctor and has amazing stories and her Mum is Italian, has a very sexy accent and is a fantastic cook. Her grandparents are going to be there as well, which'll be fun because her granddad is actually insane and can be counted on to come out with a few classics.

'Timothy?' Mel shouted over Phil.

'Melissa?'

'Where have your hands been in the last six hours?'

'Do you really want me to answer that?'

She smiled, 'Yes I do.'

'OK, at various intervals up my nose, in my bag, in your bag, I owe you a tenner by the way, in my pants, in my armpits … Why?'

'What have they just done?'

'Well they've just run themselves through my hair.'

'When did you wash your hair?'

'This morning.'

'That'll do, can you feed me a bit of a sandwich please?'

'Sure.'

Brie, Bacon and Cranberry Jam Baguette

Ridiculously easy and incredibly bad for you.

Ingredients

- Good chunk of brie

- Two rashers of bacon per person

- Cranberry jam

- Baguette

If you can, cut into the brie the day before so that on the day you come to make the sandwiches it's all mushy and smelly.

Method

- Heat the baguette for a few minutes so it's soft and warm.

- Smear the inside of the baguette with cranberry jam, then layers of brie, then the bacon, then a bit more jam.

There's really something quite touching about watching one of your best friends ripping chunks off of a baguette and placing it in another of your best friends' mouths.

'Mhmhghm,' spluttered Mel.

'Sorry, did I give you too much? My bad.'

We were now making our way down a narrow B road, the motor-way far behind us and Buxton approaching us quickly. The road wound back and forth on itself, carrying us high over hills and down into valleys and over bridges. We sat in silence, admiring the view, thinking how different it was to the crushed city we'd left two hours previously.

'Jeez, easy Mel.'

'I grew up driving down this road, chill. Look! There's my house, there's my house!'

We turned into the driveway and parked up next to a small country house standing alone from its neighbours, the front and back gardens joining together to create an oasis of green.

'OK remember, parents called Maria and Henry, thirtieth wedding anniversary. And also they still have no idea I smoke. Mum! Daddy! Happy anniversary!' She leaped out of the car and was swallowed up by a family hug.

Chapter Nine
Later that night

SITTING IN MEL'S BACK garden under the stars I thought of a young Mel growing up in this house. She'd told us this afternoon whilst we were walking that when she went through her rebellious teenage stage she used to come down here and sit amongst the trees. It created a kind of adolescent fortress, a place where you couldn't be seen from the house and a place where you could smoke and bring boys without fear of being disturbed.

'We always knew where you were, Melissa,' Maria had told us that evening, 'we are your parents, it is our job.'

Twirling some thick red wine around her glass Mel had asked, 'So why did you never tell me off or bust me?'

'You are your own person; you have to try things for yourself otherwise you can never know for real who you are or what you are made of. Besides, I would much rather my daughter got stoned in my own back garden than at some boy's house when I think she's with a friend. You will learn my dear, one day, trust me,' and with that Maria lent over to kiss her daughter on the cheek.

Mel reached over to hug her Mum and rest an arm on her father's knee. From what Mel had been saying over the last few months, her half-sister Alexia had been causing her parents problems and Mel being there this weekend was a welcome break for them. I'd met Alexia lots of times over the last few years and found her lovely, a real exuberant character but some of the stories Mel came out with were so completely different to the girl I'd met. Stories of self-harm, suicide attempts and class A drugs, all under the family roof, had meant that the last few years or so had aged Mel's parents immeasurably.

Tim looked at me questioningly and motioned towards the door, I nodded and we both began to rise.

'Boys, sit down, please.' Henry looked at us earnestly. 'We know how much you all care for each other and we consider you family, we have no secrets from you, nor do we feel any need to be embarrassed.'

'Besides,' Maria wiped her eyes, 'it's lovely to see both of you again; let's talk about happier things.' And we did. We laughed, drank expensive Italian red wine and played Monopoly and when the last of the fire changed from a glowing orange to a light grey we all went to bed. Well, the others went to bed, I came out here for a bit of air.

Maria and Henry, who seemed as in love with each other as the moment they married, had been dewy-eyed all day because of their anniversary. Maria's father just smiled a lot. As well as private presents they'd decided to give each other presents the whole family could enjoy and Henry was taking them all to see "The Lion King" in London in a few weeks' time, whereas Maria had spent most of the last week preparing the banquet that we had for lunch.

Baked Camembert with Crudités

Ingredients

- One large camembert between around four people or so, so we had two.

- Chopped vegetables, i.e. carrots, cucumbers, radishes etc.

Method

- Bake the camembert for around twenty minutes until the outside is hard but the inside is a gooey mess.

- Cut the top off, and serve with crudités, that's it. As with all good European food the emphasis is on sharing with the family and making a mess.

Roast Chicken with a Paprika, Honey and Mustard Glaze Served with Honey-Dipped Vegetables

Ingredients

- One large chicken for around four people, again we had two. Innards removed and fed to an animal (or Tim).

- Cloves of garlic
- Red onions
- Potatoes
- Sweet potatoes
- Carrots
- Parsnips

For the chicken marinade:

- Dijon mustard
- Honey
- Sprinkling of paprika
- Zest of half an orange and lemon
- Black pepper and rock salt
- Olive oil

Method

- Depends on the size of a bird but it's normally about eighty to ninety minutes' cooking time. Go for twenty minutes' cooking time per 500g plus an extra twenty minutes. Remember the meat also has to relax for ten minutes after coming out the oven, so in your calculations you want to begin cooking the chicken around a hundred minutes or so before you want to serve it.

- Ages before you want to cook your bird, like a few hours if you can but if you're stretched, around half an hour before, you need to cover the chicken with the marinade.

- Remove all the packaging and place the chicken in an oven dish. Going from left to right, diagonally, score the skin and first few millimetres of the meat with a very sharp knife. Once done, go from right to left in reverse, resulting in a diamond shape all across the bird. This helps the flavours sink down into the meat.

- In a bowl mix up a few tablespoons of olive oil, a large teaspoon

70

of mustard, the grated citrus and pepper and salt. Mix it all up then massage the mixture into the bird, taking care to cover the whole area, not just the top.

- Sprinkle generously all over with paprika and leave to chill in the fridge for a few hours if you can.

- Just before you put it in the oven chop up a few more garlic cloves and slice a red onion into quarters and bung it up its arse, for some extra flavour.

- About an hour before you want to serve, chop up the potatoes, parsnips and sweet potatoes. It's an idea to lightly boil the potatoes for ten minutes or so first as they take an age to cook.

- Place potatoes and parsnips, cut at awkward angles to make them crispy, on a baking tray and cover with honey, olive oil, rosemary and oregano. Mix it all up so each vegetable is covered with the mixture.

- About half an hour before you want to serve add the onions and carrots to the tray, once again making sure they are covered with honey so they'll caramelise.

- Every twenty minutes or so you want to be spooning the fat and juices produced by the chicken back over itself to keep it flavoursome and moist.

- When you think the chicken is done, press a knife to its thigh; if clear juices run out, it's cooked. Wrap it in foil and leave for ten minutes so the meat can relax, then serve it all up.

As Mel was a vegetarian her Mum had cooked her something different.

Lemon Scented Seabass

Ingredients
- One seabass fillet
- Two lemons, sliced
- A third of a glass of dry white wine
- Three or four sprigs of parsley
- Pinch of rock salt

Method

- Mix the lemons, wine and salt together in a bowl then empty into an ovenproof dish.

- Place the seabass on top of the lemons

- Take one lemon slice and squeeze over the fish

- Sprinkle a pinch of salt over the fish and rub in well

- Sprinkle the parsley over the fish

- Cook in the oven on around 180 degrees for around twelve minutes.

- Serve with the vegetables.

As I said, Mel's Mum is a fantastic cook so the food was naturally exquisite. Exquisite enough for me, Mel and Tim to play our favourite game, Eat and Show. Now, once again this goes back to my uni days and is fairly simple to explain. Ideally one person, sitting eating in a large group of people will look at another person across the table. Said person will then look rapidly from left to right to make sure no-one is looking before opening his or her mouth at their intended target, displaying the contents of their mouth finely chewed on their tongue. The tongue is then retracted and everything goes back to normal. If you play it enough it becomes completely normal so you really have to watch who you play it with and how often. Nuts are a really good food to choose because you can chew them up into billions of little pieces so your whole tongue is covered. Mashed potato is another good one, if a little tame. Good for a beginner perhaps. The game, and its more drunken offshoots, Drink and Show and Eat, Show and Share are played almost constantly amongst my group of friends, especially in situations such as this, family dinners or lunches with work colleagues when the horror of being caught, a twenty-four-year-old man or woman displaying a mouthful of chewed food, is unimaginable.

Tim had started the ball rolling with a good display of shredded carrot at Mel whilst her Mum was talking to her, something that had reduced Mel to hysterics and her mum to puzzlement. Mel rebounded to me with a roast potato as her Dad was earnestly telling me about a new NHS initiative and I swiftly gave Tim a view of my chicken as Mel's grandma was asking him why he wasn't married yet. Mel's granddad however, hadn't quite caught onto the rules of the game as he displayed his mouthful of chewed vegetables to the whole table before swallowing and grinning at all of us.

'Papa, not at the table! Where are your manners?!'

'But Maria, they are all doing it; I am thinking it is some new young thing to do, to show the food is good, no?' He looked at Tim and then Mel.

Mel shook her head slowly, 'No papa, I think you were imagining things again, it's very bad manners.'

'But I saw, but …'

'Enough Papa!' Maria shouted. 'Eat your food and keep your mouth closed.'

He grumbled and went back to cutting his chicken, and as the conversation moved on looked at me, opened his mouth and winked. I don't think I've ever laughed so hard.

Griddled Pears with a Wine and Pomegranate puree

Ingredients
- One pear per person, halved lengthways
- Roughly one pomegranate per person (probably up to a maximum of five or six)
- 400ml dessert wine
- One tablespoon brown sugar
- Five tablespoons of caster sugar
- Squeeze of lime
- One tub of vanilla ice cream

Method
- Mix the wine and brown sugar together and heat gently until the sugar has dissolved.

- Pour the mixture over the halved pears and leave for a few hours.

- Peel the pomegranates, leaving half of one for the garnish, and blend up until a puree has formed.

- Strain the mixture until just the pomegranate juice remains, and stir in the caster sugar and a squeeze of lime.

- Griddle the pears for a few minutes so thick brown lines appear.

- Arrange two halves of each pear on a plate and pour the pomegranate sauce over.

- Sprinkle a few pomegranate seeds over the top, and finish with a spoonful of ice cream on the top.

After lunch Mel, Tim and I went for a long walk in the Peak District. Buxton is perfectly situated right at the edge of the Peaks so there are lots of good afternoon walks to do from Mel's house. Feeling a bit boozy from lunch we clambered over sty and gate, Mel vaulting them with typical ease as Tim and I betrayed our city roots and did our best impressions of pregnant hippos climbing a staircase.

I hadn't had a chance to speak to Tim about what he'd told me that night in "The Freemasons Arms" but it had been on my mind ever since. Tim had indeed quit his job and was receiving a generous severance pay and the promise of a superb reference from his previous employers so I wondered if that counted for anything with him.

By now we'd reached the bottom of the valley we'd been slowly descending for the last twenty minutes and we stopped for a water break. A cool stream flowed next to where we sat and we dangled our toes in the water, letting the ice cold liquid massage our hot feet. Hilltops rose sharply a couple of hundred metres into the air in both directions, lightly topped by a sprinkling of snow that had fallen the previous night. The water was so cold that we no longer felt it as one by one we all lay back to look at the clear sky, and a feeling of pure contentment washed over me.

'This is perfect Mel, thank you so much for inviting us.'

She turned to me, covering her eyes with her hands so she could block out the sun and see my face. 'You're welcome, more than welcome, plus I couldn't have handled my parents on my own. With you guys here I get to see them yet also get some time out from it all.'

Tim joined the conversation, 'How do you think they're doing?'

'My parents? I've never seen them look so tired. I'm used to hearing about it on the phone but seeing them face to face, and seeing the scars on Alexia's arms, I don't know, it's just awful. I just can't understand why she's doing it.'

'Is she seeing anyone? Like professionally?'

'Yeah but she doesn't talk; I don't think it's doing much help.'

We lapsed back into silence, making shapes in the water with our feet.

Mel smiled, obviously not wanting to talk about anything further. 'Shall we play?'

Tim leapt to his feet, 'Right, who's got the oranges?'

I got the powersling out and we spent the next hour slinging oranges further and further up the hills, identifying targets in trees and shrubs, betting drinks on whether we could hit them or not.

Chapter Ten
February 7th 2008

A SOFT KNOCK ON my door.

'Hey J.'

I looked up, 'Hey Jazz.'

She stood just inside my room, looking at some place on the floor just in front of my feet. She glanced up at me before looking down again. Silence.

'How have you been?' I asked.

'Good, yeah, been a really busy week at work so I've been working lots. Well, of course I have, I just said it'd been busy, stupid comment, how about you? Heard you had a pretty fun weekend.'

'Yeah good, I mean, yeah it was.'

'Good. That's good.'

'Look J, I ju—'

'Jazz I want to—'

We both interrupted each other then stopped.

'You go, what were you going to say?'

'No, you,' she said.

Bollocks to this awkwardness. I walked over to the door and kissed her. After a few seconds she broke it off and put her arms around me, resting her head on my chest, just like she did when we danced at the wedding.

'Oh J I don't know what to say, I'm so embarrassed. I promise you I tried to tell you before, I just couldn't, I didn't have the guts. I'm so sorry, and if you're having second thoughts I completely understand.'

I looked down at her, 'Hey, hey, I'm not having second thoughts.

Look, I said some pretty horrible things to you Saturday night, things I'm not proud of and things a guy should never say to a woman, no matter what happened.' I twirled a lock of her hair in my fingers. 'I wish you'd told me but I do believe you that you tried; I realise how hard it must've been, but Jazz, if you had told me maybe I could've helped on the day, been more supportive or something instead of joking to the entire table that we met after a one night stand!'

She smiled at the memory. 'I think I needed to do that on my own,' she looked up at me, flashlights boring into my eyes, 'to see if I would be OK going back and seeing them all again, but I needed you there too just in case I stumbled.' She reached for my hand. 'I guess instead of stumbling I fell flat on my face. J, can we kind of forget about it? I know it's a lot to ask, and I know you're aching to ask me about me and Jules and everything but it can wait, can't it? Soon, I promise, just, just not now. Is that OK?'

'Yeah, it can wait, there's no rush after all, is there?' I kissed her forehead and pulled her close and we stood like that for a minute or so, not saying a word.

'Well, we've come through our first argument.'

'Baptism of fire more like,' she grinned. 'I missed you, and it really annoyed me that I missed you so much; it's been three weeks!'

'I know, same here.'

'Soooooooooooooooo,' she grinned up at me through her hair, 'can I stay over then?'

I smiled, 'Yeah, of course you can.'

'Cool, I'll go get my bag, I left it downstairs by the door.' She smiled and bounded out of the room.

I shouted down the hall, 'So you weren't sure if we were going to break up yet you brought an overnight bag?!'

'Oh shush!' she shouted back up. 'I was feeling optimistic.'

We spent the rest of the evening curled up in bed watching a film, occasionally murmuring to each other comments about the film. Before we went to sleep we had sex, actually no, it was more than that, it was slow and sensuous, our lips never leaving each other's.

I woke as usual at about four, that time of night where if you awake alone you always look at the empty half of the bed with longing, and if you awake with someone next to you a feeling of warmth invades. I hope that doesn't fade with age or familiarity. I was lying on my back and Jazz was asleep on my chest, face turned to the side and one hand resting on the chest hair she'd been toying with before she fell asleep. I always wake at around four as I can never seem to turn my brain off and, as always a billion thoughts were running around my head. Mostly I was thinking about Mel and Alexia and what the next few months had in store for them, and how they'd deal with it. Mel is convinced one of these days Alexia is going to succeed, and yeah you can argue suicide attempts are nothing more than a cry for help, but what if in this case it isn't? Or, what if it is a cry for help but she goes too far without realising?

I felt Jazz's hands stir, 'Baby, you ok?'

I started gently playing with her hair, 'Yeah, just thinking about stuff, it's cool.'

'Yeah?' Her voice was thick with sleep, not quite aware of what's going on. 'Anything you want to talk about?'

'Nah, we've got to be up soon. I was just thinking about Mel and Alexia really.'

'Are you worried about Mel?'

'Aren't you?'

'Yeah. Yeah I am.' She rolled off of me and propped her face up with her hands. 'But I'm not sure how to deal with it; she hates talking about it and has to listen to so much from her parents I just think she wants a break from it all.' She yawned, 'Plus I always feel if I keep saying "How's Alexia?" I might as well be saying "Is she dead yet?" Do you know what I mean?'

I nodded. 'Completely. I guess we just take our lead from her.'

We lapsed into silence.

'How was Tim this weekend?'

I shrugged. 'OK I guess, he still seems so down though.'

She rolled back and started playing with my chest hair again, 'It's such a shame, I know I don't know him too well but he seems like such a great guy; hell, most of my friends would kill to go out with someone like that; he's hysterical yet he seems to have this real protective caring side to him.'

'That's just it, there's so much more to him than his joker exterior. But I think how he's feeling runs deeper than not having a girlfriend.'

'Yeah but it can't help, can it? He's been single for a while, hasn't he?'

It's true, it had been a while since Tim was with anyone. He started going out with a girl, Sarah, in sixth form and that carried all through university but they broke up after they both graduated. They went straight from seeing each other twice a month at each others' unis for three years to full-blown living together over the summer and their relationship just couldn't handle it. Since then, which was coming up to two years ago, there'd been pretty much no-one, and there was no-one before Sarah.

'Weeeell, maybe I should start introducing him to a few friends from work.'

'Excuse me?! Can't I meet your friends first?!'

Jazz leant in and gently nibbled at my chest. 'No, I'm far too embarrassed to be seen with you.' And with that she kissed me and turned over and fell asleep immediately, leaving me to go back to my thoughts.

Chapter Eleven
February 8th 2008

WE TOOK THE TUBE together into town the next morning. My nearest stop is Chalk Farm and my office is near Victoria, Jazz was going to work in Holborn so we parted at King's Cross.

'Tonight?'

'I can't tonight J, I'm going to the cinema with a few girls from work. Tomorrow? My treat, I'll take you out, something fun yeah?'

'Yeah that'd be cool.'

'Great, I'll call you later. Bye babe, be good,' and with that she hopped off the train and was gone.

I minded the gap at Victoria and emerged into a chilly February Monday morning above ground in London Town. Stopping to grab an Americano from a nearby stall, I emptied a tonne of sugar into the bottomless pit of coffee that now warmed my chilled hands. I shunned the milk; not before midday. Walking whilst drinking coffee is one of the most difficult things a man is expected to do, and true to form I managed to spill most of the coffee down my chin and yet still burn my tongue without feeling any liquid work its way down, and when my colleague Rob fell in line with me as I walked down the approach to our office I felt a slight annoyance that I was now expected to indulge in clever, witty banter, walk and drink my coffee, all of this at half eight on a Monday morning.

Rob is one of those intensely annoying guys that are great at everything yet have no idea they are, and so are just really good people. He'd been at IQG, my company, for as long as I had, in fact we were both on the same grad scheme and met in an initial group interview. I knew he was the sort of person I'd get on with when after the assessment day instead of slinking off home he'd asked everyone else in the group if they felt like unwinding at the pub next door. Nine months later and I'd say he's the person I'm closest to in the company, although I never get to see much of him at work.

'Honestly, all bloody weekend running around after him and he still couldn't carry it off, and then he had the balls to blame it on the weather!' Rob had just spent the weekend coordinating a gig featuring an artist who was huge in the sixties and had just embarked on a farewell tour, his third since the early nineties. 'His agent warned us how he doesn't like being looked in the eyes, told where to go or touched, can you believe that? I mean he actually said that if we see him walking the wrong way, not to tell him where to go because if he needs help he'll ask for it! Anyway, after acting like a total prick all weekend and after being on stage for just under an hour he decides not to do an encore, 60,000 people sitting in the cold in Cardiff and he refuses to sing the one song they'd all come to see, walks off stage early and starts screaming at the work experience kid for not having his food ready when he was the one who decided to come off early! What an arsehole; you can see why the other one left the group, you really can.'

We swapped stories about our weekend (I brought him up to speed on Jazz as he was asking why I was grinning on a Monday morning) and parted as we entered the office, arranging to meet for lunch later and then for a pint maybe that evening.

Chapter Twelve
February 9th 2008

'So have you memorised the card?' I asked Rob. 'Thanks so much for doing this by the way, I'll buy you a drink after.'

'Yeah I've got it, tell me what you think.'

He cleared his throat and stood up straight, drawing whines from Mel who was still trying to tie his bow tie: 'Miss Loyland, you are cordially invited to a Valentine's evening at Mr Jonathan Camfield's flat from eight o'clock on the fourteenth. Dinner shall be served at eight-thirty, would you care to RSVP now madam?'

'Perfect.'

'I still don't see why I have to be the horse and Rob gets to sit on me? It should be the other way round, he's bigger than me.' Tim walked out of his bedroom wearing the horse outfit I'd hired for him, placed the head of the horse over his own and stood there looking from Rob, to me, to Mel.

'Rob looks better in a dinner suit hun, sorry to say it but it's true,' said Mel, wiping tears from her eyes, 'whereas you, well you make a very attractive horse. Would you like a carrot?'

'Sure, I'll show you where you can put it,' came Tim's muffled reply.

Her eyes widened and she slapped the horse's head, 'So rude!'

Parked up three doors down from Jazz's flat I watched Rob and Tim cross the road and assume positions outside the door. Tim got on his hands and knees and Rob swung his leg over and sat on Tim's back.

Rob hit the back of his horse costume, 'Shhh, you look fine Tim.'

'No I don't,' I heard Tim say, 'I look like a midget horse, anyway there should be two people in a horse costume. I look ridiculous, like a donkey or a pony. I'm a pony, a goddamn pony, aren't I?'

'No, now shh, I've rung the bell and need to look noble.'

'How can you look noble, you're sitting on a pony.'

Rob smacked Tim's ass. 'Shhhh!'

'Did you just spank me?!'

The door opened but Rob blocked my view from the car. Rob and Jazz had never met so I'm guessing Jazz was pretty confused. Rob said his piece and I heard Jazz's loud laugh and a 'Yes, of course I will.'

'Very good madam, I shall leave you now and ride my noble steed back to my castle. Come Tintin, away!'

Tim stayed still.

'I said come Tintin, away. Away!'

'I can't move, you're too heavy! I think I've pulled a disc.'

Rob shifted and I saw Jazz doubled in two resting against the door.

'Stupid Pony, adieu Madam,' Rob reached over and closed the door from the outside and the two ran back to my car.

'What was I supposed to do? Gallop?' Tim, still wearing his horse's head, pointed at me from outside the car. 'You owe me, Camfield, again.'

They both clambered into the back and I started the car. 'I know, I know, thanks so much guys, let me buy you a drink.'

'Erm,' Tim pulled his horse's head off. 'We're stopping at ours so I can get changed, right?'

I shook my head, 'Nup.'

Chapter Thirteen
February 14th 2008

I **WANTED TO MAKE** it a special night for me and Jazz, and what with Tim and Mel deciding to go out for a "fuck-you Valentine's Day" dinner I decided on a night in with food and wine. I settled on an Italian menu, easy salad and my own special recipe for Spaghetti Bolognese.

Insalata Caprese

Ingredients
- One buffalo mozzarella
- Three to four tomatoes, vine preferably as I find them juicier
- One large ripe avocado
- Black pepper and olive oil
- Fresh basil

Method
- Cut the tomatoes into thin strips, cut the avocado into small sections and the mozzarella into small discs.

- Arrange in a circle around the diameter of the plate a piece of tomato, avocado, mozzarella, tomato, avocado, mozzarella and so on.

- Cover with olive oil, shredded basil and black pepper.

Note: If you're making this some time before and leaving it in the fridge, don't put the oil on until just before serving time, as it cooks the salad.

Also if you want to beef the salad up, put some rocket or prosciutto in the middle of the plate.

Spaghetti Bolognese

Ingredients

- 200 grams fresh spaghetti
- One pack of beef mince
- One large red onion
- Three cloves garlic
- Four spring onions
- One can of chopped tomatoes
- Tomato puree
- Half a de-seeded red chilli
- Handful of mushrooms
- Half a glass of red wine
- Oregano, basil and rosemary
- Half a glass of milk
- Half an avocado
- One spoonful of sugar

Method

- Chop the onions, garlic, chilli, rosemary, basil and oregano and fry over a high heat with olive oil and a spoonful of sugar. The sugar helps to bring out the juices in the dish.

- Add the mince and turn the heat down low, brown the mince. If the mince produces a lot of fat, drain it.

- Add the tomatoes and mushrooms to the mince.

- Stir for around five minutes, adding tomato puree and more spices to taste; you want quite a runny sauce.

- A few minutes before you want to serve, add the milk and red wine and stir, it'll make it rich and creamy.

- Boil some water and boil the fresh spaghetti with a splash of oil, it will only take a few minutes, don't cook it for any longer.

- Serve and finely slice half an avocado for each person and arrange on top of the plate. A little addition a Mexican chef taught me, it works really well.

Dinner had gone great and I was glad to have the place to ourselves, it felt so much bigger. We'd both eaten far too much and were in the lounge, me sitting on the couch, Jazz lying with her head in my lap and her legs dangling over the end of the couch. I was twirling her hair around my fingers, something I never get tired of doing as my mind drifted away, intertwining with the music of an unplugged "The Cure" disc coming out of my CD player. From the looks of it Jazz was doing the same; it was her CD, she'd brought over a copy for tonight and I loved it.

Jazz turned to look at me, the angle of her head forcing her lips apart, giving the impression that she was pouting. She licked her lips, her teeth slightly stained from the bottle of Malbec we'd shared, and opened her mouth.

'One day when I was five, my Dad sat me down on a couch and told me that he and Mum were splitting up. I was only five and didn't really understand what was going on; I remember I just kept looking at both of them, grinning because we were all sitting together as a family, something we never did. Mum was crying and I didn't understand why. My Dad hugged me so tight I thought I would snap, and left. On my bed was a letter, I've still got it, it reads, "Dear Jasmine, I love you very much and I always will. See you tomorrow love Daddy." I never saw my father again. Two years later we got a postcard from Florida where we have a few cousins. He said he was doing well and apologised for running away. He left no forwarding address.'

She swallowed. 'Growing up with just Mum was tough at times but we had a lot of fun. As I grew older it seemed like we were more friends than mother and daughter and I'd often look at people's relationship with their parents and think "It doesn't matter I don't have a father, I'm so much closer to my mother than you are to both of your parents." It was when I went to uni that I realised that whilst I felt like my Mum was just one of my good friends, I was her only friend. She'd put so much energy into raising me that she'd sacrificed her social life for over a decade, so when I left there was nothing but this me-sized gap she had no idea on how to fill. But slowly she started doing stuff, meeting people; she still worked so there were things going on in her office, so all was good.' She paused and looked into the distance. 'But towards the end of my first year at university she had a massive stroke which paralysed her whole right side and severely damaged her mentally.'

'Oh God Jazz, I had no idea.'

She smiled or grimaced – I couldn't tell which – and looked at me through moist eyes. 'I didn't tell you, of course you had no idea. Anyway, she's in a home in Southend now; she always loved the sea and she's being looked after well. She knows who I am sometimes, she doesn't say it but I can tell when I look in her eyes or feel her hand grab my arm. I see her once a fortnight at least and we sit, in the garden if it's nice, if not, in her room, and I talk to her about my life and she talks to me or to the empty spaces in the room about her neighbours in the home and the nurses.' She looked up, reached to take my hand, and smiled. 'I've told her about you. Anyway, the summer she had the stroke was the worst time of my life; I was twenty, trying to care for my ill mother and look for a home to put her in and trying to sort out her finances to pay for it all. Part of me was ready to chuck in uni, but I knew she'd be so angry with me for doing that. By the time September came round Mum was in a home and I was bursting to get back to uni, to do things for me, y'know. Almost as soon as I got back, Julian, who I'd never thought of as more than a friend, started showing an interest. I began to fancy him a bit, or I thought I did, and so we got together and things went well. Then all of a sudden after a couple of months, I just collapsed on him, all the stress of my Mum came out which dug up stuff about my Dad, and I was just a mess. Julian helped me so much, got me back together, helped me catch up on missed lectures, and that's something I'm eternally grateful to him for, because without him I would've dropped out of uni. And that was it, the relationship cemented into him looking after me and me letting him. I guess I was tired of being the grown-up, and on some level must've been looking for a replacement father figure. But as uni went on I began to grow in confidence and realise that Jules wasn't right for me, but I also didn't yet have the confidence to go it alone. When he proposed I freaked out, mainly because I wasn't really in love with him anymore, yet when I listened to what he was "including in the deal", so to speak, I changed my mind. He promised to pay for private healthcare in a top residential home in Devon for my Mum for the rest of her life, and Mum's finances were running low so I said yes, because she deserved to be comfortable.'

She paused and looked up at me. 'Shall I carry on? You've gone very quiet.'

I reached down and stroked her cheek with the back of my hand; she responded like a cat and followed the movement. 'Carry on, I'm just stunned.'

'OK. Well Jules was such a nice guy that I couldn't talk to anyone at uni about my ulterior motive, I obviously couldn't talk to my Mum, so the only person I told was Mel, who promised to never tell a soul.'

'She didn't, she never said anything to me at the time or when we first got together.'

Jazz smiled. 'I know, that's what I asked her on New Year's Day in the kitchen whilst you were in the shower. She's a very good friend.'

'What did she think of what you were doing?'

'She said she'd support me either way, but that she didn't think I should marry Jules. Deep down I knew I shouldn't either, yet I was terrified about how far down the road it all was and I didn't know how to put a stop to it. Before I knew it it was the day of the wedding and I was walking down the aisle with no-one in my corner.'

'Wasn't Mel there?'

'No, I felt ashamed and didn't tell her the date. Anyway, halfway down the aisle I got an image of my Mum in her room in Southend, and how upset she would be if she knew her only daughter was getting married, not for love, hundred of miles away, all alone. I looked at Julian, and I think he knew exactly what I was thinking; maybe he'd been kidding himself too, and I turned around and ran. I got a taxi to the station and went straight to my Mum's, still in my wedding dress.

I spent my wedding night sitting in her armchair crying as she slept, unaware who this stranger was or why she was there.' She paused. 'J, I couldn't tell you all that before the wedding, it was just too much too soon, can you see that now?'

I didn't really know what to say. 'Yeah,' I croaked, 'yeah, of course I can, and now I feel even worse about the things I said to you. God, Jazz, you're amazing, you really are. The stuff you've gone through, yet you seem to be so strong.'

'No, no I'm not, anyone would've done the same, plus if I was amazing I would never have accepted Jules' proposal; that boy was devastated when I left.'

'But most people would've gone to pieces, not known how to cope with something like that, especially so young.'

I felt her shrug slightly. 'You have to though, otherwise life stops, you have to keep going because it will always get better one day. Jules and I had a great time, it should've just ended after a year, not three, and like I say, I'll never forget what he did for me.'

'But what about money and the nursing home? You said your Mum is still there?'

'Yes, I'm paying for it at the moment, and it's OK, I earn enough at work and have never been a girly girl shopper, so it's not too bad. I still go every other weekend; I went whilst you were in the Peaks, that's when I told her about you. Sometimes it's a really good release, to talk at someone for hours without fear of judgment and sometimes, even though she can't articulate it, maybe she hears what I'm saying.'

'Can I meet her one day?'

'What? No, you'd be bored out of your brain.'

'No I wouldn't, I'd love to meet her.'

She sat up and raised an eyebrow. 'Really?'

'Yeah, really.'

A smile exploded onto her face. 'OK, maybe next month or sometime, but you don't have to; if you change your mind or anything I'd completely understand.'

I playfully hit her knee with the back of my hand. 'Jazz, I wish you'd stop saying it's OK for me to change my mind; I'm not going to, about anything.'

She leant into me and we kissed and I felt the wetness of her cheeks begin to dry themselves on mine.

We carried on speaking about our childhoods and Jazz completely opened up, telling me about how tough it had been at times, yet for every sad story there had been a happy one such as being the only thirteen-year-old in class who went to see Bon Jovi at Wembley; it was a birthday present from her Mum and they queued all day so that by the time the doors opened they were right at the front. My child-hood was pretty tranquil in comparison; my parents split too when I was really young, but I still saw my Dad every fortnight or so and he helped my Mum out financially in raising me and my brother. I had never been overly close to my father, and I never sought him out for emotional guidance, but deep down I know he loved me and my brother; it's just he was never really the type who should have had kids, he didn't really know what to do with them.

'It's all because of advertising I think,' I was saying to Jazz.

'How so?'

'Well, when Matt and I were really young he was a God of adver-tising, winning prizes all over the world and being worshipped by everyone around him. Then every day he'd leave that world and return to suburbia and to an exhausted wife and two screaming children. He couldn't handle not being adored and being the centre of attention which is why I think he had an affair; this woman must've had him on this pedestal, or he had her on one. Anyway a depressed wife and screaming babies were no longer tempting to him so he left. Pretty soon I reckon he realised his mistake, but it was too late by then.'

'How do you feel about him now?'

'Fine, we have a good relationship now, it just took a bit of work.'

'Do you see him much?'

'Ish, probably about once a month for a meal. Do you miss your Dad?'

She nodded. 'I miss having a parent there to tell me what to do. But my Dad left almost twenty years ago, I could have walked past him in the street and never realised it. You make do with what you have, and right now I'm making do as best I can. Sometimes it's hard, sometimes, like tonight, I wouldn't change it for the world.' She looked up at me and squeezed my hand.

I smiled and leant down to kiss her.

Jazz arched her back and stretched like a cat. 'Mmmmmmmmmmmm. Ah J, I love having the place to ourselves, I wish Tim and Mel were away for the night, not just the evening. I'm so relaxed with you right now I can't be arsed to see them. Am I rude?'

I smiled. 'I know, I feel the same which is why ... I think it's bath time. You keen?!'

'A bath?! Hell yeah, let's do it.' She giggled and leant up to kiss me.

'OK,' I pulled her up, 'you go run it and I'll get dessert.' I pulled her close, 'I want you in a bath covered in bubbles in ten minutes, Loyland. Deal?'

She pressed herself tight against me and leant in so that her lips were millimetres from mine. 'Deal,' she whispered.

Chocolate Fondue with Sliced Fruit

I'd prepared the fondue beforehand so all I needed to do was bring the fruit into the bathroom. I'd sliced loads of strawberries, papaya and mango into strips and put them in a bowl. Now, with a fondue set all you have to do is place loads of chocolate into the little container bit, light the gas or candle and wait for the chocolate to melt. Once melted, dip away with the fruit or your fingers, whatever. I'd used about a 200g bar of dark chocolate for me and Jazz.

Ingredients
- Strawberries
- Honeydew melon
- Mango

- Papaya
- 200 grams of chocolate
- Splash of milk

Method

- Light the fondue set and add the chocolate together with a splash of milk.

- As the chocolate begins to melt, stir continuously so it's smooth.

- Serve and dip away.

N.B. if no fondue set is available, boil some water in a pan and place the chocolate in a bowl above the boiling water, for it has exactly the same effect and will melt the chocolate just as fast.

Jazz had scoured Mel's room for candles and the whole bathroom was alight with flickering flames. She was already in the bath, the water just above her breasts, rising and falling slightly with each movement she made. She'd taken the petals off of a few of the roses I'd given her and scattered them on the surface of the water and one or two, already sodden, clung to Jazz's neck just above the water line. She turned to look at me, her deep chocolate eyes reflecting the candles and burning into me deeply. 'It's pretty warm in here, do you want to come in?'

I pretty much threw the bowl and chocolate onto the floor, lighting the candle underneath as quickly as I could. I don't think I've ever got my clothes off as quickly as I did that night, and before I knew it I was in the bath, rolling around with Jazz. She giggled and splashed me with water as I tried, yet again in vain, to find where she's ticklish. Water started splashing onto the mat below and spreading towards the fondue.

'Stop, stop,' I wrapped my hands around her, 'we'll get the fruit wet; you want some chocolate fondue?'

'Mmm, do I?! Here, I'll hold the fruit, you bring the fondue over.'

She balanced the fruit precariously on the edge of the bath, resting against the wall. The fondue we could easily reach into from the bath. It took probably about five minutes of eating normally before the food fight started, Jazz smearing a chocolate-covered mango on my neck before leaning across to lick it clean. I returned the favour, making a line of chocolate on her body from the space just behind her ear down to both breasts. Pretty soon we were having awesome chocolate-covered sex in the bath, no longer caring about the water spilling over the edge and onto the floor and into the fondue.

We lay for a while, Jazz lying between my legs with her back to me, gently stroking my legs under the water.

'This is such a perfect evening.'

'Isn't it.'

She looked at her hands. 'I'm beginning to wrinkle, shall we go next door?'

'Sure, although,' I laughed as Jazz sat forward, 'you're covered in chocolate, come here.' We washed each other, got out and wrapped each other in my huge dressing-gowns and went into my bedroom. I shut the door. 'There we go, now we don't need to go out again till the morning, no Mel and Tim!'

I turned round towards my bed to find Jasmine lying on it, the dressing gown gently falling open, allowing me the most tantalising glimpse of her dark, tanned body. I joined her on the bed and she undid my robe, pushing it off of my shoulders before pushing me back on the bed. Starting at my neck she began kissing her way down my body, her hands running up and down my chest and between my legs.

The last of the candles had long since faded and my room was covered in a darkness so thick it was like a second duvet. The house was silent; Tim and Mel had got in around twelve, pretty hammered by the sounds of it, and after a bit of noise I'd heard doors shut and saw the faint tube of light under my door fade away. I was spooning Jazz, one arm under her head, the hand being held by both of Jazz's as if it were a rope or vine dangling over a river. My other arm was resting on her leg, the space between my elbow and hand exactly the same as the space between her thigh and knee. A perfect fit. I'd dozed off for about half an hour or so, I thought, and was at the moment hovering between the two worlds of sleep and waking, dream and reality. I felt Jazz slowly tracing the outline of my hand with one of hers, and realised that she'd been doing it for a while. I moved my head slightly, unsticking my cheek from her shoulder, letting her know I was awake if she wanted to chat.

'Sorry, did I wake you?'

'No, no, I just woke up anyway I think; have you been asleep yet?'

'No, but it's still early, around two, I reckon.'

I moved my arm from her leg and tucked it around her stomach, pulling her closer, keeping the cold February air out and the warmth of the two of us in. 'What a great night,' I murmured into her neck.

'The argument we had ...'

'Ah Jazz, let's forget it, it's all ...'

'Nonono, listen. That Saturday night when I told you I hadn't felt for anyone in a very long time how I feel for you; I meant it, you know. You seem to have found a way in, and I really like having you there, which seems crazy considering how recently we met but it's just all happening so fast and it's amazing.'

I kissed her shoulder. 'I know. I don't completely open up to many people and yet I've told you stuff people I've been friends with for ten years don't know. I want to be open and honest with you, and I get the feeling that when I'm with you you're one hundred percent genuine with me, and I love that.'

'Even after the wedding you feel I'm one hundred percent genuine?!'

'After what you told me tonight, even more so.'

She squeezed my hand. 'Thank you.'

There was no way I was going into work the next day. I called a sickee, the first I'd ever done, actually, and climbed out of bed. I had a special breakfast in bed treat for Jazz the next morning; I wasn't going to let her go to work either. I snuck out to get "The Times" and along with an enormous cafetière, made her breakfast in bed.

Scrambled Eggs with Smoked Salmon

Ingredients
- Four large eggs
- Splash of milk
- Oregano
- Black pepper
- Sugar
- Few slices of smoked salmon, cut into strips
- Toast, one to two rounds

Method
- In a bowl mix the eggs with the milk, oregano and black pepper, then fry up in a pan, mixing continuously to create the scrambled effect.

- Add a spoonful of sugar and mix in well.

- Serve on toast and leave to cool for a minute or two, otherwise the eggs will cook the salmon.

- Arrange the salmon on the eggs and serve.

After breakfast and a bit of morning fooling around we spent the next hour or so reading the paper and doing the enormous crossword together. Finally at about midday we heard a banging on the door.

'Guuuuuuuuuuys,' whined Mel, 'I'm hung over too and you've got both the cafetière and the papers, c'mon.'

I shouted back through the door, 'Why aren't you at work?'

'Same reason as you! Now open the goddamn door.'

Jazz put a gown on and tucked herself under the covers. 'Come in.'

The door opened and a puffy-eyed Mel, followed by a scowling Tim, entered.

'How was dinner, guys?' Jazz asked, offering up the cafetière to

Tim as if it was a sacrifice.

'I can't remember anything past the main course. You're far too …' he turned to me and pointed at Jazz, 'she's far too chirpy in the mornings J. Coffee.' He turned and left, Mel turned to leave too before adding, 'Fantastic, had a really really great night. You?'

'Yeah,' I said, 'really great. Go get your coffee and come back, there's room.'

The four of us didn't even get dressed that day. By the time we had read the papers and watched daytime TV it was time for an evening film and Chinese take-out. A perfect sick day.

Chapter Fourteen
February 22nd 2008

TIM, MEL AND I were sitting in "Crazy Bear", a funky little bar in Soho, celebrating Tim's new job at a bigger firm, for bigger money. As a thank-you for putting up with his moods he'd decided to take Mel and me out for dinner and drinks, for working weeks were over before you knew it and it was hard to carve out a time to see each other properly.

'So all in all a pretty good few weeks, I'd say. You've got a brand new job, Alexia hasn't tried to kill herself since January and you and Jazz seem to have got back on track.'

I grinned. 'Yeah we have, it's, it's going really really well; we're both just having a hell of a lot of fun.' And we were; since Valentine's things had been great. We'd seen each other pretty much every night, either going out for a drink or chilling at mine. The four of us had even gone bowling together on Tuesday, which had turned into a strangely competitive evening with Jazz and me just losing to Mel and Tim in a frantic final frame decider. We needed a spare and an eight to win it, and I'd got the spare but fucked up and only got a two on my final ball. Tim and Mel had only just stopped celebrating and now wanted to do it weekly, and for money.

'I think she's perfect for you, bud,' Tim said, clinking my glass, 'ten out of ten, great girl.'

'Really? Cool, I'm glad you like her, I've always wanted a girl-friend that's just relaxed hanging out with my mates as well.' I turned to Mel. 'Have you found it weird at all, me and Jazz?'

She poured herself another glass of white. 'No, not at all; we still go out for drinks, gossip and bitch, nothing's changed, apart from now

97

most of the gossip and bitching is about you, peachy.' She winked and smiled.

'She didn't ...'

'Peachy?!' Tim slammed his pint glass down on the table. 'Peachy?! Oh please tell me that's her pet name for him. Peachy!'

'Yup sure is, named after his pert arse apparently, that right, J?'

'Ohhhhhhhhhhhhh dude, I am never going to call you anything else. That's made my day, it really has.' Tim chuckled into his pint.

'Thanks, I really appreciate it.'

'Ah don't worry J, you don't want to know what else I know. Besides, I have to tell her to shut up sometimes, she's completely crazy about you, do you know that?'

I cracked a grin. 'Yeah I did, and it's mutual.' Feeling awkward for a second I clapped my hands. 'Anyway, how about you two, any love interests or potentials on the horizon?'

Tim shook his head, 'Dunno peachy, there are a few hotties in the new office but that's always a bit of a no-go, isn't it. Nah, no interest but I'm ok with that.'

'Me too,' Mel added hurriedly. 'I mean I've got exams in two months, and what with Alexia and everything I've just got no time really. And that's cool.'

'Well, Jazz and I were thinking about a big night sometime over the next few weeks, y'know, meet in a bar, her friends and my friends and maybe go out after, sound good?'

I saw a smile pass between Tim and Mel. 'Yeah, sounds good,' said Tim. 'But no matchmaking, I hate crap like that.' He pointed his finger at me. 'Nooo sir.' He got up to go and get another round in and Mel grinned at me.

'I think Tim's gonna be OK.'

'Yeah, the change in the last few weeks is amazing, isn't it, and you guys seem to be getting closer too.'

She paused, 'Yeah, yeah we are, he's begun to let his guard down more with me, maybe because you're not around on your own as much as you were a few months ago but yeah, I think talking to me about it has helped, plus he told me that he's really feeling better about things.'

I felt a pang of irrational jealousy. 'He told you that?'

'Yeah, we talk quite a bit; as I said, he's been opening up to me recently, it's good.'

I dismissed the pang immediately; my two best friends were getting on and that's what I wanted after all. 'Well I'll drink to that, cheers.'

MARCH

Chapter Fifteen
March 1st 2008

FROM THE OUTSIDE IT looked like a service door halfway down a tunnel running adjacent to London Bridge. Cars sped into the darkness, a swishing sound from the rain kicked up by the tyres echoed down the tunnel, its walls tinged with the yellow-orange of a London that never gets dark. I nodded to a security guard who opened the door for me and I stepped out of the club and into the tunnel to get some air and have a break. Reaching for my phone I slipped the top up with my thumb, immediately unlocking it and causing my suit jacket to glow blue. *"Jazz I'm gonna have to cancel tonight babe, we're running way behind and doubt I'll be home before midnight, sorry, I'll make it up to you this week promise xsorryx."*

I sidestepped past a face I recognised and ducked into a coffee shop by the entrance to London Bridge station.

'Double espresso please.'

The guy behind the bar raised his greyish eyebrow at me and chuckled. 'You supposed to be Britney Spears or something mate?'

A momentary confusion then I realised I was still wearing my microphone and receiver that reached down from my ear to my lips. I smiled in acknowledgement, downed the espresso, burning my tongue, paid and headed back to the club.

Built as a jail in the 1600s, "The Tunnel" is one of my favourite venues in the capital, and one I always recommend to clients because of its originality. Hidden deep in the London underworld near the river, admittance was through a long windy tunnel which emerged out onto enormous room after enormous room snaking round in a circle, with each area having only two entry and exit points. What was great about "The Tunnel" was that each door into the next room was tiny which, when combined with the metre-thick walls, created a virtually soundproof room meaning that each space could be transformed into a completely different setting. The spec for this party was pretty easy; it was the birthday of a relatively new music star, one of the ones who won a reality music show a few years back and she wanted a large party for two hundred people at a discreet London location, drinks and canapés, good music and an original theme. My boss met her just before Christmas and told her about "The Tunnel", suggested a gothic theme and she'd jumped at the idea.

I was knackered and pretty fed up that I was working tonight when my boss was at home chilling out. The downside of being on the graduate scheme was that whenever a job required a bit of evening work, we were always the ones stuck with it. I walked from room to room, checking with the bar and waiting staff that everything was going to plan. Around me hundreds of people dressed in Victorian dress sipped champagne, fresh mojitos and nibbled from Thai canapés. Torches burned from enormous candelabras, the venues' only source of light, that hung on the walls, creating a fluid, flickering reflection of light on the dark stone. I passed through the opera room where two women wearing half masks sang haunting melodies whilst a Phantom-of-the-Opera-esque pianist played with his back to the guests. Into the main room where a DJ, standing in a purpose-built box twenty feet above the floor played a set. All around me beautiful faces on beautiful bodies moved like the flames of the candles, erratically, sometimes independently, sometimes intertwined. Looking around I felt disorientated. Scanning the room, a slight gap in a black curtain hanging across a wall was my key and I slipped through it, momentarily blinded by the harsh white light of a busy kitchen.

Emma looked up from a tray of king prawn and mango kebabs she was arranging on a glass tray.

'How's it looking? Do they still look hungry?'

I glanced at my watch; half past eight. We were running late due to a London Underground strike which had huge knock-on effects on the roads. I had hoped to have all the food out by eight, leaving me an hour to help with the packing-up of everything apart from the bar and the main room. I could then sign out, leave and meet Jazz at ten, but what with the late arrivals of most of the guests the food wouldn't all be out till at least nineish, meaning I was looking at a late night.

'Yeah, all the food's going quickly, we're on about a five-minute turnaround for the trays.'

Emma placed a flower on top of the kebabs and smiled at one of the waiting staff hired for the evening, 'Good to go.' He picked up the tray and left, leaving the kitchen strangely quiet for once.

Emma undid her apron and took a swig from her water bottle. She came around from behind the work surface and leaned her head against my shoulder. 'Jesus I'm knackered.' She stifled a yawn, 'Any gossip out there that I can sell to the newspapers and retire on?'

I returned the yawn. 'Doubt it, it all looks pretty tame really.' I reached over and nabbed a ricotta and smoked salmon bite. 'Mmm mm, Em these are pretty special.' I reached over for another. Emma is a fantastic chef; she's got a real passion for food, something I share with her. We went to school together but she was never really the academic sort, something she discovered halfway through A-levels when she quit school and went off to cookery college. A heap of diplomas later she now runs her own premier catering company and I try to push for the company to use her whenever possible.

King Prawn and Mango Kebabs with a Sweet Chilli Dip

Ingredients
- One pack of king prawns, already de-shelled
- One mango, cut into inch square chunks
- Half a lime
- Sweet chilli sauce

Method
- On a skewer place one prawn followed by one cube of mango followed by one prawn etcetera etcetera. Stop at three prawns each.

- Squeeze some lime over the prawns and place under the preheated grill.

- Turn once, the prawns will take about two minutes each side to cook.

- Place a few on a plate and add a dollop of sweet chilli sauce in a bowl.

About two dozen of them were served on a tray and went pretty quickly.

Ricotta and Smoked Salmon Bites

Ingredients

- One tub of ricotta cheese
- One red chilli, diced
- One pack of smoked salmon
- Juice of one lime
- Cocktail sticks

Method

- Mix together the ricotta and chilli, and add the freshly squeezed lime juice.

- Refrigerate for a few hours to allow the cheese to firm up a bit.

- Cut the salmon into long strips and place a teaspoonful of the cheese in the middle of the strip.

- Wrap the salmon around the cheese and seal with a cocktail stick through the middle.

N.B. this also works really well with bacon instead of salmon.

Chicken Teriyaki, Carrots and Mushrooms in an Iceberg Lettuce Wrap

Ingredients

- One chicken breast, diced into centimetre pieces
- One carrot, diced
- One white onion, diced
- One garlic clove, diced
- One large field mushroom, diced
- One large iceberg lettuce

For the teriyaki sauce:

- Eight parts light soy sauce
- Two parts dark soy sauce
- Two parts sake
- Four spoonfuls of sugar

Method

- Whip up the teriyaki sauce. To do this add everything together and stir on a low heat until the sugar dissolves.

- Add the onions, garlic and the chicken and cook on a high heat, stirring continuously.

- After two minutes add the carrots and mushrooms. Because everything is diced so small it should all be cooked in around four minutes.

- Unwrap the lettuce and remove leaf by leaf.

- Spoon a generous amount into the lettuce and wrap it around so it is completely covered.

- Use a cocktail stick to hold the lettuce in place.

- Serve, but be careful of the sauce dripping out.

My key slid into the keyhole a little after half twelve and I felt my way across the hall and up the stairs. All the lights were out; Tim and Mel would've been in bed hours ago, being knackered from both the effort of a new job and medical exams next month. I could barely keep my eyes open as I opened my door, keeping the light off so it didn't hurt my eyes. I threw my clothes on the floor, set the alarm for half six and fell into bed.

'Mmmmmmm ...'

I turned quickly to see the outline of a body in my bed.

'Jazz? Hey! What the hell are you doing here?!'

'Mmm,' she made that sound you make when you're half asleep, as if you're chewing something in your mouth. 'Saw Mel instead, thought I'd surprise you. Sleepy.' She lifted her head and pulled my arm under it. 'Night.'

Chapter Sixteen
March 11th 2008

IT WAS FRIDAY NIGHT, finally. I'd had a pretty hard week at work and was now looking forward to relaxing a bit and chilling out. Tim was meeting Rob and me after work, and we were planning on a quiet few drinks, nothing hardcore, just a couple of pints, intermittent conversation and the chance to let the last five days gently unwind themselves from our minds.

Rob and I pushed open the door to "Motion", a sushi restaurant by day, bar by night kinda place round the back of Smithfield Market, and looked around. We were early yet there was electricity in the air as barmen rushed back and forth stocking up the small fridges and changing barrels, getting ready for the rush later on. Rob got two Stellas and brought them over to the heavy wooden table I'd procured opposite the bar. Clinking our glasses we both stretched our shoulders, clicked our backs and drank deeply.

'I'm knackered.' Rob yawned into his pint and rested his elbows on the table. 'When's Tim getting here?'

I looked at my watch. 'Any minute now I think, he's not really one to stay late to impress his new boss, especially on a Friday. He can probably smell the beer already and is sprinting down past "The Barbican", palming off toddlers and OAPs into the traffic.' I took a deep sip. 'Christ this tastes good, I've been craving this all afternoon.'

We lapsed into silence, enjoying the feeling of not talking about work for a change.

'Jazz out tonight?' Rob sat up, undid his collar and removed his tie.

'No, well yeah, I think so but we're not meeting up. I've seen a lot of her this week, practically every night after work and felt like a bit of man time, know what I mean? I feel like I haven't spent any time with just you and Tim in ages actually.' I laughed. 'Although obviously I take all of that back if you invited Megan out with us!'

Rob grimaced. 'No, no I haven't. Actually, er, we kinda broke up last weekend.'

I put down my pint. 'No way! You didn't say anything, what happened?'

He shrugged. 'Yeah, sorry but I really couldn't be arsed to talk about it, I needed some time to digest it first myself. I think, well, I know that whatever was there just wasn't there any more. We were at that point where we needed to move on to the next stage, y'know either move in together or get married or engaged, whatever, and I just didn't want to. I felt I should be asking her to move in, or be my wife, but I didn't feel like I wanted her to do or be either.'

'That's a huge decision though; you felt like that for a while then?'

He nodded, 'Yeah, since around Christmas I guess, we did loads of family stuff together and both our parents were hinting, and all I could think about was shit, am I gonna have to get married just because it's gonna be so goddamn awkward to break off from this? I mean she's been my everything since I was a teenager, I don't know how to exist without her but it's not a reason, is it?'

'No you're right, but must've been pretty hard to do. How'd she take it?'

'You know what women are like; she knew it was coming, she was just waiting for me to man up and admit it to both of us. She's hurting, as am I, but you can't force it, can you? It just wasn't there anymore, and you got to admit that.'

'Are you talking at the moment?'

He shook his head. 'No, no we're not. It's really hard if I'm honest with you. We both need to get over each other so need some space apart, but I'm thinking about her constantly. I want to call her and tell her about all the stupid things that happened in my day and it's so tough not to.' He sighed, 'But this is the way it has to be. I know it was the right thing to do, I think she does too, it's just this is the hard bit now,' he tapped the table, 'doing stuff without her.'

'That's shit, that really is shit. So you're sure you made the right decision?'

He nodded. 'Yeah, and the thought of getting back out there terrifies me!'

'Man, Rob single, I've never known that before.'

'Well get used to it! It's scary though; I've got absolutely no idea how to talk to girls anymore. I haven't dated since school.'

'Well not much has changed, apart from you don't need to worry about asking the girl you like for a slow dance before your Dad comes to pick you up at half ten. Oh yeah, texting is the new calling by the way.'

'Hmm, think I'm gonna give it a miss for a bit; really can't be arsed with all that yet. Rather just sit with you and Tim for a few months.' He grinned.

'Speaking of which, I'll let him know we're here.'

I pulled out my phone and dialled his number. An out of breath and sweaty Tim picked up. 'Hey, you in the pub yet?'

'Tim, you sound like a kerb crawler; slow down and get your breath back, we're not going anywhere.'

'Ok, oh, great news by the way.'

'What?'

'I just bumped into Jazz, she's joining us tonight, said her plans fell through.'

I heard her shouting 'Hey babe!' in the background.

'Oh er, OK.'

'Isn't that great?!' I could hear Tim smiling too hard.

'Sorry dude, OK see you in a minute.'

I flipped down the top on my phone. 'Jazz is coming, she just bumped into Tim outside his work.'

'What?! No, this is man night, I want to get drunk and hug you both.'

'Well, you can still do that. Look, Tim couldn't exactly say no could he? She knew we were all meeting up.'

'But you said she had plans?'

I shrugged. 'She did, but they must've fallen through.'

'And she just happened to bump into Tim after her plans had fallen through?'

'Yeah …?'

'OK.'

'What?'

He shrugged. 'Nothing.'

'No, what?'

'Well,' he paused, 'that's a bit suss, isn't it? I mean she knows where Tim works, is it anywhere near where she does?'

'No, but why wouldn't she have called me or "bumped into me" instead of Tim if she wanted to come out?'

'Because she knows you want a man night out, and if she saw you first you would've talked her out of it or palmed her onto Mel. This way Tim can't tell her not to come and you can't exactly tell her to go home when she gets here.'

I shook my head. 'No, look, I know you don't know her but she's not like that. I'm sorry, I wanted it just to be us tonight but I guess it's not, but she is cool, really, you'll like her.'

Rob held up his hands. 'No, look I'm out of line; I'm sorry mate, of course it's cool if your girlfriend comes. I'm probably just bitter about this whole Megan thing and was looking forward to the chat. Another time, huh.'

'Yeah. Another time.'

We lapsed into a brief silence, broken a few seconds later by the sight through the enormous bay windows of Tim practically jogging down the street with Jasmine a few paces behind trying to keep up yet refrain from breaking into a run. He pulled open the bar doors, flicked Rob and me a V-sign as greeting and headed straight for the bar. Jasmine came towards us, an apologetic look on her face.

'Laura cancelled at the last minute; she goes to print on Monday and apparently is nowhere near done. I was in the area; can I be an honorary boy tonight?'

I stood up to give her a kiss. 'Course you can Jazz, course you can. You remember Rob, right?'

Rob leant forward to kiss her cheek. 'Hi, the weirdo on the horse, remember me?'

She grinned. 'Do I?! That was one of the funniest moments of my life, I've told literally everyone I know about that little scene. Very well acted Rob, good to meet you.'

We were joined by Tim, who had already taken a hefty chunk out of his pint. 'Morning guys, how are we? Happy Friday.'

'Happy Friday Tim.' We clinked glasses. 'How's your day?'

'Nay bad, Rob, good to see you.' He held his hand out. 'How are you? How's the Megster?'

'Probably better off in the long run, we broke up.'

'Oh. Shit. Sorry. Erm, you OK?'

'Yeah I'm OK.' He held up his glass. 'It'll come out in a few pints' time, we don't have to do it now.'

Jazz sipped from her glass of white wine. 'Sorry guys, I'm playing catch-up, what's going on?'

Rob took a long sip. 'I've just broken up with my girlfriend.'

'How long were you together?'

'Since sixth form, seven years.'

'Wow.'

Silence.

Almost on cue the bar's sound system kicked in, making conversation across the table pretty much impossible. Tim and Rob broke off opposite, as did Jazz and I, and that's pretty much how it stayed until we finished our drinks.

I put down my empty glass and motioned to the door with my head. 'Shall we go somewhere where we can actually hear each other?'

Rob leaned over. 'Where to though? It's a Friday night in the city, everywhere'll be rammed. Stay here, it'll be fine. I'll get a round.' Tim got up to help, leaving me and Jazz alone, the table feeling unnaturally empty.

'Are you sure you don't want me to leave? You don't seem yourself tonight, J.'

I turned to her and put my hand on her knee. 'Of course I don't want you to leave' (was I lying?) 'you're my girlfriend, I want to see you. It's just a shame Laura was busy; have you rearranged?'

'Yeah some night next week; now listen, I was thinking, tomorrow do you feel like going for a long walk on the Heath? It's meant to be quite a sunny day.'

I looked confused. 'Tomorrow? I thought you were going out for lunch.'

'Oh, it er, fell through, family problem or something. So, what do you think?'

'Well, it's just I'd planned to spend the day with Tim; we were gonna go underwear shopping and drink beer.'

She stroked my cheek. 'Babe, you can do that anytime. You don't need any pants, besides you're drinking beer with Tim tonight. C'mon, me and you, Hampstead Heath, arm in arm, cold breeze and bright sunlight, big cappuccinos, it'll be great.'

'Did somebody say sambuca on an empty stomach? I think they did!' Rob and Tim had returned with two bottles of wine, four shots of sambuca and a pack of matches. 'Who's first?'

'Shotgun!' I punched my fist into the air, 'Right here buddy.' I knocked back the sambuca, swilling it round in my mouth before leaning back and opening wide. Tim walked over and leant over me, dipping the lit match into my mouth. I love sambuca, and I'm blessed, I can drink shot after shot and never get too hammered on it.

One by one we polished off the sambucas, the wine and another round of sambucas, plus another two bottles of wine. Conversation had gone in fits and starts, occasional deep and meaningfuls followed by hard banter and general drunken shouting, hugging and high-fiving.

Using a hell of a lot of effort I looked to my left.

'Where's Jasmine?'

Tim looked at me as if I'd just asked him to stamp on a kitten. 'She went to the toilet, she told all of us.'

My brow furrowed. 'Really?'

'Yeah J, get a grip, you're not being very nice tonight.'

'What are you talking about? I haven't done anything wrong?'

'You've barely spoken to her.'

'What do you mean I've hardly spoken to her? Anyway, we've seen each other all week, maybe we don't have much to say to each other tonight.'

Tim wrung his lips. 'But I think the girl feels plain uncomfortable. C'mon, you're her boyfriend, look after her a bit, maybe we should ease off the in-jokes.'

'Ah, for God's sake.' I was pissed off. 'This was supposed to be our night out, I want a night off from being the considerate boyfriend. I'm right, right Rob?'

He held his hands up. 'I dunno, I mean, you can't have it all your own way, can you? We all wanted a boys' night, it hasn't happened, no point dwelling on it, is there? I think you could include her a bit more, yeah.'

I scowled and leant back in my chair. Whoever said that sambucas didn't affect me was a liar, a liar and a thief. I was drunk. The kind of drunk where you turn your head and it takes a second or two for your eyes to catch up. How did that happen? Was everyone else as drunk as I was? Rob and Tim's bottle was half full, mine was empty and Jazz was in the toilet. Had I drunk that all myself? Were the boys right about including Jazz? Was I not? And what the fuck was all that about Hampstead Heath tomorrow? No, I don't want to do that.

'I'm gonna get another drink.'

I got a pint of London Pride and leant against the bar, suddenly finding it hard to stand perfectly still. I tried putting all my weight on one leg but that made it worse. Jazz had come back in, gone over to our table and was now walking over.

'J why did you get another drink, we all said we were gonna go after the wine. Tim's shattered by the look of him.'

I looked to her left. 'He's fine, I think I'd know if my best friend's tired or not.'

'Well, he just told me he was tired and wanted to go home, so whatever.'

My elbow slid off of the bar. 'Wonder why he wants to do that.'

'What did you say?'

'Doesn't matter.'

'Look,' she raised her voice and a few people began to turn round, 'I'm sorry my plans fell through and I'm sorry I crashed your' (she raised her fingers) "boys" night out, but I somehow thought my boyfriend would want to see me. Obviously I was wrong because he's barely said a word to me all night and is now finding it hard to stand up straight. Tim and Rob are going in a minute, I'm going with them. Finish your pint, grow up and meet us outside in five minutes.' And with that, she turned and walked out of the bar.

I slammed my pint down on the bar and followed the three of them out. I was fuming.

Rob nipped off to get the last train and Tim, Jazz and I shared a taxi, me sitting in the front with the window half open. Back home Tim threw a 'night' over his shoulder and disappeared. Jazz headed into my room and I turned on the light in the bathroom.

Looking at myself in the bright humming glare I thought, what the fuck are you doing? Why are you so pissed off? Why are you taking it out on Jazz and making her feel shit? I held on to the sink whilst I brushed my teeth, locked up and went into my room. The light was off and Jasmine was curled up against the wall in bed. I got underneath the covers and put my arm on her leg. She shrugged it off. I tried again. 'Jazz.' She shrugged it off again. 'No J, let's just leave it till the morning, I don't want to say something I'm gonna regret. Good night.'

Chapter Seventeen
March 12 2008

I AWOKE EARLY NEXT morning. Jazz was still scrunched up against the wall, the edge of the duvet wrapped around her hand and tucked underneath her chin. She was breathing pretty deeply, so from the sounds of it was a while off of waking. Not wanting to disturb her I lay in bed for a while instead of getting up, letting what I remembered of last night run through my mind. You see, at the risk of sounding like a dick, I don't know if I regret anything about what I did last night. Did I do anything that wrong? I got drunk, OK yes, a bit silly, I'd only had half a sandwich for lunch, and I should have thought to have had more food, whatever. As for ignoring Jazz … I'll be blunt, I really didn't want her there last night. Is that wrong? We'd spent so much time together recently and I'd really fancied a night out with Rob and Tim, but as Rob says, we can't always have it our own way; why didn't I just accept it and be pleased to see my girlfriend? We'd seen each other loads, but so what, there's not a set number of times you're meant to see someone, is there? Why did I act like a dick to her instead of just being normal?

Recently I've been so busy at work and been out every evening, but whenever I haven't been at work I've been with Jazz and I'm beginning to feel a little suffocated. It started off as just a niggling feeling I dismissed, but almost every night she's turned up here saying plans have fallen through, or she wanted to see Mel but Mel had too much work on or something. But why should that bother me? If I do really care about her, surely I want to see her, and the fact that she wants to come over and sleep next to me after I've been working fourteen hours straight is a sign of how close she feels to me. Why do I not want to see her that much then? Why would I rather spend the day buying underwear with my flatmate than having a picnic with my girlfriend on Hampstead Heath? Why am I not really bothered about her being pissed off with me?

I sat up to take a sip of the water by my bed. I could see Jasmine's eyelashes were open and she was looking at the wall. I put the glass down and lay back in bed, my arms behind my head, looking up at the ceiling. One of the most uncomfortable feelings in the world is sharing a bed with someone after an argument. You both know the other is awake, but no-one wants to say anything, because that brings the argument and who knows where that could lead.

I cracked first. 'Hey.'

'Hey.'

'You want some coffee?'

She shook her head and turned around, her head resting on her pillow, her eyes boring into mine. 'What happened last night, J?'

'I dunno. I honestly don't, I was pretty drunk.'

'Have I done something to piss you off?'

'No. Well, a bit, but it's not your fault, I mean no, no you haven't.'

She sat up. 'But what have I done? I thought everything was good until last night.'

'So did I, I mean it is good, it's just …'

'What?' Her eyelashes were stuck together in little groups, a mixture of mascara, sleep and an early onset of tears creeping out of her eyes. Something about her really reminded me of a wide-eyed little girl, innocent, unaware of what she had done wrong and unsure of how to fix it.

'It's too much. Seeing you all the time, having you come out all the time. I need a bit of time with my friends.'

'But you see your friends all the time, and Mel is my friend too, anyway.' Her eyebrows furrowed. 'You want to see me less? Is that what you're saying?'

'I guess so, yeah.'

She looked like she'd just been punched in the stomach. Why was I doing this? I didn't want to see her less.

She sighed. 'J, we're getting close, a by-product of that is that we see each other more, spend time together, you know, do what other couples do?'

'But do they do that after two months? Spend every night together? Want each other to cancel plans with friends, turn up unexpectedly at those friends' work saying plans have fallen through?'

'Excuse me?' She gathered the duvet around her. 'You think I made that up last night so that I could see you?'

'Well ...' Stop, what am I saying? This is Rob's idea, not yours, of course she didn't. 'Well it was a bit suss how you happened to bump into Tim, wasn't it?'

She shook her head in disbelief. 'You really think I would make up a plan so that I could spend a few hours with my precious boyfriend because I can't live without him. Is that what you want to believe?'

'I guess when you put it like that it does sound a bit stupid.'

'Stupid?' She was getting pretty loud now. 'Stupid?! J, you make up a fantasy in your head that I'm so depressed and upset that I can't deal with an evening on my own and so have to see you, and then have a go at me for wanting to spend time with a guy I thought something special was beginning to happen with. Tell me, if I wanted to see you only once or twice a week, would we be sitting here having an argument about how I was neglecting you?'

'OK OK, so you didn't plan last night then.'

'Oh, you believe me? Oh thank you, thank you. I understand now why you behaved like a total prick last night; you thought I was stalking you, well that's fine, water under the bridge, huh. Jesus J, listen to yourself.'

I wasn't, that was the problem. I could see it changing, she was changing, by the second.

'Look, I didn't think you were stalking me and I'm sorry if you felt awkward last night, but ...'

She snapped. 'I didn't feel awkward J, I felt fucking ignored.'

'But I'd just got it into my head I was seeing Rob and Tim,' I protested.

'So plans change! For fuck's sake, you're so regimented sometimes.'

I didn't know what to say. Was this heading where I thought it was heading? I turned to look at her; she was sitting up, arms folded across her chest, a stray tear or two running down her cheek. 'It's too much too soon Jazz, it feels like we've been together two years not two months. Maybe if we were to see each other once or twice during the week, then …'

'A timetable?!' She whipped around to look at me, fire burning in her eyes. 'Are you proposing we plan when to see each other? What, every Tuesday and Thursday, leaving you Friday night free to go out with the boys and fuck a random?'

'Hey, that's not fair, I am not like that and you know that, that has nothing to do with what I'm saying. Of course I'm not interested in anyone else. Look, why don't we do that picnic, get some air, forget about last night.'

'No J, you can't take that back. You can't say you don't want to see me then suggest we spend the day together. I don't even want to be anywhere near you right now.'

She got out of bed, put my robe on and started picking up her clothes from the floor. 'Just go have your coffee with your friends and have a fantastic day and whilst you're at it try and work out what the fuck it is that you want and whether you think you're actually grown up enough to handle a relationship, because that's what I'm going to be thinking about today.'

She slammed my door and I heard the bathroom generator switch on. Two minutes later I heard her feet on the stairs and the front door open and close.

That's why you should never start talking in the morning.

I opened the door a few minutes later and walked into the lounge. Mel was curled up on the couch in her pyjamas watching re-runs of

"Friends" on TV. I put a cafetière on and joined her in the lounge.

'How was your night?'

'Amazing, I was up till two learning all about colon cancer and after breakfast I'm going to write up notes from a patient who tried to feel me up last night as I was stitching up his face. How was the lash?'

I shrugged. 'Lash wasn't great. I somehow managed to get drunker than everyone else did and then had a massive argument with Jazz.'

'Yeah, I heard you both this morning.'

'Oh sorry, did we wake you?'

'No, not at all; I just turned "Hollyoaks" up. Tim around?'

'Haven't seen him, coffee's on though so he'll wake up and smell it soon. So we didn't bother you this morning then?'

Mel sighed. 'J, I'm not gonna ask you what you were arguing about OK? You tell Tim, Jazz will tell me, as will Tim, and then I'll decide who's right and wrong and get back to you. No infringements of the rules, you know the arrangements.'

'Yeah yeah yeah.'

I flicked absent-mindedley through last week's "Heat" magazine.

'Any girls last night?'

'What? That's not what we were arguing about.'

'Not you,' Mel murmured into the couch, 'Tim and Rob. Oh no, Rob's taken isn't he. How about Tim?'

'Actually he's not taken anymore, bit of a bombshell, but no, no girls.'

'Hmmm.'

'Why?'

'Just curious.'

'I've been thinking recently that it's high time Tim got a girlfriend again. I think it'd do him the world of good.'

Mel plunged the coffee, pouring out two large mugs of the stuff. 'Yeah I guess, but he seems pretty content y'know. Perhaps with all the stuff that's going on for him he's not in the right place for a girlfriend.'

'Well it doesn't have to be the most amazing, mind-blowing intense love affair, just a bit of fun.'

'I guess, but you know whoever she is we won't like her. No-one is good enough for him.'

'No, you're probably right.'

I think there's a part in every human that despises change. Sometimes, if we are brave enough to admit it to ourselves, our desire to repel change comes to the detriment of those around us. Thinking about what Mel said I had no desire for Tim to be in a relationship because that would have meant the end of the three of us, and the three of us worked incredibly well. It's such a strange feeling to think that no-one is good enough for a friend. If they are a true friend and you know them inside out then of course no-one will ever be good enough, because you're not gonna get to know the other person as well as you know the friend. Therefore, are friends ever truly accepting of girlfriends and boyfriends? I remember in my second year house at uni, there were six of us, four guys, two girls, and at one point during the year we were all going out with someone. Whilst we were all polite to them, one night we all had a drunken heart-to-heart and admitted than no-one liked each other's partner as they weren't good enough. I know I'm rambling but stick with me here. So, can friends actually hold you back then? Does there come a point in every relationship where you must choose to some extent between friends and girlfriends, and will your relationship with the losing party be irreparably damaged? That said, you've obviously known your friends for a hell of a lot longer than your girlfriend so will the girlfriend ever win? It's all very well saying if someone makes you choose, you've made the choice already but if that choice is a natural result of human character, what then? Everybody wants to be number one in someone's life, everybody feels threatened if they sense they may be being replaced. How does Jazz fit into all of this? Was she asking me this morning to choose or is that my imagination? I've found a girl that feels comfortable with my friends, and my friends feel comfortable with her, what a rarity. I've found someone that is happy dicking around with my friends as if she's known them all her life. But, is that what I want? Am I shoving this feeling of suffocation to the corner because I have everyone around me telling me what a great girl she is? What the hell do I want?

Chapter Eighteen
Later that day

'WELL, WHAT DO YOU want?'

We were in H&M in Oxford Circus having a disjointed shopping conversation, weaving our way in and out of the congregation of shoppers holding jumpers up against their chests, holding jeans up against their legs and generally just holding us up.

'I'm going for button fly today I think, not too tight, not too loose. You?'

'Idiot.' Tim put down the pants he was looking at. 'I mean what do you want with Jazz? It's crunch time.'

'You reckon? I dunno, it was just an argument.'

Tim looked around. 'We're too old for here, let's bug out. Sure it was an ultimatum. She's expecting you to think today about what you want from this relationship. The question is, Mr Camfield, what the dickens do you want, 'cause I'm having a hard time working you out on this one.'

We pushed through the crowds and emerged onto Oxford Street and turned right, heading down to "French Connection". 'I don't know Tim, I really don't. Two weeks ago, everything was great, amazing really, we couldn't bear being apart, she was getting on great with you and Mel, I was thinking about her constantly all day but now … now I feel like there's a little warning sign going off in my head and I'm not as sure about it as I was.'

Turning into "French Connection" we headed downstairs to the men's section, and spotting the pants in the corner, made a beeline. Tim picked up a pair of lime green y-fronts, his eyes lighting up. 'Should I? They're beyond repulsive. I could wear them at home, they'd go really well with the couch.'

'Awesome, get them, how much are they?'

He looked at the price tag. 'Twelve quid for a pair of pants?! Maybe not.' He hung them back up. 'Ok, let's be logical about this, you said you're not as sure about it as you were. What is it that you're not sure about?'

I was thumbing my way through a rail of light blue boxers, aimlessly picking ones out. 'Well, it's this suffocation thing, it just feels like too much. I want my independence, and right now it feels like if I want to do something I have to ask her permission to do that.'

'So in an ideal world you'd want to see her less?'

'Yeah, but after what she said this morning I know she's not up for that. So do I stay with it, and hope this is just a dip I'm in and soon enough I'll be back to how I was like with her before or do I go with my gut instinct, which is telling me that all of this is just a little too much? What do you think?'

'I need more information first. OK, if you were to break up this weekend how would you feel?'

'Appalling. I'd feel like I might have passed up the chance to see if this could turn into something pretty special.'

'That completely contradicts what you've just said dude.'

'I know. Well, OK yeah, I'd feel shit, but all feelings fade in time don't they? Maybe it's more having someone I'd miss rather than missing her.' I paused, 'Do you know what I think it is actually, it's the mystery. In two months I've found out so much shit that I just feel I know everything about her, there's no more discovering left to do.'

'And there would be more mystery if you saw each other less?'

I tapped the rail of pants. 'Exactly! Yes that makes sense. God I should really write this down.' I looked around as if expecting a pen to drop from the ceiling.

'You're kidding right?' Tim looked at me. 'C'mon, let's buy these.' We headed over to the cashier's desk, proudly presenting our pants to the shop assistant. Tim smiled at the girl before turning to me.

'Actually I owe you twenty quid from last night, I'll get these.' He turned back to the girl. 'I'll buy his pants, I owe him.' She half smiled and started packing the underwear quicker. Never knowing when to stop, Tim protested. 'Ha, that came out wrong, no we're not gay really! Yeah, we just live together, and we both needed new pants so we thought y'know, why not.'

I punched his shoulder. 'Shut up!' By now the shop assistant was beginning to laugh.

Tim handed over the money, winking as he said, 'Cute when he's angry, isn't he?' We left the shop, Tim smirking to himself, me walking as quickly as possible.

'Every time Tim, every time. And still it isn't funny.'

He laughed to himself. 'Oh I disagree, I really disagree. Anyway back to Jazz. I think we're making progress here. OK, where were we? So, you say you want to see her less as that will keep the mystery alive right? Is that gonna make you feel better?'

I nodded. 'I guess yeah, but something she said this morning, shouldn't I be wanting to see her more?'

'Hmmm. I guess the fact you don't so early on isn't really a good sign, is it?'

'No. What do you think I should do?'

We got separated by shoppers and then rejoined. 'I'm not gonna answer that, I might prod you gently in the right direction but I won't do any more.'

Pulling open the door to a pub at the bottom of Marylebone High Street we ordered a round of Guinness and some crisps. I picked up the conversation again at the table. 'OK, so you won't answer that, but you like her right? I mean you both seem to really get on.'

Tim nodded. 'Yeah we do, she's a lovely girl but I'm not sure if she's right for you. I started thinking that in January.'

I dipped a crisp in the head of my Guinness. 'Why do you say that?'

'OK, if I answer this question I'm being completely honest, you can't get angry or pissed off or whatever; you asked for my honest opinion right?'

'Right.'

'The wedding thing man, that was weird. Personally I think you should have stood up for yourself more over that.'

'But it was …'

Tim raised his hands. 'Hey hey, no interruptions, you asked my opinion OK. I know what you were about to say, that she didn't want to tell you about her Mum till later and she felt really guilty etc. etc. That's fine, I completely understand her not wanting to let all her secrets out after three weeks but, and this is what sticks with me,' he tapped the table, 'she shouldn't have taken you in the first place. She knew everyone there would be looking at both of you, and for you to walk completely unprepared into that environment, not having a clue of the history, well I think that's pretty selfish. Anyway, that made me think, there's something not quite right about the two of you. You had that huge argument after the wedding and you were depressed for days when really you'd known each other four weeks. It all just seems far too intense J. You fight, you agree to stay together and work through problems, that's not normal for a two-month relationship. You disagree, yeah, but you don't scream and walk out on each other that early on and if you do, well then that's normally the end, isn't it? I'll tell you what worries me, that you're sticking with her because either you think she needs looking after and protecting, or that you've already been through loads together so you're gonna stick it out. Any of that ring true?'

I looked down at my pint and murmured, 'Yeah. Yeah it does.'

'Well maybe you need to make a few choices today, think about what you want, not what others expect of you.'

Chapter Nineteen
That Evening

I LEFT THE FLAT and began walking to Jazz's place, a rough plan in my head and new pants on under my jeans. I had done a lot of thinking today and come to the conclusion that I didn't want to break up with Jazz, I really didn't. She was great and I knew she was, but I did need things to change.

She opened the door with a weak smile; I went to kiss her and found myself brushing cheek. We went through to her sitting room and sat on the sofa, awkwardly asking each other questions about our days. She seemed nervous. I felt nervous.

I hadn't been to Jazz's flat that many times and didn't know it that well. She lived alone so it was kinda small, the lounge and kitchen taking up the majority of the flat with a small bedroom and ensuite off to the side. Decoration was sparse yet tasteful, such as a vase of stylishly arranged flowers and twigs sitting in the old Victorian fireplace and an Edward Hopper print on the wall, you know the one of the lady alone in the bar gazing out into the night.

We were skating round the big elephant sitting in front of us, neither of us sure how to get the ball rolling. In the end she plunged in first …

'J, this morning, last night, I don't know about you but that fight seemed different. Stuff came up I wasn't really aware of y'know.'

I nodded. 'Yeah, a lot of stuff I didn't know till it came out of my mouth.'

She looked at me earnestly. 'But you meant what you said right?'

'Yeah, but Jazz,' I reached for her hands, 'I don't mean we can only see each other twice a week and no more, I just mean I want to have a bit of a life apart from you, that's all.'

She pulled her hands back. 'And you feel like I hold you back?'

'No, not at all, I just want to be able to spend time with my friends, or even on my own and not feel bad about it.'

'But I don't make you feel bad about it J. I really don't. I want you to have a life outside of me because I want one too.'

'So why do I feel so suffocated then?'

'That's something you've got to work out because I really don't think I do that. I don't know why, but you seem to have this opinion of me that if I'm not with you I'm crying my eyes out longing to see you. J, if I wanted a protector I would have married Julian. I don't. I want someone who wants to be around me and who sees me as an equal, not someone they have to wrap up and keep in their pocket and …' She stopped and sipped some water, psyching herself up. Oh God, she was going to say it wasn't she? Please don't, don't. 'And I don't think you're that guy.'

Wow.

I did not see that coming.

Now I needed the water.

'You, er, you're breaking up with me?'

Her eyes though watery, never left mine. She nodded.

'And you just decided that today?'

'Yes. This morning. You thought I'd bumped into you all last night on purpose. I don't think I've ever been so offended. That just sums it up J; you don't see me as an equal.'

'But …' I had no idea what to say.

She held her hands up. 'Don't. It's over.'

I looked up at her. 'I thought this was going somewhere amazing Jazz?'

That set her off, the tears began to roll. 'So did I J, so did I until today. I'm not going to demean myself by being with someone who wants to see me twice a week so he doesn't get bored with me. I don't want to feel I can't see my boyfriend if I saw him last night and I don't want him to get pissed off. No, I'm better than that, and I wish you could have seen that because if you could've, we might have had a future.' She looked down at the floor. 'J, I think you should go before this becomes any harder than it already is.'

I stood up and walked to the other side of the room. 'Harder? You're so clinical and cold about this, how is it hard for you? You're dumping me!'

She looked up at me from the couch and shook her head. 'I'm not gonna rise to it; I told you today's argument was different, we're not going to fight about this because I'm not going to change my mind. I've spent most of my life thinking I'm not good enough, and now that I think I am, I'm not gonna let you put me back there.'

I knelt in front of her and put my hands on her knees. 'Jazz, you're making me out to be this kind of monster; I'm not trying to make you feel shit about yourself or make you feel that you're not good enough, you are!'

She stroked my face and looked at me earnestly. 'I know that J, I know you're not trying to hurt me or demean me, really I do, but this morning I realised we had no future, or no future that would be healthy for either of us. Instead of running away as usual I'm facing up to it.' The tears began to fall again. 'And you probably won't believe me, but it's breaking my heart to do this and I'll probably regret it, but this is how it's got to be.' She trembled. 'Now please, go.'

She got up and walked past me, brushing my stomach with her hand, turned into her bedroom, closed the door and left my life.

Chapter Twenty
March 19 2008

SO I'VE BEEN EATING a lot of soup this past week.

There's no fairytale ending to this I'm afraid. Jazz didn't come running down the street after me screaming about how she'd made a mistake, she didn't call me at three o'clock that night as I was lying awake in my bed gazing up at the ceiling and she didn't come over during the week and crawl into my bed and wait for me to come home from work, even though I looked for her there every night. I went over and over what she'd said to me between the bar and us breaking up and I realised that she hadn't been in touch with me because she was right. End of story. I'd been so preoccupied trying to work out if I wanted to be with her I just took it completely for granted that she wanted to be with me. It didn't even cross my mind that I could lose her over this.

I tried to blame others. I blamed Rob for suggesting Jazz popped by on purpose and I blamed Tim for taking me pant-shopping and making me talk about Jazz and getting it into my stupid head that I wanted to see her less. However, more than anyone I blamed myself. I lost her and she's right; if the person you're with wants to see you less then they don't have the right to see you at all.

Anyway, back to the soup.

I was raised as a liberal Jew, which meant whenever I was ill or cold or tired or depressed my Mum would make me chicken soup. As a baby I was quite seriously ill and allergic to pretty much everything, and the only thing I could keep down was soup. Oh and Ribena. Anyway, I think I associate soup with comfort so I've had a bowl of it most days this past week.

Homemade Italian Chicken Broth

Serves One

Ingredients:

- One chicken breast
- One carrot
- One small onion
- Three spring onions
- Half a potato
- Handful of penne
- Handful of mushrooms
- Half a can of borlotti beans
- About a litre of water
- Parmesan, or whatever hard cheese if you don't have any parmesan
- Black pepper, salt, oregano, rosemary, basil
- Two chicken stock cubes, one vegetable stock cube

Method

- Boil up the water, herbs and stock.
- Add the diced potato and leave for around five minutes on high heat.
- Add the onions, spring onions, carrots and pasta.
- Few minutes later add the diced raw chicken breast to the pot.
- Five minutes later add the mushrooms and the beans; the beans are thick and help to thicken the broth.
- About six to eight minutes after you put the chicken in, the broth should be ready. Spoon out the mixture into a bowl, ensuring that the liquid just about covers the chicken, potato etc. Remember it's a broth, not a soup, the difference being broths are thicker.
- Grate shitloads of parmesan in to the bowl so it melts and covers the top.

I guess the fact that I got mugged on the way home didn't help.

Is that funny? Because if I wasn't me I'd think that was really funny. Get dumped, get mugged, go home. What a Saturday night.

I'd caught the tube back to Chalk Farm and turned out of the station and started walking home. It was about a ten-minute walk, and at nine o'clock in March of course it was dark. Now, I've walked that route hundreds of times at all hours and sure there are dodgy characters, but no more than there are everywhere else. I was about two hundred metres from my house and I got to this turning that takes you off the main road and into the side streets. At that corner, on the other side of the street were two guys leaning against a wall, big hoodies and scarves round their necks, pretty menacing. So I walk quicker and after fifty metres or so I give a little look round, no-one there, fine, slow down. Then it must have been what, twenty seconds later I look around again and there they are, both running at me and all of a sudden they're about three metres away from me. One dives forward and puts his arm round my face, splitting my lip, and hauls me to the ground, the other gets on top of me and starts punching my body.

He looks at me dead on, dark eyes shining out of the hoodie, all I can see. 'Give me your fucking bag now, c'mon, hurry up, your bag.'

Now, this is fine. I carry nothing of value in my bag and it's a shitty twenty-quid bag, but the dickhead has got his knees on my chest, how am I meant to give him my bag? I mean c'mon, if I'm going to get mugged for the first time in my life the least I could ask for is a little professionalism. Anyway, he realises this and gets off of my chest, punches me in the stomach so I sit up, and takes my bag from off of my shoulders. Next up, he's back on my chest saying, 'OK, now your wallet, phone, fuckin' everything, hurry up man, c'mon,' and for a split second I think, no. There's only two of you, I could get you off of me and run, I'd be home in thirty seconds; bam, he punches me in the face, OK just give it to him, they've probably got knives, there's two quid in your wallet, it doesn't matter. I gave them my wallet and after a few punches to the head they run off, leaving me lying on the pavement, all alone.

I got home and after cancelling my cards and blocking my phone I started cleaning myself up. As everyone always says about getting in fights or being mugged, it doesn't really hurt that much, it's just a shock. Shock and anger I'd say are the most dominant feelings. Apart from a bust lip I didn't really have any marks, and to be honest that paled into comparison next to how I was feeling about Jazz.

So I thought that was a pretty good time to have soup.

An hour later I'm lost in a world staring into the cracks in the kitchen table, mechanically spooning soup into my mouth when Tim walks in.

'Oh my God J, what happened to your face? Are you OK?'

I shook my head. 'Jazz dumped me. It's over.'

'And she hit you?! Why?!'

'No! Course she didn't hit me, this was after, two guys on the street.'

'She got two guys to beat you up?!'

'No! Forget about that, I was mugged OK, it's fine, I'm just a little sore. Concentrate Tim, Jazz dumped me.'

'You were mugged?! Where? Are you OK?'

'About two hundred metres away; yeah I'm fine, a little shaky but fine. What are you doing?'

Tim got out his phone. 'I'm calling the police, have you done your cards? Hello, police please.'

I sighed. I really couldn't be arsed to get the police involved. What was the chance of getting anything back? I just wanted to have a bath and forget today ever happened.

'Ten minutes? OK.' Tim closed his phone. 'They'll pick you up in ten minutes.'

'What?! Why? Where are we going? What did they say?'

Tim came closer and took my head in his hands, looking at the slight swelling on my left cheek. 'They think that they could still be in the area; they want to go for a drive round with you. Tea?'

'Gin and tonic. They want to go for a drive round with me? I can't think of anything I'd rather do less, what's that going to achieve?'

'Don't be so negative, you might see them.'

'Oh great and if I do what do they do, bundle them in the back with me, tell us all to squash in tight?'

'J calm down, I'll get you your gin, it's OK. Tell me what happened.'

'With what? Jazz or the mugging? Christ what a day.'

'Whichever you want; let's talk until the police come.'

I smiled bitterly. 'I never thought I'd hear that sentence; Mum would be so proud.'

I filled Tim in, then the police turned up and I spent the next half hour in the back of their car driving round the estates of Camden (beautiful). Needless to say the two punks weren't hanging around so it was a bit of a wasted trip. All I could think of was what if they texted Jazz from my phone? What if they sent her something crude or abusive? Hers was the last text I received, so if they're gonna piss around with anyone it's gonna be her. Also, what if Jazz was texting or calling me saying she was wrong or saying she wanted to talk? I just wanted to put the day to rest and after a long bath, bed beckoned but was followed by an even longer night; sleep and Jazz intertwined in my mind like two helium balloons, moving slowly together up and up and out of my reach.

Chapter Twenty-One
March 24th 2008

STILL ON THE SOUP.

Thai Chicken Broth

Serves one

Ingredients

- One chicken breast
- One small red onion
- One piece of lemongrass
- Three spring onions
- One large carrot, peeled and sliced
- One green chilli
- Handful of mushrooms
- Pack of creamed coconut
- One vegetable stock
- One chicken stock
- Thai seven spice
- Splash of fish sauce
- Fresh coriander
- Fresh lime

Method

- Boil up some water, about a pint and a half.

- Add the onions, spring onions, juice of half a lime, chillies, seven spice, fish sauce, stock and lemongrass and carrots

- Boil for around five minutes or so, then add the chicken.

- Wait five minutes and taste the mixture. If it's too hot add loads of coconut cream, if it's not too hot only add a bit, to give it some flavour.

- Just before it's ready, squeeze in half a lime and a handful of fresh chopped coriander.

I'm getting a bit bored with soup to be honest with you. It's been almost a fortnight since Jazz dumped me and I think I'm almost ready to move on to solid food. She hasn't been in touch with me at all and I don't have her number anymore because of the mugging and so I haven't contacted her either. I know I could always get her number off of Mel but I don't know if she'd give it to me or if I should even ask for it. I still miss Jazz like crazy but the hurt is beginning to fade a bit, or at least it's not as sharp as it was last week. I'd still prefer it if we were together obviously, but maybe it was for the best. I mean, the day it happened I was questioning if I wanted to be with her or not, which is surely a sign everything's not great? I've been mulling over some of the stuff Tim was saying too, and maybe she was kinda selfish at the wedding. Either tell me first or don't invite me, especially that early on. But every time I think of that it gets far outweighed by an image of me and Jazz lying in bed together on a Sunday morning or covered in chocolate in the bath. This does get easier, right?

Chapter Twenty-Two
March 28th 2008

THERE'S A SONG BY Counting Crows called "Have You Seen Me Lately" and there's a verse in it in which Adam Duritz, the lead singer, talks of "angels of the silences". Now, these angels of the silences are the thoughts that come to you when you're lying in bed alone, and you wake at four am and can't get back to sleep. The angels flutter around you whispering thoughts into your ears like "no-one will ever want to spend the rest of their life with you" or "if you don't do well at work this week you're gonna get fired" or "no-one texted you today, you don't have any friends". For the last few weeks I've been having angels of the silences about Jazz for a good hour each night. I've woken convinced she's having sex right now with a new boyfriend, and it's obviously the best sex she's ever had because he's better looking than me and treats her better. However, I was sitting at work this morning and I realised I hadn't thought about her yet today and I hadn't woken up at four am either. This is getting easier.

I had a boys' night in with Tim and Rob and I think that helped a lot. So, all in all it does suck me and Jazz aren't together, and it looks like we're not going to get a friendship out of it, but it's not the end of the world now, is it? Sure she's in my head, and I do still feel a little bit sick when I think about her but I'm putting my faith in the knowledge that each day is easier than the one before, and that really does help a lot. Being around Rob, who's single for the first time since 1948 also has a sobering effect, as whatever I feel really does pale in comparison to him.

'I dunno dude, I mean as I said before I do feel kinda lost without her but I still would've made the same decision if I had my time over. And yeah, we were friends and I do want the best for her as she is an amazing person, and the best isn't with me, so I want her to go find that best.'

'I don't think I could be that altruistic,' Tim said, stacking the fridge with Corona. 'There's a small part of me that wants Sarah to spend the rest of her life crying in the corner because she isn't going out with me.'

Rob looked up from the pepper he was dicing. 'Really? I mean do you honestly mean that?'

'Well, in a way yeah. I mean we had an amazing few years together and I do still love her, I think I always will, but I also like the thought that no-one she meets can measure up to me and part of her will always think that.'

I chimed in, 'I think I'm with Tim on this one. It goes back to the whole being number one doesn't it? Yeah, your girlfriend can move on but you don't want her to be with a guy who's better looking and you don't want her to be happier with him than she was with you, right?'

'I guess. Now Speedy Gonzalez, what are we doing with these nachos, shall we have them with the mojitos?'

'Well technically Tim, mojitos are Cuban, if this really was authentic we'd be having margaritas instead.'

I felt a lime splat into the back of my head. I turned round and Rob grinned at me. 'Sorry I slipped, were you being pedantic again?!'

Having spent a semester at uni studying in Mexico I am of course a complete Mexico snob, which irritates the hell out of everyone but comes in pretty handy when it comes to food. Dinner was going to be good.

Mojitos

Ingredients
- Bunch of fresh mint
- Lime
- Two spoonfuls of sugar per drink

- White or golden rum
- Ice

Method

- Rip up some fresh mint and add to a double of rum and the sugar.

- Add a squeeze of lime and shake well.

- Add some crushed ice to the mixture and shake again.

- Serve garnished with a slice of lime.

Nachos with Cheese, Tomato Salsa, Guacamole, Sour Cream and Jalapenos

Ingredients

For the tomato salsa:

- Half a dozen vine tomatoes
- Half an onion
- Two cloves of garlic
- One green chilli
- Four tablespoons olive oil
- Half a lime

Method

- Minutely slice the chilli, tomatoes, onions, coriander and garlic.

- Mix together with the olive oil and squeeze the juice of the lime in.

- Refrigerate for about half an hour.

Guacamole

Ingredients

- Roughly one avocado per two people eating
- Half a lime
- Two vine tomatoes
- Olive oil
- Spoonful of mayonnaise

- One third of a green chilli

Method

- Ideally you want a really perfect ripe avocado. Peel and slice up.

- Once again minutely slice the chilli and tomatoes.

- Add one tablespoon of olive oil, juice of half a lime and one teaspoon of mayonnaise.

- Beat with a fork until smooth and creamy.

Now the avocado turns brown pretty quick (although the lime helps to prevent this) so ideally you want to be making this just before you eat it.

- Cover a plate with tortilla crisps and grate a lot of cheddar cheese over them.

- Whack under the grill until the cheese has melted.

- Cover the plate with sliced jalapenos, sour cream, the salsa and the guacamole.

This is meant to be a big group dish, not an individual one, so do it all on one big plate and be prepared to get messy.

Chicken and Beef Fajitas

Ingredients

You want about 200 grams of meat per person, chicken or beef. For us I did two chicken breasts and one rump steak which was enough.

- One large onion
- One bunch spring onions
- Handful of mushrooms
- Couple of large tomatoes
- Three cloves garlic
- One large pepper
- One chilli
- Tortillas, probably about three per person

Method

- Cut all the ingredients into long strips (with the exception of the mushrooms, tomatoes and chilli, which you should dice).

- Place the strips on a griddle and cook on a very high heat. Add the mushrooms, tomatoes and chilli.

- Turn frequently then when ready place in a big bowl.

- Add separate bowls of grated/cubed cheese, sour cream, salsa and guacamole.

- Heat the tortillas in the oven, about 1 minute each should do it.

- Place a tortilla on a plate then smear guacamole over the entire tortillas.

- Add the strips of food (fajita means strip in Spanish) to the tortilla.

- Spoon over the salsa, sour cream and cheese, wrap up and eat it. It's amazing how quickly you'll get stuffed.

Mango and Papaya with Red Chilli

As with all Mexican food this is served with lashings of chilli, which goes surprisingly well with fruit

Ingredients
- One large mango
- One large papaya
- One red chilli
- Juice of one lime
- Some sort of fruit sorbet

Method
- Slice up the mango and papaya into cubes and place in a bowl.
- Dice the red chilli and add to the bowl.
- Squeeze over the juice of at least one lime and mix thoroughly.
- Serve with sorbet.

By now we'd had a lot of beer and to make the night even more authentic I thought it'd be a good idea to get out my seven-year aged dark tequila. What a stupid idea. The stuff is pretty potent, it's by a maker called La Cordial and comes in a big glass bottle with a thick heavy wooden cork. I bought it in the town of Tequila, a very strange town in central-western Mexico where the smell of tequila permeates everything and horse-drawn carriages amble through the dusty streets taking tourists out to the ranches where tequila is grown and fermented. Anyway, it's pretty strong stuff and it's such a quality type of tequila that downing it with lime and salt is really frowned upon in Mexico.

'Who wants to down it?' I shouted as I emerged from my room, bottle in hand. 'Tim, lime duty, Rob, salt, do that now.'

Later, after we'd knocked back a good few and sucked the hell out of a bag of limes, Tim started smiling to himself. He looked up at me and Rob, lost the smile, then looked down and started smiling again, shaking his head. Rob threw half a sucked lime at Tim's head, 'Mate, what is it?'

'Doesn't matter,' he grinned.

'Tim …'

'No really, it's nothing.' He smiled again.

I threw the lime this time. I missed and it landed on top of the toaster. Wow, I really missed. Better remember to get that out. 'Tim, stop being a dick, tell us or stop smirking.'

'I want to, but I caaaaaan't. I'm not allowed.'

'Whatever. Rob, lean in a sec.' He leant in.

I squirted the remnants of the lime in his eye.

'Ow! You little shit, come here.' He picked up the last tortilla on the table and went to slap me with it. I stood up and ran into the lounge, picking up another few limes for protection. Rob chased after me, tortilla raised and looking deadly.

'Mel and I are kinda together.'

Rob and I stopped. The tortilla dropped to the floor and landed flat out, like a stingray on the bed of the sea.

I turned to him, 'What the hell …?! When? Tim, what do you mean together?!'

He grinned sheepishly, 'Yeah, it's going great actually. Oh man you're not meant to know, she'll kill me. You got to pretend you don't know J,' he turned to Rob, 'you too.'

'Hang on, hang on.' Rob sat on the couch and patted the space next to him. 'Sit down and start from the beginning mate. When did this start?'

'February.'

My eyes widened, 'February! I don't get it, why didn't you tell me?'

Rob looked up, 'Oh come on, be happy for him! C'mon, what's the story?'

'Well, there's not much to tell really.' He shrugged, 'I guess you kinda got us together J. That night we went to the cinema just the two of us, to give you and Jazz the flat, well it was the first time I'd really spent proper time with Mel and I realised how cool she really is. I dismissed it as I thought it was a really bad idea and that she probably wouldn't think the same anyway, but then remember Valentine's when you cooked for Jazz, and Mel and I went out for dinner? Well that night we got on great, got hammered and ended up getting it on. Kinda started from there really.'

'So, it's quite serious?'

'Well, not really. I mean we don't do that much couple stuff together, mainly because we were keeping it hush, but we spend most nights together. Look dude, the only reason we didn't tell you is that firstly, we don't know where it's going so we wanted to wait and secondly, by the time we realised it was going somewhere, you broke up with Jazz, so the timing was shit, really that's it.'

'I think that's great mate.' Rob patted Tim's leg, 'Mel is a top girl, good luck to you.'

Tim looked at me. I sat down on the armrest. 'Me too, yeah it's cool, a bit weird, but yeah, I'm happy.'

He looked relieved. 'Good, I've hated keeping it from you. You still don't know though, it's just 'cause I got drunk and told you, but I'm actually really happy about it. I know it's not what you want to hear when you're getting over Jazz but ...'

I interrupted him, 'No really, I think I'm on top of that. So, every night you've been sneaking into her room?'

A grin spread across his face, 'Yup, it's actually been really fun sneaking around. Normally you're working late or just not looking when I say goodnight, but you've been close to catching me a few times.'

'You had sex on the couch?' Rob started prodding Tim.

Tim nodded, 'Yup.'

'Alriiight, where else?'

Tim started to go red. 'I'm not answering that question! C'mon, it's weird! I need much more tequila before I answer that!'

I woke the next morning with my computer on and lights shining. I was fully dressed. I stared at the ceiling for a while before lifting my head in search of water. No water and I definitely won't be lifting my head again for another hour or so. I guess I'll go back to the ceiling.

I must have drifted off again because now Rob had got off the couch and was in the kitchen making coffee and Tim had just brought me in a pint of water.

'Morning.'

'Hmmhmhmhm.'

'Tell me about it, why the hell did we drink tequila?'

I looked at the empty bottle on the floor. 'Wow all gone, how did that happen?'

Tim got out of my chair and stretched. 'Well, India it is then.'

Rob came in with a full cafetière. 'Morning guys, how we feeling?'

'Been better I guess, but fun, good night wasn't it?'

Tim poured out the coffees. 'So, India.'

Rob sipped his coffee. 'What about India?'

Tim looked at both of us. 'Us, going to India in June.'

'That's a good idea actually, we should all go away together.'

'I'm up for that,' Rob added, 'and I have always wanted to go to India.'

Tim looked from Rob to me and back again. 'You're joking, right?'

'What?'

'Neither of you remember do you?' He stood up. 'That's amazing!' He pointed at my computer, touched the mouse and the British Airways home page came up. 'We booked a flight to Delhi last night.'

'What?!! Why the hell did we do that?! When?'

Tim creased up. 'Oh that's hysterical, you both really don't remember! Jesus, yeah, we booked it last night, three weeks in India, last few weeks in June and into July, it's gonna be great!'

Rob and I looked at each other as smiles broke across our faces.

'We're going to India ...'

APRIL

Chapter Twenty-Three
April 5th 2008

Do you think you can ever hit the steering wheel so hard with your hands that your airbag comes out? I mean a sudden jolt makes it burst free right, so surely it stands to reason that hitting the steering wheel really hard with your hands would make it pop out, pinning you to the back of your seat? I hate traffic. And today, whilst stuck in a long queue on the Finchley Road, I found the best way to pass time was to indulge in a little air drumming, or steering wheel drumming as it should perhaps be called.

I felt like having a few days off of alcohol because every time I have a weekend in London I end up waking up with a sore head and a wasted day and that's not fun all the time. Saturday morning I awoke at eight, still on office time and had nothing to do except lie in bed and piss around on the internet; however I spend five days a week in front of a computer so I didn't want to do any more of that. I got up and grabbed myself a coffee, leaving a half-full cafetière for Mel and Tim. I picked up yesterday's paper and put some TV on, oh wait, Saturday morning there's only programmes on for kids with ADD, two seventeen-year-olds jumping around and making fart jokes for two hours. There was still another two hours to go before "Football Focus", what to do, what to do?

It's odd how a certain time can either be the very best part of the week or the very worst, and right now Saturday mornings were the worst part of my week. God, even three Saturdays ago I was waking up still at the same stupid time, but instead of watching a repeat of Keith Floyd on TV insulting foreigners and getting drunk whilst cooking prawns on a boat, I would've been in bed with my girlfriend.

I would have been waking up with her and we'd lie there, thinking about how we had an entire two days to do as we please. There would have been Saturday morning sex, slow and sleepy, followed by dozing, chatting and more sex. A sudden realisation dawned on me, that's exactly what Mel and Tim were doing, wasn't it? I sighed and helped myself to the remainder of the cafetière and checked my watch again. I didn't begrudge them it, not at all but I guess Saturday mornings when you're single are shit because you know what everyone else in a couple is doing at that time.

Living with a couple was a little strange if I'm honest. No-one was quite used to the idea yet, least of all Mel who would untwine herself from Tim whenever I walked into the living room. I didn't want them to feel awkward, but then again I didn't want to feel awkward either in my own house. I think in an ideal world Mel would've preferred it if I was still unaware, or I thought as much when I overheard her the other day saying to Tim, 'I leave you alone for one night and you have a tortilla fight, book a flight to India and tell J and Rob about us when I'd explicitly told you not to?! And why the hell is there half a lime in the toaster?'

Even though I don't remember putting a £400 transaction on my credit card, which if we pause to think about it is a little worrying, I was pretty chuffed about India and the prospect of travelling again. It had been a while since I'd last got my backpack over my shoulders and I was desperate to get back to that mindset.

My Mum had moved to St Albans, a small city on the cusp of the M25, around a year ago so neither me nor my brother thought of it as the family home; however, whenever I went there I really felt like I was leaving the city behind.

I finally left the A41 and turned on to the start of the M1, accelerating hard up the ramp taking me to the motorway. This was much more like it, I thought as I wound down the window and turned up the radio. I reached inside the glove compartment and put my shades on, locking myself inside the bubble of my own head.

I miss Jazz.

So, Your Girlfriend's a Vegetarian?

I know, I know, I know. I said I didn't and I told the others I didn't but let's face it, no-one really believed me, least of all myself. I thought if I said it enough times it would make it true or at least manageable. I mean don't get me wrong, I'm not grief-stricken and unable to leave my flat because I may dissolve into tears at any second, I'm just a little sad about all the small plans I'd had in my head in February that now weren't going to happen. We're not going to go away for a week or two to somewhere hot in the summer. We're not going to spend lazy days on the beach exploring islands, and we're not going to spend nights in a rented apartment making love with the windows open. I'm not a fool, I know it was only two and a bit months, I hadn't even considered anything like the possibility of something really long term but it's a shame that it got cut short before it ever really got going.

See, I've never really fucked up before. Apart from when I was fourteen, which doesn't count, I'd never caused someone to dump me because of what I'd done. Break-ups had always been done because one of us was leaving the country, or we both realised what was there was no longer there, but it's never been because of how I've acted. I mean on that Saturday Jazz must have sat and thought, 'Right, because of how he has been over the last twenty-four hours, I want to remove this guy from my life completely, I want to find someone who will be better than him.' That's it actually J, isn't it, your pride is damaged? You were rejected because of you, nothing more than that. I just wish I could have shown her that it wasn't me.

I indicated to leave the motorway, the St. Albans exit being only six junctions from where I'd started, not quite far enough. I hadn't seen my Mum for about a month as we'd both been so busy, so it was with a big grin that I unlocked her front door and shouted a 'hey' up the stairs. As usual the house was incredibly hot, smelt of incense and echoed to the sounds of whichever female solo singer was fashionable at the moment. Right now we were on Madeleine Peyroux but previous highlights had included Norah Jones, Carla Bruni, Katie Melua, Natalie Imbruglia and back in the day Alanis Morrisette.

I heard soft padding on the stairs and we hugged and kissed. Now, my Mum is approaching sixty yet she looks fantastic, like she's mid-forties at the most. Her hair is in great condition, she's got a good fashion sense and her passion for travelling means she's always kitted out in necklaces or bangles from random countries. All in all as much as a son can say this, she's a pretty good catch and always has someone after her, even if she never quite realises it.

We spent the next hour or so catching up over a cafetière and waiting for my brother so that we could eat. My brother is as into his food as I am, and whenever the family get together me and him always cook because Mum did it for us for twenty years, so I guess it's our turn. Besides, we're better at it than her. True to form, we heard in the distance the squeal of brakes and the tinny echo of late eighties heavy metal music, and a few minutes later my brother turned into the road. Now Matt, even though he was hitting thirty, going bald, wore a suit and was a die-hard neo-conservative, was once upon a time a long-haired guitarist with several piercings and three tattoos. Whilst he'd sold out and become a corporate whore, and was perfectly happy to admit that, his music and his tattoos, hidden underneath his Hawes and Curtis shirts, were promises to never forget who he was. Much like the way I refuse to take off my gap year beads I guess.

Matt lowered his cheek to my Mum, letting her kiss it, his two hands full of carrier bags preventing him from giving her a hug. He smiled in greeting to me as he entered the kitchen, placing the supermarket bags on the counter.

'Right, I just did a quick shop and got some pasta and bacon, oh and asparagus was on offer, we can do something with that.'

'Well we can do a carbonara with the pasta and bacon.'

'Yeah, that's what I was thinking, and how about smoked salmon with the asparagus?'

'I'm just defrosting some salmon,' my Mum said as she rummaged in the fridge. Of course she was, she was a Jewish mother and that's the one thing you can count on whenever you go home, that there will be a fridge full of smoked salmon.

We set about chopping and cooking whilst Mum looked on, popping back and forth, laying the table. I love my Mum's kitchen as it is enormous, as all kitchens should be. It's definitely my favourite and when I get round to being able to afford my own house the kitchen's going to be one of the most important rooms. Food is such an integral part of life that it shouldn't just be cooked in cramped surroundings and then taken to another room; it should be prepared as it should be eaten, slowly, with other people, involving all the senses and interrupted by constant conversation. That's why I love my Mum's kitchen; there is room for everyone to sit, chop, cook, rummage in the fridge and wash up, all at the same time without getting in anyone's way. When the food is cooked it tastes all the better as everyone's played a role in making it, and you're eating it in the same place you cooked it in, so the smells linger.

Asparagus Wrapped in Smoked Salmon

Works well if you make a little green salad to put the asparagus on, or if you're not that hungry just have it on its own.

Ingredients

- Four to five asparagus pieces per person

- At least one long strip of smoked salmon for each piece of asparagus

- Sliced lime

- Olive oil

- Black pepper

Method

- Boil up some water and place the asparagus in the pan, once the water is boiling.

- Add salt

- You want to cook them for around three to four minutes depending on their thickness. Ideally, cooked asparagus is neither crunchy nor too soft.

- Whilst that's going on, cut some smoked salmon into strips around an inch wide and 6 inches or so long.

- Remove the asparagus and starting from the bottom wrap the salmon around the asparagus, leaving just the head protruding.

- Arrange the four on top of each other so that they're all pointing at different angles, it looks good

- Garnish with a slice of lime, dash of olive oil and black pepper.

Spaghetti Carbonara

I'm only a recent convert since I stopped being a student but fresh pasta really does make such a huge difference.

Ingredients

- Fresh pasta
- Two to three rashers of bacon per person
- One large red onion
- Two cloves of garlic
- Handful of mushrooms

For the sauce:

- Four egg yolks
- Grated cheese
- Knobful of butter
- Milk (cream if you want, but I never bother as I always waste the rest of the can)
- Oregano, rosemary and black pepper
- Sprinkle of dried chillies (optional)

Carbonara tastes like it should be really hard to make but it really isn't. Should take you around fifteen minutes.

Method

- Dice the garlic and onions, fry up with some oregano and rosemary.

- Turn down the heat after a few minutes and cut the bacon up into little squares and add to the pan.

- Whilst the bacon cooks, make the sauce.

- To get egg yolks, crack the egg over the bin and keep pouring the egg yolk back and forth between the two halves of the shells. The egg white will gradually slip off into the bin.

- Add the butter and a handful of grated cheese to the bowl, followed by around sixty ml of milk.

- Add chillies, herbs and black pepper and mix thoroughly with a fork.

- Add the mushrooms to the bacon and onions, and boil water for the spaghetti.

- Fresh spaghetti only takes two to three minutes to cook, so if using dried pasta you need to do this before, about the time when you first start cooking the onions.

- When the spaghetti is cooked, drain and add to the bacon mixture. Turn off the heat.

- Pour the sauce into the pan and mix thoroughly. The heat of the food will kill off all bacteria in the raw eggs.

N.B. If using fatty bacon, drain off the fat before adding the sauce, otherwise the sauce will be far too runny.

Like most families, I guess the three of us had sat around a table sharing food at a lot of different times in our lives. Some I'd hated, some were uncomfortable, but most I had loved. The table had swelled to include extended families, friends, girlfriends, even a fiancée, but the three and the link between the three had always remained. Growing up, Mum used to say that she felt like a lion protecting her two cubs, but now I think that we were all lions, very independent yet fiercely protective of each other. I guess it was quite intimidating for an outsider to come into it, but once you were in it you became like one of us, protected and protective.

The last year had been pretty event-free, which is pretty good for our family, so each time we met everyone was in a good mood and today was no exception. By the time the pasta came out, both Matt and I had started bantering my Mum pretty hard about the new man in her life.

'… and that's just it, he calls me and I have to talk to him for an hour or so. I mean I've already got things I want to do during the evening and now I feel like I really should be talking to him. But when I do, it's already nineish by the time we've finished, I've still got to eat and I want to watch some TV, put a wash on, read the paper, do whatever.' She poured herself some more water, 'I mean I used to watch you two in awe; when you were teenagers you'd always walk around with the phone glued to your ears for hours and I'd always wonder what on earth you had to talk about when you saw these people every day anyway.'

'And now?'

'Well I was telling Alan about next door's new fountain in the garden. It's not exactly riveting stuff now is it?!'

My brother smiled and poured some olive oil on his plate, swirled it around with some ciabatta so it picked up the sauce, and started to chew it. 'I know what you mean though; with Claire we lived together either at uni or in the flat so we never did the phone thing. Now with Liz she calls me when I'm playing poker online and it's like, if I don't speak to her she'll get pissed off, but equally if I stop the game I might as well throw forty dollars away.'

Mum nodded her head, 'I know! And texting too! All bloody day long. That's something I hadn't realised either.' She turned to me, 'If he asks me a question I have to reply right, but if he doesn't I don't have to? Are they the rules?'

I shrugged, 'Don't ask me, I'm shit with texts but I'm impressed you're texting though! Long gone are the days when I'd text you and you'd just send me the same text back as a reply.'

'Oh shut your face, that was when you were about eighteen, I've come a long way since then.'

My brother looked over, 'I bet she still signs them, though.'

'Well of course I sign them, otherwise how would he know who the text is from?'

I sighed and shook my head, 'How's it going with Liz? It's been what, about a month?'

Matt nodded, 'Yeah, just over. Good, well yeah, good, I've met her friends, she's invited me to her parents' house one weekend, it's fun. To be honest I'm just enjoying having regular sex again.'

Mum choked on her water, 'Matthew please, there are some things the woman who changed your nappies doesn't want to know.'

'OK OK, sorry.' He shrugged. 'I dunno, it's fine, she's nice but she isn't blowing me away. I'm not sure there's a future in it but it's fun for now.'

I think that's where my brother and I differ, or maybe where I differ from a lot of people, because if I felt like that then I don't think I'd be carrying on with it. What's the point if you know that it isn't going anywhere?

They both looked at me. 'And you? How's Jasmine?'

Why did I not see this coming? Matt and Mum raving about their new people whilst single McSingleton sits in the corner.

'We er, we broke up the night I got mugged; what with every-thing going on guess I forgot to tell you. But I am going to India in two months!'

My brother raised his eyebrows. 'Why did you break up? I thought it was going well?'

I moved my head from side to side. 'It was, but then it stopped going well and we nipped it in the bud before it started getting serious.'

Mum furrowed her brow. 'So it was a mutual thing?'

I nodded. 'Yeah, I guess you could say that.'

'Oh.'

Silence reigned over the table. I really couldn't be bothered to go into detail; it wasn't something I wanted to talk about at the moment. I tried to change the subject again.

'But I am going to India!'

'Oh yeah? So how come you decided on that?'

'Well Rob, Tim and I were sitting around last week and we just thought, fuck it, let's go somewhere exciting, so we booked flights, going for three weeks.'

My leg started vibrating; it was a text from Tim. '*Dude, time to get back out there, I've got you a date next Saturday, no need to thank me.*

Chapter Twenty-Four
April 6th 2008

'SO WHO IS SHE? And what have you done?'

'Katie, she works in my office, she's awesome. You're gonna love her.'

We were all in the lounge watching "Planet Earth" and eating Revels, a Sunday night ritual. One plus of Tim and Mel being together was that I now always had an entire couch to myself.

'Tim, I appreciate the sentiment but I don't really want to start dating again. I mean I'm still thinking about Jazz.'

'Oh forget about Jazz, you can do much better; now Katie is owww what was that for?'

Mel sat up and tweaked Tim's nipple hard.

'Don't insult Jasmine, she's one of my best friends, you dick. That's what that was for!'

Tim tapped his chest. 'But this is about MY best mate....'

'Yeah but you don't need to insult ...'

I held up my hands. 'Guys, c'mon no arguing about who's looking after me or whatever.' They half eviled each other and snuggled back down together.

I reached for the half-empty bag of chocolate. 'Eugh, orange cream. Tell me about Katie. Mel, have you met her?'

'No, but I did see a picture of her on Tim's phone.'

'Well, let me see it then!'

'No, it was just to show Mel, you can't see it.'

'What?'

'Yup, deleted.'

I threw a Revel at him. Missed, again. 'Fine. Ok, tell me about her.'

'Well, she broke up with her ex-boyfriend about three months ago, has only just moved to London recently, doesn't have too many friends yet.'

'What's she like?'

He shrugged. 'Seems like a laugh, good sense of humour, yet I've also seen her be a bit tough in work too.'

'Looks?'

'Hot.'

'Hey!' Mel stuffed a Malteser in Tim's face. 'Rephrase that.'

'Ok, she's pretty, your type, dark, curvy etcetera. Anyway, she's always wanted to go rollerblading in Hyde Park, apparently it's something non-Londoners think we do all the time. Since she's moved here she's been even more desperate to go but doesn't know anyone who can blade.'

I was now watching a slow-action shot of a great white shark jumping out of the sea and was only half-listening to Tim. 'Well, she can go on her own can't she, or there must be clubs she can join.'

Mel started to giggle.

Tim picked up the remote and turned the TV up. 'Well, I told her you could blade, you're meeting her at Hyde Park at two on Saturday – wow would you look at that shark it's eno—'

I sat up and turned towards Tim. 'WHAT?!'

Mel was in hysterics now.

'What? You're going rollerblading with a hot girl, it'll be fine, something different.'

'Tim, I can't rollerblade!' I exclaimed.

'Sure you can, we used to play roller hockey at school.'

I hit the couch in frustration. 'That was eight years ago and I was shit! I hate you, you did that on purpose!'

'I did not do that on purpose,' he protested, 'I honestly thought it would be fun.'

'I'm not going, no way.' I shook my head. 'You'll have to cancel.'

'Can't. She's not in work this week.'

'Text her.'

'Don't have her number.'

'Tim!'

'You'll be fine. She used to be a county figure-skating champion so I'm sure she can help you if you've forgotten how to blade. Help screw on some stabilisers or something. Now shut up and eat your chocolate.'

Chapter Twenty-Five
April 10th 2008

IT RAINED ALL DAY.

Well actually that's a complete lie, it didn't rain all day. But I wish it had. I spent the whole of last week trying to find some rollerblades in charity shops or friends' wardrobes but couldn't find any. When I did ask people they looked at me as if I was either twelve or living in 1993 and then changed the subject. You see, I could have bought some but I decided to wait and see if we hit it off or not. If sparks flew, if you pardon the pun, then I'd be first in line at Lillywhites buying the best blades around and no-one would be any the wiser, but if we just ground to a halt instead (oh I could do these forever) then I'm not going to waste fifty quid on some blades only for them to never be used again.

Anyway, I managed to find some in the end; Rob's sister-in-law's younger brother had some I could borrow. Obviously he was fourteen and had size eight feet so not only was I going against my will on a date with someone I'd never met to do a sport I hadn't done since school, I was now going to be in agony for the whole day too. Thanks Tim.

Another thing that I realised when I was waiting for Katie at the tube turnstiles on Saturday morning, was that I had no idea what the dickens she looked like. I was on the lookout for a dark curvy chick carrying rollerblades, at Hyde Park on a Saturday. There were loads of them. Looking down at myself I realised that I was a mess. Brown flowy hippy trousers, frayed at the bottoms and with a hole between my legs that I'd only discovered as the wind blew on the way to the station, and a dark blue old uni hoodie. I guess I never really factor rollerblading in when buying clothes I like, what are you meant to wear? If I was her I'd just carry on walking past me. I looked at my watch, five minutes late, she wouldn't have done that, would she? Take one look at the scruffy hippie clutching his blades like a falling baby and just carry on walking straight past, tell Tim on Monday that she couldn't see me. Maybe she was watching me now, as yet undecided. I stood up straight and tried to look cool, maybe she'll be great, maybe I'll look back on this day in forty years' time.

'J?'

Oh God.

'J? Tim's friend?'

'Yeah, hi! Katie, right?'

'Yeah cool, cool, so shall we see if it's still raining?'

'Let's do it, lead the way.'

I followed Katie up the stairs and into Hyde Park, where the rain had actually stopped; rollerblading was definitely happening.

I limped up the stairs into the flat a few hours later. I hurt. My knees felt like they were in a vice which was being slowly tightened and my toes wouldn't unfurl from the curl they'd been in since I slipped on my blades. Never again. The corridor was shrouded in a half-light from the streetlights outside as I felt my way into the lounge to draw the curtains, imagining that the TV and the couch looked inviting.

'Hey.'

I was wrong though. Curled up in one corner of the couch was Mel, a small desk light shining over her shoulder and onto the book that lay open on her lap. Her hair was tied up and she was chewing a pen, her brow furrowed. She looked up from her work with a studious expression on her face. 'How'd it go?'

'Average, not great really. Think I was pretty piss poor company too. How's work? Am I interrupting you?' Mel had an exam on Monday, it was the culmination of her two years of being a junior doctor in Nottingham and at the Royal Free in Hampstead. A good result on Monday and she was done, a fully fledged full practice

Doctor, ready to start a career in medicine.

'No, I feel like a break anyway, come sit. Feel like an Irish coffee?'

'Yeah, want a hand?'

She lifted herself off the couch, being careful to hop over the pages of notes surrounding her. 'No, I've got it, back in a minute.'

Irish Coffee

Not really a recipe I know, but it's a pretty good winter warmer, and after the April we were having it was more than welcome.

Ingredients
- One pot of freshly brewed coffee
- Double cream
- Sugar
- Whisky
- Few whole coffee beans

Method
- Brew up the coffee and pour it into thick highball glasses.

- Add a shot of whisky (or whatever, rum, tequila, coffee liqueur etc.) and a spoonful of sugar and stir.

- Slowly pour the double cream over the back of a teaspoon, holding it over the coffee. It'll create a thick layer of cream sitting on the coffee. Around ½ to ¾ an inch is good.

- Place a few coffee beans on top of the cream for decoration.

Mel brought the glasses into the lounge and handed me one. 'So tell me about it, what was she like?'

I chewed my lip. 'She was pretty cheerless actually. She'd been out the night before and kept moaning about how hung over she was, as if I was supposed to be impressed or something.'

'So she was great company then?'

'Exactly; no chat whatsoever. I think she just wanted to be next to someone rollerblading, either that or she thought the same of me and was just bored and couldn't be arsed to make the effort.'

'And how was the rollerblading?'

I grimaced. 'It wasn't that bad y'know, it's quite fun to do. If there weren't so many speed bumps we could have gone quite fast. As it happened, every time I saw a speed bump I slowed so much I almost fell over.'

'Hmm. So not going to see her again then?'

'No.' I reached for my coffee. 'Considering the fact we didn't even swap numbers I don't think that's very likely.'

'You sure?'

I looked at Mel full on. 'Yeah I'm sure. Why, what's up?'

She put her coffee on the table and turned to face me on the couch. 'J, I don't want the Jazz thing to come between us OK. If you meet someone, I don't want you not to tell me or to downplay it because you think it's going to go straight back to her or whatever.'

I shook my head. 'Honestly, it just so happened that me and Katie didn't click at all; of course I'd tell you.'

She reached for her coffee again and took a long sip before saying, 'Would you though?' She swallowed. 'Think about it.'

I thought about it.

'Maybe I wouldn't y'know. Not that I think you're going to start telling Jazz I've moved on and doing fine, it's just … it's just I'd feel weird talking about it in front of you, when you see Jazz all the time and know how she is. You have no idea how many questions I want to ask you.'

She nodded. 'I do, she says the same.'

I lifted my hand and motioned it forward. 'See that's it, it's so weird because for me it's like she stopped existing last month 'cause I've heard literally nothing from her. She's forever walking into her room and closing the door to me whereas for you, well, I mean you probably saw her today, didn't you. Did she ask about me?'

Mel looked down and said quietly, 'I'm not sure we should be having this conversation. It's hard enough on all of us as it is. I try my hardest not to bring you up around her and her up around you. I mean this is pretty much the first time we've spoken about it, isn't it?'

I nodded. 'Yeah, yeah it is. I don't feel as close to you as I did a few months ago, and that is beginning to get to me.'

We looked at each other, neither wanting to break eye contact. She placed her hand on mine. 'I know what you mean.'

We stayed like that for a few seconds until she moved her hand to reach for her coffee.

'How's it going? That's another thing we haven't spoken about.'

She smiled. 'We haven't, have we? I didn't like keeping it from you but I …'

I waved my hands. 'It's OK, really, I completely understand your reasons and seeing you both together, well I'm really happy for you. I think you're just what each other need.'

She raised an eyebrow. 'How'd you mean?'

'Well, you're very grounded, down to earth and contained, the complete opposite of Tim. He has his head in the clouds the whole time and it seems you're more than happy to walk along the pavement with his ankle in your hands.'

She smiled at the image. 'He makes me feel good about myself, no, more than good, he makes me feel unique and special, and what with everything going on at home it's just what I need at the moment.'

'Where is he now?'

'Sainsbury's. He's cooking me dinner so I don't have to take a break from work to cook.'

'And here I am …'

She playfully slapped my wrists. 'Oh hush, if I wanted you to go I'd say.'

We stayed there for a bit, in silence with her hand loosely covering mine, the desk lamp behind Mel creating a glow in the corner as if the room contained the dying embers of a fire. Leaning her head back into the couch she half-turned and looked at me out of the corner of her eyes. Her light brown hair spread out over the dark couch like a fan, tumbling down to her black polo neck.

'So what are the things you want to ask me?'

I leant back and did the same, our heads close. 'Really?'

'Look, is there anything that you're doing now that you wouldn't want Jazz to know about?'

'Well, no.'

'Right, and if it was me and Jazz sitting here right now instead of me and you, and she asked about you, would you rather I was either honest, lied and said you were sleeping with everything that moves or just clam up and say I can't talk about it.'

'The first, I guess.'

'Right answer, and she'd say the same thing.'

'How'd you know, though?'

''Cause it was me and her here last night whilst you were down the pub with Rob and Tim, and we had the exact same conversation.'

'She was here?!' I looked around in surprise as if I expected to see her hiding in the corner or something.

'Yeah, she came over for a bottle of wine and left just before you got back.'

Mel must've seen me deflate a little. 'J, it's too soon, she can't see you yet. You got closer in two months than some people have ever got. You know how proud yet vulnerable she is, she can't see you until she feels like she can look at you and you're not looking inside of her. Her words, not mine.'

'Does she talk about me much?'

'Same as you.'

'But I never talk about her in front of you.'

'No, but you're always on the verge of asking me about her yet you always pull back at the last minute.'

'You noticed?'

'Even Tim noticed.'

I smiled. 'Hmm. So hang on, that means she doesn't talk about me then.'

'Well, no, she didn't until last night.'

'What did she say?'

Mel shook her head. 'No J, some things I can't say.'

'Does she miss me?'

Mel looked at me, the lamp causing her light eyes to almost glow.

'What do you think?'

'Did you tell her I missed her?'

'Yes.'

'What did she say?'

She sighed. 'That it sucks but that it's the way it has to be. She isn't going to change her mind about this, that's why she doesn't want to see you because she knows she'll stumble if you're there. This way she can forget about you, or try to at least. I'm not having a go or anything, but I don't think you'll ever realise how much you hurt her last month, especially considering her past.'

'How'd you mean?'

She looked at me and raised her eyebrows. 'I thought it would be obvious?'

'What?'

'I guess sometimes it takes an outsider … C'mon, think about it. Her Mum's got three, four years of life left probably, if you call what she has life, and her Dad left her when she was a toddler. Couple that with the way most of her uni friends sided with Julian after the botched wedding, and Jazz has pretty much been abandoned by everyone in her life. Then you come along, make her feel safe with you, then from what she says out of nowhere you say you don't want to see her as much, another abandonment. Yours was the final rejection J, the one that made her realise she was always better than the people who made her feel like shit. Even though she's hurting just as much as you are at the moment, I think she needed to feel like this for her own sake. That's why, and I said this to her last night too, even though I think you two could've worked, she's got to do the next bit on her own. Maybe we see what happens further down the line, maybe we don't, but for now you got to move on.'

'You know, I'd never once thought of it like that.' I leant forward and drummed my fingers on the table. 'Whatever good faith I'd managed to get her to feel after a lifetime of getting dicked on, I managed to kill in one drunken night.' I paused. 'But that's the thing,

Mel, that's all it was, one drunken night. I never cheated, I never lied, I never even ...'

'No, you didn't, you were honest with her about how you felt and how things were moving along. Surely if you do both want different things in a relationship it's better you discover it early on than a year or two down the line.'

I heard the sound of Tim's key in the lock. I picked up the glasses and stood up, feeling guilty for some reason. Turning to Mel I said, 'Maybe I'm not so sure that what I wanted was so different from Jazz.'

Mel held my eyes before looking down to the carpet and shaking her head. Looking back up at me she whispered, 'Too late.'

Chapter Twenty-Six
April 16th 2008

```
<poo shop @1?>
<k, fancy going earlier? Starving>
<12.45? Only 40 mins to go>
<sweet>
```

ON SEEING ME RISE from the other side of the office Rob also stood up and we both walked towards the door. Simultaneously changing our phones from silent to ring, we left the office to get some lunch at the poo shop. This was not as disgusting as it sounds, for the poo shop was an old disused public toilet that had now been turned into one of those London sandwich shops with a huge display of meats and salads in front of a large swinging blackboard, the many sandwich combinations carefully drawn on with multicoloured chalk.

I picked up my wrapped sandwich, and once Rob had got his we went for a walk to a small park nearby. Rob and I had been spending quite a bit of time together recently, almost all our lunchtimes actually, and I think we were both glad of the company. Work was pretty dull at the moment, well not dull, just monotonous. It was all too easy to turn up at nine, work till six getting everything done, and leave without ever really interacting with anyone else. The company was going through a period where no-one was leaving or joining and no-one seemed to be having a birthday and so social meetings were pretty rare. That's why I was pretty thankful for Rob, we were having a post-work drink two to three times a week now. What with Tim and Mel together a lot of the time I didn't really fancy going back to the flat to sit on my own each evening.

I balanced my sandwich on my knee and looked around the park. On almost every bench sat someone reading a book or paper, eating a sandwich from a plastic wrapper. After an hour, like convicts allowed their fresh air and time off, they left the park to go back to their offices. I went to take a bite of my sandwich but the movement dislodged a mayonnaise-covered tomato which fell from the bread onto my grey suit. I sighed and wiped it off with the only napkin I was given.

'Is this it?'

'Hmm?'

I motioned to the people reading their books and to the mayonnaise stain on my suit. 'Is this it? Is this what we spent thousands of pounds and four years studying for? The privilege of working forty-five hours a week in a job we don't really care about so we can afford to live in crummy flats that are worse than the ones we lived in at university, yet more than twice as expensive?'

Rob looked skyward and carried on eating his sandwiches. 'Dude, it's starting out, it's forging a career for yourself, of course it's hard and soul-destroying, but it's never going to be as bad as it is today. Each day we get more experience, we get a better idea of what we want to do and what we don't want to do and we get on with our lives. Now shut up and eat your sandwich.'

I opened my mouth '…'

'Nup, don't want to hear it. Today is a no-whingeing day, a no-talking-about-Jasmine day and a no-being-in-a-grump day, OK?'

'Have I been that bad?'

'Yes, and now enough is enough. OK?

'OK.'

We lapsed into silence and I looked around again.

'You get that email about Friday night?'

'No? What about Friday night?'

Rob bit a corner off of his egg mayo sandwich. 'Must've landed the second you got up, I got it just before we left. Friday, Lucy suggested an office outing to Victoria Rooms, go out for a drink and actually talk to other people in the office for once.'

'I dunno if I can be arsed.'

Rob slapped the side of my arm with the back of his hand, 'J, no more fucking wallowing ok! At the risk of sounding harsh, I've just broken up with a girl I thought I was going to marry and you don't catch me almost in tears about a mayonnaise stain on my jacket. Man the fuck up and get ready to come out on Friday.'

Chapter 27
April 20th 2008

As soon as it got to six o'clock on Friday there was a mass exodus towards the Victoria Rooms, our local bar just opposite the office. There was a buzz of anticipation around the office today, most people were coming tonight and were ignoring the fact it was another two weeks at least until pay day. Work had pretty much stopped after lunch with most people deciding to 'clean up their inbox' or other euphemisms for wasting time and faffing around on a Friday. Around half five all the girls from the office left to do their make-up, taking with them the eyes of most of the guys and when they returned it was a green light for people to start switching off their computers and making their way out.

Four Kronenbourgs and no dinner later and I was feeling tipsy. Actually who am I kidding, it was coming up to eight o'clock and I felt drunk, and you know what? It felt good, I hadn't been out in ages. Sitting in the middle of an enormous couch I looked around at my colleagues opposite me, next to me and standing up by the bar, all drinking, all immediately switching off from work, forgetting their roles and being themselves. I wonder how many times in our lives strangers are thrown together and have to get on. Myself included, there was no-one in the office that anyone knew before they started and now look at us, getting on like friends do. You walk into that office shy and timid on day one and as your confidence grows you express yourself more and become more like the person you show to your friends, and then when you decide to change jobs you start all over again, you walk into a new office, shy as anything, desperately waiting for someone to invite you to the office get-together after work.

So, Your Girlfriend's a Vegetarian?

I guess it's like the whole university halls thing but on a smaller scale. I was lucky at uni because in my halls I found a great group of friends on pretty much day one. Even though the group expanded and depleted as people came and went, there was a hardcore group of fifteen or so who stayed constant, lived together throughout uni and now do a pretty good job of keeping in touch with each other. We'd always say to each other how glad we were that X spoke to Y or whoever on the first day so that the group formed, otherwise we'd never have met, but then we never would have known we'd never have met. Being placed in a hall of 220 people I found people I hated, people I fancied, one or two I fell in love with and a load of people who I'm pretty sure will be friends for life. As great as that is, and as privileged as I feel to have those great friends, I have no doubt that if I was put in another hall the same thing would have happened and I would never have known about these other people. I could've been sitting in our union with my mates next to Mel one day and never known who she was. Weird. So, what made me think of that, as I looked around at my workmates, was that it was all the same but on a smaller scale. There were a few that irritated the hell out of me, a few I fancied and one or two that I was really glad I'd met for I still want them in my life when I'm not working here. Any group you enter alone and I reckon the same thing happens. We're social creatures, we crave interaction and as sad as it sounds if you weren't friends with this person it really doesn't matter as you would've been perfectly happy being friends with someone else. It's all so random and that's what I love. Think about it, if I wasn't in halls with Mel I never would have met Jazz and Mel would never have met Tim. If I hadn't got accepted for a job here I would never have met Rob, instead there would be this alternative J working with other people, going home to different friends and even going to bed with a different girl. I think that's why I get really annoyed when people harp on about soul mates. There are six billion people out there, and there must be thousands upon thousands of people that someone meets in a lifetime. The notion that there is only one person in that mixture that you could

169

feasibly spend the rest of your life with is crazy. If soul mates do exist then I reckon there are dozens of them all over the world, the challenge is to find one of them when the timing is right.

'What do you mean when the timing's right?'

I looked at Lucy. 'Huh?'

'You can't just launch into this whole diatribe about life to everyone and then stop when it gets interesting. And who do you fancy in the office?!'

My God, I'd been talking aloud. The whole table was looking at me.

I sat up and thought quickly about what to say. 'Well I mean what if you meet someone you think something amazing could happen with, and she's going out with someone, or you're about to leave the country, or you don't even speak the same language!'

Freya leant in from the corner. 'Well that's when you have to make those life-changing decisions, isn't it? Don't leave the country or do break up with your boyfriend for someone else.'

'But what if it doesn't work?' Rob joined in. 'What if you fuck up a perfectly good relationship to pursue something with someone and then when you do pursue it, you realise it's not what you wanted after all?'

'I dunno, something tells me if you're looking elsewhere anyway the relationship isn't that solid.'

'Ah c'mon!' Rob hit back at Lucy. 'We're human, everyone looks around or wonders what it would be like with someone else. That doesn't mean you're going to cheat on someone or that you're a bad person, it's normal. You can't say that in all your years with Dan you've never once looked at someone and thought, "I wonder what my life would be like if I was with you."'

She spluttered, 'Well yeah, sure, but I've never contemplated leaving him to find out. You have that split-second feeling of wonder, then you remember all the things you love about the person you're with.'

'Maybe that's it then!' I leant into the table. 'If after that split-second of wonder you don't have that flash of all the things you love about that person, then maybe that's your clue to move on.'

We all went quiet for a bit and began to drift off back to our own conversations. I was talking to Lucy about someone who had left the company a year ago and was now working for our competitor, Rob and Freya were opposite us and to our left were Donna, the office manager, and Martin, another events guy. As we all got up to get drinks and go to the toilet the group moved and reformed, until I found myself an hour or so later on the couch next to Freya.

Now, I didn't know Freya that well but she seemed nice enough. She was the kind of person you talk to in the kitchen when you're waiting for the kettle to boil or when you both happen to be walking to or from the station, but beyond that I didn't really know her. When I first started working I was incredibly intimidated by her for she seemed like she'd been working at IQG for ages, but it turned out she'd only been there six months or so longer than me. I guess I should also say I was a bit intimidated by her because when I first joined I also had a little bit of a crush on her, something that had been around for a few months and then faded into the background.

Thing is, I know I was drunk but I was kind of remembering what I'd fancied about her. She had this raw kind of sexuality about her, the look that made you think she could eat you alive, and for me there's pretty much no greater turn-on. As we were talking people around us gradually left or moved over to other parts of the bar until all of a sudden I noticed that we were alone on the couch and that there was no longer any need for us to be sitting that close to each other. Thing is, I was wedged into the corner, she was the one who could've moved yet she hadn't. Interesting.

Now, obviously I'm not going to read too much into this, but I am feeling quite drunk so why the hell not. I lifted my feet up from the ground so that they were resting on the table with my knees up. Because I was a guy and needed the space, I opened my legs so that all of a sudden my right leg was resting against her left leg. Contact made. Freya didn't move away, in fact it might have been my imagination but she actually leaned in a bit. I reached forward to pick my drink up off the table and sat back, moving slightly closer to her so that our shoulders were now touching. Done

'So.'

'Yeah, so …' By now the music was deafening so we had to lean in to hear what the other was saying. 'Up to much this weekend?'

'No, not much really, maybe a house party tomorrow. You?'

'No, not much really either, catch up on some sleep.'

My God what a dull conversation. I literally couldn't think of anything to say.

'Cool.'

'Yeah.'

'So how's your week been? I never really see you much around the office?'

'Not bad y'know, thankful it's Friday and everything.'

I don't understand, I'm pretty sure she was flirting or playing or whatever you want to call it and I'm sure she knew that I was sort of interested too, but I could not think of a single thing to talk about. I looked around.

'Nice place isn't it, I mean for your average city bar?'

Oh come on J, you can do better than this.

'Hey guys.'

Rescue. Rob slid on to the couch next to Freya.

'J, we're going,' said Rob.

'Are we?'

Freya looked at both of us. 'Yeah, are you?'

'Yeah we are, sorry, but hey what are you both doing next Friday?'

I looked at Freya who turned to look at Rob. 'Nothing,' she said, 'why?'

'I'm thinking of having a dinner party. J, you free?'

'Rob, my only social events revolve around you nowadays, yeah I'm free.'

'Excellent, thing is I'm only inviting the two of you from the office so don't tell anyone. Now come on J, we got to go.'

I shook my head a little too forcefully. 'Nah, I'm going to stay here a bit, I think, stay here with Freya.'

He took my hand and pulled me up. 'No, we're going now, say your goodbyes. Bye Freya, have a good weekend.'

I looked over my shoulder and smiled at her. We mouthed the word bye at each other and Rob and I emerged into the half-light of the London street.

'Dude, what the hell did you do that for?! It was on with Freya!'

'No it wasn't, or if it was, it shouldn't've been tonight. Mate, you're both drunk, the whole of the office is there. You guys leave together and the entire company will be talking about you, and that is something you do not want. We're leaving 'cause I'm watching your back.'

'Ach, but she was looking hot.' We stopped at a zebra crossing and waited for a car to slow. 'I couldn't think of a single thing to say to her.'

'That's because you're tired and drunk, an awful combination. Anyway, no rush. That dinner party idea? Completely made it up but it could be fun. You, me, Freya, Mel and Tim, we could see if Emma's around. That way if you do want to make a move on Freya, or her on you, you can both do it when you haven't got the whole office staring at you. I'm an awesome friend, when are you going to realise this? Now run, we want that bus.'

Chapter Twenty-Eight
April 25th 2008

AWESOME FRIEND OR NOT, Rob's flat was a dive. He had a great bedroom, as did his two flatmates, but the communal areas sucked. The bathroom was a joke and seemed to be almost an afterthought of the architects, bolted on to the side of the house on the top floor. His lounge was pretty small too, but big enough to just about fit the six of us around the table without us being too cramped; however it was his kitchen that was the real downer. It had pretty much no work spaces and only really enough room for one person to cook. Tonight that one person was me, surprise surprise. I'd got into work on Monday to find an email waiting for me from Rob saying, <FYI if I'm having a dinner party and possibly getting u some, ur cooking. Make it tasty.>

I'd replied, <no! This is ur party, u sort it. Get Emma to cook>

To which Rob replied, <fraid not bud, she spends all week cooking, besides don't really know her well enough to ask. U want to come u cook.>

So I was cooking then. As I said, we were six tonight, one couple and four others. Tim and Mel had become a firm couple by now, and I think after our chat Mel had got a bit used to the idea of acting like a smitten kitten over Tim in front of me. She'd also started coming into my room and lying on my bed with a big inane grin on her face, rabbiting on and on about Tim, just like I'd done to her about Jazz in January. Although I took the piss whenever she got soppy, the truth of it was that I hadn't seen her this happy about a bloke since uni, and the more I got used to the idea the more I could see a future for them.

Tim was obviously being a bit cagier about it, but then again that's

174

just the sort of person he is. The guard lets slip once in a while and the real him shines out, and when it does, you can tell how crazy he is about her. I guess the fact it completely took them both by surprise makes it feel even better as neither of them saw it coming, I mean on New Year's day if I would've told Mel that in a few months her and Tim would be serious, I doubt whether she'd have known whether to laugh or beat me to death with a wok.

The Freya thing was quite interesting. I'm pretty sure we'd been flirting over the last week, but then again I am a guy and so interpret any girl talking to me as flirting. That said, there had been a few emails going between us at work, mostly about food or what to wear (her not me obviously), but it was a definite change from our previous months working together. I think I fancy her. I'm not sure. Actually, I'm completely sure, she's a nice girl but I don't fancy her, well, when I'm sober at least.

Creamed Asparagus, Parmesan and Mushroom Soup

Ingredients
- Two dozen asparagus
- Vegetable stock
- Handful of chestnut mushrooms
- Wedge of parmesan cheese
- Half a tub of crème fraiche
- Black pepper and salt

Method
- Boil up the asparagus in two pints of the vegetable stock, seasoning with black pepper and salt.

- After five minutes or so remove the asparagus, cut a few heads off and put to one side then put the tails in the blender.

- Add the crème fraiche and the vegetable stock and blend.

- Crumble up the parmesan and blend again; the mixture should now be thick and bright green.

- Fry up a few mushrooms.

- Pour out the soup and sprinkle over the asparagus heads and the freshly cooked mushrooms (quartered).

Pork Chops, Sweet Potato Mash, Roasted Onions and Fried Plantains

Now, although this looks pretty complicated, cooking time is actually only around ten minutes so it really shouldn't take long to do.

For the pork chops with a jerk marinade:

- In a bowl mix a teaspoon of olive oil, paprika, grated nutmeg, cumin, cinnamon and coriander.

- Lay the pork chops out and score with a sharp knife diagonally across the meat. Do this from each side, creating a diamond effect.

- Empty the mixed spices onto some kitchen roll and place the pork on the spices, pushing down hard on them so that the marinade sticks to the meat. Flip the chop over and repeat.

- These can now chill in the fridge. They'll take about eight to ten minutes to cook under the grill and should be turned once.

For the potato and sweet potato mash:

Now even though it looks a lot, mash is pretty easy to eat so roughly use two potatoes per person.

- About fifteen minutes before you want to serve, thinly slice the normal potato and add it to a pan of boiling water, add a good helping of salt.

- Normal potatoes take longer to cook than sweet potatoes, so add the sweet after the ordinary have been boiling for about five minutes.

- Use a knife to test, but when the potatoes crumble easily, turn off the heat and drain.

- Add a good portion of butter, a splash of milk and some black pepper and mash away.

For the roasted onions and carrots:

These should go in around the same time you cook the potatoes.

- Slice the onions and carrots and place in a baking tray.

- Use the same marinade as before, but this time add a bit of olive oil and a teaspoon of honey.

- Use your hands and ensure it's all covered and leave it in the oven.

For the fried plantain:

With plantain, the greener and harder the better, as it'll hold its consistency more when it's cooked.

- Using roughly one plantain per person, slice into discs around half a centimetre wide.

- Dry fry (no oil) and add a lot of rock salt.

- Keep turning until the surfaces go brown.

- Taste it, it should be quite dry and taste a bit like potato. If it's soft you cooked it too long.

And for the veggies (Freya was one too, I mean seriously…)

Stuffed Peppers with Chilli, Cous Cous and Melted Cheese

Ingredients

- One large pepper per person
- One courgette
- Two cloves of garlic
- One red onion
- One red chilli
- Around 125 grams of cous cous per person
- Portabello mushrooms
- Parmesan
- One vegetable stock

Method

- Chop up the courgette, garlic, red chilli and mushrooms and cook with a little olive oil.

- Mix up some vegetable stock and add half a cup to the vegetables.

- Remove and drain after all the vegetables have browned and have absorbed most of the stock (around four to five minutes).

- Chop a red pepper in half and de-seed.

- Spoon the mixture into each half of the pepper and grill for eight to ten minutes.

- Empty the cous cous into a bowl and cover with around 250ml of water. If there is any left, add the vegetable stock water (this should be cold however).

- Cover the cous cous for five minutes and then fluff with a fork.

- Remove the peppers and empty the vegetables into the cous cous bowl.

- Stir so everything becomes mixed up, and then spoon back into the peppers.

- Grate parmesan over the top and grill for a further two minutes.

We were changing seats every course, with the men moving one space to the left after each dish. This lasted until after the mains when Tim pointed out that when there are only six of you, and you're all having the same conversation, musical chairs becomes a bit redundant. A lot of the conversation had revolved around work for if you included Emma, four of us worked for the same company and anyway Tim and Mel knew most of the people we were talking about. We had tried to move on to talk about Tim's job but that bored most of us to tears so we quickly reverted to IQG. The red wine was flowing freely round the table and after a nod from Rob I followed him into the kitchen to get the cheese board ready.

Cheeseboard

Emma had gone crazy and bought a tonne of cheese.
Ingredients
- Brie
- Stilton
- Camembert
- Saint Agur
- Bunch of red grapes
- Crackers
- Chutney and/or apricot jam
- Celery

Method

- Not really anything to do. Arrange all of the cheese on a board and garnish with the grapes, celery and chutney.

- Serve with a lot of crackers.

'Freya?'

'Dunno.'

We were whispering as the kitchen was only next door.

'What do you mean you don't know?!'

'Well I don't, OK! Yeah she's hot, but I don't know if I want to make a move.'

'Well, what do you think she wants?'

'Oh I don't know, I'm shit at working out if women fancy me, I can never tell.'

'I think she does.'

'Why?'

'You guys have been talking all evening! Even when you weren't sitting together.'

'Well of course we have.' I unwrapped the brie from its sellotape-like wrapping. 'Apart from you she doesn't know anyone here.'

Rob moved over to the sink and started washing the grapes. 'Still, I reckon you should go for it. Stop being so picky and waiting for perfection.'

'Rob, with all due respect, I'm not gonna listen to your advice, it hasn't exactly worked in the past.'

He picked up the board and walked towards the door. 'Low blow dude, low blow. I just think you should let your guard down once in a while, it's not that bad out here.'

We rejoined the table to find Tim pouring out the port and Emma rolling a joint, the standard mid-twenties ending to a dinner party. We all piled in and pretty soon port and weed were making their way around the table, criss-crossing over each other as the cheese was demolished.

'Nah, I'm thinking about moving on, selling the catering business, putting down a deposit on a place to turn into a restaurant.' Emma stopped to inhale deeply. 'I mean ...' she exhaled '... if it doesn't work, fuck it, but I'm twenty-four, I've got to try it now when I don't have that many strings, I'm never gonna be freer than I am now.'

Freya shook her head. 'But what about your business, you've what, spent six years building that up, what if you put all that money into a place and it sinks?'

'Then it sinks.' She nibbled some brie off of her finger. 'Then it sinks and I start from square one, but I still tried it. I'm not going to settle for what I've got now.'

'That, Emma,' said Rob, waggling his finger at her and receiving the joint in exchange, 'is the worst word in the world, "settling" is the curse of our generation.'

'Explain Rob,' asked Mel, 'enlighten us, Yoda.' We all started giggling.

'OK OK, pipe down.' He cleared his throat. 'We come out of uni and move to London and start working. Now, all is good for what, three months or so and then the exhaustion hits, you realise you're slowly becoming part of the machine and you don't think there's anything you can do to stop it. Your job is tedious, you spend your life filling in forms saying what you're about to do and forms saying what you've just done, and every day you catch a sight of yourself in the reflection of the tube and you think fuck, what am I doing? This is the same person that helped build an Aids clinic in Malawi, or worked with abused orphans in Ecuador, what am I doing?'

We all nodded, minds flying in the clouds.

'And then you think, but I can't change jobs, I don't have the time or the money. If I quit I'll have to move home, go back to square one, and so you do nothing, you settle for what it is. Now, next you have the couple in a relationship, together since uni when there were no worries and you could spend days in bed missing lectures. Now you're both working, and part of you wants to be on your own, doing your own thing and being independent, but you've just moved to

London, you have exactly the same friends, it'd be a nightmare if you break up, so you don't, you settle.

'Next up are your housemates. Some you knew, some you didn't, and for whatever reason it's not working out. The flat's too small, a flatmate irritates you, it's that bit too far from the station, but what do you do? Nothing, moving is a hassle so you settle. Soon enough you're settling for everything and you're firmly part of the machine. That part of you that would happily sleep on the side of a road in China waiting eight hours for a bus or get up in the middle of the night just to climb a mountain in the Andes for sunrise is gone forever.' Rob turned to the table. 'No, what I will never do, and what I believe no-one round this table will ever do, is settle for anything. You think something could be better and it's within your power to change it, then change it because it's far better to know something doesn't work than to settle in a comfort zone and convince yourself it wouldn't have worked anyway.'

'Rob,' Tim reached for the joint, 'with all due respect, that's bollocks OK. I have a job, sure it's not the best thing in the world but it's OK, I put up with it because the people I work with are halfway decent and it gives me money to do things I want to do. Now, sure I agree in principle, you should always strive to do what makes you happy, but if I was doing that I'd be unemployed and we wouldn't be going to India in a few months. You make choices, and I don't think I'm settling just because one aspect of my life might not be amazing.'

Freya nodded and relit the joint. Holding it up to her face, she smiled. 'It's like this is the conch, only the smoker can talk. Sorry Rob, I'm with Tim on this one I think. Nothing will ever be perfect and if you continually strive for perfection then you'll end up burnt out and alone. What we do now,' she tapped the table, 'it's real Rob, and I think it's pretty naïve to think you can be happy with all of your life at the same time.'

'You misunderstand though.' The candlelight flickered in his eyes, making him appear even more animated than he was. 'I'm not seeking perfection, I'm seeking happiness. You know that famous saying, you are truly free when you no longer strive to be free, well I want to get to a stage when I no longer try to improve my life, when I'm happy with how it's all going and not continually looking over the fence thinking "wow wish I was doing that".'

'That's your problem in a nutshell, Robin.' We turned to look at Emma. 'Who cares what the next person is doing? You continually compare yourself to others and you'll continually fail; just do your own thing and concentrate on that.'

Rob sat back in his chair and looked down, an acknowledgement that he was outnumbered. We lit another joint and smoked it slowly; a chilled hush as thick as the smoke covered the table.

The evening began to reach its end. The wine and food were gone and all of a sudden a wave of tiredness hit the table. The culmination of a lot of food, red wine, a long week and the first bit of weed in a few months meant everyone's thoughts turned to bed. Mine turned to Freya's. Our legs had been pressed up close to each other's since I'd gone into the kitchen with Rob, and every now and then we caught each other's eyes and lingered. I was drunk, a little stoned, horny and y'know what, fuck it, I'm gonna do something out of character. We all got up and started putting our coats on, and as we left the room I leant in close to Freya.

'I can't be arsed to call it a night yet, do you feel like coming back to ours for a drink?'

She turned to me, a slight smile playing on the corner of her lips. 'You're asking me back to yours?!'

I shrunk back, my confidence immediately gone. 'Well yeah, if you fancy, I mean it is still quite early.'

She shook her head. 'No J, I don't think that would be a good idea.'

'OK.' Damn. I half turned away.

'You could come have a drink at mine though?' She did up her jacket, smiled and walked past me into the hall to join the others.

The cab sped us away to Putney and as we made out in the back I wondered, like every person who kisses in the back of a taxi, just how many other people have done what I was doing, and does the cabbie really not care? A sharp corner sent us hurtling into the corner, our lips becoming unstuck, killing the mood for a second.

'Second on the left after the lights please.' A speed bump shook us again as the taxi turned into Freya's road and came to a rest at a bus stop. I paid, giving a large tip and avoiding eye contact, and followed Freya into her flat. She opened the door, flung her jacket over a couch and picked up a bottle of red from a wine rack in the corner.

'Back in a minute,' she threw a look over her left shoulder before heading into the kitchen. I made my way over to the couch and sat in the middle. Then I stood up and took my jacket off before sitting down again. I was up again and walking over to her CD collection. I walked past photo after photo of people I'd never seen before and never would see, all with their arms around Freya at various ages. I looked at myself in the mirror, my blood-red eyes and small pupils giving away my condition.

This was wrong.

I heard the pop of the cork and Freya re-emerged with two large glasses of red. Cheersing, we sat back down on the couch, the glasses in our hands preventing us from kissing.

Was this wrong?

'J, I'm not going to sleep with you.'

I almost choked on my wine.

'Erm, ok.' I put my glass down and paused. 'I'm not quite sure what to say to that. I wasn't really planning that far ahead.'

'I mean, well I just wanted to say that now, in case that was the only reason you'd come back here, 'cause I'm not, I think it's a bad idea.'

I nodded. 'OK, well that's not why I came back, I mean, it had crossed my mind but I didn't think that,' stop talking J, 'yeah anyway, that's cool.'

She smiled and clapped her hands together. 'Cool. I mean we can still do stuff, just no sex, OK.'

'OK.' Is this just me or is this a little strange? We lapsed into silence. Freya drank her wine, I drank my wine.

'So how long have you been single for? Weren't you going out with someone when I started working?'

She poured out the remaining half-bottle into our two glasses. 'Yeah I was, but we broke up about six months ago; I found out he cheated on me.'

'No way, how'd you find out?'

'He told me. He could never lie.'

'So what did you do?'

'I told him to get out and said I never wanted to see him again. Cheating isn't cool. Anyway, what about you? Are you over Jasmine?'

'Jasmine? God yeah,' lie lie lie, 'we were never that serious anyway,' lie lie lie, 'yeah she's long gone.'

Freya put down her glass and moved along the couch so we were inches apart. I reached for her and we kissed as I put my arm around her shoulders and started to run the backs of my fingers across her exposed top back.

'I like you, I think you're a nice guy,' she said, 'I can trust you, can't I? This isn't going around the office on Monday morning is it?'

I shook my head. 'Course it isn't, this is between you and me.'

She smiled. 'Good. Want to see my room?'

Freya took my hand and led me towards the stairs. She walked up the first stair and turned to kiss me, our heights equal. She put her arms around my shoulders and kissed me deeply, leaning into me with all her weight. I responded and with my arm around her back pushed her gently down onto the staircase. Our hands intertwined as I lifted them above her head and pushed them down onto the stairs. With her hands still held above her I began to bite her lower lip and then moved down to kiss her neck. She responded and pushed back, moving off the stairs so that I was now underneath her, the rounded corners of the stairs digging into my back. She ground her hips down hard on mine and arched her back as I pulled up her top, raising her arms so that I could pull it off completely. I threw it back down into the lounge as she kissed me hard, forcing my head back onto the stairs. Fumbling with my buttons she undid my shirt quickly and wrapped her hands around me, nails clutching at my back. I reached up with my hands and pulled down on her shoulders, forcing her groin down onto mine. She gripped my back harder and moved her hips back and forth, rocking on top of me.

She pulled away. 'Come upstairs.' She took my hand and I followed her upstairs. We went into her room and as she turned from shutting the door I kissed her hard, my hands reaching up to undo her bra. She removed my shirt from my shoulders, kissing and biting my neck as she did so, and led me over to the bed. Pushing me down, she clambered on top of me and we kissed again.

Reaching down for my belt she tugged at it a few times, trying to loosen it, before I intervened and undid it. Whilst still kissing me she undid my fly, pulling at my jeans. I wriggled out of them and she threw them across to the other side of the room. I pulled her on top of me and slid my hands down to grab her arse, pulling her down onto me. I moved my hand around and she started to breathe harder as I slowly undid the buttons on her trousers, sliding my hands inside. Pulling down her trousers I flung them across the room and we went back to kissing, my hands toying with the waistband of her French knickers. I eased my fingers underneath the elastic and slowly moved my hand down as her body responded to my touch and she pressed herself close towards me. Pulling down my boxers she gripped me tightly as I lightly skimmed my finger down over her hair and began to trace around and across her clit and further down. She was soaking wet. She sighed and pulled her lips away from mine, pushing her breasts into my face, gripping my hair tightly, holding me there. I pulled down her underwear and ran my fingers up and down the inside of her thighs as she responded by running her nails hard down my back. Now both naked, our arms encircled each other as we lay on top of the duvet, rolling from one edge of the bed to the other. I kissed her neck, working my way down until I took her breast in my mouth, gripping the other one hard in my hand, my fingers skimming over her already hard nipple. My fingers moved down and entered her again and as I began touching and circling her G spot she began to groan. Pulling at my hair, she lifted me to her lips and kissed me deeply, our teeth crashing against each other's as once more we swapped and she now lay on top of me, moving her body slowly against my hand. Breaking off, she began to kiss my chest, working her way downwards, taking me in her mouth. I lay back, closed my eyes and pulled her body up so that she was lying side-on across me. I reached for her thighs and she manoeuvred herself so that her legs were either side of my head as she took me in her mouth once more. My fingers entered her again as I lifted my head towards her. As I began to lick and suck on her clit I felt her nails dig hard into my thighs.

A few minutes later she lifted herself up off of me, turned around and we kissed again as once more she ground her hips down hard on me and I, gripping her waist, pushed myself towards her, holding her steady. She sat up and threw her head back, our bodies moving together, faster and faster. She looked at me through the mess of brown hair dangling over her face, her lips moist and slightly open, it was one of the sexiest looks that I've ever seen. Leaning down she began to kiss me, holding my hands back behind my head. Grinding herself down she pushed my wrists down into the pillow, her fingers interlocking and squeezing mine tightly. She opened her eyes and leant down to kiss me as I felt her quick hard breath on my cheek.

'J ...'

I reached up and pulled her head down towards me again so that we could kiss.

'J ...'

'Yeah?'

'I think, I think we should stop before we do something we'll both regret.'

She stopped moving against me. She looked down and gently kissed my lips. 'I just think we should stop.'

I looked up at her, my hands resting on her hips. We were both breathing hard, blood pumping around our bodies and hearts beating quickly.

'Really?' I asked. I caught my breath. 'I, I don't think I'd regret this, Freya.'

She smiled. 'J, we work together. We shouldn't.'

She looked down at me again through her hair. 'It's just going to complicate things.'

I sank back into the pillow; I knew she was right, even though you have no idea how much I wished she wasn't.

'Maybe you're right. Yeah, I guess we should stop.' I paused, 'You, er, you sure you don't want to carry on?'

She gave a little laugh and leant down to kiss my lips. Moving off me she lay down by my side. 'I'm cold, let's get under the duvet.'

We rolled back the covers and got in. Taking my hand she pulled my arm across her so that I was spooning her. I turned the light off and we lay in silence for a while until about ten minutes later I heard Freya breathing deeply. I pulled her closer, her hair tickling my cheek, and waited for sleep to come.

MAY

Chapter Twenty-Nine
May 2nd 2008

CROSSING LONDON AT NINE the next morning hadn't been fun. At that time there were only two types of people on the tube; those that had to work on a Saturday and hated that fact, and those that either hadn't been to bed yet, or had but had woken up on foreign ground. It was my first tube of shame in a while and as I looked at my contorted reflection in the mirror of the Northern Line train I felt conflicting emotions. In the cold light of day I knew I wasn't really interested in Freya. Sure, I was attracted to her and whilst I'd loved being thrown around and throwing her around last night, I couldn't ignore the fact that we had barely anything in common and even less to talk about. The physical stuff wasn't a good enough base to want to pursue anything more.

I didn't feel bad about being with someone else after Jazz. It had been about six weeks after all, and for all I knew she was doing the same thing. Problem was, however, it kinda made it worse and I can't really put my finger on why that is. I think it was the realisation that Freya was nothing compared to Jazz and I guess that got me wondering if I'd always be comparing and if they'd always come up short.

It was still early, just before ten as I gently slid my key into the lock and sneaked inside. I eased my way up the stairs, went into my room, threw my clothes in my washing basket and crawled under the covers. I was shattered. I knew I wasn't going to be able to sleep but I could really do with an hour or so of dozing.

The door exploded open and Tim and Mel toppled over each other into my room. Chewing on the end of a piece of toast Tim clambered over me, still in his dressing-gown, and flopped down next to me on the bed, sitting up and leaning against the wall. He ruffled my hair. 'Morning, stud.'

Mel jumped on the bed and lay across both of our legs. Resting her head on her hands she looked up at me questioningly, 'Sooooooooooooo?!?!?!'

'What?'

She slapped my knee. 'Don't you "what" me, Camfield! You were pretty sneaky last night, I turned round and you'd both gone. So, are you in love?'

'Very funny; no I'm not in love.'

Tim swallowed the remnants of his toast and started picking his ear. 'You sleep with her?'

'No I did not sleep with her!'

'Why not?'

'What do you mean why not? We just didn't sleep together, OK! Tim, you're dropping wax on my duvet!'

'She said no, right? So what did you do?' He nibbled his fingers.

'Look, fun was had by all OK, now leave me alone, I want to go to sleep.'

'Fun was had by all?!' Mel turned to look at Tim. 'What the dickens does that mean? Spill J.'

'No! Look, stuff happened OK, leave it at that.'

'OK, OK.' Mel moved up the bed and settled herself between me and Tim. 'So, do you like her?'

I looked at her and grimaced.

'Ah J, not again.'

'I know.'

She slapped my shoulder. 'Why don't you like her? She's beautiful.'

'She is, but there's no …' I gestured with my hands, clicking my fingers, 'Y'know.'

Tim rolled his eyes. 'She didn't blow you away immediately so you're giving up straight away, wow way to do something completely out of character, J.'

'Well what do you suggest then? That I fake it?!'

'No!' Tim exclaimed. 'Jesus, give it a chance, go out on a date, just don't completely dismiss her out of hand just because from day one you can't picture yourself with her for the rest of your life or just because she isn't Jazz and—'

'Hey.' I turned to look at him. 'Stop Tim, don't. You don't know what you're talking about so just shut up.'

He held his hands up. 'OK, I take that back, I just think you should stop comparing today with yesterday or with what you hope may come along tomorrow.'

'And I think you should let me be, Tim. I'm tired OK, and I'm not in the mood; just both of you give me a little space.'

'Fine. Take your space, c'mon Mel.'

I awoke a few hours later, guess I had drifted off after all. Walking around the flat I realised I was alone, an eerie silence draped over the lounge, Mel and Tim must've just left. Maybe the door shutting was what woke me up. Rays of lukewarm spring light shone through the large bay windows, distorted by the grime of the fine covering of dirt on the outer side of the glass, a window cleaner not being high on the list of things for a landlord to subscribe to. I walked through the flat, looking at the smear of ketchup covering two dirty plates on the table, betraying the fry-up Mel and Tim must've just had. It felt like the kitchen chair should be on its side.

I showered, taking an unusually long time and allowing the hot water to burn into my neck muscles, breaking up the tension in my shoulders. I stood and looked at myself in the mirror before taking a swipe at the condensation and rubbing shaving foam into my skin. Coming out of the bathroom I glanced at the clock and felt a surge of anger as I realised it was almost one. Checking myself I remembered I had nothing to do today. I almost craved the need to go shopping or to have some admin to do. It's sad how city life makes you feel compelled to go shopping and spend money when you're at a loose end. I considered texting Tim or Mel but thought better, not only was

I a little embarrassed about snapping at Tim, but their couple status made me not want to feel like a spare wheel, half deflated and not really needed.

Opening the door I felt a slight chill on my raw, shaven cheeks. I half considered taking a jacket but decided to leave it, preferring the sun instead. I hurried over to the other side of the road which was bathed in brightness, and started walking towards Primrose Hill. Feeling the new sun beat down on me I began to warm up, stretch out, uncurl from whatever sort of hibernation I felt like I'd been in for the last few months. Everything looked better in the sunlight.

Turning into the Swiss Cottage end of Primrose Hill I began climbing to the top, London's skyline as ever hidden until the very last moment. At the top a group of tourists congregated around the metal plaque detailing the sights in front of them, pointing off into the distance and trying to distinguish between Westminster Abbey and the top of St Paul's Cathedral. I paused to look at a view I'd seen a million times before yet never grew tired of, before I began making my way down the other side towards Baker Street and the West End. I looked around the park, at the groups of school kids sitting in circles pretending to revise for exams, at the couples lying on each other reading the papers, at the bikini-clad and topless North Londoners stripped off at the first sign of sun. Everything felt relaxed, even this far into central London, the city was such a different place in summer. I passed the bit of grass I'd sat at with school friends toasting a new year with cans of beer and my first ever joint and headed south. Coming close to the exit I glanced at a tree underneath which I'd picnicked with a girl in the pouring rain and never felt happier. An umbrella hung from a branch as rain water dripped into our shared glass of Pimms and for a little while I saw the rest of my life as afternoons like that.

Pushing the memory from my head I emerged onto the road, the tranquillity momentarily suspended until I made it across and into Regents Park. Joggers surrounded me, as did extended families and friends walking arm in arm. I walked on alone.

So, Your Girlfriend's a Vegetarian?

Freya had made me feel worse about everything. My inability to like her made me wonder if it was my fault that I was on my own on a Saturday, walking around London because I had nothing better to do. Tim's right, I've pushed her away without giving her a chance and now there's no going back, just an awkward office to look forward to on Monday. Much as I may want to, I can't make myself like her, and I don't want her getting too close, so I'll close off after showing a crack of daylight to her. I know I have friends, I'm comfortable that I'm not walking through this life alone, but I know that the thick jacket I wear not only doesn't let people all the way in, it pushes them away after a while too.

I looked up to see a plane arch in the air and turn gracefully away from Heathrow. Like a lot of people I yearned to be on it, immediately assuming that everything would be solved by a different view from my bedroom window. Having called four countries and nine houses home in the last five years, I knew that that wasn't true, however I would never stop believing that this was the case. In the back of my mind a plan was beginning to hatch that come January I may be off again but for now it was just an idea. Having studied languages at university I always thought my life would take me away from these shores, I'd feel almost a failure if it didn't, but I don't want to do it alone. Not because I can't travel on my own or that I think I wouldn't make any friends, but because I'd love to share the experience of leaving the country with someone I loved and thought there may be a future with. What terrifies me is that if I did leave on my own and then it didn't work out, I'd be coming home and staying at my Mum's, looking for a job at twenty-eight when everyone else would be getting on with their lives. I'd close the door to my single bedroom, look around the walls and wonder if the last few years had happened at all, for here I was again, starting from scratch but a year further down the line.

The drone of traffic grew louder as I neared Baker Street. Leaving the park I embraced the sudden rush of heat and fumes emanating from the taxis and buses that raced past. I reached the underground and contemplated catching a tube to my destination. But what was my destination? Internally assessing the condition of my legs I walked on, I was in no rush.

I felt my phone vibrating, one missed call and one message received, both from Tim. *Dude, it's the first day of summer. Cheer the hell up and join us for an outdoor pint, Southend Green, big love.* I smiled and turned around and headed back through Regents Park, regretting my earlier annoyance at Tim and looking forward to indulging in the typical English summer daytime activity, drinking. Tim was right, the sun was out and I was walking through one of the most exciting cities in the world to meet my best friends; cheer the hell up Camfield. I texted back: Inbound.

Southend Green laps at the shores of Hampstead Heath and in sunlight is a great weekend place. The main area is only about two or three roads long yet pretty much each place on the High Road is a huge pub with ample beer gardens much like "The Freemasons Arms" I knew today they'd be just round the corner in a place called "The Gate" just down from Parliament Hill. We often went there when the weather was nice for their garden was enormous and littered with giant heavy benches and couches curving round fountains and statues. Walking down Haverstock Hill I stopped off in Belsize Village, just down from where I lived a few years ago with my Mum and brother. The Saturday afternoon market which only started last year had now become pretty big. Being Hampstead it was mostly full of overpriced cheeses and pâtés but a market was still a market. I picked up a couple of avocadoes and squeezed them gently, looking for a slight resistance so that I could eat them tonight or tomorrow. Finding three I handed them over and went back to wondering. A half-dozen vine tomatoes and a good handful of large, flat mushrooms joined the avocadoes as I left the vegetable stand and moved on. I was starving, I wanted everything. When I lived in Mexico I'd always do my weekly shopping in the village market, a huge groundfloor building just behind the main square. There, for pennies you could buy any vegetable imaginable, bunches of coriander, fresh lemongrass, perfect for making tea with when ill and even freshly killed whole chickens, lined up with their broken necks hanging down. I'd also even regularly embarrass myself by asking for a cucumber, without realising the word for cucumber in Spanish, 'pepino', was actually Mexican slang for 'little willy'. The smell of a market is one that I think is intrinsically the same all over the world, that slightly acrid stench-yet-fresh smell. Not that I can afford to do it in this country but I'd always love buying a half-pound of raw prawns for next to nothing, getting them home quickly in the Mexico sun and de-shelling and de-heading them whilst listening to my music on tiny speakers. Happy.

Whole King Prawns with Garlic and White Wine

Ingredients

- Depends on if it's tapas, starters or a main course. For something light use about 6 prawns per person I reckon, for something heavier use a dozen.

- Small onion, diced

- Half a dozen or so cloves of garlic, diced

- Glass of white wine

- Knobful of butter

Method

- Melt the butter in the pan, and just before it all starts to boil, add the garlic and onions.

- Fry for a few minutes on quite a high heat, then add the wine.

- Reduce the heat and add the prawns.

- The prawns will turn from their grey colour to the normal pink-orange colour within a minute or so.

- As soon as the prawns are ready, remove from the heat as the longer you cook prawns the smaller, harder and drier they become.

That's it, just remove the heads and shell and eat. Also, use some bread to mop up the butter and wine sauce, it's pretty good.

In case you're not sure how to effectively de-shell a prawn, do the following;

- Grip the head where the shell has already broken, just at the top of the spine.

- Rip that off first, don't go any higher as you'll get a fingerful of brains, which don't taste that nice

- Next unfold the shell around the body, it should come away easily in one.

- Depending on how you like it, leave the tail on or remove. I leave it on, in Mexico it's the custom and I've got into the habit, plus I really like them actually.

Thinking to myself that I was quite in the mood for prawns I weaved myself past the fish counter, eyeing up a large chunk of tuna steak, and almost made it out before spending too much money. That is, however, until I saw the fresh Spanish tortilla stand, another dish I absolutely love and can't get enough of. Studying Spanish at school meant I was always in Spain on exchanges or work placements and so became addicted to tortillas, especially when it's boiling hot and crammed full with potatoes. The stuff is everywhere, you get it for free when you order a beer, on the side of a street, in shops, every-where. I handed over some money for a slice and happily made my way down the hill.

Spanish Tortilla

Ingredients
- Ten to twelve eggs
- One large potato, diced
- One large white onion, cut into strips
- Salt

Method
This takes a little while to do but once cooked it lasts for days in the fridge.

- Half fill a wide frying pan with vegetable oil and add the potatoes and onion. I know, it's disgustingly bad for you.

- Sort of deep fry them for around ten minutes on a high heat, or until the potato is nice and soft.

- Drain, get rid of the oil and pat the onions and potatoes dry on some kitchen towels, try to get as much oil off as possible.

- Whisk up the eggs and add a good few pinchfuls of salt.

- Pour the eggs into the pan and leave for a few seconds, until the base layer of the omelette has started to cook.

- Add the potatoes and onions equally into the eggs.

- Wait. This is the frustrating part. Turn down the heat so the bottom doesn't burn and just wait for the omelette to solidify.

- Now, after seven to ten minutes you need to flip it, which is pretty tricky. It's not a pancake; if you try tossing it you'll probably break your wrist and it won't work so instead take the pan off the heat and place a chopping board over it. Then, standing over a sink, turn the pan over so that the tortilla now rests on the chopping board. Then, using a spatula ease it back into the pan and carry on cooking. Tossed.

- A few minutes after that, remove and if you can't get it out of the pan in one go, use the chopping board again.

Spaniards eat it in a variety of different ways. Well, actually in two different ways. Either cut it like a cake and eat slices of it, or put a bit in a baguette, douse with olive oil and munch on.

'Sorry about before, guys.'

I bought Tim a beer and Mel a gin and tonic as an apology. Looking at Rob I also apologised. 'Sorry dude, didn't know you were here too. You want a drink?'

He shook his head and held up his car keys.

Tim slapped my knee and Mel leant over and gave me a loud kiss on the cheek, 'Over it. Apology accepted.'

I poured my cider into the glass and watched it fizz over the ice cubes.

'So Monday's going to be fun. Have fun with Freya?'

I shook my head. 'We didn't sleep together, Rob.'

'Oh I know all that, "fun was had by all" apparently,' he raised two fingers from each hand to indicate quote marks. 'I'm just thinking about Monday, you don't really like her do you? That's going to be awkward.' He rubbed his hands together in anticipation

'Was it awkward this morning?'

'No, not really. I mean it's never that comfortable between us anyway. Cup of coffee then I left as her Mum was coming to visit and she needed to clean …'

'Ha, she doesn't like you!'

I looked at Mel and raised my eyebrow. 'Er what?'

'Sorry J but that's the line we use when we want guys out of our place in the morning. Wow, she must have had an awful time with you …'

'Hey, her Mum might've been coming down!'

She laughed. 'Trust me on this one. When was the last time you ever heard of parents coming to the city to see their kids? It's always us escaping to see them and get some fresh country air. No, it's a lie, J.'

'Oh. Hmm.' I looked at my hands.

Mel threw an ice cube at me. 'God, men! You are all useless! You don't like her but the second you think she may not like you, you get all hurt! I bet in the last ten seconds she's just got a hell of a lot more attractive, hasn't she?'

The three of us looked at each other and nodded.

'You're all pathetic,' she laughed, shaking her head.

Chapter Thirty
May 11th 2008

I'M A FULLY FLEDGED Doctor! Ur taking me out for pasta xxx

Two hours later and I slung my suit jacket over the back of the chair and gave Mel a huge hug.

'You're amazing! I am so goddamn proud of you.'

I lifted her into the air and twirled her around as she squealed and shook her head in disbelief.

'I still can't believe it, I really really can't. All this hard work for the last seven years of my life and I've done it, I've done it.'

I smiled and squeezed her hand. 'Have you told your parents yet?'

She nodded. 'Yeah, Mum's with Alexia in Italy but Dad picked up, he's going to take me out for dinner this week, I think.'

'And did you get through to Tim?'

'No. No, annoyingly he hasn't set up his phone to work abroad so it goes straight to voicemail.'

'What a Tim thing to do.'

She grimaced and nodded her head. 'He's back by Friday, I can wait till then.'

Ripped Sausages and Shitake Mushrooms with Tomato and Chilli Over Pasta

Ingredients
- Three good quality sausages
- A handful of shitake mushrooms

- One red chilli, de-seeded
- One red onion
- Two cloves of garlic
- Fresh rosemary
- One can of chopped tomatoes
- Half a glass of red wine
- Splash of milk
- Fresh pasta

Method

- Slice up the chilli, onion and garlic and chuck in the pan.

- Add a few sprigs of fresh rosemary and some black pepper.

- De-skin the sausages. To do this, make a prick in them and pull the skin away.

- Rip up the sausages into half inch chunks and add to the pan.

- After a few minutes, tear up the mushrooms into small pieces and add to the pan.

- After the sausages have browned, after about five minutes, add the tomatoes.

- Bring to the boil then simmer, stirring continuously.

- Around two to three minutes before you want to serve add the red wine and milk, then turn up the heat and reduce.

- Cook up the fresh pasta, drain and serve as a bed for the sausages.

What with Tim being in Zurich for a conference, the flat had been quite quiet recently. Mel had been on edge all week waiting to get her exam results and I'd been working late trying to piece together an open air jazz festival for Somerset House in August. Rob and I were both taking three weeks off next month for India so there was a lot of stuff needing to be sorted as soon as possible at work. Anyway, this lunch was pretty much the first time Mel and I had had a chance to catch up all week and she was positively shining, her shoulders noticeably a lot lower than they had been for the last few months.

'How's work?'

I shrugged, 'Same old, getting a bit bored to be honest, it's becoming routine and I'm counting the days until India.'

She picked at a mushroom with her fork. 'Yeah, that's gonna suck, me on my own for three weeks in the flat.'

'Sorry about that, it's not like we didn't invite you or anything, it's just that, well what am I saying, I was hammered when I booked it, I have no idea what happened.'

'It's cool, I can't get the time off of work. I think I may go to Italy for a week at that time anyway.'

'Oh yeah? Whereabouts?'

'Northern Sicily, Jazz knows someone who has a villa there. Apparently he won't be there until July and has said we can have it before that.'

I nodded and reached for my water. 'That'll be fun. Just you and Jazz?'

'Yes J. Just me and Jazz.'

I felt like we were at a crossroads. I changed the subject.

'So if your Dad is coming to take you out for dinner soon, then that means that parents do come see their kids in London and maybe Freya was telling the truth!'

She smiled. 'Maybe, but I still think she just wanted to get rid of you.' She stuck her tongue out. 'So has it been awkward at work?'

I shook my head. 'No, well not from my point of view it hasn't. Monday morning was a bit weird, there were a few secret smiles and glances across the office but I think that's more from knowing something that no-one else knows rather than love-struck awe.'

'Well, as long as you're not leading her on. You are incredibly weak remember, so I think you should watch yourself the next time you're all drunk together.'

I touched my forehead in a mock salute. 'Will do. How about you? You missing Tim?'

She put down her spoon and fork and looked at me straight on. 'J, I'm going to ask you something you asked me four months ago. Are you OK with me seeing Tim?'

I immediately nodded. 'Absolutely. I thought you knew that.'

'I do, but what if I want to talk to you about my feelings for my boyfriend in more detail than "oh he's great, things are going well blah blah blah"? Do you have a problem if the person I want to talk to you about is your best friend?'

I hesitated. 'I don't think so.'

She nodded and took a deep breath. 'He doesn't get me, or as much as I wished he did.' She sighed. 'I'm not sure if it's going anywhere.'

I thought for a few seconds. 'What way do you want him to get you?'

'I dunno, like if I'm quiet and looking out of the window I don't want him to keep asking if I'm OK. I'm fine, just in a quiet mood. Or if I'm upset about something and start to cry, I don't want him to solve the world, I just want him to hold me.'

'That's what we do though, we see a girl crying and we try to fix things. It's easier than sitting with someone you love when they're upset knowing there's nothing you can do. You know that from an outsider point of view you get on great.'

She took my hand. 'And we do, we really do, but I just wonder if it's just mates getting on and we happen to find each other attractive or if it's ever gonna be more than that. I mean, take what me and you are doing now, I can't do that with him, he just clams up; I sometimes feel like I'm just reciting a soliloquy to him, there's no interaction.'

I took my hand back. 'I didn't realise it was that bad.'

She stopped herself and sat back. 'No, no really it isn't, it's great, it's fantastic, I'm just annoyed I couldn't speak to him today.'

'Really?'

She sighed. 'I don't know.'

'Mel, it's early days for you guys. You both look great together and if you were mates before then I guess maybe there's always going to be a transition stage, or that being mates is going to be the foundation of your relationship because that's how it started. Are you having fun?'

'Yeah,' she nodded vehemently.

'And is there anyone else you'd rather be with?'

She shook her head.

'Then just go with it, maybe he'll start getting you soon, maybe you shouldn't expect so much, it's still early days.'

Mel half nodded and returned to her food.

Chapter Thirty-One
May 14th 2008

'DUDE, WE NEED TO do something for Mel, have a celebration or something.'

Tim nodded and yawned. Due to a delayed flight he'd only just got back and Mel was out for dinner with her Dad. I was cooking him a quick teriyaki chicken stir fry whilst he unpacked and sorted himself out.

Chicken Teriyaki Stir Fry

Ingredients
- Two chicken breasts
- One onion
- Two cloves of garlic
- Half an inch of ginger
- Four spring onions
- Two carrots
- Handful of mushrooms
- Green beans
- One cupful of rice

For the teriyaki sauce:
- Eight parts light soy sauce
- Two parts dark soy sauce
- Two parts sake
- Four spoonfuls of sugar

Method
- Add all the components of the sauce into a wok, and mix on a low heat until the sugar has dissolved and the sauce becomes thick.

- Add the garlic, onions and ginger and cook on a high heat.

- Cut the chicken into chunks and add.

- Start cooking the rice, add a vegetable stock cube to it for flavour.

- If you find the chicken is absorbing a lot of the sauce, make up more.

- Add the carrots, mushrooms and beans.

- When the rice is cooked, drain and add to the pan.

- Mix it all in together and serve.

'Let's have a house party. We haven't had one in about a year.'

I turned from the counter and smiled, 'That is an awesome idea. She'd love that!'

'Thing is though, we need access to all of her friends' phone numbers. And we need to contact them without her knowing.'

'Well, you could steal her phone? Do it tonight, she would've been drinking wine all evening, she'll pass out straight away.'

Tim widened his eyes in mock surprise. 'I hope not, I haven't seen her in a week! So when shall we do it? And in all honesty are we going to get more people than just me, you and Rob? Mel actually makes friends with people remember.'

I served up and sat at the table. 'I reckon do it for … well, let's try for next Saturday, some people won't be able to make it but fuck it, there's always going to be cancellations. It'll be a surprise, right?'

He nodded and blew on his food. 'Yeah, I think so, or at least start it off as a surprise. I'll text all her friends in her phone tonight and gauge who's around.'

'We should do a theme as well.' I was getting excited now. 'Or a dress code, make everyone get into the spirit of things. She's worked so damn hard she deserves to be spoilt a bit.' I looked around the kitchen. 'I reckon we could get fifty in the flat, no probs.'

'So just to reiterate, I'm gonna text all her friends tonight, OK, that's text ALL of her friends, yeah?'

I shrugged. 'Mel's my best friend, she's always going to be in my life. Jazz is one of hers, I'm gonna have to see her eventually. Besides, it's been two months, it's OK.'

'And if it's not?'

'Then it's Mel's night and she won't find out it's not.'

Chapter Thirty-Two
May 19th 2008

You can't go wrong with Zorro. Seriously, I really don't think you can. Everything about him is awesome, from his pointy leather boots up to his ruffled open shirt and big black wide-rimmed hat.

After much arguing, Tim and I had settled on a fantasy themed evening. We initially thought that that was a bit general but then we realised if you make the dress code too tricky, no-one will bother making the effort and then the few that do will just feel ridiculous. Besides, fantasy left it nice and open, it could be a sexual fantasy or someone you fantasised about being when you were a kid. Between us we'd dressed up in some ridiculous costumes over the years and to be honest, doing this for Mel also gave us the chance to show off a little bit. Tim was refusing to tell me what he was going as, so was Rob but, as I tied my black mask around my head, I thought to myself again, you can't go wrong with Zorro. (Just to clear this up, Zorro isn't my sexual fantasy, but growing up I did want to be a cross between him and Don Juan de Marco.)

We were expecting a biggish turnout. Between us we reckoned we had about a hundred invites out, so that meant probably around fifty to sixty would show up, enough to fill the flat. Most of Mel's friends were up for it, or said they were at least, and yes, Jasmine was coming. She'd replied pretty much immediately to Tim's text saying she was *looking forward to seeing you both xxx*, and to be honest, putting my mature cap on here, I was looking forward to seeing her too; it had been two months.

Getting Mel out of the flat for the late afternoon had been tricky as hell, especially as she's such a suspicious person. Even harder was hiding all the food we'd bought from the supermarket yesterday. In the end, using a cunning diversionary ploy of Tim picking his nose until he got a nosebleed, then running upstairs to the newly qualified doctor, at which point he was whisked into the lounge and ordered to sit, I managed to get all the food upstairs and into my room or onto my shelf of the fridge. Walking back out of my room I was suddenly accosted by an irate Mel carrying towels and a big pillow.

'J, watch your driving,' she snapped, 'I can't believe how idiotic you were!'

I looked at her with utter incomprehension.

'What?'

She brushed past me. 'Tim told me how you weren't concentrating and had to brake suddenly at the zebra crossing. Honestly, how could you not see a child pushing an old woman in a wheelchair across the road? It's people like you that keep me busy at work.' She shook her head. 'Honestly.'

I looked to Tim, who told me to 'roll with it' with his eyes.

'Oh yeah, yeah, well I must've just glanced away for a second.'

'J, I'm so unimpressed. You're lucky it's just Tim's nose that's bleeding, really. How are you, baby? I'll get you some tea.'

He waited until she left the room before turning to me and laughing. 'Unlucky! And she's already told me I'm getting sex tonight to make me feel better!'

Little shit. We'd also roped Mel's family into it, and convinced her parents to take her out for dinner (again). The only thing was, when Mel got home, the only person not in fancy dress would be her ... but you can't do everything.

I sat on the edge of my bed and slipped my brother's old black leather cowboy boots on over my feet. What did looking forward to seeing you both mean? Did she mean me and Tim or did she just mean Mel and Tim? She sees Mel all the time, and I don't think she'd be spiteful, so it probably meant me and Tim, right? She better not be bringing anyone, that'd piss me right off. Hmmmm. So I'm clearly over Jazz then. Freya was coming too. That's fun, isn't it? I can't wait for them to meet each other: Jazz, this is the girl I almost slept with to get over you, but it only made it worse; Freya, this is the girl I wish you were, cheese on a stick anyone?

'So, what do you think? Do I turn you on?'

Tim walked into my room and stood in front of me, legs spread. He was wearing a wetsuit, an old one he had when he used to surf at uni; however he had made some alterations. The wetsuit was cut off completely at the thigh and top of the arms, and undone at the back, the resultant effect was a fully grown man in a tight latex suit that hugged tightly every part of him contained underneath the suit and displayed to the world every other part of his body.

'Want to see my party trick?'

I was almost lost for words.

'No, I don't think I do.'

He produced a pen and threw it on the floor next to me. Smiling, he sauntered across the room and slowly bent over to pick it up, shoving his ass in my face. He poked the pen back into the wetsuit and stood up.

'Not bad, huh.'

'Tim. What are you? Who are you and most importantly, whose fantasy are you?'

He deflated a little. 'I dunno, I didn't have time to go shopping and I've got no money. Besides, it's my house, I can wear what I want, can't I?'

I cracked up as I looked at him again. Putting my arm round him we walked out of my room. 'Come, let's get the food out, I'm pretty sure it's beer o'clock anyway.'

Food had been tricky to sort out, what with the numbers being pretty unknown. Also, neither one of us had much money at the moment and so couldn't really afford to splash out. What with Mel and some of her hippy friends being vegetarians, our hands were tied even further. We'd tried to keep it simple and cheap and at the end of the day I guess people don't come to parties expecting to get fed.

Borlotti Beans, Rosemary and Garlic on Toasted Ciabatta

Ingredients (for about forty slices of ciabatta)

- Four tins of borlotti beans
- Four large ciabattas cut into slices
- One bulb of garlic
- One diced green chilli
- One pack of rosemary
- Few sprigs of diced coriander
- Lashings of olive oil

Method

- Slice the garlic and fry in a pan with a tiny amount of olive oil.

- After a few minutes, drain the beans and add to the pan along with the chilli, rosemary and coriander.

- Cook for around ten minutes until the beans begin to become a bit crumbly.

- Turn off the heat and empty the pan into a bowl. Add loads of olive oil and mash with a fork.

- It's amazing how much oil you actually need, so keep adding until the beans are mashed to a smooth consistency.

- Spread a bit over each slice of ciabatta and bake in the oven for three to four minutes then serve straight away.

Asparagus Strips in Soy Sauce and Sesame Seeds

Ingredients

- Thirty to forty pieces of asparagus cut into one-inch chunks
- Two to three tablespoons of sesame seeds

Method

- Boil the chunks of asparagus for about three minutes in water.

- Drain and add to a pan of hot soy sauce.

- Fry on a high heat for a few minutes.

- Sprinkle sesame seeds over the asparagus.

- Serve with cocktail sticks.

Vine Tomatoes and Green Pesto and Mozzarella

This one looks good.

Ingredients for sixty portions

- Thirty vine tomatoes
- One jar green pesto
- Four to five balls of buffalo mozzarella

Method

- Slice the very top and bottom off of each tomato so it can stand freely, then cut each tomato in half.

- Arrange standing up on baking trays, and place a piece of mozzarella on top of each tomato.

- Spread a generous amount of green pesto over each slice of mozzarella.

- Bake for a few minutes, or until the cheese has just started to melt.

Serve immediately.

For dessert Tim had made some dulce de leche, a caramel-like South American thick sauce, which went really well with a load of fruit we'd got in the market

Dulce de Leche

Ingredients

- One can condensed milk
- One can evaporated milk

Method

- Mix the two together and stir over a low heat constantly for around twenty minutes or until it becomes really thick.

- Serve quickly before it solidifies

When you add all of that to the loads of crisps, dips and sweets we'd brought in, hopefully no-one would go hungry.

Chapter Thirty-Three
May 20th 2008

WE WALKED ON IN silence. There was nothing really to say to each other at the moment; neither of us wanted to bring up what had happened last night but we both knew we had to. We needed to talk about it, not just for our sake, but for the sake of everyone around us as well. We met and decided to walk over Parliament Hill and head towards a coffee house in Highgate Village, hoping that by the time we reached it, we would've sorted it out or at least tried to anyway. I cast my mind back to last night and our argument, unsure as to where it had gone so wrong and unwilling to start talking about it until I could answer that question for sure.

By about eight the house was pretty full and still more people kept coming. Costume-wise, well I was pretty impressed, it seemed everyone had made an effort as people's weird fantasies took a forefront for the night. After an afternoon spent down the army surplus store, Rob had arrived wearing a Top Gun pure white officer's outfit complete with peaked hat and sunglasses. He'd even spent an hour cutting strips from different coloured pieces of card and gluing them onto his breast so they looked like medals. He spent the majority of the evening standing at full attention with his hands behind his back, glasses on and shoulders thrust outwards until either Emma, Tim or myself, the "officers" according to Rob, would say to him "at ease".

Emma had gone full-out as well and was looking hot. She'd ordered a nurse's outfit from Ann Summers which she looked like she'd been poured into it. Black suspenders and a little hat completed the look and whilst she had half the room staring at her, Tim was not impressed after she refused to play a "picking a pen up off of the floor" contest with him.

I looked around contentedly and catching Tim's eyes, nodded at him and watched as he did the same. Mel was going to be so chuffed. A huge banner which read "Congratulations Dr Clarke!!" hung across the back wall, underneath which Dan, a friend of Tim's from work, played on his decks. He'd picked out a perfect set, and was effortlessly blending The Chemical Brothers, Kraftycuts, DJ Yoda, Hot Chip and Too Many DJs all into one unending track. Even with only one eye (he was dressed as a pirate) he was mixing pretty seamlessly.

I took out my camera and went for a few action shots. There was quite a big S&M presence, which I guess shouldn't be surprising. One guy turned up in a gimp mask and dog collar, attached to two women in thigh-high boots, corsets and whips. I think Tim was a bit put out that he was no longer the most outrageously dressed. Ace Ventura posed with Tinkerbell, I had a sword fight with a samurai warrior (I won, as I said, you can't beat Zorro), two girls wearing exactly the same short green army dresses eyeballed each other from across the room and one girl dressed as an angel with enormous white wings got upset when she was asked by Rob if she had come dressed as a swan. Perhaps the award for most random outfits of the evening went to my office, as four people (including Freya) turned up dressed as Christmas presents. The boys wore black jeans, the girls black leggings and each had a large box decorated in wrapping paper around their chests, with holes for the arms and head. Smiling at Freya and slightly raising one eyebrow, she looked at me and shrugged, 'Well, every kid dreams all year round of Christmas presents, don't they?!'

My leg vibrated. *"Hi J it's Henry, just leaving the restaurant now, see you soon"*.

'OK guys!' I shouted. 'Mel is going to be here in about ten minutes so everyone keep an eye out, we don't want her coming in without us knowing about it!'

Rob tripped over with his arm around Emma. He tipped his cap with his beer bottle. 'Dudefish, good job, excellent job.' Turning from the hips he looked around and then back again. 'Everyone's here.

Literally, all of our friends are here.' He turned from the hips again. 'We don't have many friends, do we? I don't know half these people.' Looking at a dark-haired girl dressed as a cowboy he said a little too loudly, 'You, who are you and why are you here?'

The girl turned to look at Rob, 'Hi, I'm Beth, Mel and I are gym buddies, who are you?' She proffered her hand. Rob shrugged, removed his arm from Emma's shoulders and put it around Beth's. 'Rob, you could say I organised this party. Let's get a drink.'

Emma smiled and shook her head. 'Last we'll see of him all night.'

'He's hammered! It's only nine o'clock, how did that happen?'

'Tim,' Emma said. 'He ordered him to down a bottle of wine or he'd get him shot.'

'Obviously. Can't believe I didn't think of that trick.'

Emma uncapped another bottle of beer and sidled up next to me against the wall. 'She here?'

I turned to her. 'Who?'

Pushing her right hip against my left, giving it a shove, she laughed. 'Ha, you know damn well who I'm talking about. Jasmine, is she here?'

I shrugged. 'Dunno, haven't seen her.'

'J, stop being an arse.'

'Ok no, she's not here. I keep looking at the door, though, and that pisses me off. I feel nervous and I hate the fact I feel nervous in my own house.'

'Well, if you feel nervous and it's your party, imagine how nervous she's gonna be feeling. She's got guts.'

Tim rocked up. 'Who has? And have you seen how drunk Rob is? Hysterical.'

'Jazz. Dude, I really can't look at you normally, I don't use this word often but you really do look horrific.'

'Thanks, just for that I'll show you my pen trick again.'

He threw the pen to the floor and made an even more exaggerated effort at picking it up, raising his arse high into the air and shaking it from side to side.

The lounge door swung open.

'Oh my!'

'Timothy, what are you doing?!'

Mel's parents stood shocked in the doorway. Mel's jaw was being propped up by her socks.

'What the hell is going on?! It looks like some sort of torture garden in here!'

Tim jumped up immediately. 'Mel, erm, surprise!' He opened his arms out wide. 'Wow, I really should have rehearsed this, this is your "becoming a doctor" party!'

She looked around, recognising all of her friends, noticing the banner, and a smile crept over her face.

'Tim, you organised all this for me?'

'Sure did! I wanted to do something special for you.'

I half opened my mouth, but decided to close it again.

'Ohhhhh my god, I don't know what to say!' Turning to her parents she said, 'You were in on this too weren't you! That was Tim you texted when we got out of the restaurant wasn't it?!' She hugged them, then came over to Tim and kissed him lightly.

'Thank you, it's amazing.'

As the music restarted she pulled away from Tim, squeezed his hand and started to do the rounds. She embraced all her friends one by one, laughing at how ridiculous they all looked. Reaching me and Emma she hugged me tightly and whispered in my ear, 'Thank you, this has you written all over it.'

I shrugged. 'We both did it for you; we want to show you how proud of you we both are.'

Her eyes moistened and she moved on to the next group.

I noticed Tim looking at me out of the corner of his eyes. I smiled and winked at him, mouthing the words 'good job'. He turned back to the people he was talking to.

Floating around at parties like I normally do, I quickly scanned the crowd, looking for Jazz, no sign yet. Everything was going great.

Rob was on the couch with Beth, his arm still dangled around her shoulder, work people were mingling with Mel's friends and things with Freya looked like they were definitely sorted. On my way to the toilet I noticed Tim's door ajar and the light on. Knocking gently, I stuck my head round the door. He was sitting on the side of the bed, his head resting on one of his palms, drinking whisky neat from a half-litre bottle.

'You OK?'

He nodded. 'Yeah, fine.'

I opened the door fully and leant against the frame. 'What you doing in here? Come outside and help me make faces at Rob behind Beth's back.'

He grimaced. 'I'll be out in a minute, J.'

'You sure?'

He took a long swig. 'Yeah, shut the door please.'

I closed the door and turned round, wondering what was up. Looking into the lounge I saw Mel alone at the table, refilling her glass of rum.

'Hey, how you doing?'

She smiled. 'Great, thanks, thank you again, both of you, this is amazing.'

I held up my hands. 'Enough, stop saying thank you and start enjoying yourself. Actually, speaking of which, is Tim OK?'

She raised a quizzical eyebrow. 'Yeah, as far as I know. I haven't really spoken to him much. Why?'

'No reason. Just thought he was being a bit quiet, that's all.'

She shook her head. 'No idea. I'm feeling pretty out of place here though.' She looked around. 'Everyone looks awesome and I'm in a frumpy top and black skirt. What sort of fantasy is that?!'

I poured some ginger beer into her cup. 'Shush, it's your party, you can wear what you want. You look great anyway.'

Smiling, she took the cup and placed it on the table. 'You always know what to say don't you? Come on, come here.'

She extended her arms and I stepped in. Feeling the familiar embrace I hugged her back and kissed her forehead.

'Oh, this is just fantastic isn't it? What the fuck do you guys think you're doing?'

Tim stood before us, rage written all over his face. The half-empty bottle of whisky dangled loosely in his left hand.

I separated myself from Mel. 'What are you talking about?'

'What am I talking about? I'm wondering why you're trying to grope my girlfriend, that's what I'm talking about.'

'Don't be ridiculous,' Mel snapped, 'it was a hug.'

'Not what it looks like from over here. Not "just a hug" in my eyes.'

'Well, it is just that, so deal with it.' I picked up my drink and walked past him, our shoulders brushing for an instant.

He wheeled round. 'Don't you dare push me!'

I turned. 'Tim, I didn't. Look, you're drunk, calm down before you say something you'll regret.'

By this time a crowd had gathered. Out of the corner of my eye I saw Rob weaving his way over.

'Don't you fucking tell me what to do. It's not enough you want to fuck my girlfriend, now you're telling me what to do!'

'Tim!' Mel shouted, conscious of her parents in the room. 'Shut up right now, don't you dare carry on with this conversation!'

He nodded. 'That's right, united front is it? It's written all over your faces.'

'What are you talking about Tim?! Where is this coming from?'

He took another swig. 'Do you really think I'm that stupid? I see the way you look at each other, I see the way you touch each other all the time, get the fuck off of me.' He moved his shoulder in reaction to the hand Rob had placed on it.

'Tim, stop OK. Come on, let's go for some air.'

'I'm not going anywhere until he admits he wants a piece of my girlfriend. Well …?'

'Tim,' I looked at him earnestly, 'what are you talking about?'

'Bollocks you don't know. Mel?'

'Tim,' she had fire in her eyes, 'I can't believe you are doing this to me.' She clenched her teeth. 'Get out.'

He spluttered, 'You're throwing me out of my own flat?! Fuck you.'

I'd never seen Tim like this before. He placed the whisky down hard on the table as Rob materialised next to him.

'Tim come on, let's go outside, get some food or something.'

Rob placed an arm gently round Tim's shoulders and began moving him towards the door. 'C'mon.'

He looked at me with what can only be described as pure hate in his eyes. 'And Jazz isn't coming, she cancelled yesterday. I just wanted to watch you squirm.'

We reached the crest of the hill and wandered through the long grass to a bench. Sitting in silence we looked down at the sports centre below us where dozens of kids ran round the athletics track and played football on open fields. Before us lay the city, and in the distance the Crystal Palace tower, unofficially marking the end of the city in the south. Looking at twelve million people was a concept I couldn't get my head round; each speck below was an entire life, connected to thousands of other people. How many specks had experienced a night like last night, I wondered to myself.

'J, before we start, I want to apologise for last night. It was wrong, I was out of order and I should have known when to stop. I'm sorry.'

I nodded. 'Tim, I'm not the one you should be apologising to.'

'No, you are, it's just that I need to have this with Mel too.'

We lapsed into silence, analysing the words that had been exchanged like two boxers feeling each other out during an opening round.

'Is that all you have to say?'

'No, no it isn't.'

'So where did it come from?'

He sat back on the bench. 'I dunno, when she came in and saw the surprise, I felt like she should've been more grateful to me. She just said thank you and moved on, then she goes up to you and gets all dewy-eyed and I'm like, well I'm her damn boyfriend and she doesn't get like that for me. I went into my room to change; all of a sudden I felt like I was dressed like a fool, and when I was in my room I saw the whisky and decided to have some. Then when I did come out I saw you with your hands all over each other and something in me just snapped.' He paused. 'I've never shouted at anyone like that before.'

'What did you expect Mel to do? There was a room full of people, she had to go round and say hi to everyone. And I think she got over-whelmed in general, not because she hugged me. And for the record, our hands were not all over each other, we were hugging, like we've done a million times before. Come on Tim, listen to yourself. This isn't you, I know you.'

He shrugged. 'Maybe you don't know me as well as you thought.'

I snapped. 'What's that supposed to mean?'

'Well, when was the last time we really sat down and talked about anything that's going on in my life? All we talk about is Jasmine or what you're doing; most of the time you're out with Rob anyway. I know you and Mel talk about me and her, but when have you ever asked me how I'm feeling about it?'

'Well, how are you feeling about her?'

'Amazing; I think I may be falling in love with her but that doesn't make a difference 'cause no matter how hard I try you're both going to be closer to each other than I ever will be to either of you. I'm not a fool, I know I care about her more than she does about me, but it's just hard when you think the girl you're lying next to would rather feel someone else's arms around them.'

I shook my head incredulously. 'Tim honestly, what are you talking about? You know how close me and Mel are and that we're both tactile people. I know things are different now but I don't see why you and her being in a relationship should affect how the three of us work.'

He looked off into the distance at the winking Canary Wharf.

'But that's just it, things are different. She's my girlfriend, I should be coming first now.'

'Well, then I think we have a problem.'

Tim nodded in acceptance.

A few minutes passed.

'Look,' I turned to him. 'I don't know why I'm even saying this but I am not in love with Mel, but she is, as are you, one of the most important people to me in the world. You and her being together is not going to change that, I'm sorry Tim, but it just won't.' I paused. 'But in some ways I can get where you're coming from, although I think you've gone about it in an appalling way. Maybe I should be more understanding of your feelings when we're all together, but you have got to tone down your possessiveness or I really don't think you're gonna have a relationship to protect.'

He nodded his head and looked down at his feet.

'Truth is, I had no idea you were thinking you may be falling in love with her, and I really do apologise if you think I haven't been there for you recently, but you have got to remember that as well as getting over Jazz I have had to get my head round you two.'

'So you admit that—'

'No, stop there, I mean I had to get used to the fact that my two best friends now had something I could never share and that through no fault of their own, I was now going to feel awkward in my own home.'

'It's just, you should see the way her face lights up when you come in the room, J. I want that,' he stressed. 'I haven't had that in so long with a woman, and now that I find someone amazing I still feel like I'm second best. We don't talk like the way I know she does with you. I try but I just don't know what to say, I clam up.'

'And because of that you think she's in love with me? Tim, where does she sleep every night?'

'That doesn't prove anything.'

I sighed. 'You really need to get over this. This is going to fuck everything up OK, and I am not going to let that happen. How long have you thought like this?'

He shrugged. 'A month or so; it's got worse the more I've thought about it.'

'Have you spoken to anyone about this?'

'No.'

'And do you honestly think we are in love with each other, that if you weren't here we'd be all over each other?'

He paused. 'Well no, I guess not.'

'And before you got together did you ever think me and Mel would make a good couple?'

'No, I just knew you were friends.'

'Right, and since then, the only thing that's changed is you and Mel are together, mine and Mel's friendship hasn't changed at all; if anything we're not as close as we used to be.'

'Look, J, I know I'm probably overreacting but it's just, last night should have been about me and Mel, and it wasn't.'

I slowly nodded. I think a decision had just been made in my head. 'Well I got that wrong, I thought it was meant to have been about just Mel. Look, I guess something like this was bound to happen. We need to sort this; what are we going to do?'

He shrugged. 'I don't know. I guess,' he sighed, 'I guess deep down I know you two aren't in love with each other and I need to stop being jealous, but I need you to work on this with me.'

I replied testily, 'How? I'm not gonna close myself off from Mel.'

'No I know, but I need you to step back a bit, let me try and get her to feel for me what I feel for her.'

'But what does that actually mean? You want me not to talk to her? Not to comfort her if she's upset? I can't do that.'

He was struggling. 'I don't really know what that means, I can't quite explain it.'

'What hurts is that you knew Jazz wasn't coming. Everything else I can put down to you being drunk but that, well you consciously wanted to hurt me. That's not cool.'

'I know, I've been angry with you.'

'That was harsh.'

'I apologise. Look, I feel like we're beginning to go round in circles. Can we see how we go?'

I nodded. 'I will try and let you take the lead in stuff, OK.'

He placed his hand on my shoulder. 'I'm sorry about last night, truly.'

I made a move to get up. 'Home?'

'Actually J, can you let us have the flat for a bit? I've got a lot of apologising to do.'

I sat down and turned back to the city.

Chapter Thirty-Four
Later that day

I SHRUGGED. 'I DUNNO, I've never seen him like that, it was pretty weird to be honest. All this anger came flooding out and it took me completely by surprise. Completely by surprise. How was he when you left? Thanks for looking after him, by the way.'

'No problem.' Rob put down his fork and wiped his mouth. 'He was OK, not angry anymore, probably because he wasn't around either of you and in the cold wind of a one am night, he must've realised that he'd been pretty stupid.'

'Did he say much?'

He shook his head and started mopping up his egg yolk with a piece of bread. 'No, he went pretty quiet actually.'

I plunged the cafetière on our table. 'So nothing? Not a word about why he suddenly snapped or why at a party in his house he decided to sit in his room alone and drink half a bottle of whisky?'

Rob shook his head, his mouth full of bread. 'What did he say just now?'

I filled Rob in on what Tim had said to me on Parliament Hill.

'Jesus. Where the hell did all of that come from? You and Mel? That's ridiculous, anyone can see that you're just friends.'

'I know, it's his insecurities; I didn't realise it was that bad. If I wasn't so goddamn angry with him I'd be quite worried; as it is I'm cruising between the two at the moment.'

'Come on, this is Tim we're talking about, you have to forgive him this one.'

'I know, I know. I just wonder how Mel is taking it.'

'Well, what happened after we left last night?'

223

I ripped open two sugar sachets and poured them into my coffee. 'Not much. I think Mel was more embarrassed than anything else, especially with her parents being there. It kinda wound down, to be honest. The music didn't come back on, people began to drift off, Mel stayed in her room and ...'

'Did you both speak?'

'What, about what Tim said? No, there was no need to.'

Rob nodded and we carried on eating for a few minutes in silence.

'So what are you gonna do? I mean, without making you feel worse, your house is gonna be fucking awkward for a little bit.'

I grimaced. 'I know, in a dream world he will have gone back and it'll be sorted and then me and Tim will get sorted and everything will go back to normal, but I have a feeling it's not gonna happen.'

He held my eyes. 'Well, being selfish here, make it happen. I'm not going to India in a month with two guys that aren't even talking.'

I put down my mug a little too hard. 'Crap, I'd completely forgotten about that.' I chewed my lip. 'I mean, it is a month away, I'm sure it will have been resolved either way by then.'

'It better be or I'm not coming, I'm saying that now.'

I ran my fingers through my hair. 'Jesus, what a weekend. You're not the only one who's put a countdown on getting this solved, anyway.'

'How do you mean?'

'Well. It suddenly dawned on me when I was talking to Tim today that maybe our time together as a three has been and gone. Maybe it's time we went our separate ways.'

Rob almost choked on his coffee. 'That's ridiculous, you can't cut Tim out of your life for one little mistake.'

'No no no, I meant us living together, maybe it's all a little too much, maybe I should start looking around.'

'Really? You being serious?'

'Well, I'm twenty-four and I claim to be from London although I only really know north-west London. There's people scattered all over that live in London but I never see; I'd quite like to explore some new areas. You know me, I can't stay still for long.'

'Hmm.'

'Also, I would have said this before last night anyway, but I'm not over the moon about living with a couple either, even if they are my best friends. I felt awkward enough as it was whenever they start kissing on the couch or getting all coupley, and I don't really want to feel awkward in my own home.'

'Interesting, very interesting.'

I raised an eyebrow. 'Why do you say that?'

'Well, I'm thinking, or at least beginning to think, about buying. I had thought about buying a one-bedroom, but with two people you could get a much bigger place.'

'What, me and you, split a mortgage?'

'Well it's an option, isn't it? You may want to move, I want to buy. Either we split it or I buy it and charge you rent. What do you think?'

'Erm, I dunno really, I'd never thought about it before.'

'I mean, I don't want Tim to think I'm taking sides, 'cause I'm honestly not, so I don't think any decisions should be made yet …'

'When are you thinking of moving?'

'Next few months. Look, why don't we keep this between ourselves for now and see how you and Tim go. I'll look for two beds anyway, and I mean it when I say no pressure, I'm more than happy to rent the room out to a stranger, I'll just give you first refusal. How about that?'

My brow furrowed. 'Yeah, I mean, provisionally yeah. Where you looking?'

He shrugged, 'Dunno, that's the freedom of it. I've never been keen on North, like round here,' he raised his hands, 'and West is such a hassle to get anywhere from. I dunno, Clapham or Balham, that kind of area, maybe? I don't know them that well so we could go on research trips down south, sampling the local pubs and bars wherever we go!'

I smiled and raised my coffee cup. 'Between you and me though, right?'

He nodded. 'Between you and me.'

JUNE

Chapter Thirty Five
June 1st 2008

```
<So this is what we do
Week 1-Running 40 mins x5, sit-ups x200, daily
Week 2-Running 1 hr x5, sit-ups x300, daily
Week 3-Running 1hr x5, swimming 40mins, x2, sit-
ups x300 daily.
We start tomorrow after work ok?>
<What are you babbling about?>
<Have you seen me in boardies recently?>
<Thankfully no>
<Exactly, I am not displaying my pasty white flabby
belly to anyone. We are getting in shape before
India, tell Tim tonight. We start tomorrow. This goes
for food and drink too, alcohol in moderation and
healthy food>
```

I picked up a muffin I'd got at lunch and stuffed a chunk of it in my mouth before eat and showing it at Rob from across the office.

```
<you make me sick>
<good, I'm helping you lose weight>
```

I smiled to myself and got on with my work; three weeks and counting. I was aching to leave the country and every day at work just seemed to drag. India was all I could think about and I knew that if we planned it right we could make three weeks feel like months. A rough itinerary had been planned, well by rough itinerary I mean we knew we flew in and out of Delhi and had some time to kill in between, what we did with that time was the complicated bit. I'd had a quick glance at a Lonely Planet but always found them hard to read before you're actually there, or on the plane on your way. From talking to friends and my Lonely Planet reading (I looked at the pictures), a route was beginning to emerge, the only question was in which way we took it. Closest to Delhi was Agra, home of the Taj Mahal, and from there we could head northwest into the state of Rajasthan, one of the most remote, rural yet interesting states in the country. A whistle-stop tour of there and we could then head south, pausing at Mumbai before ending up in Goa or Kerala on the southwestern coast for some much-deserved sun, beach and chill. An internal flight up to Delhi a few days later then home, sorted, or we could do the same thing but in the completely opposite direction, beach first, hardcore travelling second. I guess our minds were made up when Tim, who had actually done more than look at the pictures in the Lonely Planet, read that the whole of southern India is pretty much underwater until at the earliest, mid-July.

Turning from my desk to look at me where I was sitting on my bed reading the paper, he shut the book decisively. 'Sorted, Rajasthan first, Kerala second.'

'If it's not underwater.'

'If it's not underwater. Who the hell chose India anyway?!'

I shrugged then paused. 'Didn't you choose India?'

He turned back to the book. 'Oh yeah.'

'Jackass,' I muttered.

'Heard that.'

I think me and Tim are going to be OK. The last ten days or so had been pretty hard but then again, they were over and hopefully each day would be easier than the previous one. We'd kept a bit of a distance from each other for the first few days, but the weekend after her party Mel went home and that forced Tim and I to spend time together and try to move on from whatever had happened last month. We hadn't talked about it again, well not at length and for the time being it felt like everything had been said up on a hill in Hampstead Heath, now all we had to do was show each other some respect and try to do what was a lot easier to promise. Mel returned after the weekend to a house in which Tim and I had reverted back to our usual dicking around selves, but it would have been stupid to suggest things were back to how they were, and perhaps it was naïve to think that they would be. I dunno, in the back of my mind I figured that spending three weeks solid with Tim would be plenty of time in which we could talk about all of this; right now all that mattered was that we were getting on again.

The same however, could not be said for Tim and Mel, for I returned from my meal with Rob to find a relationship in tatters. Mel had ended it with Tim and was indescribably angry with him for getting so abusive in front of her parents. The bottom line was that Tim had scared her that night with his anger, and she couldn't be with someone she was scared of. She'd moved back into her room and was spending a lot of the time out of the flat, mostly at Jazz's, I presumed. I wondered what Jazz made of all of this.

Tim had accepted Mel's decision a little too meekly, I thought. They were still talking, they weren't arguing, in fact I thought the inane small talk that they were making was worse than arguing, as so much was still left unsaid, but at the end of the day whenever Mel left a room she left behind Tim looking longingly after her, his legs rooted to the spot. I never quite understood why he never moved to follow her.

I tried desperately hard not to take sides, I really did. Even though I thought Tim was completely in the wrong and I was still angry at him for what he'd done, part of me felt sorry for him, a big part of me, to be honest. For all his possessiveness and extreme overreaction that night, wasn't all he wanted was to be number one in Mel's eyes? He was her former good-friend-now-boyfriend, so was that such an unreasonable thing to ask for, and was I really the one who had denied him that wish? If I was in Tim's position how would I feel? If I was with Mel yet knew she was closer to Tim, would I be paranoid every time they spoke alone? Would I wonder if they were talking about me? Would I get a shiver of jealousy and anger whenever I heard about the two of them having lunch because one was in the same area? I guess I would. I'd try to man up and pretend that it didn't affect me but at some point all that pent-up anger and jealousy would come out like a shaken bottle of Coke and there'd be no way of controlling it until it was all out. Now the guy has lost his girlfriend and fucked off his best friend and probably doesn't feel like he can talk to me as in his paranoid head it's gonna go back to Mel. What a mess. Sure, Mel and I had spoken about it, but never about what Tim had actually said. I'd been into her room a few times to see if she was OK, and mostly, apart from a few tearful episodes, she was. She wasn't jumping with joy and doing cartwheels around the flat but she was getting her head down and getting on with being a newly qualified doctor.

Chapter Thirty-Six
June 5th 2008

I LOOKED ABSOLUTELY RIDICULOUS. Leaning against the gates at the Baker Street end of Regents Park I watched Tim doing star jumps, his arms flailing wildly and endangering the small crowd that had gathered to watch this man in tight lycra skipping around like a fairy.

We were on day four of Rob's pre-India routine and to be honest with you, we were all beginning to notice early results. Looking in the mirror I could see a slight difference; I definitely felt a lot fitter and I knew that if we could carry it on until India we'd be going in great shape. Credit to Rob, his narcissistic tendencies had actually ended up getting us in shape, and more importantly had given time for some much-needed bonding between the three of us, especially so soon before spending an entire three weeks together.

'Evening fellas, how are we?' Rob touched his head in salute to all of us. 'Not feeling the burn after yesterday, I hope.'

'I can't sit down.'

'Well that's fine Timothy that'll go, it's all about training your muscles. After such a period of total inactivity they're bound to hurt after a while.'

Tim looked up from the ground from where he was doing press-ups. 'You're no Mr fucking Motivator y'know, I saw you yesterday and you struggled just as much as we did.'

I chimed in, 'That's true actually, Tim and I were talking all the way round yesterday, you hardly said a word after ten minutes – feeling a bit tired, were we?'

Rob shook his head and began putting his headphones in. 'Focusing on the route, dear boy, don't want the responsibility of getting you guys lost.' He nodded towards the lake. 'C'mon, forty minutes starts now.' He turned and began jogging towards the bridge.

It was a beautiful evening for a run, it really was. It was around seven o'clock, the sort of time where the summer air becomes thick and murky. Running round the lake we felt like we were cutting through the air, causing it to ripple before reforming behind us once more. As usual Rob was ahead, setting the pace and moving his head in time to his iPod, his reason for not wanting to talk today. Tim and I followed a few metres behind, the path not being wide enough to run three abreast. We both ran in the same rhythm, pushing each other on, already feeling a bit tired after only fifteen minutes or so of running. We reached the complete circuit of the lake as I began to feel the lactic acid dissolve away inside me and began to peel off to the right to run along the bottom of the park and then north up to the canal. Coming into the wide carriageway that runs through the middle of the park, Tim and I stepped up and began running level with Rob, this was more like it. Here we were, three guys completely at ease, not a care in the world, about to leave the continent and explore somewhere new, cruise around the extremes of our comfort zones and come home more knowledgeable people.

Rob's eyes grew larger as he ran a few paces in front of us, touched his arse then slotted back into the row, the official call sign for an approaching troop of hot joggers. Subconsciously (men have been trained in this since adolescence) we simultaneously puffed out our chests and sucked in our stomachs and began to run faster. We smiled and nodded at the two girls running in the opposite direction, who obviously totally ignored us. Rob turned to look at the disappearing girls before turning back, the multitasking causing him to collide into me and almost take me down.

'Rob! Stop chasing ass and concentrate on the pavement. You're not breaking any bones before India.'

'God, you're such a whinger today J! I'm sure you just said something but all I heard was "whinge whinge whinge". You better cheer up before the end of the month or we're leaving you behind!'

I smiled and pushed him gently in the back.

'Right, that's it.'

He turned to chase me and I headed off the path and onto the grass, sprinting as fast as I could. Tim joined in the chase as I tried to lose them by weaving my way in and out of the trees.

'Whinge whinge whinge, don't run over a pebble J, you may hurt yourself.'

I took refuge behind a tree and started throwing sticks. 'You little shit, I just don't want you not to come! I'm not helping you up and down mountains with a cast on your leg.'

The three of us were now at either end of a bench.

Tim held his hands up, panting, 'OK fair enough.'

'Yup, it's press-up time anyway.'

I edged away from the bench and walked towards the path, not trusting them an inch.

'Bundle!'

Tim leapt for me, taking me out and hurling me to the ground. Rob, who had taken a run-up, launched himself on top of all of us and landed with all his weight. Both Tim and I exhaled sharply and tried to move him off of us, but he stayed put.

'Mmmmm, forty minutes running, I bet I really smell.'

Back at Rob's we both watched in amazement as Rob took a carton of melon juice out of the fridge, shook it, opened it and poured it into three small-sized glasses. I picked up the glass and looked at it, turning it in my hands and looking at the underneath of it.

'What the dickens is this? I don't think I've drunk out of glasses this small since I was at school!'

'Not only that dear Jonathan, but he seems to have filled them with a liquid that,' Tim leant in to smell it, 'that doesn't appear to be water or beer. Jonathan, have you ever heard of such a liquid?'

I shook my head. 'I have heard rumours from some folk as to a world of liquids that exist outside of beer and water, but I never thought I'd see one first-hand. Shall we try it?'

Rob was just looking at us, arms folded with a wry smile on his face, shaking his head.

'Yes we shall, chin chin.' Tim raised the glass, pinched his nose and took a sip. Pausing, he smacked his lips together. 'Interesting.'

'Well?'

He shook his head. 'Nothing, it literally tastes of nothing.'

'Funny guys, very funny.' He reached into the fridge and took out a big bowl. 'Now eat your salad.'

'Woah woah woah,' Tim stood up, pushing back his chair and causing a squeak to echo around the room. 'Now you may have got us to eat salad last night but you promised steak tonight. Rob we told you last night, you don't make friends with salad.'

I nodded vigorously. 'It's true Tim, didn't I almost get floored by a little gust of wind whilst on the way back yesterday?'

Tim became very serious. 'Yes Rob he did, do you want that to happen again?'

'Look! Just sit down and eat your salad, you'll like it, in fact tell me which one you prefer, last night's or this one.'

'What, which bit of lettuce tasted nicer?'

Rob threw a wooden salad server across the room. 'Eat your salad, Tim!'

Chicken Summer Salad

Ingredients

- Two chicken breasts
- One heart of romaine lettuce
- Cucumber
- Vine tomatoes
- Sun-dried tomatoes
- One avocado
- Cheddar cheese

- One red apple, cubed
- Handful of black olives
- Fresh rosemary, thyme and oregano
- Olive oil
- Black pepper
- Balsamic vinegar

Method

- Rip the washed lettuce into bite-size chunks and put at the bottom of the bowl.

- Cut the vine tomatoes into cubes and with the diced cucumber, add to the bowl.

- Making sure your avocado is ripe, cut in half, remove the stone then dice and add.

- Throw in the olives and sun-dried tomatoes.

- Dice the cheese and red apple and add.

- Cut the chicken breasts into strips and place on an oven tray. Sprinkle with a little bit of olive oil and the fresh herbs.

- Grill for around seven to ten minutes, turning at least once.

- When the chicken is ready, add to the bowl then pour in some olive oil and balsamic vinegar, mix with your hands and serve immediately.

The reason you serve salads immediately after making them is not just for the freshness of the vegetables. The olive oil starts cooking the salad as soon as you add it, so either make the dressing on the side and add just before serving, or just put it in at the end and serve immediately.

Tuna, Egg and Asparagus Salad

Serves 3

Ingredients

- Hearts of romaine lettuce, ripped into bite-size chunks
- Diced cucumber and vine tomatoes

- One avocado
- Green beans
- Sun-dried tomatoes and olives
- Handful of fresh asparagus
- Two eggs
- Two fresh tuna steaks
- Olive oil
- Balsamic vinegar

Method

- As before with the lettuce, cucumber, avocado and tomatoes.

- Cut the green beans in half and add.

- In the same pan, boil the two eggs and the asparagus.

- Remove both after five minutes, slice the asparagus into inch-long strips and add to the salad.

- Cook the tuna steaks in a little olive oil and turn after a few minutes. Slice into small chunks and add to the bowl along with the olive oil, black pepper and vinegar.

- Mix with your hands.

- Peel the eggs and cut into slices, it should still be nice and runny.

- Arrange eggs on top of salad and serve.

Chapter Thirty-Seven
June 16th 2008

FOUR MORE DAYS TO go then I am out of here, and thank God. After another week of eating salad, running, feeling faint in the mornings and generally feeling tired all the time we'd decided (well Tim and I had decided) that enough was enough and Rob's hardcore training, whilst good for a few weeks, really had run its course (hahahahaha) and that there was more to life. The crowning moment came when Tim read in his Lonely Planet that alcohol was banned almost everywhere in northern India and only sold sporadically in the south. If we weren't going to be drinking for the first two weeks anyway and doing some hardcore travelling, well we could afford to slack off the pace in the final week. So that was exactly what we did. Tim called a "meeting to discuss the trip" in the "Freemasons" and we happily exchanged an hour's run round the park for a good sesh in the pub. Tim and I got there early, choosing to play a few games of darts before Rob turned up (he was shit and whined whenever we played). Engrossed in a particularly dire game, time flew by until we realised Rob was over half an hour late. Calling him he picked up and said he was still a good half-hour away before mumbling something about 'bloody gypsies'.

'What he say?'

'He's walking, be here in about half an hour.'

'Walking? Where from? He lives miles away.'

'I know, he said he'd explain all when he got there, mumbled something about gypsies.'

Tim paused as if to ask something further before shaking his head and taking his three throws.

'Double tops finish, no pressure.'

'Feeling none.' I held my arm up and lined the dart up with the double twenty. I missed, again.

Tim rolled his eyes. 'Jesus, will this game never end.'

'You got anything major to do before we leave?'

Tim shook his head. 'Nup, might go see the parents on the Sunday but no, nothing major. You around over the weekend?'

'Yeah.'

He nodded and I knew full well that in his mind he was thinking about all the eventual possibilities of me and Mel together in the flat for a weekend. I decided not to bring it up and we played on.

A disgruntled Rob slumped down on the chair before looking up and asking, 'Can someone buy me a pint, I haven't got any money.'

'Sure, what took you so long?'

'I gave all my money away to a gypsy who then cursed me.'

Tim looked at Rob. 'Riiiight. You want to expand on that?'

He shook his head. 'I was just leaving work when a gypsy stopped me and thrust this herb or plant or something into my hand. I tried to give it back to her but she was having none of it. She said she would curse me if I gave the present back, and that I should give her some money too. I'm pretty superstitious, don't really want to be cursed before India, so I gave her a couple of quid. She looked me up and down, saw I was in a suit, asked for more and I said no so she cursed me. I buckled and gave her a tenner, she scarpered and I don't know if she lifted the curse or not!' He sighed, 'And she took the present.'

'So you got mugged by a gypsy?'

He nodded. 'Yeah, mugged and cursed, and it put me in such a foul mood especially seeing as I had no money and had to walk here.'

'Why didn't you get some money out?'

He looked confused. 'Y'know, I didn't actually think of that. I need a beer.'

I squeezed his shoulder. 'Come on, I'll get you a drink.'

I turned around to go to the bar and there she was, ten metres away and looking straight at me. In my head everything stopped; the music, everyone's conversations, Tim's dart in mid-air. Wearing a business suit and with her long black hair tumbling down to her shoulders and then beyond she looked strong, confident, self-assured. And then she smiled and I saw that little tooth pointing through.

'Jasmine.'

She grinned. 'J.' She looked over my shoulder. 'Hey Rob, Tim, how are you guys?'

They both smiled, Tim waved from the dartboard. She turned to me. 'J, you remember Andy and Laura don't you?' Hands were shook, cheeks were kissed, a slightly embarrassed Laura avoided eye contact, probably still regretting drunkenly exploding Jazz's life story into my ear at Jules' wedding.

We stood in silence; I put my hands in my jacket pocket.

'I-I-I'm sorry about the party,' she stammered, 'I wanted to come, really, but I had to go to Southend in a rush.'

A sudden remembrance. 'Everything ok?'

She nodded and smiled. 'Yeah, yeah, fine.'

'Good. So,' I looked around, 'this is kinda random, I didn't know you drank around here?'

'No, well I don't normally, I've only ever been with you guys but apparently Andy and Laura come here all the time, don't you?'

She turned to them in an attempt to bring them into the conversation; she must've felt awkward, I felt hurt that she was.

'Never miss a Sunday lunch here, best roast this side of the river.'

We stood in awkward silence again. Tim went back to the darts, Laura got out her phone to see if she had any text messages.

'Do you want to …' she tilted her head towards the bar, 'that's where you were headed, wasn't it?'

'Yeah, good idea. Rob, pint of Pride, right?'

He gave me the thumbs up and Jazz and I weaved our way towards the bar. Reaching the side we both leant down on the counter, both looking forward, watching ourselves and each other in the mirror in front of us.

'Well, that was awkward.'

I smiled. 'Tell me about it, never thought I'd see those two again!'

'And you and Tim in the pub playing darts, wow you've changed!'

'Hey! There is nothing wrong with playing darts in a pub.'

She shook her head. 'No, no there isn't. I'm glad you guys are OK, Mel told me about what happened at her party.'

'Yeah well,' I made a hand gesture for no reason at all. I turned to her and leant on the side of the bar. 'So how are you Jazz? How have you been?'

She bobbed her head. 'I've been good. Nothing really major to report. Still same flat, same job, same going to see Mum when I can, plodding along really. How about you?'

'Yeah same really, the whole Tim and Mel thing has been the big story since we, er, I mean since I, since I last saw you.'

She flinched. 'How's work?'

I shrugged. 'Same as really, it starts at nine, more often than not ends at six and when I walk out the door I don't remember a thing about it until the next morning. Just the way it should be.'

'I'll drink to that.' She turned to face me, those familiar flash-light eyes reacquainting themselves with my face. She still took my breath away.

'It's good to see you J.'

So we talked, and we talked, and we forgot why we were at that bar in the first place. Sure it was a bit awkward, sure there were things that had happened over the last three months that I didn't tell her about, but I'm sure she was doing exactly the same. We laughed and we smiled and we reminisced and during the entire time we spent at that bar, our minds projected one combined thought onto the wall behind the barman that we ignored, I've missed you.

'So Sunday night in a pub huh, really taking work seriously at the moment, are we?!' She looked at me and smiled, sticking her tongue out between her teeth.

'Hey,' I held up my hands, 'for your information I haven't been in a pub for weeks, the three of us have been running almost every day recently.'

'You running?! God, why?'

'Don't act so surprised! Anyway, we wanted to get fit for India.'

She swallowed. 'India?! You're going to India? When?!'

'Wednesday, I thought you knew?'

She motioned with her hands. 'How would I know?'

'Well I would've thought Mel might have said something.'

She shook her head. 'Mel barely speaks to me about you, she finds the whole thing really awkward.'

'What, still?'

Jazz looked a little hurt. 'It wasn't that long ago J. Some things take time y'know.' She looked down at the bar, she'd clammed up. My God, she wasn't over me was she? I looked away. Am I over you?

She looked back up at me, her lips slightly parted; she looked like a deer caught in my headlights. You could cut the tension with a rusty spoon.

'Are you?'

'Am I what?'

'J, do you still think about us?'

I paused, not sure if this was a conversation I wanted to be having.

'Yes.'

'Much?'

'It's got easier. At the start it was pretty tough to be honest, I was so angry at myself for what happened and how it'd got fucked up so quickly. I don't think I realised how much I cared for you.' I paused again. 'And how much I'd miss you.'

She held my gaze and then turned her head towards the bar.

I continued, 'And then it got a bit easier, although I was pretty nervous at the prospect of seeing you at the party last month.'

She smiled.

'OK, your turn, do you still think about us?'

She nodded. 'Yeah, yeah I do. I meant what I said that day, it was one of the hardest decisions I've had to take and since then I've always wondered what would—'

'Where the hell have you guys been? I asked for that pint about thirty minutes ago.'

Rob put his arm on my shoulder and gave it a squeeze for a fraction of a second longer than necessary. He caught the barman's eye. 'Pint of Pride please mate.'

We ordered our drinks and headed back to the group. Jazz led the way, followed by Rob, then me. He turned to me as we left the bar and whispered, 'Saving you from the awkward ex chat, mate.'

I didn't need him to save me.

The two groups converged a bit but never really merged, Jazz stayed with Laura and Andy whilst Rob, Tim and I stayed around the darts board. Last orders rang and we began to put on our coats and pack the darts away. Jazz weaved her way through the chairs and said, 'Laura and Andy are taking the bus home, could you please walk me to the station? I don't really want to walk on my own.'

I nodded, then motioned at my half-full pint. 'Sure, just give me two minutes.'

Her cheeks were red with embarrassment. 'Thanks, I'll meet you outside.' She turned and left.

Tim raised an eyebrow. 'Want us to come with you?'

'No, I've got it.'

'Sure?'

'Yeah it's, it's just genuinely nice to see her, y'know I wouldn't mind spending a bit more time with her.'

'Be careful, OK?'

I waved my hand. 'It's fine it's fine, I'll see you at home.'

Walking up the hill towards Hampstead station, the late evening wind that blew against us made us walk slower. All around the clack-clack of women in heels leaving bars and noises of over-revved car engines made up for the lack of conversation between Jazz and me.

Suddenly she spoke out. 'Yeah I do think about you, I think about it a lot. I'm not sure if that means I acted wrong, or you acted wrong or whatever, I guess it was just one of those things.'

I didn't say anything, I sensed there was more to come.

'And seeing Mel just made it worse, all I wanted to do was to ask her about your life. I spent most of the following weeks in tears, did she tell you that?'

I shook my head. 'No.'

We walked on, the tension between us growing, it was all I could do not to reach out and take her hand in mine, yet something stopped me.

'So India, how come?'

I smiled. 'You want to know the real story?'

'Of course I do!'

'We drunkenly booked it one night when Rob and Tim were trying to help me get over you. We didn't remember a thing about it until the next morning.'

She smiled and shook her head. 'That doesn't surprise me at all. How long are you gone for?'

'Three weeks.'

'Wow.'

The station was in sight, our pace slowed. We stopped a few metres down from the entrance.

'Well, thanks for walking me here.'

'You're welcome, it was, er, it was good to see you again.'

We stood in silence for a second. What to do, what to do.

'And have a great time in India.'

'Thanks and you, have a good time if you go to Italy.'

'Thanks.'

'Well,' I began to back away, 'see you.'

'See you.'

She held my eyes for a second before turning up the hill. I turned and began walking away. One loud clear voice began to echo around my head and I decided to listen to it for once.

'Jasmine.'

She turned and within a few seconds I'd reached her. Taking her head in my hands I kissed her, lightly, gently on those lips I'd gotten so used to but had missed so much. I recognised her taste, I recognised the way her hands ran through the hair at the back of my head. I remembered this feeling of helplessness and desire, and I remembered how hard it was to kiss her when I couldn't stop myself from smiling.

'Make sure you call me when you get back from India.'

She kissed me lightly and turned to go into the station.

Chapter Thirty-Eight
June 25th 2008

WE LEFT ROB BURIED underneath our three rucksacks, jumped out of the tuc-tuc, splashed through the rain and headed into the third hotel we'd been shown so far this evening.

'Do they have a swimming pool?'

'Yes, certainly,' said our tuc-tuc driver.

'And are there fans in the room?'

'Absolutely, fully air-conditioning Sir.'

We removed our flip flops, crossed the lobby and headed towards the check-in desk. Clasping our hands in front of our chests we bowed our heads slightly in the typical Hindu greeting.

'Namaste.'

'Namaste,' replied the hotel clerk and bowed his head back.

I took the lead. 'Do you have a room for tonight please, for three people?'

The man behind the desk waggled his head. 'Certainly we do.'

'And how much is that room?'

'Three hundred rupees.'

Tim and I exchanged looks, that was a good price.

'And does it have air-conditioning?'

'Fully air-conditioning, yes sir,' he nodded.

'Can we see it?'

'Certainly.'

We followed the hotel guy up three flights of marble, rain-covered stairs.

From behind me Tim asked, 'Where is the swimming pool?'

He shook his head. 'No swimming pool sir.' He looked upwards and raised his hands. 'We don't need it!'

Arriving at the room he unlocked the heavy padlock and swung the door open. Bugs swarmed in through the door, the continuous drone of crickets and mosquitoes hung heavy in the air.

I looked at the ceiling and around the room. 'There's no fan or air-conditioning here?'

'No sir.'

'But you said there was air-conditioning?'

He smiled and nodded energetically. 'Yes sir.'

Sighing, Tim turned to our tuc-tuc driver. 'Look, all we want to do is go to the Udaipur Palace Hostel, please, just take us there.'

He held up his hands and waggled his head. 'No problem, we go now.'

Emerging onto the street our driver pointed fifty metres up the hill. 'Udaipur Palace Hostel.'

He jumped in and started the engine as Tim stuck his head around the side. 'Rob, it's just up there, we'll walk.'

The tuc-tuc moved off and with the weight of Rob and three heavy backpacks, began slowly climbing the hill. Then it slowed a bit, and then it slowed right down. Then it stopped. Then it began to roll backwards.

'Guuuuuuuuys!!!!'

We jumped behind the tuc-tuc and stopped it from rolling whilst the driver pulled up the handbrake. Giving him twenty rupees we unloaded our backpacks and decided to walk the remaining bit.

It was a very strange experience. For all our travelling, and between the three of us we'd all been to every populated continent a few times over, we were all experiencing our first ever culture shock. We'd been in India for over a week now, and whilst we'd done enough in that week to make it feel like a month, none of us yet felt a hundred percent comfortable.

I guess we'd been on the back foot since the second we woke up in London and tried to leave the country. Owing to a major security threat almost all European flights were cancelled from Heathrow, and only a smidge of intercontinental flights were taking off, meaning that not only was it a battle trying to get to Heathrow, but we had no idea what would be in store for us when we did finally get there.

Absurdly, after all the hype we were only delayed by eight minutes, but a consequence of the security alert was that no hand luggage was allowed on board, everything apart from wallets and passports had to be stored in the hold which meant we'd suddenly lost our chance at planning the trip. For weeks we'd been saying how we had nine hours on the plane in which to work out a route from Delhi to Rajasthan and then south to Kerala, but instead we now found ourselves with nine hours to kill on a flight, whilst our travel guides were locked in our bags some five feet below us. Landing in Delhi on no sleep, no itinerary and being greeted by a forty-five degree wall of heat meant that the holiday started on a quiet note. Before we knew it we'd crossed Delhi by taxi and were at the train station waiting to catch a train four hours south to Agra, home of the Taj Mahal and former capital of India. I'm sure there were great things about Delhi, but our first impressions were pretty poor, so we just decided to get out as quickly as possible and maybe explore Delhi on the way back.

The train station was probably our first real culture shock. The platforms were enormous, about a quarter of a mile long and were rammed full of bustling commuter trains, all painted light blue with bars covering the windows. From the dark inside all that could be seen were hands dangling limply down and faces that stared openly at the three rich, white foreigners who stood defensively together around their bags, unsure if they were being overly protective or just offensive.

All around us shoeless kids ran over the tracks and followed in hordes any tourist or middle-class Indian that walked down the platform. One thing that immediately surprised me was that, in contrast to South America where the poor are constantly ignored, middle-class Indians dished out money to all who came asking and those that asked accepted without any obvious gratitude. It seemed I was witnessing first-hand a form of self-regulated benefit, those that had gave a small amount to those that did not have, and neither one questioned it. This was such a contrast to the streets of London, where sure, people give to guys on the street, but if a man came up to you on the tube and unapologetically shoved a hand in your face you can bet your life no-one would even so much as acknowledge him.

Feeling peckish I wandered over to a little kiosk on the platform and asked for a pack of crisps and three bottles of water. A beautiful girl who could only have been about five or so ran over to me and began pulling at my T-shirt. She simultaneously pointed at a pastry behind the counter and motioned to her mouth. Looking into her enormous brown eyes I felt like the typical western stereotype yet I also couldn't say no. The vendor handed over the pastry which I passed onto the girl who, after giving me a wicked smile, turned and ran off to a group of kids down the platform. Sure enough they all ran after me, motioning to the kiosk and rubbing their stomachs. I returned to Rob and Tim with a half-dozen kids following me, and any joy I'd felt at giving the little girl food was eradicated by the guilt I felt at having to turn away six more.

Finding the right carriage proved a lot more difficult than you might have thought. After walking the length of the platform with our bags and not seeing a sign that we so much as remotely recognised, we asked for help, a fatal mistake to make in India. The first guy we asked had absolutely no idea, nor did the ten people who gathered around us to hear what was going on. The second guy vehemently pointed us to one end of the platform, which obviously turned out to be wrong, as did the advice of the third person we asked who was, note, someone who worked for the train company. As we ran down the platform for the third time the train started to pull away, and lunging for the door we all bundled onto the nearest carriage and collapsed down onto the hard foam-covered benches.

'Jesus Christ, what a mission!'

I looked down at the hand-scrawled train ticket in my hand.

'Yeah, this definitely isn't our carriage.' Tapping the second row of benches above our heads I said, 'This is a sleeper carriage, we want third class.'

Rob stood up and peered over the benches above us. 'That's a sleeper? We are definitely not training it down south, sod it, let's pay fifty quid and get a flight and be there in two hours.'

We finished our waters and watched as the outskirts of Delhi slowly passed us by. Still wearing our clothes from England and the flight, we were exhausted and must've smelt pretty bad. Our three rucksacks and day packs filled the booth as one by one Rob and Tim began to doze, lying down on the benches and using bags or one of our legs as pillows. Just before sleep completely consumed Tim he squinted at me. 'Dude, we can do sleeping shifts, keep an eye on our stuff. Wake me in an hour if you want?'

I shook my head. 'It's cool, I'm not gonna sleep.'

He nodded and closed his eyes.

I slumped down in my seat and rested my feet on the opposite bench. It was mid-afternoon and the sun was on its climb down, the earlier heat of the morning gone for the day. For an enormous train that probably hadn't changed since the British left sixty years ago, we were travelling at quite a decent speed. Fields flew by, interspersed by the occasional settlement perched on the edge of a river, its rubbish spilling down into the water in which people washed and cows bathed.

We arrived in Agra around dusk and tuc-tuc'ed it to a hostel within walking distance of the Taj Mahal. Absolutely ravenous, we dumped our bags and immediately went straight up to the rooftop restaurant to tuck into our first Indian meal. Wanting to ease ourselves into it slowly, and delay getting sick for as long as possible, we all decided to become vegetarian for the first few days, just to give our stomachs time to accustom before bombarding them with chicken and goat.

The view as we climbed the stairs to the roof was one I'll never forget. By this point the sun had completely vanished and the full moon had risen high above and lit up the Taj Mahal a few hundred metres in front of us. Obviously being closed at night the whole area around the temple was lit up, yet being deserted and with all the fountains turned off it was eerily quiet. The reflection of the Taj rippled in each pool as if the temple itself was moving in the moonlight. Because of the stone used to create it, a greenish hue, a product of the moonlight, emanated from the enormous curved dome.

Pulling up a few plastic chairs we sat at our table, lit a few candles in glasses and turned to soak up the view, the glow of the candles, the moon and the Taj being the only light we could see.

Vegetable Biriyani

Ingredients
- Cup and a half of basmati rice
- One onion
- Two cloves of garlic
- One big potato
- Two carrots
- Handful of green beans
- 400 ml vegetable stock

Spices:
- Two cloves
- Two cardamom pods
- One tablespoon cumin
- One tablespoon coriander
- One tablespoon turmeric
- Half a tablespoon chilli powder
- Salt and black pepper

Method
- Boil the washed rice in the stock, and add the cloves and cardamom. Cook until the water has been absorbed, probably takes about twenty minutes.

- Blend the garlic cloves and all the spices with two tablespoons of water in a blender.

- Pour the mixture into an oven dish and cook for two minutes.

- Add the chopped vegetables and six tablespoons of water to the oven dish, ensuring the paste covers the vegetables, cover and cook for twelve minutes.

- Spoon the rice over the vegetables and cook for a further twenty minutes.

We ordered three banana lassis to go with our biriyanis. A lassi is exactly like a smoothie and contains a variety of different fruits and spices. We found banana lassis to be the tastiest.

Banana Lassi

Ingredients for each individual lassi
- Two bananas
- 250 grams yoghurt
- Two tablespoons sugar
- A sprinkling of cinammon

Method
Pretty self explanatory, just blend everything together for a few seconds and serve.

Cheersing our drinks we relaxed into a comfortable silence, enjoying stopping for the first time in over twenty-four hours. Even though we were three stories up and completely exposed on the roof, only the lightest breeze ruffled our tops. After the anticlimactic start to the summer we'd had in England the heat was a welcome change.

'You know what,' Rob said, turning from the view of the Taj and facing the table as the waiter brought out the three biriyanis, 'this is exactly what I wanted, this is exactly what I needed.'

We nodded our heads in agreement and began scooping up the rice in our right hands, as is the Indian custom. None of us really had the hang of it yet and we ended up with more rice down our tops than in our mouths.

'Best of all, we're being paid to be here!'

I smiled and raised my lassi. 'I'll drink to that.'

'So I was thinking on the train,' Tim said in between mouthfuls of chapatti, 'that we need to set out a series of rules for the next three weeks, y'know, just to make sure we're doing as much as we can.'

Rob and I exchanged glances. 'Rules, like what? A schedule?!'

He shook his head. 'Nonono, I don't mean hardcore rules like we have to be up by seven every day, I mean tasks, missions.'

'Such as?'

'Erm, eat and show? We have to get a local on camera doing eat and show?'

I smiled. 'Like it, like it, photographic evidence is essential. What about,' I drummed my fingers on the table, '… we have to take as many different forms of transport as possible? Plane, train, car, tuc-tuc, moped, boat that sort of thing?'

'Well we already jumped on a speeding train this afternoon.'

'Alriiite, it was speeding, wasn't it?!'

We high-fived.

'I've got one for now.' Rob held up three chapattis. 'Who can fit an entire chapatti in their mouths? No liquids.'

We crammed the chapattis in our mouths and attempted to chew. The dryness of the dough combined with the ban on liquids meant it was impossible to chew and swallow, so we all sat there with our cheeks full, trying to get it down. Tim began to eat and show, Rob and I quickly followed. Our waiter came over to see if everything was OK. Rob eat-and-showed the waiter.

'OK, more rules.'

'Weeee have to motorbike it down to the tip of India and stand as far south as possible.'

'What, from Agra?!'

'No you jackass, from Kerala, the southern point is in the state below.'

'Oh yeah,' I chimed in, 'we have to go to as many states as possible.'

'Swim in as many oceans as possible.'

I came out with the classic, 'Climb something high and watch the sunrise.'

'Get in at least one dodgy situation where we think we're going to die.'

'I think that about covers it.' Tim downed the rest of his lassi. 'And we're not leaving this country till we've done them all!'

'Ha, I can just imagine us on our last day in Delhi getting someone to eat and show whilst riding a motorbike up a hill for sunrise and getting held up by robbers.'

'And I'll be severely disappointed if we don't! Now, guys,' I looked at Rob and Tim, 'we also need to get our teams going.'

Rob raised his eyebrow. 'Teams?'

I smiled. 'Let me explain. Now, you know when you see someone hot in the street you say "shotgun", yeah?'

They nodded. 'Yes J we have been playing that game for over ten years now.'

'Well, it's the opposite, when you see someone incredibly ugly you put them on someone's team. For example, if Rob's Mum was walking down the road I'd say to you,' I looked at Tim, 'she's on your team. With me?'

'Yup.'

'Good, now this develops further and can work for anything. You see a guy with appalling hair, two strands combed over his bald head and you can say "that guy's your team's hairdresser" or you see a bombed-out car and you say "that's your team's mode of transport". You see?'

Tim nodded. 'Yeah, so it works in conjunction with shotgun, right?'

'Right.'

'So,' Rob looked around and pointed at the Taj, 'I can say shotgun the Taj for my team's headquarters?'

'Yup, good shotgun.'

'Excellent. Now, final rule, we all have to pull a traveller here.'

Tim and I looked uneasy. 'Rob, have you so much as even seen another traveller in India? It's the end of the season, it's dead.'

'Yeah, and I'm not that keen on that rule anyway.'

He raised his eyebrows. 'I didn't realise I was travelling with two fun sponges, why the hell not?'

I shrugged. 'I dunno, I can't help but compare ...'

'Oh no, don't you do this, you've done well so far and not mentioned her all day. If you are gonna tell me some bullshit like you feel you'd be cheating on Jasmine I am gonna slap you so hard with this chapatti!'

'Well ...'

He picked up the chapatti.

I raised my hand to block it. 'Well, who knows Rob, I mean we did kiss a few days ago, and she did tell me to get in touch with her when I got back.'

Rob threw the chapatti back on the plate. 'I don't trust her. She dumps you then clicks her fingers and now you're putting your life on hold.'

'Rob, not wanting to drunkenly pull a hippie tie-die traveller that hasn't washed in a week isn't exactly putting my life on hold, is it? And she didn't click her fingers, you haven't heard the full story OK.'

'OK, poor excuse. Fun hoover, what's yours?' he turned to Tim.

He shrugged. 'Dunno, just not really in the mood for it all y'know, still quite soon after Mel.'

Rob slumped back in his chair and sighed. 'You're both on each others' teams.'

Chapter Thirty-Nine
June 26th 2008

WE LEFT AGRA THE following evening; apart from the Taj there wasn't that much else to see or do there. We woke at sunrise to go to the palace but after an hour of wandering around it and sitting in the gardens doing Princess Diana impressions on the famous bench we felt like we'd kinda done it all. As is so often the case when you see famous buildings or statues, the image itself is so familiar to you for you've been looking at it all of your life, so seeing it in front of you is always a slight disappointment because it looks exactly how you'd imagine it to look.

Another train ride, this time a seven-hour one, took us west into Rajasthan and into Jaipur, the state capital. Jaipur was an enormous city that spread around the basin of snow-capped mountains and as one of the former capitals of British Imperialism retained grandiose buildings and palaces, former homes of the Raj. The heart of Jaipur was a bustling square mile of identically painted pink houses gathered around two main thoroughfares. At either end of the pink city, as it was known, stood elaborate temples and palaces rising high into the burning blue sky. The pink city itself was awash with colour and noise as tuc-tucs, cows, horses, camels, elephants, people, mopeds and cars weaved in and out of each other, shouting, honking and braying whenever right of way wasn't given.

Hopping out of a tuc-tuc we decided that the pink city would be better explored on foot and so we plunged into one of the dozens of side streets where all around us the air was filled with a mixture of spices being sold openly on the street and the stench of litter and human waste. We stopped at a group of women sitting cross-legged on the floor, busy nattering amongst themselves. In between the three women, mounds of freshly ground turmeric, cumin and garam masala rose high into the air. In one swift action the women emptied half-cupfuls of the spices into small see-through bags, flipped them over once and tied them up, without breaking conversational stride and without even looking at their customers.

The poverty had got to us. Everywhere we went we were followed by kids asking for food or the odd rupee, and the genuine confusion on their faces if we turned them away was truly humbling. As with other places in the world that we'd visited, the whole idea of travelling was such a foreign concept to the people we spoke to. No judgement was made on why we'd chosen to spend such vast sums of money on flying to India when it could in their eyes, be put to better use, but having to continually explain what you were doing here in front of people whose average wage was ten pounds a month never got any easier. In fact the most uncomfortable thing to do was explain to a tuc-tuc driver how long he'd have to work for just to be able to buy Tim's iPod.

After half an hour or so of wandering around the pink city we began to feel a bit aimless and our minds started drifting to the evening ahead. We were still exhausted from the flight and travelling so didn't really want to do anything big, yet it still would have been nice to do something a bit different for our first night in Jaipur.

'Could climb it for sunset?' Rob nodded towards the hills.

We turned to follow his head. Far up on one of the highest hills overlooking Jaipur sat Jaigarh Fort, its long arms unfurling over the two nearest hills.

'We can't walk that?!'

'No, I know we can't, lets get a tuc-tuc. The Planet says there's a restaurant up there. Let's treat ourselves.'

'Let's do it, bug out.'

We turned to walk back to the main road and hire a tuc-tuc. A completely naked man walked past us and turned to go into one of the spice shops. Rob turned to Tim. 'Dude, definitely your team.'

Jaipur fell away from us as our tuc-tuc rounded another corner and continued its climb. The sun had started its descent and I reckoned if we made good time we'd still have half an hour up top before it got completely dark. We'd found a two-row tuc-tuc, with the second row facing out towards the traffic behind us. Lying on that seat now I was surprised at the amount of people that smiled and waved as we passed them. India was amazing me, there was something so completely different about this country but I just couldn't put my finger on it. There was an incredible naivety, especially about love and sex which was thought of as something risqué, naughty, something to be laughed at. Maybe that was it, it was a very young naïve country, but about as naïve as a twelve-year-old is about sex. Giggling about it, thinking about it constantly, aware of it going on around you and aware that in time your turn will come. India's modernisation was on, they knew within a matter of years they'd be world competitors if not leaders, and like impatient teenagers they were desperate to get on with it, yet also not that sure what to do when they did get it.

Mens' views about women in particular were something alien to me, and what they thought happened in the west came as a big shock. The number of times I'd got strange looks from people who found out I was twenty-four and not married was increasing hourly. Rob got it worse though; on explaining to a guy in a restaurant that he was single but had been going out with a girl for seven years until recently he was asked with eyes wide open, 'But why did you not marry her?'

He shrugged. 'Just didn't feel right.'

'And that is normal?'

'What, to go out with someone and not marry them? Sure, happens all the time.'

He shook his head. 'But weren't your parents angry?'

'Why would they be?'

'Well, after finding you a bride you didn't marry her ...'

'Well no, my parents didn't find my girlfriend, I found my

girlfriend.'

His jaw literally dropped open.

'It's what we do in England; you can go out with who you want for as long as you want.'

'But how do you find them?'

Being out of season, the fort was mostly empty. All along the walls tables and chairs were set out, facing out into the open and onto the city of Jaipur several hundred metres below. We ordered a few sundowners and settled into our seats with our beers and complimentary chilli peanuts and watched the sun fall.

'It's a lot bigger than I thought it was. Look, there's the pink city, it's like a twentieth of the city.'

Rob pointed. 'Look, there's the polo club and golf course.'

'And there's the slum next to it.'

'And the palace next to that, sums it all up really doesn't it?'

We sat in silence for a while, enjoying the cool feeling of the light breeze on our cheeks.

'So we gonna talk about it?'

I turned to look at Tim out of the corner of my eye. 'Hmm?'

'Are we going to talk about it? Mel? It's been a good few days and it hasn't come up yet. I feel like we have some air to clear, don't you?'

I sat up and took a handful of peanuts, Rob sat back and said nothing.

'Well, what more is there to say? We're OK, aren't we?'

Tim nodded. 'Yeah, we're mostly OK. It's just, well, has she said anything about me? Do you think she'll change her mind?'

I turned to look at him. He was looking at me so earnestly, I had to pick my words carefully.

I hesitated. 'I haven't spoken to her that much about it. After what we talked about on Parliament Hill I wanted to give both of you a little space to sort it all out, but I don't think she's going to change her mind.'

'Did she say that?'

'Not in as many words, but I just don't think it'll happen; she was pretty angry with you for a long time dude.'

He slumped back in his chair. 'That's what I thought, I guess I just needed to hear it from you.'

'But you guys talked about it, right?' I asked.

'Not since the day after her party.'

'What? How come, we live together!'

'I dunno', he shrugged. 'I never knew how to bring it up, I never knew what to say.'

'Yeah, but Tim, you had to say something, you fought for it didn't you?'

He shook his head. 'After that night I didn't really feel like I had a leg to stand on. I humiliated her. I kinda thought the decision on this was down to her.'

'Does she know you were falling in love with her?'

He shook his head. 'No point telling her now.'

'Why?'

'She won't have me back. I fucked it up.'

He got up to go find a toilet, another Tim indicator that this particular conversation was over for tonight. By the time he got back our food had arrived and all conversation stalled as we munched on our kormas and watched the city fire up beneath us.

Rajasthani cooking is famous all over India for its fantastic, rich meaty dishes. After a few days of veggie food we'd decided we could handle meat now, and had even gone so far as to try mutton (goat) once or twice. Our mutton and tomato korma was perhaps the nicest dish we'd had so far.

Mutton and Tomato Korma

Ingredients

- 200g per person fresh goat, or lamb if the supermarket is all out

- Two red onions
- Two cloves garlic
- Twelve sliced tomatoes
- Coconut milk
- Served with basmati rice

Spices:

- Tablespoons of turmeric, ground coriander, garam masala and cumin
- Two black cardamoms
- Two cloves
- An inch of ginger, diced
- Half a teaspoon chilli powder

Method

- Cook up the onions, garlic and ginger.
- After a few minutes add the tomatoes and the meat.
- Finally, add the tomatoes, all spices and half a cup of water.
- Stir vigorously to ensure the sauce gets mixed into everything.
- If the sauce starts running a bit dry add more water.
- A few minutes before you think it's ready, try the sauce, if it's too hot, add a splash of coconut milk and stir in.
- Serve over basmati rice with some naan or chapatti.

We ate in what I thought was a relaxed silence. The air trembled with the sounds of insects and the honks of the mopeds and tuc-tucs below us.

'Guys, I'm sorry if I was a bit harsh.'

We looked at Rob quizzically.

'About the whole pulling travellers and Jazz and Mel and everything. I know you're probably both pretty focused on what you think is waiting for you back in England.'

I shook my head. 'On the contrary, there's no place I'd rather be, I want to get away from everything, even if it is just for a few weeks.' I looked around the table and continued, 'I don't know about you both but I'm exhausted. These last few months have been so busy and stressful, and I hate the fact that all of a sudden we've become these stressy city workers. No, mate, if I didn't think I'd be able to do something like this once a year, I'd go crazy.'

Tim put down his mango lassi. 'It does help that you've got someone to go back to though J.'

'Have I though?'

'Well, you tell us? I mean from what you said it sounded pretty certain.'

I chewed my lip. 'I dunno, I mean we spent what, about an hour together after not seeing each other for three months.'

'Yeah, but it was clear when you saw each other how you both felt, right?'

I slumped back in my chair and looked up at the full moon. 'I felt over her up until the point I saw her again.'

Rob moved his chair round so we were all sitting in a line, looking down onto the city and up at the stars. 'And now?'

I turned to him. 'Like if I don't tread carefully I could undo three months' work and get hurt again. What you said a few days ago about her snapping her fingers ...'

'J, I didn't mean that ...'

'Nonono it's OK, in some ways you're right.'

'But then you're the one that kissed her.'

'Yeah, but only because I was pretty sure she wouldn't coil away in disgust.'

'So what are you saying?'

I shrugged. 'I dunno, I've been thinking about her a lot this week, you always do when you're away from home don't you? I think, I think I do want to see if this is going anywhere, I mean when I look back at us earlier this year I felt so good with her, but I think I'm gonna try and take it slow. We were on the rocks from the start in January what with that damn wedding, but now ... I mean we both know each other a lot better, she seems to be seeing her uni mates which is great, yeah I think it could work, nice and slow.'

'You see, that's maybe why I snapped at you guys.' Rob put his drink down. 'I got nothing, no-one. Since Megan I haven't even had a whiff of any excitement.'

'Yeah but Rob you were with her forever, it's gonna take time.'

'I know it is, but I'm not talking about starting up a relationship, I'm just talking about that feeling where you're in a bar and you can tell someone is looking at you, or you hear from someone that this girl has a crush on you. I haven't had that feeling in ages.'

Tim put his hand on his shoulder. 'Oh come on dude, I'm sure there are plenty of women that fancy you, you just don't know about it, you're male, we're shit at that kinda stuff.'

He shrugged. 'Well I'm just bored at the moment, and can't be arsed with the prospect of going back to London and carrying on with the same shit. Maybe London isn't for me.'

A brief silence passed over us; it was pretty rare for Rob to let his guard down like this. Although I called him one of my best friends there was still a hell of a lot of stuff I didn't know about him. I pushed a bit further.

'Do you miss Megan?'

He took a while to answer and I wondered if I'd gone too far.

'… Yes and no,' he paused. 'I miss someone, I'm not sure if it's her. I miss someone I can text about all the stupid things that happen to me each day; I miss closing my bedroom door and not feeling like I'm out of the world until the next morning, but as soon as I think about her I begin to think about all the reasons we broke up. I think it had run its course and because there's no anger or resentment on either side, it's almost worse.'

We continued to stargaze for a few more minutes. The sky was lit up by the lights of the city below and the glow of the moon. We all had our legs up on the balcony, our feet lying at awkward angles on the ledge.

'Believe me, Rob, it's worse when there's anger on one side.'

We stayed quiet, letting Tim get ready to speak again.

'I feel so humiliated around her. J, you know you asked me why I never fought for it? Well I feel like she's completely justified in her choice. Hell, I wouldn't want to go out with me after what I did. Can you imagine what it must feel like to be scared of the person you're waking up with?'

'I was always a little scared of Megan actually.'

'Yeah, Jazz's temper scared me too.'

Tim hesitated for a second. 'Stop winding me up, you know what I mean.' We nodded.

'I'm sure she didn't think you were gonna hit her or anything stupid like that, she just saw your temper, something we all have.'

'Yeah but I lost it completely.'

'You were drunk.'

'That's no excuse. Everyone was drunk.'

Rob looked up to the stars. 'I think you're being too hard on yourself. You said some out of order stuff and it cost you your relationship, but come on, you were never going to hit Mel were you? I mean that's something else completely.'

'I know I know, but for her to feel like I might have. God that just turns me so cold. And now all I've got to look forward to is going back to a house in which my ex-girlfriend lives. And every time she walks out the door it's all I can do not to follow her or,' he turned to me, 'ask you where she's going.'

'So what are you going to do?'

He shrugged. 'Get over her, hope it gets easier.'

Rob sat up and turned to Tim. 'Not going to give it one more shot?'

He shook his head. 'I don't think so.'

We were quiet once again as we spent time looking for shooting stars. Rob rubbed his arms and put his hoodie on. I felt so relaxed.

'So two nights here?'

We nodded

'Let's chill out a bit tomorrow, find a pool.'

I nodded. 'Good idea'

'Then travelling all day, three nights Pushkar, onto Udaipur then south, yeah?'

'Yeah.'

'Sweet.'

Tim looked around at the darkened fort. 'How the hell do you get down from here anyway?'

JULY

Chapter Forty
July 2nd 2008

PUSHKAR DID EXACTLY WHAT it said on the tin: it was absolute hippy central. A small village around a sacred lake, deep in the mountains had ballooned from its 1960s' starting point as a village where a few gringos went to take drugs to a town where thousands of gringos, mostly Israelis, went to take drugs. We decided to stay a little out of town, away from the twenty-four-hour drug-fuelled parties.

Because of the holy nature of Pushkar alcohol, meat and dairy products were banned, something we'd only discovered when we were sitting in a restaurant overlooking the lake and looking through the menus. Whilst we could cope without a beer or an egg for the evening we were quite worried about the absence of meat, as the next day was to be our most strenuous yet and we wanted to keep our energy levels up. Overlooking the lake, atop an 800-metre mountain (ok, hill) stood a place of pilgrimage, a temple devoted to Savitr, the Hindu Sun God, and our aim was to climb it before sunrise the next day. One may question the logic of climbing a hill in the pitch darkness with no guide and a faulty torch that acted as if it was doing the owner a favour by turning itself on but we were determined to do it, after all it was one of the rules of the trip.

We spent the afternoon wandering around the town, making a concerted effort to "hippy the fuck up" by buying gap year beads and flowy tops. Armed with our purchases and in some cases wearing them (Tim had gone out topless in an attempt to force himself to buy some new clothes) we headed for a restaurant perched on top of a hostel overlooking the lake. Photos of the lake were prohibited, which only added to its mystical nature as all around us holy men dressed in

orange prayed and offered sacrifices at the lake shore. Flowers, illuminated by the candles which they supported, flowed effortlessly to
the centre of the lake where they converged in some sort of pyre. The
sound of chanting and drums filled the air and for a little while no
other sound was needed, as all was inferior.

In an attempt to compensate for the lack of meat we ordered enough
naan bread to kill a small goat, determined to boost our carbohy-
drate levels before our climb a few hours later. Our favourites, which
accompanied every meal, were garlic naan although Peshwari naans
were also a winner, but they were quite rare in Rajasthan.

Garlic Naan

Ingredients for three naan
- 280g white bread flour
- One teaspoon salt
- One teaspoon dried yeast
- One tablespoon butter
- Two garlic cloves, sliced

Method
- Mix the flour and salt together.
- In another bowl add the yeast to the butter and garlic.
- Mix thoroughly until you create a dough.
- Tip onto a pre-floured surface and keand for around ten minutes.
- Wrap the dough in lightly oiled clingfilm and leave to rise for
45 minutes.
- Knead the dough once more and divide into three portions,
shaping as you wish but ensure a good centimetre of thickness
throughout.
- Sprinkle the dough with a little water and bake for 3-4 minutes.
To make Peshwari naan:
- When kneading the dough for the first time add some sliced
coconut and sultanas, easy as that.

Our vegetarian food was quite good actually. Seeing as beef and pork
are forbidden, a lot of the country is vegetarian anyway and so meat-

free dishes aren't as in the minority as much as they are in the UK. Still unsure as to the names of a lot of the foods we ordered blind and mostly got some good stuff in return.

Vegetable Kashmiri

Ingredients

- Two tablespoons cumin seeds
- One tablespoon black peppercorns
- One cinnamon stick
- Pinch of grated nutmeg
- One chopped green chilli
- One inch ginger, chopped
- One teaspoon chilli powder
- Two large potatoes cut into chunks
- One handful of cauliflower
- One large onion
- Two cloves of garlic
- One handful of green beans
- Two tomatoes
- One glass of yoghurt
- One glass of vegetable stock
- Fresh coriander

Method

- Fry the ginger, chilli and onions for a few minutes.
- Add the spices and a dash of water.
- Add the potatoes, stir to make sure they are all covered with spices and leave for 10 minutes or so.
- Add the remaining vegetables, yogurt and stock and simmer for 10 minutes or so until the vegetables are tender.
- Serve with fresh coriander.

N.B. If you want to add meat, slice up some lamb or chicken and add after the potatoes have been cooking for five minutes or so.

Chapter Forty-One
July 3rd 2008

THE ALARM SOUNDED, WAKING me from the deepest sleep I'd been in since we got here. I sat up in bed, it was pitch black. What the hell was going on, why was I awake? I looked across to where I could faintly see the outline of Rob and Tim sharing a double bed and remembered why I was rubbing my eyes at three forty-five am. They slept on and I half considered turning over and going back to sleep. With reluctance I dismissed the temptation; this was why we were here.

'Wakey wakey! It's another beautiful day in paradise!'

I felt my way over to the side of the wall and switched the light on, sending a billion insects into a supercharged frenzy. Rob and Tim opened their eyes and looked up at me with pure hatred before rubbing the sleep from their eyes and sitting up. Ten minutes later we stumbled out of the hotel and with our one remaining torch tried to find our way to the foot of the hill. We stopped outside the hotel gate and looked up; the entire sky was covered with stars, illuminating the ground below us. Crickets hummed as before us we saw a small flickering light burning 800 metres up. This was our destination; the only problem was there was an enormous lake in front of us and our dying torch was failing to pick up a path around it. We figured we had around an hour, say an hour and fifteen, to make it to the top before sunrise and after all this effort we'd be damned if we'd miss it. As usual our questions as to when the sun rises and how long it would take to climb the hill varied from four am and two hours to the ludicrous eight am and half an hour, but by now the answers just washed over us like a summer storm.

We took a left and gingerly walked onwards. Unable to see where we were walking we didn't want to step on any snakes or sleeping creatures. It was far too early for any kind of conversation. Following the rough outline of a path we skirted around the lake and through the part of the town the druggies don't see, the part where people lived and worked. Amazingly people were also beginning to get up even though it was just a little after four. In the haze of the pre-dawn men nodded at us as they made their way down to the water's edge to wash and women blushed, stopped their clothes' washing and looked down as we passed their houses. Dogs and goats lay curled up outside, their eyes tucked underneath their paws, desperately trying to block out the fast-approaching light.

Rounding another corner we saw the outline of a few steep stone steps and 800 metres above, the temple perching on the hill's ledge. Our pace increased as the light began to grow. Looking at the mountain on the other side of the valley we probably had about half an hour until the sun breached the top and shone down onto the lake and we were determined to be up top by the time that happened. The stone stairs were high, some were up to a foot tall, and as we continued to climb we continued to slow until we were pausing every ten steps or so to catch our breath or drink some water.

Rob began to pull away and climbed the last flight without stopping. Tim and I, taking slightly longer, got to the top a minute or so after Rob, high-fiving on the finish line and too exhausted for words. The sun had not yet risen above the opposing mountain; we'd made it. We swung our legs over the wall on the edge and sat facing out; the place was deserted. Finishing our water we sat in quiet contemplation, alone with our thoughts as slowly a burning white line appeared in the distance. Growing larger and larger the ball turned first to a dark orange and then a blood red as it burst through the clouds and shone down on the lake below, its rays rippling on the water and reflecting into the white stonewashed houses of the town. In the distance we could just about make out a few people washing themselves and their clothes in the water as the bells began to ring, awakening those that weren't already getting up.

I found myself lost, first swimming through the water below, kicking hard with my legs and propelling myself forward and then flying high over the town, the strong wind ruffling my clothes and taking me higher, higher. If travelling was a drug I felt it coursing through my veins right now, seeking out a bigger rush, another experience.

'Shall we go explore?'

Tim's voice startled Rob and I from our respective daydreams. We nodded in agreement and began to explore the edge of the hill we were on; there was still not another soul in sight. Making our way towards the back of the hill we posed for a few photos on a huge stone protruding from the cliff face before boulder-hopping our way around the hill. When we could go no further we turned back and almost made it back to the stairs down when we all stopped. Ten metres or so in front of us, sitting on the rock we'd been on a few minutes previously, was an enormous monkey, perched on the edge and looking out onto the town below. We stood for a few seconds, amazed to be this close to nature without anyone else around us. All of a sudden, leaping out of the bushes, the monkey was joined by three others, then four, then five until about a dozen monkeys, some huge some tiny, were all perched on the ledge, staring down. We crouched to watch them watching the world and wondered what they were thinking, if they were as amazed by the view as we were.

'Is anyone else feeling a little bit threatened?' Rob whispered.

I shook my head. 'We're nowhere near them.'

'No, but the only way down goes right past them, and they aren't showing any signs of moving. If one of them goes for us we've had it, they'll all pile in.' He looked around. 'And there still aren't any other people up here.'

'Come on,' Tim motioned with his head, 'just go slow, don't make eye contact and walk with your palms facing inwards, that way if they do go for you they won't slash a vein.'

'Oh great,' muttered Rob, 'well you go first then.'

We moved slowly towards the group and as we got to about five metres away they suddenly all scattered.

'See,' Tim turned to us, 'no problem.'

'Guess again, look behind you.'

He turned. The monkeys had indeed run off but they had now positioned themselves at metre intervals on the path back down.

'Fuck.'

'Let's do it.' I began walking forward. 'Think of the stories.'

We edged past each monkey one by one, with our arms at our sides and our heads down. As we passed each one it ran past us and took up another position further down the path. Our hearts began to thud loudly. We approached a mother, an enormous monkey with a baby hanging on around her neck, sitting slap bang in the middle of the path, who showed no signs of moving. As Tim took the lead and began edging towards and past her she suddenly hissed, baring her teeth and raising her claws. We all recoiled back and got past her as quickly as possible before breaking into a jog as the remaining monkeys gave up the game of chase the foreigner. We eventually made it down completely dehydrated and covered in sweat, our hands still shaking from our encounter with the female monkey. As we headed up into town to get some breakfast Tim turned to us and said, 'Well that's another one down, I thought we were all goners up there!'

Chapter Forty-Two
July 5th 2008

AFTER CHILLING OUT FOR a few days we caught a bus six hours south to Udaipur, a city with the reputation for being the most romantic city in India because of its floating palace, an enormous beautiful pure white building dating from the Raj which was positioned in the middle of a large lake around which the city perched. This was to be our last stop in Rajasthan before an overnight bus south to Mumbai and a plane down to Kerala. Even though we'd only been in Rajasthan for ten days or so we had grown quite attached to it and were acutely aware that this was a very different part of India compared to where we would be in a few days' time.

Udaipur consisted of a series of windy roads around the lake. Because the lake was the central attraction of the town the buildings tended to rise upwards rather than outwards, and every second building, which was either a hostel or a restaurant, was three or four stories high with a rooftop restaurant overlooking the lake. The water was at a low but as the north was preparing for the onslaught of monsoon season, the town had an end of season feel as most restaurants and hotels were only ever half full. By this point we'd seen so many temples that they were all beginning to merge into one and so as beautiful as they were, we weren't too fussed about seeing more. Our aims for the next few days were to visit the famous mausoleum, try and get to the palace on the lake and check out a few of the Rajasthani art galleries that Udaipur was famous for.

Unfortunately it didn't stop raining for three days. Hello monsoon season, welcome to Rajasthan, how was the South?

On our first full day we took a tuc-tuc to the city mausoleum on the outskirts. During the days of the Raj, whenever a nobleman died they were buried beneath an enormous stone memorial, and obviously the bigger the memorial the richer the family. Healthy competition meant that there were over two hundred memorials, some as big as mansions and some as small as cupboards all standing independently, proud in the darkening light. Because of bandits we were accompanied around the mausoleum by the gate-keeper who kept watch as we wandered in and out of the monuments. All of a sudden the heavens opened and the clouds closed in until all that could be seen was a thick wall of greyness, obliterating the space between ground and sky. We had no choice but to run for cover to the nearest monument which happened to be the largest and tallest, but also the one with the least amount of cover. A wise choice, I think. We huddled together, our t-shirts and shorts providing scant shelter from the rain. We waited half an hour, still no let up in the rain, then forty-five minutes, then an hour, nothing. Far in the distance we could see our tuc-tuc driver sheltering under the tarpaulin of his roof, watching as the road slowly filled with water. All around us lightning shook the ground and thunder crackled; the fact that we were alone in a mausoleum only added to the electric, eerie atmosphere.

Eventually, clambering into the tuc-tuc, we were amazed at how the town had come to a complete standstill because of the rain. The lake had burst its banks and water came crashing down a nearby road, making the route completely impassable. All around us people migrated to watch the flowing water as the sounds of honking tuc-tucs and cars filled the air. Sticking his head out of the tuc-tuc and receiving a face full of water in return, Tim turned to us 'I think we're leaving Rajasthan at just the right moment guys.'

Finding ourselves with the task of filling two days with indoor activities we spent a lot of time drinking coffee in deserted cafés and playing cards. It was only when we started talking to our hotel owner that we found out about the legendary Mr Shakti's Indian Cookery School. For a tiny price we would receive a four-hour lesson in the fundamentals of Indian cooking, cook several dishes and eat them all under the tutelage of Mr Shakti, the self-proclaimed Gordon Ramsay of India. Salivating at the prospect we immediately signed ourselves up for a class the following morning.

Just over twelve hours later we found ourselves sitting in a bare room on the second floor of a small house in the centre of the city. There were no windows or doors in the flat, just empty frames which echoed with the sound of water monotonously dripping down onto the wet concrete floor. In our hands we clasped a dozen-page recipe book, its faded writing betraying years of photocopying. In front of us, hunched over a small individual stove, sat our teacher Mr Shakti, possibly the nicest man in India. Through his unique Indian English he taught us how to make a basic curry sauce (one that works with anything), chapattis and best of all, the delicious Khadai Paneer, a fresh vegetable curry topped with cubes of crumbed Indian cheese, much like the European goats' cheese.

Basic Curry Sauce

Ingredients

One teaspoon of each of the following:

- Brown cumin
- Fennel seeds
- Turmeric
- Coriander seeds powder
- Red chilli powder (only half a spoon if you want it mild)
- Fenugreek seeds
- Two cloves
- Two pieces black cardamom
- Diced red onion
- One inch diced ginger
- Two cloves of garlic, diced

Method

- Heat the oil until sizzling and then add the onion, ginger and garlic.

- When the onions have started to brown add all the spices and around 120 ml of water.

This is now your basic curry mix. Add tomatoes to make a darker curry and yoghurt to make a korma. Add chicken and vegetables as you see fit and serve over rice.

Chapatti

Ingredients

- 100 grams flour
- Pinch of salt
- Cup of water

Method

- Add the flour and salt together and mix well.

- Add the water bit by bit and mix well with both hands. The ultimate consistency you want is akin to that of chewing gum.

- Divide the mixture into individual ping pong size balls.

- Flatten each ball with a rolling pin.

- Heat a pan but do not add any oil or butter.

- When the pan is hot, place the chapatti on the heat and leave for a minute, until air bubbles start to rise.

- Turn and do the same until bubbles rise again.

- Pat the bubbles down with a cloth and carry on turning another three to four times.

Khadai Paneer

Ingredients

- Basic curry mix (see above)
- Two tomatoes
- Two small green peppers
- 100 grams paneer (Indian cheese made from goat's milk)

Method

- Cook up the basic curry paste (see above).

- Add diced tomatoes and wait for the sauce to thicken.

- Add the green peppers and onions and cook for a further few minutes.

- Stir in the paneer and cook for a further minute then remove from the heat and serve immediately, either with rice or just with some chapatti or naan.

Following Mr Shakti's instructions one of us would cook the recipe for the others, who would then eat and give their opinions. Needless to say we told whoever cooked that the food we were eating was disgusting.

Chapter Forty-Three
July 9th 2008

ROB STOOD UP TO his waist in the Indian Ocean and turned to look at the sun slowly making its descent. In a few moments the sun would hit the surface, bursting its bubble and spilling light into the water. In the distance Rob was silhouetted against the light and he appeared relaxed, at peace with wherever he was and whatever was going on. The warm water raced around him and embraced him and he appeared relaxed, the worries of London left far behind. The tranquillity of the scene was one no words could do justice to.

Tim and I decided that now was the perfect opportunity to viciously tackle him into the sea.

He collapsed quicker than an empty juice carton and immediately went under. Wriggling, we let him stand and cough the sea water out of his lungs.

'Thanks guys,' he spluttered, 'pleasure being with you.'

Tim rested his elbow on Rob's shoulders and tilted his head. 'Anytime, couldn't get you going all sentimental on us and talking about the sunset, could we?'

The three of us stood there and watched the sunset without speaking. When dusk approached we turned back to the shore and began slowly making our way towards a bar up on the cliff top that served fantastic gin and tonics.

This had been the ritual for the last few days and we were beginning to get comfortable in Kerala. Our beach retreat in Kovalam was paradisaical; a small hut nestled up in the hills overlooking the Indian Ocean made a huge change to the hustle and bustle of Rajasthan two thousand miles north. We took siestas in hammocks rather than taking tuc-tucs in monsoons, and our biggest worry was whether to have fresh tuna or squid for dinner. Beers had been drunk aplenty and our morning hangovers were easily brushed away by a fresh lassi on the beach followed by a swim or surf.

We checked our watches as we arranged our chairs in a line facing out onto the sea.

'Half six, we got an hour till we're meeting, that's enough time for a gin and a shower isn't it?'

'Sure is. Aww, you're nervous about seeing her aren't you?'

'Shut up.'

Earlier that day we'd all decided to rent surfboards for the first time, but unfortunately there were only two boards available to rent and so we had to take it in turns to surf. I opted out first, and feeling full from breakfast and groggy from the night before had felt like a mid-morning nap. I made myself a pillow with the sand, lay out my sarong and curled up, resting my hands on the sand above my head, unconsciously running my fingers through the grains. The sun was too bright to keep my eyes open and so after watching Rob and Tim get wiped out constantly I decided to close my eyes and drift away, the roar of the sea making me feel like I was drifting back and forth with the waves. The exhaustion of our hardcore two weeks in Rajasthan had hit us all and it was a surprise if any of us could now function on anything less than ten hours' sleep. I was not in the least bit surprised to feel sleep knocking and peering its head around the door as I surrendered to the sand.

I awoke what must have been ten minutes later and opened my eyes. Ow. Big mistake. Let's try that again. I slowly squinted until I became accustomed to the light and could open my eyes fully. A girl now sat about ten metres in front of me, between my sarong and the water's edge. She was dressed in combat trousers and a strappy top and carried a small backpack with her, giving the impression that she'd just arrived in town. Listening to her music and hugging her knees she gazed out into the distance, smiling broadly. Wondering what she was thinking I sat up to try and find the boys, the strong current forcing them down the coast almost to the furthest point of the beach. Leaning back I rested on my elbows and let my head dangle back, closing my eyes to the sun above me. Over the sound of the waves I heard a rustling and on opening my eyes I was treated to the incredibly good sight of the girl in front taking off her clothes to reveal a tiny bikini and a sun-kissed toned body. Turning to put her clothes back into her bag she caught my eyes, smiled and turned back to the ocean.

Do I go talk to her? Do I go and try and start a conversation? Starting travelling conversations were pretty easy yet they were also pretty generic as well. Much like in London where you have to get by the whole "what do you do" chat, when you're travelling you also have to do the whole "so where have you just come from" chat. Still I suppose there are worse ice breakers than talking about this incredible country whilst watching the light twinkle in the Indian Ocean. I lay back down in the sand, still sleepy. Another five minutes to wake up and I'll go talk to her.

I opened my eyes a few minutes later to find Tim dangling a dripping surfboard above my stomach.

'You're up next, dude, I'm knackered.'

I smiled and jumped to my feet. I loved surfing and it had been a good few years since I'd last had a chance to do it properly (i.e. without a wetsuit in a freezing Cornish sea). Taking the thin lycra protective top from Tim and strapping the cord to my left ankle I looked for Rob and found him far out waiting beyond the break, looking for the perfect wave.

'How's the surf?'

'Awesome but watch the rocks at the far end, we got swept near them a few times and the current's pretty strong.'

I grinned and ran out to join Rob.

Ducking under the break I surfaced and swam over to where Rob was. Seeing a swell coming towards us I slipped down my board and began to swim, my head looking over my left shoulder, watching the approaching wave. When I felt the wave lift my board I swam for a few seconds and then jumped up, reaching out with my hands to steady myself. I was pretty rusty, my weight was too far forward and as the tip of the surfboard began to dip under the water I jumped off, avoiding the wave breaking over me. I swam back to Rob who shook his head, 'It's not as easy as we remember it being, is it?'

I shook my head, spitting out saltwater, grinned and rubbed my eyes. 'I blame the boards obviously, old and falling apart.'

Rob smiled and began swimming for a wave, 'Definitely, all the board's fault.'

It slowly began to come back to me after a while, and after a few minutes I began to catch some waves. I still made a tit of myself and fell off pretty much every time but at least now I was getting a few more seconds of surfing first. After a while our forearms gave out and we were pretty relieved to see the lifeguard signal to us that our rental time was up. We'd drifted a bit and I scanned the beach looking for Tim, unable to see him. Maybe he was lying down asleep, out of sight.

'Dude, look!'

Rob grabbed my shoulder and pointed into the distance.

'Who the hell is Tim talking to?! She looks hot!'

True enough, fifty metres or so in front of us I could make out Tim talking to the girl that was sitting in front of our sarongs. As we neared we could see that she'd moved closer to Tim and that her sarong had joined our group of three. All of a sudden, in reaction to something Tim said she threw her head back and laughed, before tapping him playfully on the arm. Rob turned to me and raised an eyebrow, 'We leave him alone for twenty minutes …'

'Guys,' Tim looked up at us and motioned us over, 'come meet Gabi, she's from Holland.'

Making our way through the candlelight we saw a girl sitting alone in the corner. The candle on her table flickered across her hands, casting half her face into shadow, the other into a faded yellow. Tim turned to us and whispered, 'Is that her?'

Rob and I shrugged. 'I dunno, it might be, but she looks different to before.'

'Well of course she looks different, she was in a bloody bikini and covered in sand!'

'Tim, go up to her, see if she recognises you.'

'Come with me.'

'No! Man the hell up!' Rob exclaimed, 'Look, I'll create a diversion.'

Rob sneezed loudly, causing the whole restaurant to turn towards us. The girl alone looked our way, smiled and waved. Tim waved back and we began to move over.

Rob grinned. 'And that's how it's done.'

Gabi was pretty cool. She was travelling on her own, she had been for just over two months and that, especially in India takes guts. She was only twenty-two and this was her first time away from home, it was also stop one of her round-the-world tour. For the last six weeks or so she'd been volunteering in an orphanage in northern Kerala, and this was her first weekend away in six, and we her first foreigners since she arrived in Southern India.

'You see, that completely puts us to shame,' Rob was saying, 'here we are on a three-week break from work and here you are, single-handedly saving the world, alone in an orphanage where you don't even speak the language.'

She shook her blonde hair. 'I'm not saving the world single-handedly, I'm actually being quite selfish. See if I do this for three months I'm going to reward myself with nine months of fun around the globe. Plus, I'm doing this more to test myself; I've had a comfortable upbringing, I want to see what life is like for those who aren't as lucky, I want to live outside my comfort zone for a little bit.'

We paused as the waiter came over to take our drinks' orders. I looked round the table, 'Gin and tonics? Gabi, what are you drinking?'

'Oh just some water, I don't really drink.'

Tim kicked me hard underneath the table and raised his eyebrows as I tried not to smile.

'So where's next?' Tim asked.

'Erm, Thailand in a month. I'm leaving Kerala in three weeks, going to Rajasthan, then flying from Delhi to Bangkok, then my brother's coming over for my birthday in August.'

Tim launched into a description of his gap year spent in Laos, Cambodia, Vietnam and Thailand. It wasn't too long before his favourite story came out of contracting dysentery, being hospitalised in Vietnam, then helicoptered across the border to Thailand on the brink of death. Gabi's mouth and eyes dropped lower and lower as Tim told of how he'd asked for a private room in the hospital, only to be put in a room with another patient. When he complained he was told, 'Oh, she'll be dead in a few hours.'

The conversation flowed easily and Rob and I took a back seat as Tim pressed forward. They both seemed to be getting on well and as the evening grew darker, the more intimate and closer the restaurant felt. We were eating at one of a half-dozen restaurants on the cliff edge, a small narrow path being the only barrier between us and the pounding waves below. Each restaurant, plying for the gringo trade, offered its catches of the day on large white ceramic tables by the entrance. Enormous king prawns, red snapper, tuna, shark and octopus lay flat out on the ceramic as live lobsters felt their way around the plastic buckets they were confined to. Southern Indian food is very different to its northern rival. The south, being so close to Sri Lanka and Thailand, uses much more lime and lemongrass, as opposed to more traditional Indian spices such as garam masala and cumin, and noodle or soup-based dishes were the norm over rice. We'd all opted for a Keralian fish soup, a speciality from Kerala (obviously).

Keralian Fish Soup

Ingredients

- 400g of monkfish, sea bass or tuna, cut into chunks
- A dozen or so large prawns
- Two large onions
- Two green chillies
- 400ml coconut milk
- One and a half teaspoons turmeric
- One tsp salt
- One tbsp lime juice
- One tsp cumin
- One tsp coriander seeds
- One tsp black peppercorns
- One garlic clove
- One inch fresh ginger
- Twenty-five grams tamarind paste

Method

- Sprinkle fish with the lime juice, then rub the turmeric and salt into them so all the pieces are covered.

- Fry the onions in a little oil.

- Add the fish and fry on a high heat for a few minutes, then remove the fish and onions.

- Add all the spices, tamarind, 120ml boiling water, coconut milk, garlic, ginger and chillies and bring to the boil.

- Place onions and fish in an oven-proof dish, and cover with the spice mixture.

- Cook for ten minutes.

- Add the prawns and cook for another five minutes.

- Serve with fresh coriander.

Gabi began to relax more and more as the food was served and even got herself a gin and tonic. The more she began to talk, the more she began to feel part of the group and it wasn't too long before she was joining in eat-and-show and taking the piss out of

Rob's unusually round head.

'Guys, I'm so glad I met you, I've been so unhappy these last few weeks,' she said between mouthfuls of prawns.

'What's the orphanage like?' I asked.

'Awful!' she exclaimed. 'I feel so sorry for the kids and I try as hard as I can to help them but I feel like no-one even notices that I'm there.'

'How'd you mean?'

'Well, the kids are great, don't get me wrong, I love them, but it's the staff that irritate me. They either ignore me or treat me like a slave; I have a tiny boiling hot room with a straw mattress and a tiny window and a door that barely shuts.' She sighed. 'After coming here the thought of going back there in two days fills me with absolute dread.'

Rob looked thoughtful. 'So don't.'

She looked at him quizically. 'What do you mean?'

'Well what would your orphanage do if you took two more days off?'

'Well technically I can do what I want.'

I joined in, 'So come with us. We were thinking about going to Varkala tomorrow. Come with us, then on Tuesday when we fly back to Delhi you can go back upstate.'

She looked around. 'You mean that?'

Tim nodded and smiled. 'Definitely, we'd love to have you, and Varkala is only a few hours north, easy to get back from there after.'

She broke into a huge grin. 'You sure?!'

We nodded.

'OK then!'

Tim raised his glass. 'To the next few days!'

We raised our glasses and ordered another round.

We carried on drinking into the small hours. All around us the restaurants began to empty as the effects of a boiling hot sun began to take their toll on the travellers. By now, due to the armchair-like nature of the chairs we had more or less separated into two groups, me and Rob on one side of the table and Tim and Gabi on the other.

'It's the perfect cure,' Rob said to me in a low voice.

I raised my eyebrow and he nodded slightly at Gabi and Tim. 'This, meeting someone else, feeling a spark.'

I chewed the straw of my gin and tonic. 'I didn't realise how much he was affected, y'know.'

He nodded. 'I know, it sucks and I don't see how any of it is going to be any better when we get home.'

I hit his shoulder. 'Don't mention that word, we still have five days left.'

'God, five days.' He put his glass on the table. 'It feels like we've been here for months, we've crammed so much in!'

I sat back and looked up at the star-studded sky, 'Getting on that plane is going to be one of the hardest things to do.'

Rob laughed. 'I think finding our way round Delhi first will be the hardest!'

Deciding it was the last drink, we paid and made to move home. Now, before in our bungalow Tim had given us clear instructions. If he wanted to make a move on Gabi, he'd say, 'I'm gonna walk Gabi back to her hotel,' but if he decided he didn't want to, he was gonna say, 'Shall we walk Gabi back to her hotel?' We waited with bated breath.

'I'm just going to walk Gabi back to her hotel, I'll see you back at the room.'

Rob smiled. 'Fair dos, Gabi, see you for breakfast, train leaves at eleven.' We exchanged kisses and turned to leave.

'Will do and guys, thanks for inviting me again, you have no idea what it means! Night.'

Waiting until Tim and Gabi had turned the corner away from the restaurant, Rob and I high-fived.

'Alllriiiite, thank God for that!'

I smiled, 'Think it'll happen?'

'Yeah,' he nodded, 'yeah I think it will.'

We walked along the dimly lit path and turned up to our hotel, 'Nice girl, good call on inviting her along.'

'She is, isn't she, think she'll fit in perfectly. I just hope if Tim makes a move he doesn't get kicked back, otherwise I think I made a mistake in inviting her!' Rob chuckled.'

Reaching our bungalow we took turns in showering and setting up mosquito nets. We'd just got into our beds and turned off the light when we heard a light tap on the door. We opened the door to Tim's smile, which entered and was followed a few minutes later by Tim.

'Evening.'

'Well?'

He shrugged. 'Well what?'

'Tim! You're grinning! What happened?'

He nodded. 'Yeah, we kissed.'

We high-fived and ruffled his hair. Settling down under the sheet Rob said, 'Talk us through it.'

'Well, we were walking down the path and her hotel was coming up quick so I just said, "So, do you have a boyfriend in Holland?"'

'And she said?'

'She said, "No I don't, do you have a girlfriend?" I said no and we kinda carried on walking in this thick silence.'

'Go on,' I prodded

'Then we get to the entrance and stop, I say something stupid like, "Oh I'm really glad you're travelling with us," and we stand in this silence again. So I thought fuck it, and I kissed her.'

'Good work,' I said, 'then what happened?'

'Nothing, I came back here.'

Rob look confused. 'Tim, we left you forty minutes ago, have you been kissing for all that time?'

He looked down and grinned sheepishly. 'Yeah, what with the waves, stars, the whole Indian Ocean and being in India thing, we didn't really stop. It felt like I was fourteen again!'

Chapter Forty-Four
July 14th 2008

WE ALL LAY ON our backpacks, resting in the hot midday sun. The platform was boiling, the train was delayed and our clothes were sticking to our skin. I lay on my back on my bag, using the sleeping bag compartment as a headrest. I sucked on my bottle of water like a baby on a dummy and watched the heat mirage flicker along the track. Reaching into my pocket I pulled out my train ticket, some unintelligible words written on the back of a square cut out from a cornflake box. Over two hours late. At around twelve we'd wandered over to the station controller and asked where the train was. After smiling and waggling his head for a few minutes he assured us it was 'coming right now, two minutes'. An hour and a half after that and there was still no train in sight. All around us kids ran amongst the tracks, pulling at our clothes and motioning towards their stomachs. The culture shock I'd felt towards this in Delhi over two weeks ago had now gone, but I'm not sure if that's such a good sign. Am I merely more immune to poverty?

A tinny unintelligible voice echoed from the PA. A friendly Keralian smiled at us, pointed at the PA and waggled his head; we were rocking. As usual we had absolutely no idea which was our carriage so we just stood on the platform and waited for the best. In the distance we could see a shimmer of blue and the faint sound of a train approaching began to reach our ears. The train pulled into the station and came to a stop, emptying its guts out onto the station floor. Of course, this being India the train had pulled into the opposite platform so after two hours of inactivity we were forced to put our packs on and sprint down the huge platform, up over the bridge and down again to the next platform. We jumped onto the train just as it started to move off again;- this was beginning to become a habit.

The train was rammed and it was impossible to stand and keep our backpacks with us. Working our way into a carriage we formed a chain and lifted the backpacks up onto the luggage holders and moved out from the carriage to stand by the door where there was more air. By now we'd spent quite a long time travelling around on trains and were used to people staring at us, especially when we travelled in the non-air-conditioned third and fourth class sections that were normally a gringo-free zone. However, this was the first time we'd travelled with a woman and some of the looks Gabi was getting were beginning to really get on our nerves. Men would gawk at her if she leant over to pick up her bag, or try to peer down her top by standing close to her yet she just seemed to brush it off as if it wasn't happening. Noticing our evils at the rest of the carriage she shrugged her shoulders. 'You get used to it, it's all harmless curiosity really.'

'Doesn't it fuck you off?' I asked.

She shook her head. 'Not really, I just ignore it, but that said, if I was on my own I wouldn't be doing this, but with you guys I'm fine, I've got three bodyguards!'

After a few hours the train snaked its way out towards the coast and began to slow as it approached the station. By now the carriage was suffocating and there was barely any room to move around. As the station came into sight the train began to mobilise as people moved from all parts of the carriage towards the open doors. Rob, who towered above everyone, reached across and tapped me on the shoulder.

'Erm guys, we may have a bit of a problem.'

'What's up?' Tim shouted from the other side.

'Well, there's a million Indians around us, and our bags are twenty metres that way.' He jerked his thumb towards the back of the carriage.

'Well that's OK,' Gabi said, 'we just wait until everyone has got off then get our bags.'

'Uh oh.' We followed Rob's eyes and looked out towards the platform. The platform was absolutely full, five or six people deep, all getting ready to cram themselves onto the train. We felt those around us surge towards the exit as if the two groups were about to meet in some sort of medieval battle re-enactment.

'OK, action stations.' Tim took control. 'Gabs, take all our day bags and get off the train. Rob, you get into the carriage and get the bags. J, you stay here and take the bags from Rob, I'll get off and you pass them to me through the door; let's go!' He took Gabi's hand, pushed through the crowd and jumped off the train. Rob fought back against the sea of people to take the first bag. Passing it over their heads I took the bags from Rob, holding them in place on my own head and moved towards the exit. All around people pushed against me, fighting to get a seat, unwilling to stand for however long it was until the next stop.

'Beep beep beep.' I turned to look behind me and saw Rob with a backpack on his head fighting his way through the crowds, 'Go go go, last one!'

We reached the exit and handed the last bags to Tim before bursting off the train and collapsing down onto the platform. Gabi was in hysterics and was pointing her camera at us, taking a video.

'That was the funniest thing I've ever seen in my life!' She bent down and put her hands on her knees. 'Honestly, you've just made my day, you really have!'

We tuc-tuc'd to our hotel, a beautiful building on the edge of a cliff top, nestling to the left of the main beach and protected by a giant lighthouse watching guard. As it was our last place on our trip we decided to spoil ourselves a bit and had doubled our allowance for room rent. The result was a stunning three-bed room with windows on three sides overlooking the sea which crashed onto rocks below. The room also came with a balcony to the side, which joined forces with Gabi's balcony next door.

It was much of the same for the next few days, it was just that we had changed location. We still spent the days on the beach or by a pool and the evenings in open-air beachfront restaurants, eating huge amounts of fish whilst sitting on rickety plastic chairs and listening to loud eighties' music. The more time we spent with her, the more we got to really like Gabi. She made a fantastic addition to the group and had completely lit Tim up, for the change that had come over him in the last few days was incredible. He was smiling, he was charming, he was relaxed, more so than I'd seen him in months.

Over the last day or two Gabi and Tim had been a lot more chilled out around us, and more obvious in the fact that they were now a "travelling couple". They'd play around in the surf together, and not our kind of playing around where you genuinely try and hurt each other but playful playing around where it's really just an excuse to touch and kiss. They'd now pretty much separated off into a two whenever we walked anywhere and would always have their hands dangling next to the other's, never holding, just brushing the other, letting them know they were there.

Night times had been pretty enjoyable for both of them too from what I could gather. On our first night in Kovalam we'd all been chilling on our balcony and I could tell Tim and Gabi wanted to go next door to Gabi's room but were having difficulties in standing up in front of both of us and walking out. Eventually Gabi announced she was off to bed and left, leaving Rob and I to make gestures at Tim to follow. He raised his hands, telling us to calm down and waited for Gabi to leave the room.

'It's cool, I'm going over there in a bit.'

'How'd you know she wants you to?!'

He smiled and threw over our photocopied cookery leaflets from Mr Shakti's school in Udaipur. 'Look at page four.'

I turned through the recipes to page four. We'd been showing Gabi these to give her some ideas as to what she could do when in Rajasthan. Sure enough, written above the chapatti recipe in Tim's scrawly handwriting was the phrase 'shall I come say good night to you later?'

I looked up, 'And what did she say?'

'Did you not notice her a few minutes ago say yes when no-one asked her a question?'

He grinned and got up. 'Think I'll go next door, night guys.'

Our last day together was spent on a deserted beach ten minutes or so north of Varkala. Palm trees stretched in all directions and white sand glistened as far as the eye could see. There wasn't a single person apart from us in sight and if it hadn't have been for the dozens of enormous purple jellyfish populating the sea, it would have been absolute heaven. Instead of swimming we spent the morning burying each other in the sand, playing games and generally just chilling out. We were planning a big one tonight and it was to be the beginning of an absolutely crazy few days that would see us pack up and leave. We had a plane to catch at five the next morning which would take us into Delhi for ten. We then had the entire day in Delhi to kill, before catching our plane back to London at two that night, landing in Heathrow at six the next morning, giving us enough time to get home, shower and make it into work for nine. Lying on the beach thinking that I wouldn't be in a bed for more than a few hours for the next three days filled me with dread and made me want to bury myself deeper in the sand.

'I've got a plan,' Rob announced to the sun.

'We're listening,' said Gabi, lying side on and resting her head on Tim's chest.

'Well, this afternoon when we're chilling by the pool we pick names out of a hat and one by one go off and buy something for 100 rupees for the person whose name we drew. That person has to wear that item for the whole of tonight.'

I smiled and launched a pebble into the sea. 'Sounds good to me.'

'Yup,' added Tim, 'although remember where we are, nudity is a criminal offence.'

'Don't worry, we can do nice and tasteful.'

We walked into our local restaurant and pulled up our chairs, the cringeing sound of plastic chair on concrete filled the restaurant. Our waiter whom we'd made friends with over the last few nights came up to us with arms outstretched.

'Evening friends, four gin and tonics, yes?'

We all shook hands with our new friend, 'Hell yeah!'

A few people at other tables turned to look at us strangely.

'I feel like such a jackass,' said Tim as he slumped down into his chair.

Gabi started to laugh. 'Well you are wearing a lampshade on your head.'

Rob laughed. 'Well picked Gabs, Tim, you look like a fool.'

He threw a napkin at Rob. 'Shut the fuck up, look at you!'

'What? I look like a local, it's fine.'

'No, you look like you're taking the piss out of a local, even worse!'

Rob was wearing my gift to him, a garish salmon-coloured sarong. The condition of use was that he had to wear it like the locals did, tucked up so that it looked like a giant nappy, showing off his legs up to his thighs.

'I don't care, I'm nice and cool; anyway I think Gabi did the best out of all of us.'

She took off her square cap and put it on the table. 'I quite like it actually, I'll probably wear it.'

'Well I can't see me wearing this at home.'

'If you do, you'll probably need to hand out sunglasses in the street.'

I looked down at my bright orange and red flowy hippy top which was open to halfway down my chest. 'What are you trying to say?'

My God we got drunk. Gin and beer and more gin flowed like there was no tomorrow, and I guess for us in a way there was no tomorrow. Morning would take us away and as much as that sucked it was probably a hundred times worse for Gabi.

'I'm going to wake up tomorrow morning and you'll be gone. This time tomorrow I'm going to be back in the orphanage with people I hate and it'll be like the last few days never happened.'

She looked on the verge of tears as she clasped Tim's hand that was now resting on hers.

He leant over and kissed her cheek gently. 'It's only for a couple more weeks Gabs, and then you're free.' Squeezing her shoulder he said, 'You met us on your first weekend away; imagine how many more people you've got to meet in nine months of travelling! We'll be a distant memory by the time you get home.'

'Exactly,' I added, 'there are so many cooler people you've got to meet. We will just be the weirdos you met at the start of the trip who dressed up in lampshades and nappies and couldn't do anything without a gin and tonic.'

She smiled and shook her head. 'No you won't guys, and you know it.'

'Enough of this, come on and let's celebrate our last night.' Rob raised his glass. 'Let's play a game.'

More drinks were drunk as we played truth or dare. This then turned into dare or dare as the alcohol continued to flow. Gabi ended up jumping up and down in an old ship on the beach shouting, 'I'm from Holland!' whilst Rob had to stand outside the restaurant gesturing inside and telling passers-by it was 'happy hour … in my ass'.

It was now about one and we still had to pack and be in a cab at five so we decided to call it a night. We slowly wandered back across the sand to the hotel, delaying the inevitable, delaying the start of the return process. Tim and Gabs dawdled behind Rob and me, their arms wrapped tightly around each other, trying to push the hotel further and further away into the night.

'Guys,' Tim said softly. We turned around, by now Gabi's head was resting against his chest, looking down. 'I'll see you back at the hotel, we're going to chill out here for a bit.'

'OK, in that case,' I made my way back to Gabi, 'this is goodbye.'

She hugged me and Rob tightly, smiling through tears and saying again how glad she was to have met us. Tim threw a half-grimace over his shoulder as he and Gabi wandered back down to the water. Rob and I watched them for a few minutes as Tim, holding Gabi's hand in his, spun her gently under his arm. They embraced and kissed, their bodies silhouetted against the glow of the moon. Turning back, Rob and I climbed the road to the hotel, neither of us envying the goodbye the two of them would have to go through over the next few hours.

Chapter Forty-Five
July 16th 2008

DELHI SPUN OUT BENEATH us, its twinkling lights echoing into the distance and merging with that of its more upmarket neighbour, New Delhi. It was nine o'clock at night and in two hours' time we had to leave where we were to get to the airport. London beckoned with outstretched hands and with a heavy heart we walked towards the light.

But not before one last evening.

We were at one of the most exclusive restaurants in Delhi, a revolving restaurant forty stories up at the top of one of the city's new skyscrapers. It felt apt as we slowly turned to face all parts of the city, as beyond the horizon in all directions we saw Agra and the Taj Mahal to the east, hectic yet amazing Rajasthan to the west and beautiful Kerala to the south. We raised our heavy bottles of Kingfishers and cheersed to the last few weeks.

Spice Infused Red Snapper with Basmati Rice

Ingredients
- One large red snapper
- Shallots
- An inch of ginger, diced
- One tablespoon each of
    - Cumin
    - Fenugreek seeds
    - Anise
    - Ground coriander

- Turmeric
- Chilli powder
- Grated nutmeg
- Basmati Rice

Method

- Slice into the red snapper about three or four times each side.
- Mix the spices together with a little oil to bind.
- Rub the mix all over the fish, ensuring a large part of it enters through the slits.
- Wrap in foil and cook for around twenty minutes.
- Cook up some basmati rice.
- Fry the onion and ginger and add to the rice.
- Remove the fish from the oven and place over the rice, pouring the juices around the plate.

'I think we've pretty much covered all we wanted to cover, haven't we?'

I nodded. 'Fantastic trip guys, there isn't a single thing I would've done differently.'

'God,' Rob said, 'can you imagine if we'd have done it the other way round? Monsoon in Kerala first only to have it follow us up to Rajasthan a week later. That would've been shit!'

'As it was,' I smiled, 'we only really had those few days of rain. Apart from that,' I looked at my arms, 'well, we've all got a pretty kickass suntan, haven't we?!'

Tim played with the label on his beer. 'That's it though isn't it, chance we decided to go south second, chance we decided to go to that beach not the other.'

'You gonna miss her?'

He nodded slowly. 'Yeah.'

We fell silent.

Rob piped up, 'I wonder how she's getting on now. That girl's got guts, I've said it before.'

Tim nodded again and carried on playing with the beer label.

'Yeah I am gonna miss her, a lot actually.' He looked up. 'Which is silly really isn't it, we only met her six days ago.'

I shrugged. 'Yeah, but you can't put a figure on stuff like that can you? It might have been only a few days but it was constant.'

'Do you think you'll see her again?'

He shrugged. 'Dunno, I'd like to but nine months is a hell of a long time. Plus as you said last night, think of all the people she's got to meet. I'll be a distant memory.'

'No you won't, mate, I think we all made quite a deep impression on her, you especially. Give yourself more credit for once!'

He smiled. 'She was gorgeous, wasn't she?!'

I laughed. 'Yes she was, good work!'

He grinned again. 'Nah, all joking aside, I thought she was fantastic, such a strong thirst for life, it really gave me a kick up the arse.'

'How'd you mean?'

'Well these last few months, I've just felt like I've been existing, not really doing anything. I was going out with Mel but that didn't really change anything; sure it was great to be with her but we never did exciting things or went places together, and looking back, that's pretty crucial isn't it?'

He poured himself some more beer. 'These last few weeks, especially these last few days with Gabs, I've felt so alive. She's given me back the feeling that anything in the world is possible, that I can do whatever I want, that I don't have to settle for anything.'

Rob's head snapped up. 'See, this is what I've been talking about! We do not have to settle for anything in this life! Tim, you want to be with Gabs then you tell her, or you wait nine months and see what happens, whatever, but don't lose sight of that feeling you've got right now. Boys,' he looked round the table, 'tomorrow morning we are going to be sitting in work and this now,' he tapped the table, 'will feel like a dream. I don't know about you, but I only ever feel alive when I do stuff like what we've just done over the last few weeks. We need to help each other not to forget this conversation, we need to remind each other that out there,' he gestured to the window, 'is a world we have barely seen and that whatever little stresses or complaints are awaiting us in the office or at home, don't matter one little bit.'

'I know Rob, I know.' I calmed him down. 'We won't OK?'

Checking himself he looked at Tim. 'Sorry, you were saying?'

Tim shook his head. 'Anyway, yeah, she's given me such energy. I'm thinking about taking some time out actually.'

Our food arrived and we waited until the waiter had left before resuming. I tore apart some naan and looked at Tim. 'Time out to do what?'

He shrugged. 'Dunno, look for a new career, do a course, do some travelling, just change something about what my life is about, 'cause it's not making me happy.'

'Was any of that to do with Mel?' I asked.

He shook his head. 'I don't think so, I mean yeah, when we were together it was great, but I haven't really been thinking about her recently, and the prospect of now having to share a house with her again is one I really think I'm OK with. You know, looking back I don't think I was in love with her, or falling in love, whatever, I think I just wanted to be as I was looking for someone.' He looked at me. 'Don't worry, I'm not saying the second we get home I'm going to book a flight and run away, I'm just saying I'm gonna have a long hard think about myself and what I'm doing.' He slowly nodded his head as he drank from his glass. 'I'm going to be OK J, it's OK.'

I nodded. 'I have been worried about you.'

'I know you have but really, whatever happened at the party, let's just move on from it yeah? It's all good. I'm fine.'

I held out my hand which he clasped. 'Moved on.'

'Exciting times for you though.'

I turned to look at Rob. 'Yeah, they could be. Seeing you and Gabi together,' I looked at Tim, 'has really made me think about her a lot.'

'You haven't heard from her have you?'

'No, nothing since that night but we haven't been online have we?'

'So what are you going to do?'

I shrugged. 'Give her a call tomorrow evening I guess, arrange a day to meet up during the week.'

Rob nodded slowly. 'I can see this being quite a big deal.'

I smiled. 'You know what so can I, and I'm ready for that. I feel we've got some stuff out of our system, we both know each other so well, we can just start having some fun together.' I paused as Tim poured out another round of beers. 'My mind's been all over the place these last few weeks. Yeah, I will try and take it slow, but maybe we're just not those kind of people. We're both hot-headed and spontaneous, trying to keep it slow may be a bad idea, so I'm just gonna go with it, call her tomorrow and see how I feel.'

'Do you know how you feel?' Rob asked.

I nodded. 'As you said, I can see this being pretty serious, in my head a pretty major part of my life could be starting tomorrow. I was a fool in March and I've missed her like crazy ever since. When I saw her in the pub something just clicked between us, as if we both knew we were meant to see each other again and probably get back together, but we still had to go through the rituals of being embarrassed around each other, hesitating to kiss her, going on a new first date when we get back.' I swallowed some rice and wiped my mouth. 'Tim, you were saying these three weeks have given you time to think about what you want, well I've done the same thing; I know what I want.'

Our food was taken away and we all sat in silence for a while gazing out onto the city below. My mind was everywhere, filled with the last few weeks, yet I could also feel London J beginning to creep in, thinking about carrying my backpack on the tube, about what was waiting for me at work. I pushed him away for now, not yet. I hadn't really spoken about Jazz in that way in India before, and I mulled over what I'd just said. I really do think I am ready for something with her, and now I'm just excited to see what it will be and where it will take us.

I still wasn't sure what to do about houses, though. I'd kinda given myself the deadline of leaving India to decide, but I really didn't know. Living with Rob would be cool but I didn't know if I wanted to live with just one person. Plus the thought of telling Mel and Tim made me feel sick, especially if Tim now said he thought I would be OK living with Mel again. But then again I'd stayed there for a while now, I wanted to explore some more parts of London, do something a bit different. My greatest fear was routine, getting stuck in a rut, so should I move on?

I gazed out at the stars; my haunting white reflection sprawled itself across the sky. A close of the eyes and this would all be in the past.

Rob looked at his watch. 'Time to go home, guys.'

Chapter Forty-Six
July 22nd 2008

FOUR DAYS LATER AND India feels like a lifetime ago. Did we really do that? As I poured myself onto the Northern Line the morning we got back, I looked around at the rest of the carriage all getting ready to go to work and wanted to shout out that twelve hours ago I was in India! Forty minutes ago I had a T-shirt and shorts on and a backpack on my shoulders instead of a suit and tie.

Work was shit too. Rob and I spent the whole day emailing each other back and forth saying how much we hated being back, still holding on to that link between us that made us remember what we had just done. Tim's email came to us out of the blue

```
<I've just handed in my notice.>
```

I'm proud of you Tim.

Mel had been in when we got back and had been delighted to see us.

'I've been going crazy having no-one to talk to!' she said as she draped her arms around us both. 'Now no offence, but you both stink, go get cleaned up.'

All three of us had to get off to work as soon as we got back so there was no time to catch up but as Mel, Tim and I walked together towards the station, I knew I believed Tim when he told me it was going to be OK between them.

I'd been thinking about Jazz all day but I promised myself I'd wait until I got home before calling her, much as I'd wanted to text her during the day. I rang her, it went straight to answerphone. "Hey Jazz it's J, just got back from India, had an amazing time, hope you're well, give me a call and we can chat, yeah, it'd be great to meet up soon." Jet lag and exhaustion overcame me and I passed out.

The next day was more of the same. Work dragged on and as we were in the midst of summer, the tube was unbearably hot and so everyone was irritable. Tim had to work a four-week notice and was going to use that time to work out what he wanted to do, Mel was working insane shifts at the hospital and so was barely around, a catch-up would have to wait for a week or so.

I called her. It went straight to answerphone. I texted her. *Hey hey, how's it going? India was incredible, have to tell you all about it, feel like doing something fun this week?x*

I didn't receive a reply. Was she OK?

I awoke the next morning pretty confused, still no reply. Mel wasn't around so I couldn't ask her if Jazz was OK, why wasn't she answering her phone?

I called her at lunchtime; this time it rang, but it wasn't a sound I recognised, it was a foreign ringtone. It rang and rang and rang. Eventually someone picked up.

'Hello? Jasmine's phone.'

'Er hi, is Jasmine there?'

'No she's not at the moment, can I take a message? Who is this?'

'It's J, er, is she around later?'

'Not sure mate, she's on the beach at the moment, I'm just about to go join her.'

Someone kicked a football into my stomach. 'The beach?! Where am I calling? And who am I speaking to?'

'Italy, and I'm Keith, her boyfriend. Mate, this is costing her a bomb, I'll tell her you called.'

The line went dead.

AUGUST

Chapter Forty-Seven
August 3rd 2008

'ARE YOU NOT GOING to answer it?'

I looked at my phone and shook my head. 'No.'

'Well, are you not going to reject it at least, that ring tone is pretty annoying?'

I shook my head again. 'Not going to reject it, 'cause then she'll know I'm rejecting her call.'

Tim nodded. 'I see, because otherwise she thinks you just haven't bothered checking your phone for the last ten days.'

'Shut up, I said that I'm not going to answer it.'

He sighed and collapsed down on the couch. Looking across to Mel he asked, 'Any ideas?'

She shrugged and looked at her phone which was now beginning to ring. 'Oh great, what do I say?'

'That you don't know where I am.'

Mel grimaced and got up to leave the room. She flipped her phone up. 'Hey Jazz.'

Tim moved across to fill Mel's indentation on the couch. 'Why the hell can't she get the message?'

'I dunno and I don't care, I just wish she'd stop calling me.'

We'd been back from India for nearly two weeks now, and Jazz had been calling me pretty much non-stop. At first I thought about answering the phone and hearing her out but after thinking about it I changed my mind. I was so angry with her. Indescribably angry with her, and nothing she could say would make the blindest bit of difference. I guess it wouldn't change anything because I was really angrier with myself. I'd based three weeks' worth of daydreaming about my future on one little kiss outside Hampstead tube station. We'd kissed, so what, she said call me when you get back, so what, she wasn't pledging to be mine forever but I'd acted like she had. I knew nothing about Keith, I didn't want to, I just hoped he hadn't been around last month because that would hurt, really hurt a lot more than the hurt now.

She never left a message so I could never answer that question. Mel knew nothing either and hadn't even known about our meeting last month; in fact the whole thing was making Mel pretty angry with Jazz too. Not only had she hurt me, but she'd been lying too and as is always the case with liars, once one lie is uncovered you wonder how many more there are.

Mel came back into the lounge and flopped down next to Tim. 'I hate this.'

'What did she say?'

'Same as always, she asked where you were and asked me to ask you to call her.'

I snorted. 'Well that's not going to happen; what did you say about tonight?'

'I told her. I'm sorry but I hate lying to my friends. She asked me out down the pub and I said I couldn't because we were having a barbeque.'

'And?'

'And she asked if she could come.'

Tim's head snapped round. 'You didn't.'

She slapped his shoulder. 'No of course I didn't, still doesn't make it any less awkward for me though.'

I sighed. 'God what a mess, I would've thought that this would've blown over by now. I mean it's been over two weeks!'

'And it will, come,' she reached out to both of us with her hands, 'I'll make some drinks, you guys light the barbie.'

We'd returned from India to some boiling hot British weather. England was experiencing one of its hottest summers on record and even though we only had a tiny bit of square turf outside the front of the house we were determined to use it to its full capacity. Because of the way the house faced, the sun set in front of us and so our 'garden' retained the sunlight till quite late on. This meant our cooker had pretty much become redundant and the barbeque Tim and I had built last weekend was the new centre of our lives. Hell, if we had more time in the mornings we'd barbecue our toast out there too.

Tonight, the three of us had decided to stay in, get drunk, catch up and eat meat (or in Mel's case tuna); God knows it had been a while since we'd all done that. On the menu tonight was a feast. Mel was in charge of cocktails and Tim and I were in charge of the barbie, and neither one of us wanted to be outdone by the other.

Drinking-wise, there were two choices. The first, an invention of Mel's was a Brown Russian and was, according to Mel, a perfect sundowner intended to be sipped slowly at the start of an evening. Following that, Mel was making the Brazilian national drink, Caipirinha, a tricky, time-consuming cocktail that she had perfected on her travels.

Brown Russian

Ingredients
- Chocolate milk
- Ice
- Vodka
- Kahlua

Method
- Shake the vodka and Kahlua together, then add the chocolate milk. Pour over ice.

Caipirinha

Ingredients (per person)
- One lime
- Double shot cachaça
- Two tablespoons sugar

- Four ice cubes

Method

Time-consuming, as each cocktail has to be made individually.

- Slice the lime into very small pieces and add to a glass with the sugar and cachaça.

- Using a pestle if you have it, grind the mixture as much as you can.

- Add the crushed ice and shake incredibly well.

- Serve.

Tim and I were cooking as much food as possible. In addition to my stilton and mushroom hamburgers we were also doing grilled corn on the cob with lime and chilli and marinated chicken strips whilst also cooking tuna kebabs for Mel. Combine that with the salad Mel was making upstairs, the jacket potatoes cooking in the coals and the surprise dessert we had in store (banana and chocolate), and we were in for a treat.

Yoghurt and Mint Marinated Chicken Strips

Ingredients

- Two chicken breasts cut into strips
- Four spoonfuls of natural yoghurt
- Few sprigs of mint, diced
- Paprika
- Turmeric
- Wooden skewers

Method

- Mix the yoghurt, spices and mint in a bowl and then cover the chicken with the mixture.

- Refrigerate for a few hours.

- Run a skewer through the strips and when the time comes cook on the barbie for around ten minutes.

Corn on the Cob with Chilli and Lime

Ingredients

- One corn on the cob
- Half a lime
- Diced chilli
- Decent pinch of rock salt

Method

- Easy, barbecue the corn for around ten minutes, remembering to turn frequently.

- Rub the chilli and salt into the corn and squeeze lime over it.

Teriyaki Tuna Kebabs

This works either with a teriyaki sauce or a more basic soy and garlic sauce.

Ingredients

- One tuna steak
- Eight tablespoons soy sauce
- One garlic clove diced
- Two spoonfuls of sugar
- Splash of sake
- One red onion, cut into large strips
- One Portabello mushroom, cut into chunks

Method

- Cut the tuna into inch chunks.

- Mix the soy, garlic and sugar together and pour over the tuna.

- Leave to chill in the fridge in an airtight bag or container for a few hours.

- Make up the tuna kebabs. Skewer one piece of onion, followed by the tuna and then the mushroom.

- Repeat so you have six chunks on each kebab.

- Pour the remaining teriyaki sauce over the kebabs and cook on the barbie for around five minutes or so, it depends how well you like the tuna cooked.

If you don't want to use a teriyaki sauce, just marinate it in garlic and soy, maybe with a bit of diced ginger too. This also works well with beef.

The three of us hadn't spent much time together since we'd got back from India and by now the moment had passed where we'd sit down and tell Mel all about our trip. She'd watched a few videos we'd made on our cameras and flicked through the best pictures but we hadn't really pushed it. From the sounds of it she'd been working pretty hard, and if Jazz was in Italy Mel didn't have that many other people she was close to living round here in London. After a few weeks like that the last thing you really want to hear about is the amazing holiday your friends had just been on. Also, and I was taking my lead from Tim here, talking about it meant bringing up Gabi's name, a name he hadn't yet mentioned in front of her.

Sitting on our front wall with our legs dangling into the weeds below, it was easy to fall back into how we were. Mel was sitting in between us, a glass of Brown Russian resting in her hands, staring at the burgers sizzling and roasting on the coals, when she said out loud, to no-one in particular, 'Alexia was sectioned whilst you were in India.'

Tim and I exchanged glances.

'What happened?' he said softly.

'Mum found her trying to slit her wrists.'

'Is she OK?'

She nodded, 'Yeah, she sliced across instead of down, making the doctors think it is an attention disorder. If she really wanted to kill herself she would have cut down her veins.'

'So, and sorry for sounding stupid,' I apologised, 'what does it mean?'

She downed her drink and reached for the jug. 'It means she's in a psychiatric ward and can't leave until the doctors say so. She's on a constant watch.'

'Then,' I trod carefully, 'is this such a bad thing?'

She shook her head. 'No it isn't, but it's just,' she looked at me through watery eyes, 'you should have heard the sort of things she was shouting at my parents when they had to take her away. Mum just doesn't know what to do anymore, I don't know what to do anymore.'

I reached out and put my arm around her and she allowed her head to rest on my shoulder. Tim reached out and rested his hand on her knee and for a little while we just sat there, all three of us, interconnected. I felt a wave of protectiveness for Mel surge through me and I squeezed her shoulder with my hand.

'It was so hard with both of you gone, I had no-one to turn to. I'm just so scared that one day I'm going to get that phone call I've been dreading, and when I do …'

Tim stroked her hair. 'Hey, you don't know for sure that that will happen. Where she is now is the best place for her, she won't be able to do anything like that under constant supervision.'

'And she's going to be getting daily help from professionals, and she'll have to sit there and listen to them instead of running away,' I added.

Checking herself she sat up and rubbed her eyes; the moment was gone. 'I'm sorry, you're right, you both are; it's the best place for her and if anything goes wrong there are people there twenty-four hours a day.' Getting up to turn the burgers and put the tuna on, she turned to us. 'Anyway, I just wanted to let you both know, there wasn't a reason I didn't tell you before, I just didn't really want to blurt it out at seven in the morning. Anyway,' she exhaled, 'onto happier topics; Tim, you sorted out your life yet?' She looked up at him and smiled.

'Alright alright,' he raised his hands, 'give me a while, no I haven't. But I'm in no rush.'

'What's the atmosphere like at work?'

'Well, they're a little bit pissed off if I'm honest with you; after all I've only been there a few months and now I'm leaving.'

'How long till you leave?' Mel asked.

'Erm, I think it's two weeks next Friday, what with the bank holiday but I'm not sure. To be honest I probably need to pull my finger out; I've just got absolutely no idea what to do.'

'Well, what was your dream when you were growing up?'

'To be an astronaut. I think it's too late for that.'

Mel joined in, 'Well what was a more realistic dream then?'

He shrugged. 'I dunno, I've never really had a burning conviction about what I want to do. In some ways I envy you; since you were a kid you knew you wanted to be a doctor and now here you are, being a doctor. It must be so satisfying.'

'It is, but there's also a certain amount of, "well I've worked so hard and waited so long to be here, and now that I am, I'm just wondering what to do next", so it's not as satisfying as you may think.'

'I guess,' he chewed his lip, 'but I have absolutely no idea what I want to do. Earning loads of money doesn't motivate me enough to carry on with banking but I don't know what I can transfer into. I just hate the way we all have to find something to do, a place to fit in and a cog to turn.'

'God, you sound like Rob!' I muttered.

He smiled. 'I see his point though. Look, I'm realistic, I know I have to get a job, I'm just not going to rush myself into finding one I'm not sure I want.' He looked at Mel. 'I'm even thinking about studying again; I miss going to classes and researching topics and writing essays. I used to love politics and international relations at school; I'd jump at the chance to study them again.'

'Yeah, but you still need to work to pay for it.'

'Yeah yeah yeah, I know. All I'm saying is that I'm keeping my options open.'

I doled out the food from the barbecue and for a while we didn't speak as we all sat or leaned against the house and ate our food. It was beginning to get dark so Mel lit a few candles that stood in glasses on the wall.

'J, I know you don't want to talk about it but what am I gonna do about Jazz? I feel like I'm betraying you by seeing her.'

I grimaced. 'No, you're not betraying me by seeing her. I'm just fucking angry with her and I have no real desire to see her ever again.'

Tim impatiently prodded Mel. 'What actually happened when we were in India? Who is this Keith guy?'

She shrugged. 'I dunno, Jazz has been pretty distant recently. She works with Keith. I met him a few months back one evening.'

My lips tightened. 'Were they together then?'

She shook her head. 'It was obvious he fancied her, he ...' She paused. 'Tell me if you don't want to hear any of this?'

I waved my hand.

'OK, it was obvious he fancied her. We met him after work one night; he bought champagne all evening for no reason, that sort of guy.'

I shuddered. 'Carry on.'

'I thought he was a bit of a prick to be honest with you. I asked her that night if she fancied him and she said no, although she was enjoying the attention. Everything goes dead for a while, I hadn't seen Keith in ages and Jazz hadn't spoken about him at all. Then a few days before you get back I get a message on my answerphone from Jazz saying how she had finally given in to Keith and was going to Italy for a week. That's it, that's all I know. Jazz never told me about you both meeting before you left so I never saw the point in telling you about Keith, because I thought you and Jazz were completely over.'

'I know, I know, don't worry, I know you're not taking sides.'

Mel laughed. 'Ha, no I am taking sides J, I'm just taking yours! I don't like saying this about a friend of mine but I've realised you definitely can do much better.'

'Amen to that!' Tim lifted his drink. Looking at me he said, 'If you ever go back to her I will kill you.'

I nodded. 'I know you would, and that won't be happening. Even if I did think we would really work, I've got to get some self-respect going. She can't do this then call me and expect it to all be OK.'

'Thing is dude, at the risk of sounding harsh, you seem more angry than upset.'

I raised an eyebrow. 'How'd you mean?'

'Well yeah she screwed you over and you deservedly are fucked off with her, but are you just lamenting the fact you're not together or are you just angry at the situation?'

I shrugged. I hadn't really thought about it like that.

'What I mean,' he continued, 'is that all the stuff you thought about in India, such as you guys being together for a long time, that isn't going to happen anymore but are you more angry at the fact that you wasted all that time thinking about her rather than at the fact that she isn't here right now?'

I thought about it. Pointing his glass at me he added, 'I think you were never sure about you both working, you just wanted it to.'

'I agree with Tim here. Right from the start I could never see you both working.'

I filled up my glass from the jug. 'Great, guys, couldn't you have told me this in January?!'

Mel shook her head. 'Got to make our own mistakes.'

'Just make sure you learn from them, dude.'

I went upstairs to get the desserts together.

Barbequed Bananas Stuffed with Chocolate

Ingredients

- Tough one this, bananas and chocolate.

Method

- Peel about an inch wide skin of banana all the way down.

- Score the banana a centimetre or so deep all the way down.

- Break up some chocolate and stuff into the banana.

- Cover with the peel and wrap tightly in cling film.

- BBQ for ten to fifteen minutes or until the chocolate has melted.

I think Tim was probably right y'know. Much as I'd been thinking about Jazz over the last week or so, the dominant feeling had been anger rather than yearning. It wasn't like last time where I missed her, where I was devastated at the thought of us not being together. Instead it was anger that for her to do what she did, I must have felt for her so much more than she felt for me, and that hurt. No-one likes the realisation that you're not someone's number one anymore.

I walked over to the sink to wash my hands. The window was open and unknown to them, Mel and Tim's voices wafted upwards with the smoke and entered into the kitchen.

'… I really wouldn't be so hard on yourself. He doesn't expect you to all of a sudden stop talking to her. You've been friends for ages, it's not that easy.'

'Yeah, but I'm just so disappointed in her, even more so than J is maybe.'

The voices went quiet. Then I heard Mel again.

'I've missed this.'

'Me too.'

'Just hanging out, no tension, no pretence. I did quite a bit of thinking whilst you were away, about it all.'

'And?'

'And I'm sorry if you found it awkward before. I just wasn't sure how to act around you after we broke up. I found it easier to run away from it all when maybe we should've talked about it more.'

'I dunno, I'm not sure we could've talked about it. I know I said this at the time but I really am sorry, you know that, right?'

'Yeah I do, and I also know it was a one-off and that the Tim I saw that night isn't the real you.'

'India was just what I needed; I chilled out a lot out there, and one of the things I was determined to do was make sure me and you are OK. At the end of the day, when we first met J was our link and I don't want to have to go back to that. I still want you to feel like you can come to me, and that I can come to you.'

'I can, and I do.'

'Good. And even though it might have gone tits up in the end, I think we're all the closer for it.'

I heard her smile. 'That's for sure.' She cleared her throat. 'So you don't know what you're going to do, then?'

'No, it's all a bit of a head fuck at the moment. Especially because, well tell me if you don't want to know but I kinda met someone in India.'

'Oh?'

'Yeah, she ended up travelling with us for the last few days.'

'Oh right. Well no, of course I want to hear about her. What happened? What's her name?'

'Gabi, she's from Holland and is taking a year out to travel. She's cool, we got on well, but just her mentality of taking time out until she knows what she wants to do, well it's something that I really relate to and it's really her that got me wondering about what I'm doing with my life and what I want to be doing.'

'So are you guys together?'

'No. I mean we only knew each other for a few days and she won't be back in Europe for another nine months, if ever, but we've been emailing each other a lot. I said this to the guys but I think she was the kick up the arse I needed. Anyway, I wanted to tell you because I don't want to have to keep anything from you.'

'Tim really, it's cool, I'm happy for you, we're friends, good friends, I want you to be happy.'

I heard the chair creak as he sat back. 'OK. I'm glad, that was a bit of a weight actually. How about you, anyone?'

'No, work's been so hectic and I'm so tired all the time. I can't see where it's going to come from to be honest with you ...' She paused. 'Anyway, I'm glad you told me, thanks, I know it probably wasn't easy.'

I closed the window (feeling slightly weird for eavesdropping on my friends). Wrapping the bananas in foil I made my way down the stairs to rejoin my flatmates outside.

Chapter Forty-Eight
August 8th 2008

WHAT WITH THE UNDERGROUND being hotter than the sun I had begun walking to work in the mornings, and seeing as Tim no longer gave a shit about his job and his punctuality, he had begun walking with me as well. Starting the day with some air and a chat instead of someone else's iPod in your face and the top corner of a free newspaper that you don't even have the space to read put me in such a better mood in which to start the day. The change that comes over this city when the sun is shining is incredible and so infectious that you can't help but smile as you walk along the street. Restaurants start to put their tables outside and parks become busy places to spend afternoons in as opposed to places to put your head down and walk through.

Tim nodded at an obese woman in tight clothes eating a pain au chocolat on the other side of the street. 'She's your team's gym instructor.'

'Damnit.' I scanned the street, nothing good in sight, I sighed.

'Least I've got a job,' I muttered under my breath.

'Ha!' He pushed me towards the park railing. 'Whatever, I'm free,' he stretched his arms out, 'whereas you are still a big whore to the system.'

'Au contraire, dipshit, you're just trying to find a different whore to be, it's all the same at the end of the day.'

'You never know J, I still haven't seen anything I like yet.'

We turned into Regents Park. 'Well, what are you going to do then? You need to find something quick.'

He shrugged. 'Something'll come up, it'll work out.'

I turned to him. 'Yeah, but Tim, where is your money gonna come from? You need six hundred a month just to live here, let alone do

317

anything. Come on, you need to start interviewing, you're being too picky.'

'Picky! J, I'm not going to do something I don't really want to do just so I can live in a city I'm not sure I want to live in,' he protested. 'Just to have to do exactly the same thing again in six months' time. Nup,' he shook his head, 'I'm not going to rush this decision, this is a biggie. Thing is,' he continued, 'I feel that at this point I should go for it, try to do something I'm passionate about, but the problem is, I'm not really passionate about anything, so what do I do?!'

'You really got no ideas at all then?'

He shrugged. 'Dunno, but I'm not going to apply for something I don't give a shit about, otherwise I'm just wasting time and that's something we shouldn't be doing at this point in our lives.'

We came out of the Great Portland Street exit of Regents Park and walked east along the Euston Road, like a swimmer dipping his toe in the water, not wanting to cross over and plunge into the city. Walking past the new skyscrapers that had jumped up over the last few years I thought about my own job.

'I'm not passionate about my job either though.'

'No shit, J.'

'Shut up.'

'Well of course you aren't, you complain about it all the time.'

'I mean the gigs and parties are great fun but some of it is so tedious. But I'm like you dude, I don't know what I want to do either.'

'What are you passionate about?'

I shrugged. 'Job-wise, nothing really. I'd love to own a restaurant but I've got no idea about how to go about it.'

'Well, what about Emma? She's a chef, wants her own place, go into business with her.'

'I guess, but …'

'No buts J, if you're not happy, do something about it.'

We crossed over and plunged into the water.

I feel so restless at the moment. What with India still fresh in my mind, thoughts about moving and Tim looking for a new job I was finding it really hard to settle back, and was also annoyed at myself for trying to settle back. Tim jacking in his job in favour of doing something he really wanted to do was not only a pretty brave decision, but one I admired enormously. For all his laid-back approach he knew what he was doing, it was just frustrating for an outsider to watch.

I guess India had unearthed him a lot more than me and Rob. We were on a graduate programme, and although that was coming to an end in December it still gave you a certain amount of structure to your life, as opposed to Tim who had to walk into each job alone. Even though I wasn't desperately happy in my job it was a decision I knew I wouldn't have to think about until the scheme was over, and it was a decision I could put to the back of my mind for the time being.

Maybe that's why I was seriously considering moving in with Rob. Where I live is the only thing in my life at the moment that I feel I can change. Maybe my restlessness will be cured by moving south, by having to make a home in a new place. London is definitely a two-city place separated by the river and a move to South London would really feel like I had moved cities. So that's it then is it? Not content with your life then change it, but the only change I can think of is moving ten miles south, how lame is that?! I wished I could snap my fingers and have a girlfriend, as that would be a whole new area to channel my energies into, but as it stood I guess moving was what I might have to settle for, but as Rob would say should I be settling for anything at age twenty-four?

Is settling such a bad thing though? Is there something wrong in wanting to put down a few roots after several years of constantly moving on? Let's face it, renting with your friends is fun but one day it's going to end. If Rob buys a place and I move in, I know he'll rent it to me for cheap so I can save and look to buy in a few years. Thing is, I don't really think I even want to do that. I feel like I'm on a conveyor belt heading towards somewhere, but I just can't bring myself to be interested in where I'm going or what I'm passing, I'm just staring at the belt, watching it move a few inches in front of me. Is any of this going to be any better just because I'm living someplace else?

Chapter Forty-Nine
August 10th 2008

'LOOK, I'M NOT PROMISING you the world, I just think it could be fun, and different.'

'I know, I just really can't decide at the moment.'

'Chicken and bacon, brown bap to go?'

I held my hand up and reached over to take my lunch. We turned to leave the poo shop and head down to the park for a half hour.

'Well look, I know I said I wasn't going to put any pressure on you but well, I am. I need to know quite soon. I'm going south this week-end; come with me and just have a look around, see what's there.'

I shook my head. 'No, I don't want to look before I make a decision, I don't want to go behind Mel and Tim's backs.'

'God you're not, you're just looking with me. They don't have to know.'

'Dude I'm sorry, you're gonna have to look without me for a while, at least till I've decided what I want to do.'

We entered the park and headed over to a bench by a little fountain. Rob sat down in a huff.

'Fine, fine, just hurry up OK, prices are going up by the week.'

I sat down next to him. 'I will, but I thought you were going to look for two bedrooms anyway?'

'I am, I just … I dunno, just hurry up OK, don't analyse this all too much. Whatever happens, Mel and Tim aren't gonna hate you for moving out.'

'No but still, leaving the two of them together when they've only just got back on speaking terms isn't the best thing I can do, is it?'

'No, but when it comes to stuff like this you have to be selfish and go for what you want.'

'I know, but a little bit of tact never went amiss, did it?'

He sighed. 'Well if you're gonna take this long I don't know if I want to live with you. Jesus, Sainsbury's would be a nightmare, "Hmmm, green apples or red, I just can't decide, I'll let you know next month."'

'Shut the fuck up!'

Rob took a bite of his sandwich and said through his food, 'So, speaking of them, how are Tim and Mel?'

'I think they're fine really. We all had a chat about it a few nights ago, and they seem to be ok. I think they've both moved on from it all yet both want to try and keep a friendship there, which is great 'cause things could've been really awkward.'

'And Jazz?'

'What about her?'

'She still calling?'

'Less and less, I think it's dwindling down now.'

'That OK with you?'

'Of course it is, I told you, that's definitely not gonna happen.'

'Yeah I know, but now that that is out of your life there's nothing left to take its place. I know you, you're the same as me, and you're beginning to get fed up with being on your own.'

I nodded and munched on my sandwich. 'You're right, I think that's why I got so ahead of myself thinking about her in India. I'm getting pretty bored with being single.'

Chapter Fifty
August 16th 2008

BY NOW THE PLASTIC bag handles had become thin and were digging into my palms, resulting in a criss-cross pattern of pain on my hands. Between the Pimms, lemonade, food and wine the bags were pretty heavy and as I watched her skip on ahead I wasn't impressed by Mel's noble gesture to carry the blanket and French bread.

Reaching the top of Hampstead we headed down past the "Spaniards Inn", an ancient London pub that imposes itself so much on the road that cars have to bypass it in single file. Crossing over we rounded the corner and entered Kenwood House, walking through the tiny car park and on to the main entrance.

'Oh good, a space. I'm glad I left my car at home because this has been fun!'

'Shut up J,' Mel snapped. 'Of course you couldn't drive otherwise you'd have had to watch me drink. Now hold the blanket whilst I find the tickets.' She launched the blanket at me, which landed on my head, and opened her handbag.

'Mel I can't see, my hands are full.'

'Now where did I put them? J, you're mumbling, aha, here they are.'

She flashed them at the attendant and guided me into the park. 'Now where shall we go? Left looks good I reckon.'

The Kenwood concerts had become something of an institution and I'd been going to them for about a decade now. Throughout the summer a series of open-air concerts take place overlooking a lake in the grounds of Kenwood House, a large stately home which sits clinging to the edge of Hampstead Heath. The house throws open its doors and lets in a few thousand Londoners armed with lots of alcohol and picnic hampers bursting to the brim. The aim is to sit on the grass, eat, drink, chill and listen to whoever is performing on the stage on the other side of a small purpose-built lake.

We found a spot, laid out our large blanket and began to unpack our hamper.

'I'm off to do the sweep,' announced Mel, who stood up and sauntered off towards the hospitality tents. As I watched Mel get swamped by dozens of people dressed in black handing out food, I remembered how many freebies you get here. The whole event is always sponsored by chocolate and wine companies and there are always the odd handfuls of chocolate and half bottles to be had.

Mel returned a little while later with chocolate round her mouth, in her hands and in her pockets. Dumping them in the middle she smiled. 'That should keep us going for now I think. You can do the second round when it gets dark!'

I sat up and began taking lids off of food. 'That's dessert sorted, now we just need to get rid of this ton of food.'

'Which we will J, doesn't matter the others aren't here!'

I nodded and emptied the chorizo out onto a plate, enjoying the deep smell of the red wine. We had a mountain of food, we really did, and it was all Tim and Rob's fault, who up until yesterday were meant to be coming with us. Tim had decided to go home last minute because he wanted to see his parents and Rob had decided he didn't fancy the Heath and so both had bailed late last night.

Chorizo, Garlic and Red wine

Ingredients

- One large chorizo, cut into centimetre discs
- About a third of a bottle of red wine
- Two cloves of garlic
- Black Pepper

Method

- First of all, make sure you've removed the wax from the chorizo.

- Heat up a little oil in a pan and when it gets really hot, add the chorizo and garlic.

- Fry on a high heat for a little while and then add the red wine.

- Cook for a further five minutes or so until the majority of the wine has been absorbed into the chorizo.

- Drain and serve or keep in the fridge, but eat within twenty-four hours.

Cheese, Bacon and Tomato on Portabello Mushrooms

Ingredients

For four mushrooms

- One large Portabello mushroom, stalk removed
- Two rashers bacon
- One small green chilli
- One egg
- Splash of milk
- Grated parmesan
- Coriander
- One large buffalo tomato, cut into slices

Method

- Remove the stalk and dry fry or grill the mushrooms for a few minutes, then set aside.

- In a pan, fry up the coriander, chilli and bacon with a bit of black pepper and salt.

- When the bacon is half cooked, crack an egg over the mixture and add a splash of milk.

- Mix well with a spatula as if you were having scrambled eggs.

- Grate over some parmesan and stir in so it melts.

- Remove from the heat after a few minutes, you want to keep the egg still a bit runny, and spoon the mixture into the mushrooms.

- Place a slice of tomato on top and either serve immediately or wrap tightly in clingfilm and refrigerate, so the mixture solidifies a bit. Again, eat within twenty-four hours.

- Also, if eating with a vegetarian, just remove the bacon (sigh).

Homemade Hummus

Ingredients

- One can or around 350 grams of chickpeas, ready to eat
- One garlic clove
- Juice of one lemon
- Four tablespoons of tahini
- Olive oil, salt and pepper

Method

- Blend the chickpeas up with a splash of olive oil and two tablespoons of water.

- When smooth, chop up the garlic and add to the paste along with the tahini, lemon, olive oil, salt and pepper. Blend again.

I always sprinkle paprika and olive oil over my hummus, I think it tastes nicer, but this is optional. Serve as you wish, either as a great butter substitute in sandwiches or as a dip for vegetables.

Calamari Salad

Ingredients

- 400g calamari tubes
- One garlic clove
- Fresh coriander
- One chopped green chilli
- One teaspoon paprika
- Juice of half a lime
- Black pepper and salt
- Rocket and spinach leaves
- Sun-dried tomatoes

Method

- In a bowl mix the chilli, coriander, lime juice, black pepper, salt and garlic.

- Preheat a saucepan, add the oil and when hot add the mixture.

- Add the calamari and cook for around four to five minutes on a high heat.

- Serve over the pre-tossed leaves and tomato.

As the sun set and dusk dawned a host of lanterns illuminated themselves, guiding the audiences eyes down past the shimmering lake and up onto the stage in front of us. The support band had left ages ago and a hush washed over the crowd as we expected the arrival of Damien Rice. A single microphone stand stood at the front of the stage, looking commanding and imposing, requesting silence from the audience in front. The lights dimmed and we all rose to greet him, just about being able to make out a single hand raised in welcome, shining out like a beacon across the water.

The set began and we all settled back down onto the grass, relaxing into the warm evening air. Song after song from his first two albums washed over us and it wasn't too long before we were both lying flat out on the grass, not craning our necks to see Damien but just gazing up into the night sky.

'I feel like we're sitting round a campfire!' Mel whispered into the air.

All around us people murmured into each other, not wanting to disturb it for everyone else but also not wanting to sit in silence. Every now and then the odd sweet smell of weed wafted over us and we turned to find the toker, a raised spliff returning our grins.

Mel lifted herself up so she was resting on her elbows and allowed her head to drop back, still gazing upwards. 'This is so cool; Tim and Rob would've loved this.'

'I know, I can't believe how they both just wimped out of it so quickly. I mean, when does Tim ever want to go see his parents?'

'Yeah, that was a bit odd. Do you think he's telling the truth?'

I nodded. 'I think he is, just think it was a bit of a strange decision to go home when we already had something booked.'

'And what did Rob say?'

'I can't work him out, he said he wasn't really in the mood.'

Mel lay back down. 'What, to sit outside, listen to great music and eat awesome food? Yeah,' she picked up a strawberry, 'this is torture.'

'Ha well,' I raised my Pimms, 'their loss.'

We cheersed and turned to watch the last song of the first half.

I stood up and walked over to the wine tent. Hmm, the tent seems to have moved to the other side of the stage, that's weird. I made my way past the deckchair seating in front of the stage, tripping up over outstuck legs and bags. Feeling the effects of a bottle of wine and shit-loads of Pimms I think. I bought a bottle of wine and made my way back to Mel. As I approached our big Mexican blanket I saw a guy sitting down next to her. Who the fuck are you?

'Alright.'

He looked up and smiled. 'Hey bruv, how's it going?'

I nodded, sat down on my blanket, looked at Mel and raised an eyebrow.

'J, this is Paul, Paul, my best friend and housemate J.'

He extended his hand which I shook, or at least attempted to for it was one of those dangling, wet fish handshakes where you don't know whether to shake it or slap the owner round the face with it. 'How's it going?'

He turned back to Mel. 'So anyway, so like I saw Damien in Manchester a few years back and it was sweet, much better than tonight, he sounds so pop now, real sellout.'

Mel nodded. 'Is that right? I've only just really got into him to be honest. J, what do you think?'

I raised my antlers. 'I don't agree with you at all to be honest Paul. Yeah, he sounds different now, but you can't call him a sellout just because he's now successful, I think that's rather naïve to be honest.' I downed my wine, opened the bottle and filled up mine and Mel's glass.

The lights went up on the stage and Damien Rice walked on again.

327

We all stood to applaud. I took a step back on the blanket, moving Paul off of it.

He looked at me as he stepped off of the blanket. I turned my back to him to look towards the stage. 'Yeah, well I guess I should get back to my mates, nice meeting you Mel,' he leant in to kiss her cheek which Mel gave rather reluctantly. He looked to me and nodded. 'J.'

I nodded back. 'Paul.'

Mel waited until he had gone before dissolving into laughter. 'That was hysterical!'

'What? That guy was a dick, what the hell was he doing talking to you?'

She smiled. 'You are so protective, it's adorable! Your face when you saw him here, priceless!'

'Oh please, if Tim was here he would have drowned him in the pond.'

She shook her head. 'You still can't admit it, can you? You're still annoyed!' she laughed.

'Shut up,' I barked, 'lie down.'

'Oh how nineteenth century. Yes sir.'

I shook my head and lay back on the ground. Mel lay side on, resting her head on my chest, looking out towards the stage. I propped myself up with a hand behind my head. I didn't know what to do with my other hand, and so let it rest on my chest. We lay there in silence for a good few songs, her head rising and falling with my breathing. Gradually the set began to build to a crescendo, the female vocalist joining Damien on stage, making the entire crowd shiver. I felt Mel move her head a little. 'I love my hair being played with.'

I looked down. Unconsciously I'd been twirling her hair in my fingers. I stopped and Mel sat up and looked away for a moment. For a few seconds neither of us spoke as we listened to the music.

Chapter Fifty-One
August 23rd 2008

I WAS GOING TO move out.

I'd decided a few days ago that I was going to move; now all that remained was breaking the news to my housemates. I had literally been losing sleep over it, worried about how I was just gonna come out and say it, and what the possible repercussions for all of us were going to be, especially if I moved south which for North Londoners was miles away.

I felt like nothing was changing in my life, and as I said before even if my house was the only big thing in my life I felt like I could change then so be it, that's what I'll change, and I'd resolved to tell them over dinner tonight.

Tim was cooking the three of us a huge joint of beef, as if we hadn't been eating enough meat recently off of the bbq. As usual Mel was getting something else which I was cooking as Tim refused to cook for vegetarians, labelling them as selfish. He'd been on really good form since his weekend at home, almost as if he'd now made his decision and was ready to properly start looking for a job that excited him and he could really get something out of. He'd spent the last few days online and making list upon list, hopefully getting his CV together and applying for jobs on the internet.

I still felt sick. Even as I was peeling the carrots and chatting easily with Tim I still felt this albatross around my neck, this piece of news I had to deliver, knowing full well that after it was uttered some things may never really be the same again. Sometimes I really hate change. Sometimes I hate the little voice in my head that tells me to move on just as I think about getting comfortable. I looked around at our homely kitchen, at my best friend massaging black pepper into a joint of beef and at the photograph on the wall of the three of us all pulling the ugliest expressions we could manage. I don't think I'd ever felt as lonely as I did at that moment and I wondered how many more times in my life I'd be standing alone preparing to say goodbye to the present.

I heard the key in the lock and the door open. Mel armed with bags climbed the stairs and announced herself in the kitchen. She immediately headed over to the fridge and started unpacking her shopping.

'Mel, if you're going to cook the starters the whole point of it is that you're here cooking before us.'

She slapped Tim's arse in passing. 'Shut it, I'm here now. Anyway there was a huge queue at the shops, you couldn't find any asparagus for love nor money.'

'Oh we're having asparagus, great, how exciting.'

She turned to me and tried to evil me, but failed miserably. 'Don't you start, Camfield.'

We all cooked on together, singing along to the radio, hiding each other's food in cupboards and generally dicking around. Tim put his beef in the oven, I put the fish in and Mel started to flash fry the starters. Uncorking a deep red Argentinean Malbec we emptied the bottle into three glasses and made our way through to the lounge.

Asparagus, Mushroom and Chilli Baby Omelettes

Ingredients
- Six sticks of asparagus
- Two eggs
- One large field or Portabello mushroom
- One green chilli
- Sweet chilli sauce
- Three slices of bread
- Handful of green leaves

Method

Pure genius by Mel, this one.

- Using a circular pastry cutter, cut out three round discs from a loaf of bread and set aside.

- Boil the asparagus for three minutes in boiling water, remove and slice into 1cm discs.

- Slice the mushroom into small bits and dice the chilli.

- Fry all three up together on a high heat and then, putting the pastry cutters into the pan, divide the mixture into three.

- In a bowl whisk up the two eggs with a splash of milk.

- Pour a third of the mixture into the pastry cutter, covering the chilli, mushroom and asparagus.

- Place the bread on a plate and put a handful of leaves on top.

- When the mixture is firm, remove and place on top of the leaves.

- Drizzle with a little sweet chilli sauce.

Tim and I cut into the omelettes and buried a forkful each. Looking at each other we frowned before spitting the food back onto the plate.

'That is disgusting!'

Mel looked at both of us in horror,

'But, I made … but …'

I began to cough hard and beat my chestbone.

Tim cracked a smile and cut into the omelette again. 'Relax, only joking, it's great.'

Mel slammed down her fork. 'I am fed up with being bullied by you two!'

Tim and I high-fived. Polishing off the starters we sat back; the fish wasn't done yet and the beef was still relaxing on the hob. Tell them now. I opened my mouth, and closed it again. I couldn't do it.

'Shall we go out for a drink after this?' Mel asked.

Tim nodded. 'Yeah, we should, rather than just sit around here.'

Shit shit shit, OK I have got to tell them before we go to the pub, I want to tell them here. After the mains, I'll tell them then, it'll be fine.

Whole Red Snapper à la Veracruzana

Picked this one up in Mexico

Ingredients

- One whole red snapper, a really good, meaty fish
- One red onion
- Good handful of black olives
- Two garlic cloves
- Three to four vine tomatoes, skin off
- One green chilli
- Rice
- Juice of one lime

Method

- First of all, boil some water and pour over the tomatoes. Prick the skin lightly and then remove the skin after a few minutes when it has begun to shrivel.

- Slice up the onion, garlic, tomatoes and chilli and pan fry for one to two minutes.

- Make an indentation in the olives so they release their flavour and then add to the pan.

- Remove from the heat.

- Pour a little oil on some kitchen foil and place the fish on top.

- Pour the mixture over the fish, making sure every bit is covered.

- Fold over the foil and cook for twenty minutes.

- Cook some rice and add the lime juice to it when cooked.

- Place the fish on top of the rice and spoon over the mixture.

This can be eaten as it is, but is also great in tortillas. To get all the meat off, make an indentation below the neck and rip the head off. Then carefully lift out the spine; this should remove all the bones.

Roast Beef with Black Pepper Crust

Ingredients

- About 500g rump or sirloin

- Few sprigs of rosemary
- Two garlic cloves, sliced
- Handful of black peppercorns, whole

Method

- First you need to seal the meat.

- Put a little olive oil in a pan and heat until very very hot.

- Using tongs cook the meat for about five seconds on each side, then take off the heat.

- Put the peppercorns inside some kitchen paper, cover then loosely crush with a heavy implement like a jar or a hammer.

- To the kitchen paper add the rosemary and garlic, mix with your hands and then sprinkle over the top of the beef. Rub in any bits that fall down the side.

- Cook on around 180° C for twenty minutes plus twenty minutes per 500g for well done, fifteen minutes per 500g for medium and ten minutes per 500g for rare.

- When you take the beef out, leave to rest for ten minutes or so; this lets the juices soak into the meat so it's more tender.

For the gravy

Ingredients

- Spring onions
- Red wine
- Cornflour
- One beef stock

Method

- Slice the spring onions long ways and boil up in some water.

- Reduce down, then add the stock and wine.

- Add the cornflour and stir until nice and thick.

I finished off the remaining carrots and sat back, loosening my belt, absolutely stuffed.

'Guys, there's a reason I suggested a meal tonight, I've actually got something to tell you. I'm, er, I'm going to be leaving next month.'

I almost choked on my wine and looked at Tim. 'What did you say?!'

Tim nodded. 'Yeah, I've made a decision about the next step and I'm gonna go for it.' He looked at me. 'I'm gonna go find her.'

'Who?!'

'Gabi, you fool! Who'd you think?!'

Mel looked confused. 'B-b-b-but, I don't get it, you're gonna find her? You're leaving?'

'Yeah,' he pulled his chair up to the table and rested his arms on the wood, 'I've been thinking this for a while and since we got back from India the only thing I've wanted to do is be with her, so that's what I'm going to go do.'

Mel looked confused. 'Find her?'

Tim smiled sheepishly. 'Well, not find her, I know exactly where she is; maybe that was a bit too dramatic, I'm going to meet her.'

'And what? Tim this is crazy, you've known her for a week.'

He shrugged. 'And as you said to me on our last night in India, that doesn't matter. We're gonna travel together, I've already bought my round the world ticket, I leave September twentieth. I'm going to meet her in Laos, spend a month or so round there then head over to Central America and work our way south.'

'Hang on Tim,' Mel put her hand on his, 'what about Gabi, what does she think of it?'

He smiled. 'It was her idea. You know we've been emailing all the time, well she said something about a fortnight ago; I mulled it over, went home to talk it through with the folks and then booked my ticket a few days ago. Guys, I'm sure about this OK, this is what I want to do.'

'But Tim, whatever you're running away from now, not knowing what you want to do, not liking where you live, it'll all be here when you get back and it'll be worse.'

He turned to look at me. 'J, I don't know if I'm planning on coming back, at least not for a long time. This,' he raised his hands, 'it doesn't feel right. It is for some people, and I've tried it now so I know for myself but London isn't for me and so now I need to find where is, and maybe more importantly, who is for me.'

We sat in silence. I was stunned.

'And it's booked?'

'Yeah, in about a month. Look guys, I'm not going to screw you over, I'll bust a gut trying to find a flatmate whilst I'm still here, and if you don't like anyone by the time I leave I'll carry on paying full rent until you do find someone.' He shrugged. 'You could always ask Rob, I know he's not happy where he is now.'

I put my head in my hands, fuck.

'I'm not living with Rob,' Mel said, 'but anyway that's not important right now.' She took Tim's hand again. 'Are you sure this is what you want to do?'

He nodded emphatically. 'Yes it is; India reminded me how amazing it was to travel. I have no real strings here apart from you guys and family, and I have a girl on the other side of the world who I'm crazy about. I want to go see where it leads. If it leads back here then at least I can say I tried.'

Mel's eyes were beginning to well. 'Then I'm happy for you babe, I really am. You go for it.' She reached over and hugged him tightly. 'But I'll miss you like crazy.'

He smiled, hugged her back and then looked to me. The reflected light betrayed the gathering water in his eyes. 'J?'

I hesitated. Would the knowledge that Tim was doing exactly what he wanted to do outweigh the pain I would feel at watching him leave? Yes, of course it would.

'Go for it.'

'I'll get the dessert ready'

I pushed my chair back and went into the kitchen. I couldn't believe he was going to do it, I couldn't believe he was going to leave. Opening the fridge door I bent down and rested my head on my extended arm. What the hell was I going to do now? OK, one problem is gone in that I don't have to tell Tim but I can't just leave Mel, and she already said she doesn't want to live with Rob. Fuck fuck fuck, but I've got to tell them, haven't I? If Tim starts placing ads for a housemate tomorrow then I have to tell them tonight. Unless I stay here with Mel and we get a random to move in. But that wouldn't work as I'd be screwing Rob over, and more importantly – I looked into the lounge where Tim and Mel now sat on the couch – I don't want a stranger living with us here. But double whammy, Mel, both your flatmates are moving out, do you want some dessert?

I removed the oranges from the fridge and arranged them on a plate. Does this change things? Do I still want to move? I stood still, my mind gazing into the oranges; take Tim out of the equation, yes I do still want to move, I need a change in my life. I took a deep breath, picked up the plates and got ready to change my life.

Hollowed Oranges with Berries, Rum and Ice Cream

Ingredients
- One large orange per person
- Handful of strawberries, raspberries and blueberries
- Dark rum
- Spoonful of caster sugar
- Vanilla ice cream

Method
- Slice the top off of the oranges and hollow out using a spoon and knife. Set the orange pieces aside.

- Place a large scoop of ice cream in the bottom of each orange.

- Cut up the strawberries, blueberries, raspberries and orange into bite size chunks.

- Place the fruit in the orange.

- Stir the sugar into a shot of rum and mix until it dissolves.

- Pour the rum into the oranges, place the tops back on and serve.

I walked over to the couches and handed out the oranges. Walking around the couch Tim and Mel were sitting on, I put my plate down and sat on the coffee table in front of them.

'There was something actually I was going to say before Tim told us his news.'

They both turned to me; Mel's spoon froze in her mouth and her hand rushed out to my arm. 'Are you OK?'

I squeezed her hand. 'Yeah I am, I'm er, I'm going to be moving out as well.'

There, the next bombshell. From this evening forth the three of us will never ever be the same again.

'J? What are you talking about?'

I looked directly at Mel. 'Rob is buying a flat, and he's asked me to move in. I'll be renting the second bedroom.'

'You're moving out too!' She looked frantically between me and Tim. 'Is this some sort of joke? Did you plan this?'

I shook my head. 'I've been trying to tell you both for days; I had no idea about Tim.'

She sat back in the couch and squeezed her forehead with her hand. 'Fuck.'

'Have you got somewhere lined up?'

My gaze left Mel and focused on Tim. 'No, Rob's been looking a bit but I didn't want to look until I told you guys first.'

'Where?'

'South, Clapham, Balham I think.'

'South?!' She sat up. 'But that's miles away!'

'Look Mel,' I put my hand on her knee, 'it won't be for a month, and like Tim I'll do everything to find new housemates.'

'Oh no no no,' she sat up on the couch, 'I'm not staying here, not with both of you going, I couldn't face two randoms moving in. If you go,' she looked to Tim, 'and you go, I'm going too but,' she hesitated, 'who the hell would I live with? I love living with you guys, I don't want that to change!'

I felt so guilty. 'So do I; some of my best times have been in this room.'

'So why are you leaving?' Tim asked.

I shrugged. 'Similar to you I think. I need a change, I need to do something different. I don't have someone to cross the world for so …'

'So you'll cross the river for Rob.'

I smiled. 'So I'll change something. I'm not going to change jobs for a bit so I need to do something, feel like I still have a bit of control over my life.'

'It's not to do with us is it?'

I squeezed Mel's knee. 'Of course it isn't, it's just time y'know, it's just time to take another step.'

'But why? If you're happy here?'

'I am but, well look, what with Tim going as well would you want to have a random living in his room, 'cause I know I wouldn't.'

'I guess.'

'I just think it's the right thing to do, I feel like I'm in a bit of a rut at the moment.'

Tim nodded. 'I know how you feel dude, and if it makes you happy, then go for it.'

He'd already left us hadn't he? In his mind he'd moved on. He stood up. 'I think we deserve a drink.'

'Good idea.' I looked to Mel who was deep in thought. 'Coming?'

She shook her head and moved towards her bedroom. 'I've got some phone calls to make.'

SEPTEMBER

Chapter Fifty-Two
September 4th 2008

I SAW ROB FROM the other side of the road and raised my hand in greeting. I dodged the traffic and made it over to his side and we high-fived.

'So this is Clapham.' I looked around. 'Looks shit.'

'Shut it, I know you feel sick for having left North London but you can leave your sarky comments behind, thank you very much.'

I held up my passport. 'Do I need to get this stamped?'

He threw my passport to the floor. 'Dick, come on, we'll be late.'

I looked at my watch. 'Really? What's the time difference down here?'

He sighed and shook his head. 'Rising above it. OK, we got three properties to see today, two round here and a third down in Balham.'

I stooped to pick up my passport. 'Which is which?'

'Well coincidentally each house gets better than the previous, so the one in Balham is the one I like the most, but all three are good y'know. Either way we need to get moving on this; I want to make a decision today.'

We walked up Clapham High Street and headed towards Clapham North. I looked around, it was like being back at uni again. Almost everyone I passed was about my age and every place we passed was either a bar, deli or restaurant. The pavements were full of people sitting reading the papers and drinking coffee or having a few pints, soaking up the sun. I turned to Rob. 'Dude, this is awesome!'

He grinned. 'I'm telling you, south is where it's at right now.' He nodded to the left. 'Down here.'

We turned off of the High Street and walked towards the leisure centre. 'Now, the one thing I'm not too keen on about this is that it's ex-local authority, but then again that's why this place is cheaper than the others.'

'Well that doesn't mean it's dodgy.' I turned back. 'I mean we're still near the High Street, aren't we?'

'Yup,' he motioned with his hand, 'here on the right.'

We entered the estate and walked across the car park. Arriving at a ground floor flat we knocked and waited. Then we knocked again. Two minutes later what can only be described as a troll answered the door. 'Yeah?'

'Hi, I'm Rob, I was here last weekend. I arranged with the agents to look round here at twelve.'

He stepped aside. 'Well come on in, sorry dude, place is a mess, we've only just got up.'

We wiped our feet and walked into the kitchen. Stifling a yawn, troll boy waved his hands. 'Knock yourself out.' He lifted the hood of his dressing gown and walked off towards the lounge.

We climbed the stairs to the bedrooms, ignoring the foul smell of hung over sleep.

'Right, this would be my room, yours would be in there on the left.' I had a brief look round Rob's palatial bedroom and went next door.

'Rob.'

'Yeah.'

'You're kidding, right?'

He popped his head round the door. 'What?'

'You can't even fit a double bed in here. Come on, we're not living here!'

'But I love my bedroom, have you seen the bay windows?!'

'Rob!'

We headed back towards the High Street and walked down to Clapham Common. This was my first day of house-hunting with Rob and it wasn't off to a great start. We'd all given our one-month notice to our landlord, and now the countdown was hovering at three weeks. Tim left in just over two weeks and Mel and I would follow him a few days later. I'd follow Rob to South London and Mel would follow Jazz to West London. Mel had only just told me that she was going to be renting with Jazz and even though I was annoyed at the fact that I would now have to see Jazz again, I didn't really feel like it was something I could say to Mel. For Mel it made sense so that was all that mattered.

Tim was bouncing off the walls. He was ridiculously excited and couldn't sit still for a second. In his mind he was already with Gabi, which was sad for those left here with him especially as our days together were now numbered. I guess the consequences of a decision come into effect the second you make it. We were trying to think up a good send-off for Tim and had decided that instead of a house party we were going to take advantage of the weather and have an evening picnic on top of Primrose Hill for him. Something laid back and small, close friends only.

Rob and I reached the end of the High Street and crossed over into the common. All around us groups of people sat sunbathing, cooking meat on BBQs and drinking. To my left I saw a group playing bongo drums on the grass and a constant stream of joggers dodge around the families and prams hogging the central path.

'I had no idea any of this existed. I thought Clapham Common was a small deserted park where gay people go to have sex. Rob this is enormous!'

His eyes widened. 'You can't say things like that! Jeez you North Londoners are so arrogant.' He smiled. 'But yeah, there's so much more space down here. Imagine if this was your local park, it's amazing. And during the summer they have gigs and film screenings too.'

We crossed the common and entered Clapham Junction which seemed to me to be a replica of Clapham North. Road upon road of bars and restaurants offered their tables onto the pavements where sun seekers sat. The flat we saw was right on Lavender Hill, just behind the High Street, and it was nice enough, but there was no outdoor space and I didn't like the thought of being kept in during a hot day. We took a break for a well deserved pint and headed off into Balham to look at the third property.

I'd never been to Balham before either. We took the overland past Wandsworth Common (how many commons does South London need?!) and got off two minutes later in Balham. Coming out of the station and crossing the High Street I have to admit I was pretty blown away.

'Rob, have we ended up in Surrey or something?'

'Huh?'

I gestured around me. 'This place, it doesn't even feel like we're in London anymore!'

'I know, and because you're an inch inside zone three the houses are cheaper too.' He looked at his watch. 'We've got ten minutes to kill, let's wander.'

We wandered up Balham Hill, stopping to look at all the delis and restaurants. There were Nepalese, Italian, Argentinean, Indian, French, Moroccan and Sri Lankan restaurants as well as gastro pubs; it was all wall to wall eateries, posh supermarkets and ethnic shops. Caribbean wholesalers stood next to Halal specialising butchers and organic fishmongers.

I pulled on Rob's sleeve. 'I want to live here.'

'You haven't even seen the place yet!'

'I know but still, I want to live here.' I pointed to the other side of the road. 'They sell plantains!'

'Dude, don't base a decision on green bananas, you may not like it. Come, it's down here.'

We passed a huge three-storey bar; I looked up. 'What's that?'

'Ground floor bar, middle floor restaurant, top floor stand-up comedy venue and cinema, nice huh?'

I shook my head. 'Oohhhh man I'm building this flat up.'

'Well don't, open minds! But if it's any help, I love this place too! Hit the bell, flat A.'

I rang the buzzer and we stepped inside. The flat was on the bottom two floors of a converted Victorian house two minutes down from the High Street and station. It was currently unoccupied, the previous owners had rented it out but now wanted to sell and seemed to be in quite a rush. Downstairs consisted of an open plan kitchen and separate lounge and opened up onto a small garden. Strangely enough the bathroom was also tacked onto the side of the kitchen.

'Ok, liking it so far, good open space, I like open plan kitchens, space to cook and space to chill.'

'Good stuff, now head upstairs, your room would be straight on.'

I climbed up and opened the door. It would easily fit a double and more. It had lots of built-in cupboards and was a good fifty percent bigger than my current room.

'I love it.'

'Excellent, I knew you would.'

'How much are they asking?'

'Two-ninety but I'm gonna offer two-eighty I think.'

I chewed my lip. 'And what would you charge me?'

'One-twenty a week, same as you do now. What do you think? Shall I put an offer in?'

I put my arm round his shoulder. 'Let's do it.'

Chapter Fifty-Three
September 9th 2008

'GUYS, IT'S GREAT HAVING you here but really,' he turned round to look at us, his hands full of neatly folded underwear, 'where am I supposed to put stuff?'

Mel lifted her leg off the bed and kicked at the underwear in Tim's hands.

'You got no underwear now, you're gonna have to stay.'

'Mel,' he crouched down to scoop up the underwear, 'it doesn't get any funnier, no matter how many times you do it.'

She broke into a grin and stuck her tongue out. 'Have to disagree with you there, Timothy.'

She extended her arms and stretched out before resting her head on my knees. 'My God I'm tired. I can't believe how many shit places there are out there.'

'Well if you will move West …'

She looked up at me sharply. 'Shut up J, I still haven't worked out if I forgive you completely. Anyway,' she looked to Tim, 'at least I'm staying in the city rather than moving miles away.'

'It's zone three Mel, not Devon!'

She shrugged. 'Well I only have a zone one to two travel card so I guess I'll never come see you.'

I lifted my knees up and down, making her head rise and fall. 'Good, wouldn't want you in my house anyway.'

'Good. Cause I'm not coming.'

'Good.'

'Good.'

'Jesus, both of you shut up will you?!' Tim stuck his hand in a drawer and pulled out a bundle of socks. 'One, two, three.'

'Twelve, nine, seventy-three.'

'Stop it!' He threw the socks to the floor. 'Shut the hell up!'

'Oh relax Tim, it's only a practice pack, you've still got a fortnight.'

He sat down on the bed. 'I know, I know, it's just there's so much to do.'

'Well,' I sat up, 'anything we can do to help?'

He grinned. 'Make me dinner?'

'Nup, Mel can do that.'

She shook her head. 'No she can't, she's knackered from house-hunting.' She sat up and pushed me towards the door. 'G'wan, you know you want to.'

Grilled Hoki with Pesto over Pasta

Ingredients

- 200 grams each of fresh hoki
- One lime
- Black olives
- Two garlic cloves
- Fresh rosemary and oregano
- Mushrooms
- Two red onions
- Bag of fresh spaghetti
- Green pesto

Method

Hoki is a lot like cod, but is from New Zealand and there's loads of it so the government is trying to get us to eat it instead of depleting cod supplies.

- Rub some lime juice into the fish, cover with a thin spread of pesto and wrap in foil and grill for seven to eight minutes.

- Slice up the onion, a teaspoon of pesto, garlic, mushrooms, rosemary, oregano, olives and cook up on a high heat.

- Cook the spaghetti for two minutes, then drain and add to the onions etc.

- Stir in two teaspoons of pesto and stir the mixture thoroughly.

- Remove the fish from the oven and place on top of the spaghetti.

Tim put his plate on his desk and continued to sort out his clothes. I handed Mel her food and got back on his bed, my back resting against his headboard. Mel lifted her fork to her mouth before coughing and spitting it back onto the plate. 'That is disgusting,' she said, wiping her mouth.

Tim and I looked at each other and smiled. 'She's learning!'

'You won't be able to do this kind of behaviour with Jazz though.'

She nodded. 'Yeah I know, she can be a bit too serious at times.'

Tim walked over to the stereo and turned the music down a bit. 'I'd say more intense than serious. You apprehensive about it at all?'

She nodded. 'Yeah, but it'll be OK. I mean much as I'm going to miss living with you both so much it'll hurt, I guess it will be nice to live with a girl for a bit.'

I chipped in. 'And it's definitely going to be just the two of you?'

She nodded. 'Yeah, I'm too old for randoms. Plus, I guess it will be nice just living with Jazz, I think it'll be a lot more chilled than here, no offence or anything.'

'None taken, you're probably right. So, er, is Jazz still with this bloke then?' Tim asked.

I raised my eyebrow at Tim, he looked back at me. 'What? You don't care, do you?'

'No, course not.' I turned and caught Mel looking straight at me. 'So?'

She looked at Tim then looked at me. 'No she isn't, she broke up with him last month, she finally realised the guy was indeed a prick.'

'Interesting. J, isn't that interesting?'

'Not really, no, I think I'm more interested in pubic lice than

347

Jazz's love life.'

Tim ruffled my hair. 'Atta boy.' Turning to Mel he said, 'With me gone you're going to have to take my place, J, you listen to her now, stay clear.'

I nodded. 'Because that's really possible when Mel and her are living together!'

'Hey, don't have a go at me Camfield! This is all your fault remember!'

She put down her plate and rested her head on my legs again. 'Anyway, I'll slap you so hard if you do anything with her again.'

'Excellent, and if you do I'll fly home and nail both your hands to a wall. Anyway, leaving J aside are you actually OK with moving in with Jazz or are you just saying that?'

'Nonono, I really do mean that, it'll be fun, plus Fulham is lovely; it's just a shame we haven't seen any nice places yet, but we will, we will.'

I gently tapped her on her head. 'What's it like? I've never really been there.'

'Well,' she sat up, 'it's not Chelsea, it's on the fringes of it but it feels quite villagey. It feels nice and homely, like there's a proper community there. And it's just on the river so it's pretty central. All joking aside, it's easy to get south from there once I work out the bus routes. And, most importantly,' she tapped my hand, 'there's this cake shop where Jazz and I went after work, that gives you the most enormous portions of incredible cakes, and serves them along with a pint of tea or coffee. It's amazing, you have to see it.'

'I will, I will, I'll probably be helping you move in, remember.'

'Ha,' laughed Tim, 'glad I'm missing that one. "Hi Jazz, where do you want this lamp and whilst we're at it, what the fuck happened over the summer?" That'll be a fun one to see.'

I changed the subject. 'Aaaanyway, did I tell you Rob has had his offer accepted and the survey has come through fine? Fingers crossed I won't have to stay on a couch somewhere and we can actually move when the lease is up.'

'So it's true, I will have to actually come to the South to see you?'

I nodded. 'Yup.'

'It's weird,' Tim said, 'I still can't really picture you and Rob living together.'

'No, nor can I actually.'

'Really?'

Mel shook her head.

'Well, like you it'll probably be a bit quieter than with you guys, but it is going to be fun.'

Tim looked at Mel. 'Unlikely.'

'J, face it, this is the best your life is ever going to be.'

I picked up a pillow and covered Mel's laughing face with it. 'Shut it. Me and Rob are going to get on fine. Yeah I'm a little bit apprehensive but that's 'cause living in a two is so much more grown-up I think. It's like you're living together not just with each other.'

'Christ J, you're not a gay couple, you're just renting his second bedroom.'

Mel raised her fingers. 'Renting his second bedroom.'

'Mel that is not an innuendo! I'm trying to be serious here.'

'Fine fine fine I was just trying to lighten the load.'

Tim sniggered. I looked over. 'Hey, you're emigrating, you're going to need to be a lot more mature now!'

He scrunched his face up. 'No I'm not, I'm going to have no strings apart from Gabs, no worries.'

'You heard from her much?'

He nodded. 'Yeah we're emailing all the time. She's leaving India at the weekend and flying to Thailand and then that's it,' he grinned, 'it's Tim time.'

Mel smiled. 'Still hundred percent sure?'

He nodded. 'Completely. Since I made the decision, actually no, since I told you guys I feel like a huge weight has been lifted. Besides, I know you both think I'm doing the right thing for me and that helps a lot too. I just can't wait to get on with the next stage you know.' He held his hands up. 'That doesn't mean I'm not upset at leaving you both though, yeah?'

I nodded. 'We know dude.'

He turned from his wardrobe and held up two shirts. 'So which one?'

Chapter Fifty-Four
September 13th 2008

THE BALL LEFT MY arm straight on and followed the arrows up towards the pins. At the last second it careered off to the right, clipping two skittles before wimpishly hiding in the corner.

'Ha, unlucky! I win, fancy another game?'

I turned to Tim and nodded. 'Dude we both failed to get into triple figures, that's hardly something to celebrate.'

He looked up from the plastic buttons beneath the screen and grinned. 'I know, but you failed by more than me!'

'By two pins! Anyway, I let you.'

'Course you did.'

'I did!' I protested. 'I know it'll be the last time you bowl in a very long time so I want you to go out on a high.'

'Obviously J, thanks for that. Now bowl, losers start first.'

I reached for a twelve pound and hurtled it down the runway, strike! I turned round and made a fist. From behind Tim two kids looked at the screen and laughed, pointing. I looked up. 'Tim, did you change my bowling name to Jack Ass again?'

He got up and picked up a ball. 'Yes I did, but remember it'll be the last time I go bowling in a while so please let me.'

'You're such a dick.'

'Shush Jack, I'm concentrating.'

I won the second game, setting it up nicely for the decider. We ordered another round of beers and potato skins and played on.

Halfway through the final game Tim wheeled around. 'That's not fair! The grease from the skins made the ball slip out of my hand! I want that cancelled.' He moved towards the keypad.

I intercepted him and pushed him to the bench. 'Don't you dare! That one counts, it's your own fault if you can't clean your hands properly.'

'Fine, but if you win it doesn't count.'

'Oh my God you are so annoying, how soon are you leaving again?'

He reached for another potato skin. 'One week today, don't pretend like you're not gonna miss me.'

I picked up a ball and walked towards the line. 'I won't, maybe I can find some friends that know how to bowl.' I took a run up and raised the ball behind me.

'Ahughaghaaagh. Woah, excuse me.'

I turned to Tim as the ball careered off to the side. 'You shit!'

He banged his chest. 'Horrible cough there. Ohh poor bowl J, guess we both had a bad round there. So, talk to me about the weekend, what's planned?'

I sat down and reached for my beer. 'Well it's up to you really, when are you coming back from your parents?'

He twisted his lips. 'Erm not sure. I think I can only take a day of the tearful goodbyes so if I go up Friday night, I'll be back Saturday afternoon, how does that work?'

I nodded. 'That works, we'll do it Saturday night. So are they not coming to the airport then?'

'Who?'

'Your parents?'

He shook his head. 'No, it's too far for them. My Mum would just get upset and Dad doesn't want to take a day off work so it's easier if I say goodbye on Friday.'

'He can't take a day off work to watch his son emigrate?'

He shrugged. I left it. 'So how are you getting to Heathrow on Tuesday?'

He grinned.

'Do I have to?'

He nodded. 'Yup, pull a sickie.'

'Great, that won't look suss, me and Rob being ill on the same day.'

'So let's just do me and you, or Mel as well if she can get the time off. Anyway, it's an early flight, you can go into work in the afternoon.'

'OK, that's cool, I'll have a twelve hour bug.'

He picked up the ball to begin again. 'Then how long you got?'

'Huh?'

'Until you move?'

'Just a few days really, we move the following weekend. Well, I'm moving, Mel's going to stay at Jazz's for a week and then moving.'

He turned from the alley. 'But we've still got another week of tenancy left, why is she leaving?'

I shrugged and walked over to pick up a ball. 'Dunno, probably doesn't want to be in the flat alone after us.'

Tim nodded. 'That's true. I always remember whenever anyone moved out at uni the saddest thing was walking into someone's room after they'd left and looking at the blank spaces, picturing all the memories that you'd created.'

I nodded. 'Well we're going to have to do that next week.'

He caught my eye and looked down.

'Yeah I know.'

I tapped his shoulder. 'Hey, I didn't mean to make you feel bad, I'm just saying it how it is.'

'I know, J.' He sat down on the bench, the bowling ball resting on the ground between his feet. 'I am fucking terrified.'

I sat down next to him. 'Of what?'

He shrugged. 'Everything. Leaving you guys, having no job, going to meet someone I barely know. Jesus,' he raised his hands to his hair, 'what the hell am I doing?!'

'Come on, no doubts. You know this is what you want to do.'

'I know, I know, but now that I've made that choice and things are in place, it's just feeling a little bit too real. I guess I'm also gearing up for saying bye to Mum and Dad.'

'Yeah but they'll come visit if you end up settling somewhere.'

He smiled. 'J, have you met my parents? They cling to each other for help if they have to come to London let alone Lima; they won't come see me and if I get settled I'm not gonna want to visit England, it'll be too hard.'

'You're being too tough on yourself, remember if it doesn't work out it doesn't work out, it won't make you a failure.'

He picked up the ball, rested it on his lap and began playing with the holes. 'I know, I'm not worried about having to face people if it doesn't work out, I'm worried about facing myself, because I want this to work more than anything.'

'Yeah but remember, settling somewhere and starting up a life isn't the same as settling somewhere with Gabi and starting up a life. You may find that it just doesn't work between the two of you when you get there, but that doesn't mean you have to come home.'

He got up, stretched and prepared to take his bowl. 'I know, actually the Gabi thing is the thing I'm worried about least.'

All the pins fell down. 'Alriiight.'

I got up to take my turn. 'Really? I'd be worried about that the most I think.'

'Yeah but that's because you've done the whole living abroad thing so you know that you can do it, whereas I've done the whole living with a girlfriend thing so I know that I can do that.'

'I guess, I hadn't thought of it like that before.'

He gave me a little nudge. 'Come on, your go.'

I took a run up and swung forward, strike. I turned and smiled. 'Getting towards a tight finish now!'

He waved his hand. 'You'll fall away. So how do you think Mel's gonna be? I think this is the hardest on her.'

'Definitely, she's been forced into moving whereas it was something we both wanted to do.' I chewed my lip. 'I dunno, I mean living one on one with Jazz will be quite intense I reckon, and that coupled with working in a hospital, yeah it's gonna be tough.'

'Well you're still gonna see her all the time though aren't you? The Jazz thing won't put you off will it?'

I shook my head. 'No way, course I'm gonna see her all the time. That Jazz thing really isn't an issue anymore, I just don't want to have to see her.'

'Well that's cool then.'

I carried on. 'I'm not sure what to do about that actually.'

'What?'

'Well, seeing Mel, having to go over to their flat and make polite small talk with Jazz. I dunno if it's just easier to meet her out.'

He got up to take his final bowl. 'Yeah but you can't just see Mel out, she works such long hours and anyway, people are always a little bit different in a bar to how they are at home.'

'You think?'

'Definitely, especially once you've lived with someone. Trust me, work through the awkwardness, if not for you then for Mel's sake.'

He took a run up and released the ball, nine pins toppled over.

'Shit!' He looked up at the screen. 'Jonathan Camfield, you require a strike to win.'

I picked up the ball. 'You just watch this.'

Chapter Fifty-Five
September 18th 2008

THE SETTING SUN GLINTED against the Gherkin, making it look like a burning torch watching over the city. Far in the distance Big Ben, dwarfed by the Millennium Wheel, chimed eight o'clock and from all directions they came. Well maybe that's a bit of an exaggeration seeing as Tim, Mel and I were already here and Rob and Emma arrived together. So, from the tube they came, armed with whatever food and drink they wanted to share. The premise was simple. No-one wanted to waste money by going to a club, getting hammered and forgetting chunks of the entire evening, so instead we decided to eat, drink, smoke weed and chill on top of Primrose Hill. I guess it was a befitting send off, a few close friends and a chilled out, laid back evening, just like Tim.

He was in a bit of a fragile state having just come from his parents' house. Saying goodbye must have been unimaginably hard for all concerned, and it was something I couldn't really relate to. I'd only ever left the country for a finite amount of time, like a year or six months, I always knew I was going to be walking back through those arrival gates. Tim wasn't sure about anything at the moment.

There was quite a melancholic atmosphere around, no-one was sure if they should be celebrating or commiserating or doing a bit of both. The hill was pretty busy, full of little groups like us gathered around a makeshift fire, huddled together on blankets, pretending summer was still here and pushing back hard with both hands and feet the encroaching autumn. A thick smell of weed and barbecue swirled around the top as people lay back to contemplate the view and at the same time everything else in the stratosphere.

Rob unzipped his cool bag and pulled out a bottle of champagne. 'Right, this is far too downbeat, Em get the glasses and Archers out.'

She reached into her bag and pulled out five plastic champagne flutes and filled each one with a shot of peach schnapps. Rob uncorked the champagne and poured the bottle out evenly between us. We all raised our glasses and paused, unsure of what we should drink to.

'To Tim?' Emma proposed but was immediately shouted down.

'To us?' said Rob, making Mel pretend to be sick on the grass.

'Fuck it,' Tim held his glass up. 'To good times gone and good times to come, wherever they may be.'

We raised our glasses and cheersed for what was the first but by no means the last time of the night.

Warm Salmon Salad with Asparagus, Carrot and Cucumber

Ingredients

- One salmon fillet
- Four to five sticks of asparagus
- Two carrots
- Handful of lettuce
- Half a cucumber
- Soy sauce
- Sake
- Sugar

Method

- Using a peeler, peel the whole of the carrots and cucumber; i.e. act as if you are just taking the outer skin off, but don't stop. The effect is a bed of noodles made from cucumber and carrot.

- Tear up the lettuce.

- Whip up some teriyaki sauce and cook the asparagus.

- After two minutes add the carrot, cucumber and lettuce.

- After two minutes more, add the salmon.

- Cook the salmon how you want, I literally do it for twenty seconds each side.

Adam Shaw

- Remove the mixture and place it all in a bowl (except the salmon).

- Remove the skin of the salmon (this should fall away easily).

- Using a sharp knife cut the salmon into about ten slices.

- Arrange salmon on top and pour over the remaining teriyaki sauce.

The streetlights surrounding the park were now our only source of light as we looked down on the twinkling city. Our alcohol was almost all gone and Rob was rolling up our last joint of the evening. We were all lying on our backs in a circle, heads resting against each other, gazing up and across. Like a game of pass the parcel the joint made its way round the circle, pausing every now and then to rest in someone's outstretched hands.

'Do you think she's the one Tim?'

I felt him shrug next to me. 'Dunno, she may be one of them.'

Emma laughed. 'But are you going out there thinking this is gonna be it?'

'No, I'm going out there to see if it'll work. I know full well I barely know her.'

'You say that but we did live with her for a week, I mean when you travel with someone you get to know them pretty quickly, get to know what they're made of.'

He turned his head to the side to look at Rob. 'That's true but I think you only get to know the travelling side of that person, not the person who'll work nine to five or work out which gas supplier to go with, y'know, the mundane things that we all have to do.'

'So you think she'll be different?'

He shrugged again. 'Maybe, but remember, whatever happens we're planning on at least nine months' travelling first before we even think about stopping. It could have gone tits up by then or I may know for sure that it's her. Either way I can't wait to find out.'

'So jealous.' Mel turned over and rested her head on her hands, 'Apart from you Tim, and you don't count anyway as you're leaving

358

us, we are all single here. That's ridiculous, there are people much uglier than us out there who have partners.'

'Well we're picky aren't we?'

Mel smiled at Emma and poked Tim in the ribs. 'You may be Emma, but I'm not!'

'Objection!' Tim said.

'No seriously,' Emma continued, 'I mean it's not as if we haven't been getting any action, we're just choosing not to do anything more with it.'

Rob turned to Emma. 'Are you sure you're talking to the right people? Ems, do you know the last time I had sex?'

She pushed his shoulder. 'No, and I don't want to either, but I do know you pulled someone last weekend.'

'Yeah but that was nothing, just a random pull.'

'But that's it,' she insisted. 'It was nothing because you chose not to do anything about it. I think we're doing OK.'

'I'm with Rob on this one here', I added, 'no one's interested in me at the moment.'

'Oh that's crap J, you had a great three months with Jazz ...'

'In January, and it was more like two months.'

'Hush, you practically sleep with a girl in the office who is clearly crazy about you and if it wasn't for some fat rich twerp with a house in Italy, Jazz would probably be here right now. No, you're OK, I wouldn't worry!'

'Exactly,' Mel said, 'I think out of all of us here I'm doing the worst. Apart from you,' she prodded Tim, 'I can't remember the last person who showed an ounce of interest in me and it's getting me down.'

Tim reached out and rested his hand on her leg. 'Mel, you're look-ing too hard, plus there are plenty of guys who would kill to be with you, I know I did. Just be like you were around me when we first got together and you'll be beating them away with a stick.'

I heard her smile. 'How was I when I was first around you?'

Tim paused. 'Drunk.'

The circle dissolved into hysterics.

'Tim!' She began hitting him as hard as she could. He put up his hands to block her.

He laughed. 'I'm sorry, but you walked into that one! But I mean it, you are looking too hard, concentrate on other stuff, friends, whatever, and the rest will come.'

She turned back to the stars and lay down with a sigh. 'It better.'

Chapter Fifty-Six
September 22nd 2008

INDICATING TO LEAVE THE motorway and following the signs to Terminal Four, I glanced in the mirror at Mel, her head resting on Tim's red rucksack, eyes vacantly gazing out of the window at the passing scenery. Tim was to my left, studying his air tickets intensely, checking for the hundredth time that the words hadn't changed themselves around to read something different. He kept checking his watch whilst intermittently drumming his fingers on the dashboard. There wasn't really that much more to say to be honest. Goodbyes had been said and done over the last few days, and now that we had left the house, well Tim was pretty much gone. My thoughts drifted to this afternoon, about whether I could be arsed to go into work and when I should start my packing. I looked at Tim again and realised that all of these thoughts no longer involved him for they belonged to another time. I found it really sad that Tim would probably never know what I would have for dinner tonight, or what work would be like tomorrow, and I would never know what film he would watch on the plane. When you spend months or years hearing the every ins and outs of someone's life, to have it suddenly cease is a very strange concept. Would we now always be telling each other about each other's lives rather than making new memories?

I parked in the short stay and grabbed a trolley. I reached for Tim's rucksack but he intercepted me and grabbed my forearm. 'My silly tradition remember, from the minute I leave to the minute I come back home I have to carry my own bag. I've done it since I was fourteen and nothing bad has ever really happened, humour my superstitions OK?'

I stepped aside and watched him reach into the car.

We waited for the automatic doors to open and made our way slowly to the bank of computer screens.

Scanning the destinations Mel pointed and said, 'Bangkok, cancelled indefinitely. Tim, you have to stay now, let's go home,' she reached for his hand.

He smiled and gripped it. 'There it is, check in desk seventy-two. You guys gonna walk me to passport control?'

I sighed. 'If we have to.'

We ambled towards the check in desk. The queue was annoyingly short and within a few minutes Tim was free of his bag. There was nothing left to do now.

Mel lunged for his passport. 'OK, I'm gonna eat it, then you can't go.' She opened her mouth and tried to fit it in. She began to cough and choke, pulled the passport out and handed it back to Tim. 'I should have thought that through more. Here, something to remember me by.'

He reached for it. 'Thanks Mel, I'll never wash my passport again.'

'You're welcome.'

We all stood around, shifting our weight from foot to foot. He looked at his watch. 'I should ...' he jerked his thumb towards the open doorway.

I nodded. 'Yeah, I guess you probably should.'

He walked towards me and hugged me tightly. 'You take care OK.'

I squeezed him back. 'Email me when you get there OK, and say hi to Gabs for me. Good luck dude.'

We separated and he turned to Mel. She smiled at him through her tears. 'I'm very proud of you Tim, it's gonna be amazing.'

He smiled, enveloped her with his arms and kissed her cheek. 'Thank you.'

He looked to both of us and began to back away, he opened his mouth and then closed it again. Smiling he looked at us once more before turning round and walking towards passport control.

I put my arm around Mel and watched him walk away. He reached the chain before pausing, turning round and walking back quickly towards us.

'Look, I just want to say that you guys,' he raised his hands, 'you guys mean so much to me. Really, you're my family, leaving you is killing me.'

He walked towards Mel and put his arms around her. 'I was in love with you, and it was amazing.' He leaned forward and kissed her forehead gently, letting his lips linger. 'Thank you for giving me that feeling and I'm so sorry if I ever hurt you.'

She hugged him tighter. 'No need to apologise Tim.'

'And you,' he looked at me, 'well J, I don't know what I would've done if it wasn't for you. I can't count the amount of times you've been there for me.'

I put my arms around him and hugged him tightly. 'And you for me Tim, you're my best friend, I love you.'

I let him go and he looked at both of us. Tears ran down his cheeks but his smile shone through.

'That was a much better goodbye.' He swallowed. 'Take care guys.'

He turned around, walked towards the desk and disappeared.

Leaving Heathrow my eyes followed each plane that took off and even though I knew he wasn't on any of them, I said goodbye each time the wings disappeared into the clouds. I drove home slowly as if my driving reflected my thoughts, aimless and lethargic. We didn't say much in the car, once again there wasn't a whole much to say and in a way, I think we both would've preferred it if we were leaving the flat today too instead of being in this long drawn-out goodbye that the three of us had started enacting.

Mel turned to look at me and rested her hand on my hand that covered the gear stick. 'I don't want to go to work today, I'm exhausted. These last few weeks,' she gestured with her hands as if the weeks were right in front of her, 'have just wiped me out. Especially today.'

I moved out of the fast lane to let a Bentley pass, breaking off the contact with Mel. 'Don't then, you work too hard anyway. Give work a call now.'

'Will you stay home with me?'

I glanced to my left and caught her looking at me. 'I dunno, I'm pretty busy at the moment.'

'Ah come on, you already pulled a sickie this morning, just tell them it hasn't lifted yet. Let's shut ourselves away from the world just for today.'

I indicated and pulled back in to the fast lane. It was almost twelve; I wouldn't be in work until well after two, to do what, three hours' work? Fuck it.

'OK, let's get a DVD on the way home.'

'Good, I knew you'd fold.' She smiled and turned back to looking at the road ahead.

I opened the door and climbed the stairs to the kitchen. I did a subconscious double take at Tim's closed door before going in to unpack the shopping. Neither of us had much money at the moment and what with us moving at the weekend we had barely any food. Most meat was off the menu as there was no point freezing packets of chicken breast or mince and so I'd just picked up a few eggs and vegetables for a Mexican omelette.

Mexican Omelette

Ingredients
- Four eggs
- One green chilli
- Six asparagus stalks
- Two vine tomatoes
- Fresh coriander
- Fresh spinach

- One white onion
- Splash of milk
- Black pepper
- Fresh rosemary

Method

- Boil up the asparagus in a little salt for two minutes or so.

- Slice the chilli and onions and cook on a low heat for a few minutes.

- Whisk up the eggs with a little milk and rosemary.

- Pour the eggs into the pan and add the sliced tomatoes.

- Slice the asparagus into about four to five pieces per stalk and add to the pan.

- Finally rip up the spinach and coriander, add to the pan and stir quickly before the eggs set.

- Once it's all mixed in let the eggs set, flip the omelette and serve.

- If you're hungry, serve on some bread and a bit of green salad. You only want to just cook it so it's all runny.

I poured the mixture into the pan and put two plates into the oven to warm up.

'Two minutes Mel!' I shouted into the lounge. I flipped the eggs and carried on cooking for a further minute; Mel still hadn't come into the kitchen. I took the pan off of the heat and went into the lounge to find her but the room was empty. Turning around I saw Tim's door ajar, the sunlight reflecting brightly on the white walls. Entering the room I saw Mel standing in the middle looking out of the window. I went up to her and put my arms around her from behind and felt as her head moved backwards slightly and rested on my chest.

'It's just so empty. It's horrible.' Her voice echoed around the bare room. 'Can you imagine if I'd have stayed and you both left, how horrible this flat would be right now.'

'I know, you almost can't picture him here now, even though this room was so him.'

'It doesn't even smell of him anymore.'

'And the problem with that is …?'

She bucked her hips against me and pushed me back. 'Shush, you know what I mean.'

I pulled her tighter. 'Yeah I know.' I looked around, only the mattress remained on the bed whilst the pine wardrobe door hung almost apologetically half open, like some sad sort of dog. His bookcase was covered in circles of unbleached wood where his whisky collection once stood and the walls still had small blue blotches on from where he had stuck pictures up with blu-tac. Mel broke the silence. 'Let's eat, I'm starving.'

We polished off the omelettes and washed up with the radio on. I emptied our packets of Revels into a bowl and walked into the lounge to find Mel drawing the curtains. I hovered in the doorway. 'Fancy watching it in one of our rooms? I feel like lying down.'

She smiled. 'Sounds good, shot not mine, it's a tip.'

I pushed my door open with my foot and began turning on my laptop whilst Mel drew my curtains. I loaded the DVD and turned to find her already curled up under the covers. I pressed play, lifted up one side of the duvet and slid in beside her.

'This was such a good idea, I can't imagine being in work right now.'

'No me neither.' She glanced at her watch. 'Two o'clock, he's just taken off. I bet he's fast asleep.'

'Speaking of which …'

'Hey,' she pinched me, 'you are staying awake for this film, it's amazing. Now pay attention, I'll quiz you at the end.' She lifted my arm and put it around her shoulders, snuggling underneath it.

I opened my eyes and was immediately confused by the blue glare around the room. I moved my head and saw that the light was coming from my laptop and after a quick glance to my left that it was also coming up to six o'clock. I remembered nothing from the film. Mel was also asleep, her head resting underneath my arm and her hands clasping my other arm that encircled her. I ignored the cracks of light around my curtains telling me it was a beautiful late summer evening and closed my eyes once more.

I opened my eyes again later and lay there, still. I was thick with sleep, still too groggy to move. I felt all fuzzy, aware that I could go back to sleep but also aware that if I slept now, I'd never sleep later. I listened to Mel's breathing; it was shallow so she must be coming out of a deep sleep too. I pulled her closer, enjoying her heat even though it was warm enough in the flat and under the covers. Her hands twitched and separated from mine as she slightly adjusted her body. My hand, no longer supported by hers, dangled down and brushed past her hand again. Ever so slowly, almost unconsciously, she began to trace around my fingers with her own, as if she were holding a pencil in her hands and trying to find a way out of a maze in a puzzle book. I gently took her other hand in mine and began doing the same thing, rhythmically, thoroughly and sleepily, as if every part of her hand had to be covered inch by inch.

Her hand left my hand and began to trace its way up and down my forearm, her nails causing shivers to run throughout my arm. Once again she did it rhythmically, sweeping her hand up and down as if conducting an orchestra. My hand dangled down by her stomach and using my little finger to lift up her top I began to do the same. My hand hovered just above her belly button and as I extended and then closed my hand again and again so that my fingers lightly brushed her, I felt her stomach convulse with exactly the same kind of shivers she was giving me.

Leaving my forearm, her hand travelled up towards my shoulders and neck before raising her hand to my mouth and running a finger across my lips. Opening my eye a crack I could make out her closed eyes in the half light, a small smile playing at the end of her mouth. She began to push down slightly on my lip, pressing her finger millimetre by millimetre into my mouth. I began to nibble on the top of her finger as with her other hand she clasped mine, our fingers interlocking.

Mel slid her hand down my chest and wormed her way under my shirt. Gently scratching me she ran her fingers up and down my side across the sensitive skin. I pushed all thoughts from my head and carried on toying with her stomach, my fingers running across her abdomen as if they were trying to stretch out and escape my wrists. She turned into me so her head lay on my chest and her hand dropped down to my waist. I began to trace an S shape into the small of her back, the lightness of my touch causing Mel to arch her back in pleasure and press herself closer to me. Her hand moved across and began to touch first my stomach and then my chest. Fingers directed themselves to my nipples, which she grazed ever so slightly with the tips of her fingers, her hands tracing a figure of eight across my chest.

She whispered into the darkness, 'I feel like I'm exploring you.'

I reached up and ran my fingers firmly down her back as she completely arched her back and opened her eyes. She lifted her head and looked at me, gently moving her face towards mine. I looked up, angling my face towards hers, our eyes never separating from each other's. She was millimetres away from me, I could feel her breathing. I lifted my head and we kissed deeply, our lips pressing hard against each other's. Extending my fingers around the base of her head I pushed her down onto me and breathed deeply.

She rolled over, pulled me on top of her and ran her hands up my back. Moving her hands round to the front she began unbuttoning my shirt as, to support myself, my hands dug deep either side of her into the mattress. Mel wrapped her arms around my now bare shoulders and pulled me down onto her, my body pressing down on top of hers.

I ran my fingers down her T-shirt and lifted the cotton up. Her skin felt warm and I began to trace a line up her chest as she broke off from kissing me and began working her lips towards my neck and ear. My hand reached her bra and cupped her right breast, fingers skimming over the already exposed nipple. Her lips brushed my ear and I felt her hot breath on my face as I reached around to unhook her bra. I sat up and pulled her up, lifting her T-shirt off of her and dropping it to the foot of the bed. For a second as I took her top off our lips separated and we looked at each other straight in the eyes. I smiled, she smiled but still neither of us spoke, still neither of us needed to.

Now both sitting we kissed again as my hands found her breasts. I cupped each in my hands and raised my thumbs across her nipples, tracing my way back and forth over them as they began to harden. My hands gripped firmer as she reached around and ran her nails down my back. I pulled her down on top of me and we kissed once more, both of us enjoying the thrill of new skin on new skin. I bent my leg, which lay in between hers and pressed it close and up towards her. She moved her body down and up hard against my leg as I felt her heat through her trousers.

Gradually we kissed deeper and started pulling at each other's lips with our teeth as first my hands and then Mel's began to move down each other's chests. Her hand hovered over my belt before working its way down, feeling me through my jeans, gripping me and ever so slightly squeezing. As my hands moved down her body she opened her legs to me, slightly raising her hips and letting my fingers press firmly against her. Almost simultaneously we began reaching for each other's belts, pulling at them frantically as if we were running out of time. Not wanting to break away from her I moved her hands away from me and concentrated on undoing her belt and trousers. I undid her belt and pulled at one side of her trousers, loosening the zip and letting me pull them down and eventually off of her. She did the same to me and then clambered on top, her legs either side of me, her groin burning down onto mine. I sat up, wrapping my arms around her, and enveloped her in my arms. She pushed me back and lay to my side, pulling my face towards hers. She slid her fingers down under my waistband and took me in her hand, holding me tightly. With my left hand I lifted her thigh to me and began touching her through her thong. Running my fingers across the material she sighed into my mouth and began moving her hand quicker. I hooked my thumbs underneath her thong and began pulling it down. She pulled me back to her lips as one finger followed by another moved down and slowly entered her. Raising my thumb I moved it across her clit, encircling and brushing it, causing her to groan and lean into me. Motioning to me that I should take my boxers off, I eased them down without breaking contact with her lips. Pushing me back down onto the bed her hands traced the inside of my thighs as I continued to move in and out of her. As my fingers began to quicken, so did hers.

Mel broke off and placed her hands either side of my head. Kissing me on the lips she looked at me intently. 'J, shall we …?'

This felt so completely right, how had I not seen it before?

'Yes,' I answered.

She leant in to kiss me and clambered on top. My hands raised themselves to her breasts and pulled them towards my mouth as she sighed and closed her eyes. Lifting herself slightly above me she gripped me with her hand and began touching herself with me. Moving me back and forth, up to her clit and down she smiled as she bit her lower lip. I placed my hands on her hips and pulled her slowly down on to me, that incredible, warm feeling invading and taking me over. She leant forward and placed her hands behind my head and pushed down on me, moving her lips down onto mine. I pressed them hard against hers and bit her lip. Resting her hands on my chest Mel sat up and back, groaning softly. I licked my thumb and moved it down to play with her and she pressed it close to her body. Our eyes locked in on each other's as she took my other hand and lifted it up to her breast, then taking both my hands gripped them and pushed them down onto the bed so that I could go deeper. She took the lead and began moving to her own rhythm, her tongue pressing deep inside my mouth as her hips moved back and forth and then around and around in a circle. We began to quicken and I moved my hands down to grip her from behind, pushing her down harder onto me. As I raised my hips towards her she pushed herself down on to me, quicker and quicker until her lips broke off from mine and she began to sigh deeply. We moved quicker still as she ground herself down on to me. A loud groan escaped her lips, followed by another and another as I pushed myself up inside her for the last time until finally both of us collapsed back onto each other, our heavy breathing filling up the darkened room.

For a little while neither of us spoke. She lay on top of me, her cheek resting on my chest, her hand gently toying with the hair around my left nipple. I was still inside of her and neither one of us moved to change that. Mel lifted her head up, her long hair falling down onto my chest and looked at me, smiling sleepily. 'I can't believe we just did that!'

I smiled back. 'I know, where did that come from?!'

She paused. 'You don't regret that do you?' she asked anxiously.

I shook my head. 'God no, that was incredible! Why, do you?'

'No, not at all.'

She folded herself back down onto me and ran her hand down to my stomach. I rested my hand on the small of her back and looked up to the ceiling.

'What are you thinking?' I asked.

'That I always knew we'd do that one day. Did you?'

I nodded. 'Yeah, yeah I guess so.' I grinned. 'There's always been something, hasn't there?'

She smiled and moved up to kiss me, 'Yeah, there has, I guess neither of us know what that something is yet.' She bit her lip and moved her hand down my body. 'Do you want to see if we can find out what that something is again?'

Chapter Fifty-Seven
September 25th 2008

I HADN'T BEEN TO work since Monday. Mel hadn't been to work since Monday. We hadn't really left the flat since Tuesday and I was having the time of my life. Mel and I didn't make it out of bed that night, well we did make it out of bed but only so far as the floor, the kitchen table and the couch, followed by the shower the next morning.

I don't think either of us knows where this was heading, if anywhere, but neither of us were questioning it right now. The whole thing, well it feels good and it feels good for both of us so we're just going with it. Sure if I analysed myself I may think, well our best friend had just left the country, we were both feeling low and we reached out for each other, or we were both feeling low at the prospect of moving away from each other and reached out, but I believe thinking that would undermine it. All I know is that I'm loving being with her at the moment, and what we've got going on makes the thought of moving out a hell of a lot easier. We've talked about it and decided to just see what happens, no pressure. I guess starting something up with your best friend carries with it so many risks that we'd be foolish to plunge into it head first, but then again locking yourself away from the world and spending all day in bed together for four days, well that's kinda plunging in isn't it?

We were both packing up the flat, something that was taking a lot longer to do than we'd thought. I was in my room, Mel was in hers, the radio on the stairs was turned up loud enough for us both to hear and aid us in our packing. I was tired of packing my life up, tired of being able to cram all my belongings into the back of a one-litre-engine car. I really did wonder if I was doing the right thing, heading south and moving in with just Rob, when at the moment all I really wanted to do was stay here with Mel.

Feeling her arms wrap themselves around my waist I leant back and turned my head, kissing her lightly on the lips.

'Hows the packing going?'

I shrugged. 'OK, how about yours?'

'Same, I just can't be arsed to be honest, it's such a hassle.'

'When's Jazz coming?'

She looked at her watch. 'About two hours I think. I reckon two trips in her car will do it. You going to stay around and help lift boxes?'

I shook my head. 'We've got to go to the estate agents to pick up the keys. The office is in Battersea so it'll take ages.'

She nodded. 'I'll be gone by the time you're back y'know.'

'I know. I'm not looking forward to being here on my own really.'

She pushed me lightly. 'Man up, Rob will be here won't he?'

'Yeah I guess so.'

I put my arms around her and held her close, my chin resting on the top of her head. We stood there for a while gently rocking back and forth, thinking about the new places we'd both be sleeping in that night.

'I'm going to miss this.'

I looked down. 'What do you mean?'

'This, living together. It's so comfortable with you.'

'I know, it's been what, four years out of six living together already?'

She nodded. 'Yeah. Can you imagine telling our nineteen-year-old selves about the week we've just had?!'

I smiled. 'I'd be over the moon, you know I fancied you in freshers' week!'

'And it only took you six years, you fast mover you.'

I kissed her. 'Shush you. And anyway, it's not as if we're not gonna be seeing each other much, especially now, especially after this week.'

She looked up at me. 'You promise the whole Jazz thing isn't gonna be a problem?'

I shook my head. 'Promise, and if I do find it awkward I'll get over it, nothing is going to keep me from seeing you.'

She turned coy. 'Really?'

'Really, this is feeling pretty amazing Mel.'

She grinned, 'It is isn't it'

She looked at her watch, reached for my hand and pulled me towards the door. 'Want to help me pack? We've still got a few hours ∴..'

I pulled her towards me and kissed her deeply, 'Lead the way.'

OCTOBER

Chapter Fifty-Eight
October 3rd 2008

I WALKED OUT OF Fulham Broadway station, reached for my A to Z of London and after glancing at the right page took a left. Winter was on its way, making me do up the top button on my trench coat for the first time since March. Suits filed past me, sure of their destination, not wanting to waste another minute in the cold and away from their loved ones. I stepped into a Sainsbury's Local, something that seems to have popped up outside every tube station in the last few years and headed for the limited wine section. My eyes scanned the prices for the offer of the week before hesitating and reaching for the more expensive bottle. I'm going to be twenty-five in December, the time has come to choose wine that costs more than a fiver. The enormous queue was thankfully matched by the dozen checkout guys who smiled and processed us through the tills, the booming computer voice directing us to till numbers prohibited any small talk with the cashiers.

Clutching my bag I left the shop and carried on, the biting wind whipping against my hand that clasped the wine and making it ice cold immediately. I sank the bottle into my deep pocket, scrunched my hand up inside my jacket and looked for a florist. I found myself making the usual London presumption that there must be whatever shop I want within eyeshot and I became irritated when I saw no flowers on show. Scanning the parade I cursed myself for not buying flowers in Victoria when I first left work. Oh well, flowers and wine are a crummy housewarming anyway, I'll get her something nice over the weekend.

Mel had moved in a few days ago and I was yet to see the place as Rob and I had been so busy trying to get our own flat sorted. It was so far so good with him, the house was great, I loved my room and we weren't winding each other up, in fact now we were living together we were seeing each other less to be honest. Balham was going great too, and making the move to South London really hadn't proved that different. I was still pouring myself onto the Northern Line each morning, just from a different end.

Mel had ended up spending most of last week at mine, as sharing Jasmine's room and bed until they both moved had proved to be pretty tricky. Things had gone well between us and it now seemed something real. Taking those four days off of work last month and shutting ourselves away in the flat was brilliant but at some point you have to go back to real life, which was exactly what we were now doing. It had taken me a while to tell Rob, perhaps that was to do with the whole not-seeming-real aspect of it at the start, but he wasn't surprised at all when I did. I waited a few days until after we'd moved in as there was so much else going on, but when Mel called me to tell me she was coming over the next day I figured I had to tell him everything.

'Yeah I figured she'd be coming over a bit this week, that's cool. Are you gonna give her the couch or let her share your bed?'

'My bed for sure.' I looked at the couch. 'It's a nice couch, don't get me wrong, but it doesn't look that great to sleep on.'

Rob looked hurt. 'But I picked this one out, I thought it went with the curtains and carpet.'

'If by that Rob you mean they're all blue, then yes it does go, anyway I'm not talking about the colour, I just mean it's a bit hard to sleep on. Besides, it's getting cold, the lounge will be freezing in the mornings.'

He looked at me.

'What?'

'You're hiding something.'

'What? What are you talking about?'

'You're grinning and won't look me in the eye, what's up?'

I reached for my jacket. 'Let's go find our local, I've got a few things I want to talk to you about.'

We headed down to "The Bedford", an enormous, sprawling pub just by Balham station that would now become our local. Doubling as a comedy venue, music venue and club on the weekends "The Bedford" was a landmark of Balham, the sort of place that everyone knows. I ordered two pints of Bombardier and went over to the table where Rob was studying a local newspaper for upcoming events. Looking up and seeing me coming he smiled and folded the newspaper away.

'So, something's happening with Mel then?'

My eyes widened. 'Impressive! How the hell did you guess?'

'Dude, everyone in the world has been seeing it coming for months, we just always wondered if you'd ever take the plunge or not.'

I sat back and drank from my glass. 'Well I guess I did then.'

'How's the water?'

I smiled. 'Getting better every day.'

He nodded his head slowly. 'You and Mel, you and Mel, Jeez I don't know where to start. OK, talk me through it.' He paused. 'Hang on, last week you weren't ill at all were you?!'

I gave a pathetic cough. 'Course I was.'

'You were in bed with Mel weren't you?!'

I grinned. 'We left the house once in four days, and that was to go to the deli to get food for a picnic in bed.'

'Wow,' he sat back, 'I didn't realise it was like that. OK, how you feeling about it all?'

'Ha,' I put my drink down, 'where shall I start? How am I feeling about starting something up with my best friend, how am I feeling about possibly betraying my other best friend who may be still in love with her, or how am I feeling about how the girl I'm with is now living with a girl who up until two months ago I was crazy about. Where shall I start?!'

Rob shook his finger at me as he drank his pint. 'No dramatics from you J, half of what you've just said doesn't apply. Listen, you two might never have seen this coming but as I said everyone else did, including Tim.'

I cocked my head. 'Really? What, did you speak about this recently?'

'Well obviously not that recently but yeah, a week or so before he left. I think it was the night after you guys went bowling.'

'Oh yeah, so what did he say?'

'Well it was all hypothetical 'cause no-one knew what would happen but, hang on …' He raised his empty glass and held up two fingers at the girl behind the bar who nodded and started to pour another two pints. 'What was I saying? Oh yeah, I don't think he does feel that way about her anymore. I think we haven't given him enough credit about Gabi, he's properly smitten you know.'

We paused as the barmaid brought over the two drinks.

'Thanks, yeah I know he is, but being smitten for someone new doesn't necessarily change what you feel for someone else.'

'Dude I think it does, stop looking for obstacles because there aren't any. He said he can see you guys together and that he'd be OK with that.'

'Yeah but he has to say that, he's on the other side of the world. He can't expect Mel to sit and cry in the corner for the rest of her life, he wants her to be happy, we both know that.'

Rob shook his head. 'He doesn't have to say that, God you're really not hearing what I'm saying are you? Listen, Tim cares about Mel, wants her to be happy, he cares about you, wants you to be happy and he has actually said that you both getting together would be for the best as he'd know you were both happy and he wouldn't have to worry about either of you.'

I cocked my head. 'Really?'

'Yes really,' he said exasperatedly. 'Why would I lie? Now whether he'll still say that when it's a reality as opposed to a fantasy I dunno. I take it you haven't told him?'

I shook my head. 'No, not yet, I want to see what this is going to be first.'

Rob changed the subject. 'Have you heard from him much? I got that two-liner email saying he'd landed and it was all good but nothing since then.'

'No me neither, I guess he's too caught up in it all for the moment.'

'I hope it's going OK ...' Rob pondered.

'I'm sure it will be, if she asked him to come out then she's got to feel just what he does,' I shrugged, 'more maybe.'

He nodded. 'Yeah I guess. Anyway, onto Jazz.'

'You mean Mel?'

He laughed. 'No I actually meant Jazz, ahh this is going to be funny.'

'What?!'

'Them living together, it's hysterical. Anyway, you're worried about the Tim factor; not a worry, same goes for Jazz.'

'Really? I just can't be arsed to see her.'

'Yeah but firstly, you're gonna have to and after a while it'll be fine, and secondly Mel is gonna feel as uncomfortable about it as you are, more so in fact so will probably come to ours more, it's fine. Anyway,' he looked at me straight on, 'all of that was in the past, wasn't it?'

I nodded. 'Yeah, yeah it was.'

'Good, 'cause I think I speak for all of our friends when I say that you guys are gonna be great together, but screw her around and I'll kill you, Mel's awesome.'

I smiled. 'Firstly we don't have any other friends and secondly I'm not gonna screw her around, Rob, I know how awesome she is.'

He looked at his empty glass. 'Shall we get another?'

I nodded. 'Shot not.'

He sighed and moved over to the bar. Returning grinning he set the drinks down and threw a few bags of crisps at me. I opened the crisps, tearing three sides of the packets so they lay open on the table. Picking up one I dipped it in my bitter before crunching it. Rob looked at me in disgust. 'After all this time that still makes me sick.'

I shrugged my shoulders. 'After all this time your face still makes me sick. I've gotten over it, you can do the same.'

He shook his head slowly from side to side in a 'you're so funny' kind of way. 'Anyway, so now we've got Tim and Jazz out of the way, onto Mel.'

I dipped another crisp. 'What about her?'

'Well, what are you feeling, what's going on? And stop dipping those damn crisps!' He reached out and hit my hand.

I wiped my hands on my jeans and paused before answering, 'I can feel myself getting swept up in it very quickly. It's weird, I really really want to go for it, but it's Mel, there's so much to lose if it goes tits up.'

'And if it doesn't?'

'Then it's amazing.'

'Then you got to go for it, surely?'

I nodded. 'This is the first time it's felt real.'

'Well this is the first time you've talked about it isn't it?'

'Yeah it is. I am going to go for it, I know full well it will be amazing and if it doesn't work then hey,' I shrugged, 'it doesn't work, at least we'll both know. I guess I was saying I was worried about Tim and Jazz because once you take them out of the equation there's nothing stopping us, and that scares me a little bit.'

Rob sat back and nodded in a 'well done J, tell me something I don't know' kind of way.

I looked up from my pint. 'Have you ever been out with your best friend before?'

He shook his head. 'No. Megan became my best friend, but no we were never best friends to start with. Is it different?'

I paused for a moment. 'Yeah it is, because you already know pretty much everything about each other anyway so there's no getting to know each other. You know the whole post-sex lying in bed talking for hours about your past thing, well I started doing that a few days ago with Mel before realising I've told her every story at least six times.'

Rob laughed. 'It must make it awkward in a way.'

'A bit, but then again it's also more comfortable, neither of you have to pretend to be anything you're not.'

'And how's the sex?'

'You really want to know?!'

'Well no, I don't mean a blow by blow detail, believe it or not the thought of you both together actually makes me feel sick; I just mean how is it with your best friend?'

'Well the same as how it was with Megan when you were together I guess; it's amazing, it's so much better when you're with someone you love.'

He raised an eyebrow. 'Love?'

I paused then nodded. 'That's the thing, when you start something with your best friend you sort of bypass the early stuff. It's pretty hard taking it slow when you're used to seeing each other every day.'

'Yeah but love, J? Already?'

I shook my head. 'No no no, I personally believe you can never be in love with someone until you're actually going out with them, and we've only been together for like a week, but …'

'What?'

'Well I already love her as a person and this last week has been amazing.' I shrugged. 'I dunno, I just can't see it being that far off. That's all.'

I leapt up the two steps to the door and rang the bell. She opened the door and smiled, extending her cheek for me to kiss it.

'Hey J! Come in.'

I avoided the outstretched cheek and walked past her and into the hallway.

'Hey, Mel in?'

She pulled her head back and shut the door. 'Yeah she's in her room unpacking.'

I nodded and looked at the door behind her, avoiding eye contact. 'And where's that? I haven't been here before.'

'Oh right yeah, first on the left upstairs. I'm just about to put the kettle on, you want something?' asked Jazz.

I shook my head and climbed the stairs. Fuck you.

Mel smiled at me and opened her arms. I walked towards her and gathered her up, kissing her on the lips.

'So, what do you think?! I love this room.'

I looked around. A big double bed was the centrepiece, jutting out from the wall in the middle of the room, either side of which stood two built-in wardrobes. Her open window faced out onto the setting October sun, casting rays of light all over the cream walls that were quickly becoming covered in pictures of Mel's travels and uni days.

I grinned. 'I like it, I like it a lot. How's it going? You settling in ok?'

She nodded. 'Yeah.' She lowered her voice, 'Did you guys speak?'

'Well she opened the door, we had to.'

'And how was it?'

'Fine, I just came straight up here.'

She hit my chest with the back of my hand, 'Why did you do that?!'

'What?! I've got nothing to say to her.'

She let me go and went back to sticking blu-tac on the back of her pictures. 'Yeah, but for me OK, make the effort.'

I sighed, 'Fine, I will when I have to, OK. The real reason was that I wanted to get up here as soon as possible and not waste time talking with her because I've missed you too much.'

Mel looked at me and shook her head. 'You are such a bullshitter, Camfield!'

I shrugged. 'What?! Believe it or not Clarke, I'm actually telling the truth!'

She smiled. 'Uhuh. You get an email from Tim today?'

I shook my head. 'Nup, why did you?'

She nodded. 'Yeah, quite a long one.'

I frowned. 'Really, what time was that? I haven't been online for a few hours.'

'No, it was first thing this morning, they're ahead, he'll be in bed by now.'

'Oh.'

She came over and pinched my cheek. 'Look at you! You're so jealous!'

I shrugged her off. 'No I'm not.'

Mel put her arms around me and looked up. 'Yes you are, it's adorable.'

I kissed her forehead. 'Fine, maybe a little bit, how is he?'

She backed away. 'Well I don't know if I should tell you, that email was meant for me.'

'Mel!'

'What?' She smiled at me from across the room, a playful look in her eyes.

I moved towards her. 'How's Tim?'

She shrugged and moved back towards the bed. 'Dunno, he didn't really say.'

'Yes he did.'

She giggled. 'You're right he did, but I won't tell you.'

I smiled. 'Oh you'll tell me.'

She raised an eyebrow and whispered. 'Make me.'

I leapt round and tackled her onto the bed. We landed on top of each other and rolled to the side. I leant in to kiss her and she moved her head back. 'And just what do you think you're doing?'

In between kissing her neck and biting the soft skin under her jaw I whispered, 'Turning you on.'

She smiled and looked down at me. 'And why would you want to do that?'

I rolled on top of her and carried on kissing, my hands pushing her back down into the soft bed. 'Because I want to.'

She arched her back and raised herself towards me, 'And what, what if I don't want you to?'

I moved my hands down and lifted her skirt, my hands running up her legs. 'So ask me to stop,' I murmured into her neck. I moved my lips across, brushing hers. She moved to kiss me again but I pulled away, unzipped her hoodie and began to kiss her stomach, lips brushing over the slight bulge of muscle. I could feel her press herself against my hand as she lay back, head resting on a pillow.

'So is this how you make me tell you then? Turn me on and expect, expect me to tell you anything?'

I moved down off of the bed so that I was kneeling on the floor between Mel's legs which dangled off of the bed and rested on each shoulder of mine. I began to kiss my way up her thighs, reached up and slowly began to pull her underwear down.

I smiled as I tossed her French knickers to the floor and pulled her close to my lips. 'Pretty much.'

The CD finished and all went quiet. We both lay naked and intertwined, wanting and requiring nothing more from the world for tonight.

'So how is he?'

She laughed. 'I'd forgotten about that, he's good, great.' She turned around and faced me. 'He said everything with Gabi was going amazingly and that he's never been happier.'

I smiled. 'Awesome, what else?'

'Erm, not much really, it was quite rambling. Bangkok is as hectic and dirty as ever so they're getting out of there as soon as. They're both heading to an island together, just the two of them to get some space from everyone, chill out and probably shag each other's brains out.'

I shrugged. 'Well why not?'

Laughing she rolled on top of me and kissed me hard. 'Exactly, if we're doing it why shouldn't they?!'

I reached up and held her tight. 'I'm so glad it seems to be working out, he must have been shitting himself.'

She nodded into my chest. 'Mmhhmm, but just goes to show, Carpe Diem and all that.'

'Too true, seize the day and never look back.'

We lapsed into silence as we both flew into the clouds in our minds.

'Did you reply?' I said to the ceiling.

I felt her shake her head. 'No, I was at work, I was too busy to sit down and type him a proper one. Why?'

'Dunno, just wondering.'

'Jaaaaaay, what is it?' she nudged my shoulder.

'Do you think we should tell him?'

She paused and then sat up. 'Absolutely, we have nothing to hide.'

I reached for her and pulled her back down. 'No, I know that, I didn't mean it like that, I just meant when and how shall we tell him?'

'I think it needs to come from you.'

I nodded. 'I agree. I should do it soon shouldn't I?'

Mel nodded. 'Yeah do it, he said he was gonna be in touch after his week on that island.'

'OK.'

'How do you think he'll take it?'

Her head moved up and down on my chest as I shrugged my shoulders. 'Dunno, I was speaking to Rob about that last week actually.'

I felt her eyebrows rise. 'And?'

'Well apparently they'd already talked about it. Apparently we were the only ones in the world who didn't see this coming.'

'Yeah, Jazz said the same.'

'Really?'

She nodded and yawned. 'Yeah, anyway what did Rob say?'

'Well he said that Tim had said that he'd be cool with it, he knew we'd not only be good for each other but care about each other too.'

'Ha, what rubbish!'

I gently prodded her for taking the piss.

She kissed me. 'You know I'm joking, so when was that?'

'Last month apparently, just before he left.'

She reached out and began stroking my side. 'You believe him?'

'I have no reason not to. I mean, like I said to Rob whether that's still the case when he's confronted with it who knows, but I think it'll be OK.' I paused. 'So what did Jazz say?'

She sat up again. 'I knew you'd say that!' Mel moved across to the other side of the bed and began getting under the duvet.

'Mel, what are you doing?'

'I'm cold.'

'All of a sudden?'

'Yes.'

She lifted the duvet so it was covering her and lay down, her back to me.

I got under the other side of the duvet and rolled towards her. Finding ourselves halfway down the bed in the hot semi-darkness of the duvet I took her hand. She refused to catch my eye, instead looking down.

'Mel.'

'What?'

'Mel, I can't change what happened, or what I felt but,' I pulled her hand, 'hey, look at me.' She lifted her head. 'But there is no other place on this planet I'd rather be right now, and no other person I'd rather be with.'

I felt her soften in my hand, I carried on. 'I was just wondering what she'd said to you about us OK, that's all.'

She nodded and lay back down on my chest. I pulled the duvet down, reached around and began to play with her hair.

'I know J, I know it's just weird OK, something comes over me when you ask me about her and I feel it every time I mention you in front of her, she goes all quiet. At first she appeared not to care, that as long as I was happy and knew what I was doing it was fine but now, I dunno, it's like she's deliberately not asking me about anything, just to provoke a reaction.'

She sighed. 'I dunno, we've chosen something pretty complicated.'

I nodded and put my arm underneath her neck, pulling her towards me. 'I know, I know.'

We lapsed back into silence. I heard her stomach growl.

'Hungry?'

'Starving.'

'Mmm, me too actually.'

'Weeeell …'

I pushed her off me. 'No, you just stop there!'

'Ah go on J, you're much better than me, my shelf is the top one in the fridge, I've got some broccoli and mushrooms, I think there's some cheese about too.'

She began pushing me away with her feet; my God she was strong. 'Go on, I'll keep the bed warm.'

I fell to the floor and stood up. 'Every time! Fine, fine! I'll go see what you've got, but you better still be naked by the time I get back!'

I put Mel's dressing-gown on and opened the door quietly. By now it was quite late and the house was covered in darkness. I walked gently to the stairs, past the bathroom and caught a reflection of myself in the mirror, I looked ridiculous. Mel's dressing-gown was far too small for me, was tight across the arms and arse and only reached to above my knees. I sucked my stomach in and tightened the cord.

I felt blindly along the wall for the light switch and opened the door to the open plan kitchen and lounge.

'Oh, hey.'

Jazz looked up from the magazine she was reading. 'Hey J.'

'Sorry, I thought everyone would be in bed, I was just gonna get some food.'

She sat up. 'What's this everyone? There's only me! Come in, help yourself, go crazy, it's fine.'

I shut the door and walked over to the fridge. I could feel her eyes on me, I felt ridiculous.

'Looking good J.'

I turned. 'As I said, I didn't think anyone was up.'

She shrugged. 'Doesn't bother me, I've seen it all before anyway.'

I ignored her and turned back to the fridge.

Broccoli, Pine Nuts and Mushrooms with Creamed Ricotta and Green Pesto over Fresh Pasta

Ingredients

- One bunch of fresh broccoli, cut into chunks
- One large field/Portabello mushroom, or a handful of smaller mushrooms, cut up
- One red onion, sliced
- Two cloves of garlic, crushed and diced
- Large handful of pine nuts
- Fresh pasta
- One jar of green pesto
- Half a tub of ricotta cheese
- Black pepper

Method

- First, roast the pine nuts. Cook them in a dry pan (no oil) for around two minutes until they brown. Leave aside.

- Cook up the onions and garlic in a little oil, spoonful of pesto and some black pepper.

- Boil some water and boil the broccoli for around three to four minutes.

- Add the mushrooms, drain the broccoli and add that too.

- Use the same water for boiling the pasta. If fresh it should only take around two minutes.

- Add the pine nuts back into the pan, drain the pasta and add to the pan as well.

- Remove the pan from the heat and add in two large spoonfuls of pesto and two large spoonfuls of ricotta.

- Mix thoroughly so the pesto and cheese mix in and cover everything in sight.

- Divide up on to two plates and serve.

I was stuck. It would take at least ten minutes to cook all of this and Jazz didn't look like she was going anywhere. I wanted to rise above it, prove that I could have a polite conversation with her but I really couldn't be arsed. I almost felt sorry for her.

'So how do you like our new house?'

I turned from the stove. 'Yeah it's cool.' I turned back to the counter.

She continued, 'Yeah I like it here, we can both be in but give each other space if we need to. How's yours? You're with Rob aren't you?'

I turned again. 'Yeah it's going well.'

She stretched out on the couch. 'Not as nice as here though, right? I guess you'll be over here more then. God I'm tired.'

'Why don't you go to bed then?'

'Because I don't want to, I haven't seen you in ages.'

'Yeah well, we all know why that was Jasmine,' I snapped. Where had that come from I wondered?

She looked down. 'I didn't mean …' She paused. 'I just meant it's been a while.'

I added the mushrooms to the pan. 'It has, a lot's changed.'

'Like you and Mel.'

'Like me and Mel.'

'How's it going?'

'That's none of your business.'

She nodded to herself. 'OK, I guess I deserve that.'

I bit my tongue, you deserve a lot more than that.

She opened her mouth to speak again. 'Look J, about the summer, I never meant for it to happen like it did, I never meant for you to find out like you did, that must've been horrible.'

I refused to give her the satisfaction. 'It was what it was, and it's over. I hope you'll both be very happy.'

'We broke up, I know that you know that. You forget that in those few months not only did you get to know me inside out, but I got to know you.'

I turned from the stove and leant across the side. 'And what the hell is that supposed to mean?'

'Nothing, just that I know you're putting on an act for me right now, some big tough guy act.'

I laughed out loud, 'Oh Jazz, you really think I still care about you? No, you're my girlfriend's flatmate, someone I have to make small talk with when she's not around.'

I saw anger flash in her eyes. 'And when we go out together, what? J, you're not cutting her off from me, she's my best friend.'

'And I'm not trying to, I'm just saying that this,' I moved my hand between us, 'is nothing, there is nothing, not even anger, so don't try and make this into something it's not.'

She stood up and walked towards me. 'Sure, no anger, because you're being perfectly calm about all of this aren't you? I'm sorry I screwed you over, I messed up OK, just like you messed up before, it happens and I wish it hadn't but it had.'

'And I wish I'd never bumped into you in the pub.'

She turned around and ran her fingers through her hair. 'Well I'm glad you did because I meant everything I said that night, and I know you did too. You had to cope with losing me in March, now I've had to cope with losing you. The only difference is that when I broke up with you I didn't start fucking Tim the next day.'

I emptied the food roughly on to two plates and picked them up. 'Don't you dare make this about you Jazz, you moved on. Who the fuck do you think you are for saying I can't do the same? Now get out of my way.'

I walked past her, eyes blazing and headed for the door. My dramatic exit was ruined by the fact I couldn't open the door holding two plates of food. Damn.

Chapter Fifty-Nine
October 9th 2008

HEY BUD!!

How are things? How were the last few days in the flat and how was the move? How's Rob's new place? You settling in OK? Can I actually ask you any more questions? What's the capital of Chad?

So, I'm in Thailand, that's pretty weird isn't it?! Sorry I haven't written in a while but things have been really hectic since I arrived. After about two days I remembered why I hated Bangkok so much and Gabs was equally unimpressed so we got the hell out of there and took a boat over to an island called Koh Rong, far away from everyone and everything. Just got back from that first thing this morning which is why I haven't been in touch much.

Dude, I've got so much to tell you, I don't know where to start. That flight over from London, I was absolutely shitting myself. I started thinking about what I'd just walked away from all for a girl I barely knew. I was sitting next to this French guy on the plane and I was explaining what I was doing to him and he just looked at me in utter incomprehension, as if he thought I was insane for jacking it all in. But, the second I saw her, J I know I've made the right choice. I know I'm doing the best thing for me right now. I walked towards the gates, I could see her through the screens with her huge grin bursting through and I just ran to her. I've never done something like that before, but I just ran and picked her up and spun her around and kissed her and hugged her and maybe cried a little bit (again) and it was amazing. We headed straight back to the hotel; she'd booked us into this really nice place thinking I'd be exhausted after the flight and everything, and J we didn't leave the room for two days! We spent the entire time in bed, talking about wherever we see this going, about what we're scared of happening, all that shit.

She's incredible, she really is. I've never met anyone like her, not even Sarah if I'm honest with you. After this last week where we've barely slept I now feel like I know her so well and I think we're in this for exactly the same things. Neither of us is settled, neither of us knows where to settle so I guess we're gonna plod on for a while until we do know where we pause. Off to Cambodia tomorrow then Laos at the end of the month before we head over to South America. We've got a 3 day stop over in New York, which will be slightly weird as we'll be back in the Western World for a weekend and then we fly south to Mexico. From there it's buses all the way and yes J I will be asking for your advice so calm down, you can get planning now.

Anyway, I'm rambling.

So we left Bangkok after a few days in this amazing hotel and we get a lift in a boat over to Koh Rong. There's nothing on this island, absolutely nothing apart from the most beautiful beaches and a small hotel with 6 or 7 rooms on the shore. I don't think I've ever seen a place like that before, and so cheap! I think we paid something like 6 quid a night each for this huge room, en suite, big comfortable bed and balcony. You step off the balcony and you're on the beach, a good twenty metres or so away from any other rooms, in fact the sea was closer to us than the other huts. We spent a week lying on the beach (I am so brown now, especially as I've still got my India tan, unlucky!), walking round the island, having copious amounts of sex, eating fish and planning the next few months. The sand is a brilliant white here, I can't even look at it without squinting, and the sea is so blue and warm it's like lying in a bath, a very, very big bath. Each night we'd lie in bed with a sundowner and watch the sunset through the open windows, I tell you mate, it's at those times that I think what the hell have I been doing with myself for the last few years, why haven't I been doing this!

So that's about it. Thailand is as Thailand does, it hasn't really changed much, and I've told you about it enough times before so I won't bother. Suffice to say that you see things through a completely different eye when you're travelling with a girl, everything becomes that much more fun, that much more special.

Dunno if I'll be in touch much in the next week or so, can't remember how good the internet is in Laos. Mail me your news, let me know how work goes and how everyone is. I guess it must be getting pretty cold now huh? Clocks go back soon don't they? Give Mel a kiss from me and slap Rob round the face. Got to rush, time running out and I don't want to pay for an extra half hour. Miss you bud, you'd love it out here, you're wasted in London. Speak soon.

Big love

Tim

Chapter Sixty
October 10th 2008

TIM!

N'Djamena is the capital of Chad, obviously. Lovely in springtime. Good to hear from you dude, can't believe you've only been gone just over two weeks, it feels like ages! Glad to hear everything has worked out so well between the two of you and that all the worries you had before amounted to nothing in the end. A beautiful beach, fresh fish, a bag on your shoulders and a stunning girl by your side, what more do you need in life?!

So Bangkok sucked? No surprise there. How's Laos for the second time? Do you feel like you know it already or has it changed? I guess it's opened up a hell of a lot more since you were last there, has it gone the way of Thailand? Love the idea about busing it down Central and South America, let me know where you're thinking of going and I can put you in touch with a few friends, give you the odd free night's sleep and a few locals to go out with.

Everything still amazing with Gabi? What are you guys like at travelling together when it's just the two of you? Have you had any arguments yet or are you still like lovesick kittens? Does she really like your face first thing in the morning and are you trying hard to repress all your annoying character-istics? Can I ask you any more questions? Where did the word yacht come from?

Things here are good, really good actually. It was sad leaving our flat, and it's weird to think that there are now three strangers living there. Rob and

I are getting on great; he's a pretty chilled out person to live with and as you know he's always up for a beer and talking things to death which is perfect for me. Work is OK, same as really, I'm not happy and I haven't been happy for months, now I just need to take your lead, man up and do something about it. Haven't really looked around at other jobs in a while but maybe I should start doing that, the lead up to Christmas and all it'd be great to have something sorted before the New Year rush.

Dude, I've got something I need to tell you, something I've been keeping from you for a few weeks. Let me explain and I hope you'll understand why I didn't say anything before. Don't worry, it's nothing bad, everything's fine it's just, well look….

That week after you left when it was just me and Mel in the flat for a few days, well something started happening between us. I didn't tell you straight off as I'm not sure what it was, if it was a reaction to us all breaking off from each other or because we were both upset that you'd gone but it's been a few weeks now and it's still going on. Tim, I think I'm falling for her, I'm falling for her big time. I know this may be quite hard for you to read but I want to be as honest with you as I can. We've been acting like a couple, no, we have been a couple for well over a week now and it's going well. Don't get me wrong, I'm terrified about starting something up with her as there is so much to lose, and I think she feels the same but I think we both realised that if there is this thing here between us, well we have to see what it is don't we?

Now, these feelings, I absolutely promise you that they only came on when you left. When you guys were together I never even considered anything like that, and even if I had I would never have acted on it.

Rob told me that you guys had actually spoken about it a few weeks ago, and that you said you thought it was a good idea. Did you mean that? Are you pissed off? What do you think about it? All I know is that whatever you say you're feeling for Gabi, I think I'm with you. It's happening so fast, I'm getting completely caught up in it but I have just realised that perhaps it was always meant to be like this between us. Please let me know what you're thinking about this, even if you think I'm a cunt just let me know. I hope you can see that this was never meant to hurt you but I think it's something we both have to do.

OK dude, I've got to go. I'm at work and I've been on off writing this email for about an hour now! Rob sends his love as does Mel. Don't think she was lying to you by not telling you about us, we both knew it had to come from me first.

Be safe and give Gabs a hug from me. Does she still have that ridiculous cap we bought for her in Kerala? Write me soon, I really want to know what you think about all of this.

Big love

J

Chapter Sixty-One
October 18th 2008

'ARE YOU FREE THIS weekend?'

I looked up from my lunch and nodded. 'Yeah, why?'

'I've got a surprise for you.'

I raised my eyebrow and looked at her from across the table. 'What have you done?'

She shrugged. 'Dunno, just saying I've got a surprise for you.'

I smiled. 'Mel, you're the worst person in the world at keeping secrets. Look at you, you're grinning!'

'Well you'll have to just wait and see.'

I picked up my orange juice and looked out of the window. 'Fine, it's almost two anyway, I should be getting back to work.' I got to my feet. 'See you tonight?'

She reached up and pulled me back down into the chair. 'OK OK, I'll tell you.'

I sat down excitedly. 'What have you done?'

She toyed with the straw in her hands. 'Well I was just wondering if you'd like to do something, go somewhere maybe?'

I started smiling. 'Mel what have you done?'

She looked coyly at the table. 'Well I may have booked us a flight to Barcelona.'

My eyes widened. 'Barcelona?! You're kidding?!'

Her grin spread from ear to ear. 'Nope, we leave after work tomorrow, two nights, I found a deal online, do I rock or not?'

I got up and put my arms around her. 'Oh you rock, that's amazing! Thank you!'

She kissed me on the lips. 'Well I wanted to go anyway, but I thought I'd get bored so may as well bring you along.' She slapped my arse through my trousers. 'Now go to work, I'll tell you about it all tonight.'

I felt the wheels extend from beneath my seat as we made our descent into Reus airport, an hour north of Barcelona. What with my South America obsession it had been a few years since I'd been to Spain and I'd missed it a hell of a lot. Plus I really felt like my Spanish had slipped recently; this was a chance to give it a bit of a refresher course.

I looked out of the window at the bright lights of Barcelona twinkling off into the distance. I felt Mel lean against my shoulder, craning her head to get a view out of the window. I reached for her hand and squeezed it. 'Thank you.'

She hit my shoulder. 'Enough with the thank yous, that's about the twentieth today. One more thank you at the end of the weekend if we have a good time, apart from that no more, OK!'

'OK.' I turned back to the window and watched the ground rush up to meet us.

We bused into town and walked down the Ramblas to our hotel, a gorgeous Gaudí-esque place right by the sea, opposite the statue of Christopher Columbus pointing out across the waves. It was late evening but Barcelona was only just getting going. The Ramblas, a long paved area full of restaurants and bars that runs from the centre of the city down to the water, was full of people, standing either in the doorways of the bars or converging in the streets. Quickly dumping our bags in the hotel we changed, showered and left to explore. Arm in arm we walked the length of the Ramblas and up to Plaza de Catalunya before peeling off and getting lost in the Gothic Quarter. Shops, still open, beckoned us in with outstretched doors and feeling on a high from escaping London we allowed ourselves to be seduced. Like the Latin Quarter and Left Bank in Paris, the Gothic Quarter in Barcelona is where the city gets its heart and its sway from. It's home to the most eclectic shops, where African drums sit alongside Peruvian panpipes, and Che Guevara t-shirts share shop space with outrageous leather boots and bone carved earrings. Bars range from traditional Spanish cantinas where for five euros you can have a greasy burger and a bottle of Cava (no glasses) to chic, cool minimalist places echoing of red wine and bossa nova.

We decided to do a tapas and beer/wine crawl around the quarter, knowing that if we followed the roads down they'd eventually lead us to the sea and ultimately our hotel. Following a path that looked familiar to the eighteen-year-old in my head that was leading us around we suddenly burst out from the darkened cobbled alleys and into a large square where Barcelona's original cathedral stood. Bathed in an eerie white light, the golden arches shot up into the night sky like a hand waving at the city's unfinished, modern cathedral, La Sagrada Familia two miles to the north.

'This is beautiful,' she clutched my arm and pointed at a bar facing the cathedral, "El Diseño del Tapas", roughly translated as "The Art (or Design) of Tapas", 'let's go there and have a snack.'

We pulled up a table, the light metal making a screeching sound as its legs ran over the cobbles, and looked at the menu. The bar was a new creation, a place where tapas was produced like works of art.

Jamon Serrano and Sweet Pepper Jam Smothered Goats' Cheese

Ingredients
- Two individual round portions of goats' cheese
- One baguette
- A few slices of jamon serrano
- Sweet pepper jam

Method
- Slice the baguette at an angle so you end up with two wide slices that sit flat on a plate.
- Pour a little olive oil on each baguette and smear with a knife so that it's covered.
- Place the goats' cheese on the bread and cut the ham so that it covers the cheese. Try and style it so that no ham overhangs the

cheese, it looks cool.

- Smear the jam over the ham, again make sure the jam stays on the ham.

King Prawn Kebabs in a Coriander, Ginger, Garlic, Chilli and Lime Marinade

Ingredients

- Three king prawns per kebab
- Two cloves of garlic, diced
- An inch cubed of ginger, diced
- A few sprigs of coriander, diced
- Fresh lime juice
- Splash of olive oil

Method

- De-shell the prawns so that only the tails remain.

- Mix all of the ingredients with a little olive oil in a bowl and leave to marinade in the fridge for as long as possible, at least a few hours.

- Skewer three prawns onto a bamboo stick and cover the prawns with a bit from the marinade.

- As they're cooking, squeeze some lime juice over them.

- Prawns cook very quickly. Turn once and they'll be done in about four minutes.

Patatas Bravas

Ingredients

- Four large potatoes, peeled and cut into chunks around two inches long
- One red chilli
- Five cloves of garlic
- One can of chopped tomatoes
- Salt and black pepper
- Two tablespoons of olive oil

- Paprika
- Mayonnaise

Method

- Place the oil in an oven-proof dish and heat in the oven on around 200 degrees.

- When the oil is hot add the potatoes, black pepper and salt.

- Remove after ten minutes and stir in the tomatoes, garlic, chilli and paprika.

- Return to the oven for another half an hour.

- Remove the potatoes and place on some kitchen paper.

- Stir two spoonfuls of mayonnaise into the remaining mixture, this is now the dipping sauce.

- Add more mayonnaise to make the sauce creamier if desired.

We asked for a few cañas (Spanish for glass of beer) and sat back to watch the cathedral. A service had just finished and the doors to the cathedral were open wide, its gold, reddish gaze projecting out onto the square. Spaniards poured from the cathedral and out into the night, strict Catholics about to go out all night and party. Almost on cue two guitarists appeared from behind us and started to play to the emerging crowd, the rhythmical sound of the Spanish guitar rising up into the night sky.

'I can't believe we were in work this afternoon, and now we're here.'

I turned to Mel. 'We should do this every weekend. It's like a drug.'

My hand dangled from the metal chair and sought hers. By now a crowd had formed around the guitarists and some people had started to dance. Old couples mixed with young as men smiled and women twirled in the evening glow. We sat in silence, tired from the week and the journey behind us and content to be sitting there quietly. Mel's hand gently squeezed mine in rhythm to the music as she gazed upon the square, now almost half full of couples moving together. All the chairs around the square faced to the middle as those that didn't dance looked on. Wiping a crumb from her lip Mel pulled out five euros and slid it half under the plate. Getting to her feet and pulling the band from her hair she shook her head, allowing her half-wet hair to fall to her shoulders. She held out her hand towards me and pulled me to my feet. 'We're dancing.'

Mel led me over to the crowd and turned to face me. Reaching for her other hand I pulled her close and we began to move slowly together, following the beat of the flamenco guitar. The guitarist began to sing softly as two women standing beside him raised their hands above their shoulders and began to clap. The guy next to the guitarist who was sitting on a wooden box, opened his legs and began to tap the box, his hands followed the beat and his eyes followed the hips of the girls moving in front of him.

I put my hand around Mel's waist, raised my left hand and turned her underneath my arm. Her summer dress flowed around me, caressing my trousers as she passed and turned back round to face me. She looked at me through her hair, grinned a silly 'what are we doing here' grin and raised my hand to turn away from me again. I spun her out so we stood a full two arms' length apart before I gently tugged on her hand, twirling her back to me. She folded back into my arms and for a few seconds we moved together, her back pressed up against my chest, my arms wrapped around her waist.

'J.'

Her head, which rested against my shoulders turned up towards me.

'Yeah?'

She paused. 'Doesn't matter.' She looked up to the sky, a few stars were beginning to peek out. 'This is perfect.'

We carried on moving for a while until a few songs later Mel let go of my hands, kissed me on the lips and said, 'Come, let's get another caña.'

We eased our way between the dancing couples as the guitarists struck up again and headed towards the edge. As I passed an elderly couple the man looked at us and put his hand on my shoulder.

'Señor, perdoname pero mi esposa quiere bailar contigo.' He looked to Mel and smiled. 'Y yo tengo ganas de bailar con tu novia. Le molesto?'

Mel looked to me. 'What did he say?'

I smiled. 'That he and his wife want to dance with us. Game?'

I released Mel's hand and turned towards the couple. 'Claro que no.' I held my hand out to the man's wife. 'Vamos?'

We split up and began to dance slowly. Being an elderly Spanish woman my partner was about three foot four but could still dance expertly. She ended up instructing me what to do and before I knew it we were both spinning all over the place. I looked over my date's head at Mel, who smiled at me from behind her partner's back. Even though the guy didn't speak English, and Mel didn't speak Spanish they were still smiling and laughing with each other. I caught Mel's eye from behind her partner's back and blew her a kiss which she returned. I began to speak to my date a little and found out that her and her husband had been coming to the square regularly to dance for over forty years. As she spoke you could almost see the yearning in her eyes for a time long gone, a time that now perhaps only existed in the arms of her husband.

The song ended and cheeks were kissed. The old man shook my hand, squeezed my shoulder with the other and grinned an almost toothless grin at me. 'Hombre que mujer es ella! Como se mueve! Que usted nunca la pierda.'

I smiled and squeezed his shoulder in return. 'Pues lo intentaré!'

He smiled back and nodded. We watched him walk back to his table arm in arm with his wife. As he sat down heavily in his chair they smiled again and raised their drinks towards us. We waved good-bye, left the square and headed for another bar.

'What did he say to you?'

I grinned at her and put my arm around her waist. 'Nothing, I'll tell you another time.'

Picking up the two pint glasses, I made my way over to the cushions.

Mel had already got the shisha going and was trying to blow smoke rings. I stopped at the edge of the carpet, slipped my shoes off and joined her on the enormous cushions.

We were in "Sahara", the fourth and definitely best bar of the evening. It was a shisha bar, decked out in cushions and rugs and wherever you looked couples and groups lay on the cushions on the floor, drinking and smoking shisha. We were stuffed after our tapas but were still in the mood for drinking, and were having our second roncoca of the evening. The drink, a mixture of rum and Coke, was served in typical Spanish portions, about a quadruple shot measure of rum and a bit of Coke for decoration.

I lay back on the cushion and inhaled deeply, the sweet apple tobacco filling my lungs and relaxing my already pretty much coma-tose body. I passed the pipe to Mel who put her drink down and brought the pipe to her lips. The water in the shisha bubbled away as she inhaled.

'What made you think of Barcelona?'

She passed me the pipe and smiled sleepily. Shrugging she said, 'I dunno, I wanted to spend some time with you, just you. Those few days just after Tim left when it felt like we were the only people in the world, well I wanted that again.'

I smiled sleepily. 'I can't think of anything better.'

Mel took the pipe off of me and hesitated. 'I know we both said we always saw each other sleeping together one day, but did you ever imagine this?'

'Feeling like I do about you?'

'Yeah.'

I shook my head. 'I guess not, but then again I don't know what I thought. It would never have been just a random night between us would it?'

'I guess not.'

I looked to her. 'What are you thinking?'

'That it's funny how things work out, are working out I mean.'

I nodded. 'I never saw this coming, me and you. You know I can't stop thinking about you.'

She grinned. 'And me about you, I feel like such a kid.'

'Everything I do or think comes round to you. I read about a new play and I think that it's something you'd like, or I walk around Sainsbury's and I buy Earl Grey tea because I know it's your favourite drink in the morning and you only went along with coffee because of me and Tim.'

'It's true, I couldn't stand the stuff first thing.' She paused then said, 'You know if you ever have doubts that you can tell me, right?'

I looked at her. 'How on earth can I have any doubts? I love being with you.'

'Yeah but let's face it, if this goes wrong it'll kill us.'

'But I'm not even thinking about that happening; why would it go wrong?'

She shrugged and looked down. 'Dunno. I just meant if you want to get out now, y'know, before it gets even more serious and go back to friends then I'd, I'd understand.'

'Mel, where has this insecurity come from? I have no doubts whatsoever. Why, do you?'

She shook her head. 'No, none at all, but you must admit, you must've wondered what would happen if it does go wrong.'

I paused. 'I guess, but I just thought we'd deal with that if we ever needed to, and not before. This, with you, it's amazing, it's blown me away. I know it's soon and I know there's a lot at risk but fuck it. Let's see what happens.'

She smiled. 'I'm sorry, I don't know what came over me. I guess with everything that's happened I'm a little scared of getting burnt.'

'I'm not gonna burn you.'

'I know, I guess I just needed to hear you say that.'

She sat up, finished her drink and looked at her watch. 'Jesus it's almost three! Shall we go back to the hotel?'

I downed my drink. 'Why, you tired?'

She smiled. 'No.'

Chapter Sixty-Two
October 20th 2008

WE SPENT THE NEXT day wandering around the city. Both Mel and I had been to Barcelona before so weren't too fussed about doing all the tourist things so instead we just wandered around, sat in bars, went in shops and generally just spent some time together. She was right, we were acting like teenagers. We held hands constantly, each hand subconsciously seeking out the other whenever it was separated. Even though it was October it was still pretty warm so we spent the afternoon on the beach at Barceloneta, making out on the sand. Mel's idea had worked perfectly for once again it felt like there was no-one else in the world.

At the risk of sounding like Tim, this really felt different to anything I'd experienced. I felt completely consumed by her. It's weird, but I think a certain change comes over you when you go from early to mid-twenties and even though no-one will admit this, you do begin to wonder what a life could be like with someone. Now, I'm not getting ahead of myself, I'm not going to propose to Mel tomorrow but yes I have thought about what it would be like with her. I think if you can't imagine that life, or don't think it would work then there'd be no point carrying on, it's all just wasted effort really isn't it? I mean Rob, Tim and I, we're all a certain type of guy, a type that doesn't fuck around, that is actually quite happy in a relationship and so anyone we go out with, well as much as we'd like to pretend it is, it's never going to be just a bit of fun. We've all had one-night stands and yeah they're fun sometimes but they're not satisfying if I'm honest, and at this point in my life I want to be satisfied. That's why I think Tim's right in following Gabi halfway across the world,

Rob was right in breaking it off with Megan if there was no future in it and I think I'm right for going for it with Mel.

I still haven't heard from Tim. I know he said he was going to be out of touch for a few days but it just so happens that those few days would have been straight after he would have read my email. When someone's away it's so hard to explain things through a computer screen.

That evening Mel and I went out for more food on the seafront where the tables all perched nervously around the dock and candles in glasses flickered in the moonlight and reflected on our foreheads. We had a ridiculously early flight the next morning, one of the reasons they'd been so cheap in the first place, and neither of us wanted to go home. Work was now becoming something I dreaded rather than looked forward to; I was clockwatching from nine in the morning and that was no way to live. Feeling my Spanish coming back to me over the weekend also made me more determined to do something that used what I'd spent four years at uni learning. That combined with Mel's disappointment at what it meant to be a newly qualified doctor on the NHS meant that the journey home would be a long and painful one.

Beef and Mushrooms Infused with Red Wine

Ingredients
- 200 grams braising steak
- Handful of mushrooms
- Half a dozen shallots
- A can of chopped tomatoes
- Beef stock
- Fresh rosemary

Method
- Slice the beef into chunks and seal in a pan.
- Peel the shallots but leave them whole.
- Add the beef stock to a cupful of water and combine in a pan with the shallots, fresh rosemary, mushrooms, wine and tomato.

- Heat gently and stir until the mixture starts to get hot.
- Add the beef and cook in the oven for around half an hour.
- Serve with patatas bravas and crusty bread.

Our plates were cleared away and we moved our chairs closer to each other's. Both gazing out to sea, I felt the cool wind ruffling my shirt and cooling my face.

'Let's not go back.'

'I wish we could.'

She tugged my hand. 'No I mean it, get a job here with your Spanish, I'll be a doctor, perfect.'

I laughed. 'Mel you don't speak Spanish! How would you be a doctor?'

She waved her hand. 'Ah it'd be fine, all the body parts come from Latin words anyway, I'd understand.'

'Uhuh.'

She pushed my shoulder. 'Fine, ruin my fantasy, let's go back to London and separate beds at different ends of the city.'

'Maybe we could get Rob and Jazz to move in together.'

She laughed and sat up. 'Yes! Fix them up, then they can move in together and we can live together! Shotgun living in my house! Unlucky Jazz, South London it is for you.'

'And what is so wrong with South London?'

She rolled her eyes. 'Nothing, I was only kidding.'

'Hmm.'

We lapsed into silence and turned back to the sea.

'I mean it though, I'm getting bored with London.'

'Really?'

She rested her hand on my arm. 'Yeah I am, this whole moving house thing, I thought I'd be full of energy and ready to start afresh but I'm not, I'm exhausted. Is this what working in London is, being permanently exhausted?'

'I think that's just what working is like, London or anywhere. You know what, working has given me so much more respect for my

409

parents, how the hell do you raise a family whilst working? There's just no time.'

She nodded. 'I know, I'm worried about that; I'm a doctor, my hours are shit; I'll never see my kids and my husband will have to be pretty understanding.'

'Well that's it then, we can never get married, I wouldn't be understanding.'

She pinched my arm. 'Whatever, you'd do what I told you to do.'

'Ha! Oh really?!'

She smiled and kissed me. 'Yup, round my little finger. Anyway, I could always go private in a few years, more money less hours.'

'And I'd be running my restaurant in the evenings so you can be at home with the kids then and I'd be home during the day.'

'Oh great, so we'd never see each other?!'

We both went quiet.

She shook her head. 'This is so weird.'

I squeezed her hand. 'I know.'

She paused. 'You know yesterday, that man I danced with?'

'Yeah.'

'What did he say to you when we were leaving?'

I paused. 'That you were an amazing woman and that I should never do anything to make me lose you.'

She blushed and looked into her glass.

'And what did you say?'

I looked at her through the candlelight, she caught my eyes and held them, her lips slightly parted and her eyes smiling brightly.

'That I had no intention of ever losing you.'

Chapter Sixty-Three
October 24th 2006

DUDEFISH

Sorry I haven't written in a while, things have been pretty hectic and I haven't been in sniffing distance of a t'internet café.

I'm now in Laos (again) and everything is going great. Gabi and I are still rocking all over the place and getting on like a house on fire. Mate if you could see me now you'd laugh pretty hard; I'm smitten, the happiest I've been in ages, probably all year. We're still to have our first argument but we've come through the first few weeks (jeez almost a month!) and there's still no place else I'd rather be.

So, to business. No I don't think you were a cunt. Look, I'll be honest with you, it's a little bit weird for me but I can't say I'm surprised. Sure, when I was with Mel I was paranoid about you even though the whole Jazz thing was going on, and I know part of that was down to my own insecurities but I think some of it was based on truth. Now J, I can see you raising your hands in protest and I'm not accusing you of fancying Mel when we were together or whatever, I'm just saying there must have been something there to make you both act on it now. It must be the same from her side as well otherwise I don't think I would have felt like I did. So, to summarise, you're not a dick, but I do think I was right.

I am happy for you, both of you. I think you'd be amazing together, I always did. Rob and I talked about it once and I know he thinks the same. Right now I can't picture it because I'm not there living

with you both anymore but I'm sure it is going great.
J if there's one thing I've learnt recently it's that
if you think there's the slightest hope that by going
for something your life will improve, you've got to
go for it. I guess maybe Rob was right after all, that
if you're not happy with what you have or what you
do, change, it's really not that big a deal. Right now
I can't remember what it feels like to work behind
a desk looking at numbers all day, but when I was
doing it, it seemed like there was no end in sight. I
manned up and decided to leave, which yeah terrified
me last month, but now I know it's the best decision
I ever made. I guess that's how I see things with
Mel; you both went for it rather than pussyfooting
around each other and now I can see it being nothing short of incredible for both of you (not that I'm
putting any pressure on either of you or anything!).
The Jazz thing is on the side, don't let it dominate.
She means nothing to you, and to be honest I think
she's beginning to mean less and less to Mel so don't
worry, you don't have to be her best friend.

How's Rob? Tell him to pull his finger out and
email me, I haven't heard from him since I left. Is
he OK? How's South London going?

Right, this email got a lot more sentimental than
I'd intended. I was just going to email you a line
saying I hated you and see what you'd do but I figured
that might be a bit cruel.

I know you've just got back from Barcelona but I
have a suggestion, so listen up. We're heading to
Central and South America in a bit, but a week next
Thursday we have a few days' stopover in New York.
I think the three of you should take Thursday and
Friday off and come out here. I've looked at flights,
there's one at 7am Thursday morning, gets you in
around midday, then one back Sunday evening which
gets you in before work Monday morning. Also, it's
quite cheap, £312 return. What do you think? I think
it's an amazing idea, and I know Gabs really wants
to see you and Rob. Think about it, but let me know

```
soon, I want to book somewhere to stay.
  Chat soon
  Tim x
```

I looked up from my laptop. 'He's right you know, including tax it's £312. Two days off which leaves me with none remaining until Christmas but that doesn't matter. What do you think, guys?'

Mel chewed her lip. 'I dunno, it's a great idea, I just dunno if I can get the time off work. What do you think Rob?'

'I'd love to, I'd absolutely love to but I want to go skiing in January; mate I don't think I can afford it, well I can, I just can't afford to do it if I want to go skiing.'

I sighed. 'I guess when you include all the stuff we'd probably buy, it's a hell of a lot of money for four days.'

Rob got up and headed towards his bedroom. 'I'm out, if I stay here I'd buckle and book a ticket and I really want to go skiing. Sorry guys.'

I watched him leave the room then turned to Mel.

'Soooo?'

'What?'

'I really want to go.'

'I know you do, so do I, I've never been to New York.'

'And it'd be the three of us again!'

'And Gabi.'

'And Gabi, but she's great, you'd get on.'

She thought about it for a few seconds. 'I guess I could work a few double shifts the week before and after …'

'Yes! Yes you could!'

'But I'd be knackered and probably grumpy.'

I shrugged. 'You could sleep on the plane, and I promise to wait on you hand and foot when we get back. Shall we do it? Come on.'

A half smile played on her lips. 'It would be so good to see Tim and meet this girl he's changed his life for. Fuck it! Book the tickets!'

NOVEMBER

Chapter Sixty-Four
November 5th 2008

WHERE ARE YOU?

I stood by the pond and scanned the crowds. My phone vibrated in my hands.

By the pond, u?

I texted back, *I'm by the pond! Walk to the side nearest to the tube.*

I leaned back against the railing, jamming my hands deep into my trenchcoat and wrapping it tightly around me. Winter was well and truly here and we'd now entered the four-month depressing cycle of going to and leaving work in complete darkness. The build-up to Christmas was still a few weeks off so for now people were just pissed off at the vanishing sun and the return of the intermittent drizzling rain.

I looked around, still no sign. Slightly irritated that I had to take my hand out of the warmth of my pocket I flipped up my phone and dialled Rob's number.

'Where are you?!' He snapped.

'I'm by the pond where I said I was!' I replied. 'Where the dickens are you?!'

'I'm by the pond!'

'Well you can't be, as I'm there too.'

'J, I can see water and railings OK, it's a fucking pond. Are you sure you're not confused and waiting by a puddle or something?'

I went on tiptoes and looked around the common. 'Ahh OK, that makes sense, so Clapham Common has two ponds apparently.'

He sighed. 'Right I'll stay put, come to me.'

'No! You come to me!'

'Fuck off! I'm staying put.'

'Shot not moving! Ha!' I laughed.

'Damnit! Fine, see you in two.'

I smiled, put my hand back in my pocket and awaited Rob's arrival. It was our first fireworks night in South London and we'd come to Clapham Common to see the apparently famous firework display. It was Friday and I was shattered having spent the week travelling between Birmingham, Nottingham, Manchester and Warwick Universities promoting the IQC Graduate Scheme that I was about to complete. Whilst it had been fun doing the evening talks in bars to a load of wide-eyed finalists I'd had to do that whilst working from the hotel during the day. All in all there'd been four of us on the tour and we'd all got on fine, but I'd found it hard to keep myself motivated whilst representing a company I wasn't sure I wanted to be a part of anymore.

'Hello dickchops!'

I smiled and leant in to hug Rob back. I pulled back and slapped his chest. 'How's tricks? Good week?'

He shrugged. 'Office has been pretty dead to be honest, not much chat around with you four gone. How was the North?'

I shrugged. 'Cold, rainy, pretty cheerless really.'

We turned and began walking towards the centre of the common. 'What even the kids? Did they not think you were Gods because you actually had jobs?'

I shook my head. 'No, they were cool, that was the fun bit, it's just the days that were boring, sitting on cold stools in the hotel business centre trying to do some work.'

'Much lash?'

I grimaced. 'Baby lash I'm afraid, I didn't realise how boring Craig, Sarah and Alex can be.'

'Yeah, I should have warned you, I did a gig in Newcastle with Craig once, he barely said a word for the whole trip. Come we got time, let's get some food and a beer.'

We joined a queue by a food van parked on the common and waited patiently hunchbacked against the rain.

'So what about you?' I said to the ground. 'Screw IQC, what else have you been up to?'

Rob chewed his lip. 'Not much really to be honest. I've been so busy during the day it's been quite nice coming home, having the place to myself and just chilling out watching a DVD. I did go out Wednesday with a mate from home but apart from that, absolutely nothing. Oh yeah, I finally got around to replying to Tim!'

'About time!'

'Yeah I know, you know when you know you have to do something and the longer you leave it the worse you feel but the less you want to do it and acknowledge that you've left it so long? Well I was getting myself into all sorts of those vicious circles. Anyway, he replied yesterday, says he's pretty much creaming himself at the thought of seeing you both next week.'

I smiled. 'I can't wait! It feels like he's been gone such a long time.'

He nodded. 'Well it's, what, been just under two months? I guess that is a bit of time. But I think we're the only ones counting the days; he's in no rush to come back is he?'

I shook my head. 'Don't think so, guess I'll find out next week.'

We reached the front, got our lamb tortillas and two beers and walked on.

Lamb Tortilla with Fresh Salsa, Salad and Crème Fraiche

Ingredients
- 200 grams of lamb, cut into cubes
- Fresh salsa
- A handful of rocket and spinach leaves
- Crème fraiche
- Fresh rosemary

- One tortilla per serving

To make the fresh salsa:

- Half a dozen vine tomatoes
- Half an onion
- Two cloves of garlic
- One green chilli
- Four tablespoons olive oil
- Half a lime

Method

- Minutely slice the chilli, tomatoes, onions, coriander and garlic.

- Mix together with the olive oil and squeeze the juice of the lime in.

- Refrigerate for about half an hour.

- Cook the lamb in a little oil and fresh rosemary.

- Spread a layer of crème fraiche over the tortilla.

- Place a handful of the rocket and spinach leaves over the crème fraiche.

- Add a tablespoonful of the salsa.

- Add around eight cubes of lamb to the tortilla, top with a spoonful of crème fraiche and serve.

'Oh, I booked my skiing holiday, that's why I saw my mate on Wednesday.'

'Sweet, when and where?'

'Well, we've got a six-bedroom chalet in Verbier, so all in all there are twelve of us going.' Rob grinned. 'I can't fucking wait.'

'That's gonna rock, they all from school?'

'Yeah well most are, two or three are bringing boyfriends and girlfriends but yeah.'

I shook my head. 'I could never do that with my school friends, that's great Rob, very envious.'

He smiled. 'Anyway, it's over New Year so count me out for anything on New Year's Eve.'

'No way! Ah that's a shame.'

'Well, I think it all works out, because I figured you were proba- bly gonna be with Mel and I was gonna be bored.'

'You know we'd never …'

He shook his head. 'Nonono I know, I'm just saying I figured you'd probably be doing something and they happened to have a vacancy over New Year, and this way I don't use up as much holiday. Everyone's a winner.'

'I guess. Hang on, less holiday, does that mean you can come to New York?'

He smiled. 'Nice try, still no money.'

We stopped to drink deeply and looked around the common. People were coming from all sides with sparklers, scarves, warm jackets, thermos flasks of Irish coffee and plastic glasses of beer. The fireworks were due to be starting at eight, in just under five minutes' time, and the girls were late.

I looked at my watch. 'Why are women incapable of being on time?'

Rob shrugged. 'Because they're women, they accept it when they're growing up and never try to change it. And they walk slower.'

I smiled and looked at my watch again.

'J chill out, remember you're doing this as a favour to Mel, you just have to be polite and slightly friendly.'

'I know I know, I just wish it was only Mel coming, not Mel and Jazz; I really can't be arsed.'

'Well, you got to, for her. Anyway if this is the first time we do this, each time after will be easier. Plus I'm here remember.'

I nodded. 'That's true, you're good at filling awkward silences.'

'I'll do my animals of Africa impressions. Look, is that them in the distance?'

Even though it had only been five days, I'd found myself missing Mel a lot. She'd been working nights all week, and a few doubles in preparation for New York and so we hadn't spoken much. Even when

Mel wasn't working she was so exhausted that to be honest any time spent talking on the phone to me was wasted time when she could have been sleeping. Tonight was her first evening off all week and we had always planned to spend it together; however a few days ago she'd brought up the notion of Jazz coming with us, and seeing as Rob was already gonna be coming to the fireworks I hadn't kicked up a fuss about it. At the end of the day Mel knew I didn't really want to be around Jazz, yet I also knew she desperately wanted me to try and make an effort so she wouldn't feel so awkward all the time, and for me, that was more important. Who knows, I'll give it a shot. We'll never be great friends but Mel is right, we do have to try and find a way to get along.

She was wearing a tight fitted pink bobble hat and a cream jacket done up tightly with the collar folded up. In the dull yellow street-light glow all that could be seen was her green eyes, cute little nose and smiling mouth. She unfolded her arm from Jazz's, skipped a few paces forward and fell into me, her lips and arms simultaneously wrapping themselves around mine.

'Hey you.'

I smiled and kissed her lightly again. 'Hey you.'

She squeezed my hand and moved off to greet Rob, leaving me standing face to face with Jazz. As Mel leant in to kiss Rob I saw her watching from the corner of her eyes.

'Hey Jazz, how you doing?'

I leant in to give her a kiss which turned into one of those half hugs where only one person initiates it but both feel like they have to go through with it half-heartedly.

'Good thanks, how are you doing?'

'Yeah I'm good,' I replied.

'How was Barcelona?' Jazz asked. 'I hear you spent all night dancing in squares with pensioners!' She turned towards Mel, drawing her into the conversation.

'Ha we did, and I met an old man who dances better than J!'

'Well that's not really saying much now is it. Hey Jazz, how are you doing?' Rob leant over and kissed her cheeks.

We made our way over to the firework display and joined the crowds milling around a huge bonfire. The heat from the fire pressed itself upon our cheeks, causing the girls to strip pretty quickly out of their hats and gloves. Mel delved her hand into my pocket, seeking out my warm hand as for a while we all just stood there, warming ourselves and entranced by the dancing flames.

An announcement over the tannoy informed us there was a slight delay in the fireworks and as a groan swept through the crowd Rob turned away from the fire and tapped his glass. 'Drinks orders guys, J, beer?'

I nodded. 'Yes please, you want some money?'

Rob held up his hand. 'Don't worry about it. Girls?'

Mel got to her feet. 'I need to pay by card, no cash, I'll come with you. Jazz, white wine yeah?'

'Yeah thanks Mel.'

They both disappeared off into the distance, leaving Jazz and I alone, looking at the flames and standing in a thick silence.

After a few seconds Jazz turned to me and cocked her head towards the bonfire. 'You're not gonna tie me to a chair and throw me in are you?'

She actually made me laugh out loud. 'No Jazz, I'm not gonna do that, how would I explain it to Mel?'

She smiled. 'True, she probably wouldn't find it that funny.'

'She is very subtle though isn't she?'

'What, the whole paying by card thing? Yeah she's a crap liar, we stopped at a cashpoint on the way here.'

I watched as the flames flickered like snakes' tongues into a box, breaking it in two, causing each half to roll glowing down the bonfire and to the bottom.

'So how's living together going?' I asked.

'Great actually, better than I thought. It was a bit tricky to start off with, but I think that's because it coincided with you guys

421

getting together.'

I forgot how blunt Jazz could be. 'How'd you mean?'

'Well whatever either of us say, Mel is always going to have an issue with our past, and that's just something we both have to accept.'

'I guess you're right.'

She nodded. 'Yeah, she'd always get nervous when she brought up your name around me.'

I raised my head and turned. 'And now?'

She matched my eyes. 'Better. I think you not being around for a few days have helped as we've been forced to spend time together. Before if I'm honest I think she ran to yours a lot to avoid us having to see each other.'

I turned back to the fire and thought about what she'd said.

'So now it's all OK?'

She shrugged. 'Who knows, it's all baby steps isn't it? Look,' she took a deep breath, 'I'm sorry about some of the things I said to you last time we saw each other. At the end of the day you're going out with my best friend, so we need to get on and besides once upon a time there was something between us, something that came from us liking each other and getting on so I guess what I'm saying is, I'm game for trying if you are. Let's draw a line.'

I looked into the flames and thought for a few seconds.

'Yeah, yeah I don't want Mel to feel uncomfortable and feel like she has to run to mine all of the time. I guess I probably said a few things that weren't that nice either.' I nodded. 'OK, line drawn.'

She smiled. 'Good, because believe it or not I do like you J, and I do want to be your friend.'

I opened my mouth to speak, to tell her that I didn't really feel the same way, but I decided to keep it shut. I saw Mel and Rob weaving their way through the crowds and I raised my hand to wave them over.

Chapter Sixty-Five

November 13th 2008

A WAVE OF COLDNESS ran though Mel's body as she violently shivered, turned to me, undid the buttons on my trenchcoat and stepped in. Lifting up my jumper she put her hands around my back, linking them behind me as she hugged me hard for warmth. I recoiled and tried to move away but she stood firm. 'Ow, Mel, your hands are freezing!'

She laughed. 'Just a few seconds more J, you're warming them up. Just be thankful I didn't put them down your pants.'

I hugged her close in an attempt to speed up the heat transfer and tried to look at my watch over Mel's shivering body.

'What time is it?'

'Half seven. I wonder if we'll recognise him.'

Her shivering slowed to a casual chatter as she relaxed herself into me and loosened her grip around my waist. 'If he's tanned I'm gonna be so annoyed.'

'Well at least it won't show up, it'll fade in seconds in this weather.'

Mel rested her head against my chest and looked at the small Ferris wheel inside The Disney Store. 'Bit of a strange place to meet really.'

'Really? He's probably late because he's still inside playing with the stuffed animals.'

Mel smiled and turned her gaze to Times Square, spread out before us. As far as the eyes could see skyscrapers shot up into the sky as if caught in a never-ending race against their neighbour. Bright lights twinkled everywhere, creating a constant artificial daylight as from the corners of each block, electronic news headlines sprinted underneath enormous adverts for whatever new series NBC was starting over Thanksgiving. Times Square was crazy, a trashier, brighter, more expensive version of Leicester Square in London and perhaps the greatest and worst advert for twenty-first century capitalist instant satisfaction consumerism there was. Just before coming to meet Tim and Gabi we'd wandered around the square, dipping our toes into the Hershey's store and the M&M's store before the sickly chocolate aroma made us retreat. All around us dollars were thrust and snatched for gimmicky Hershey's mugs, M&M toys or huge bags of chocolate pick and mix bought by enormous families who struggled to fit the wall of 100 jellybean flavours (and themselves) into a single camera frame. Intrigued and amazed by New York we looked around, wondering if this was where London would be in five years' time, unable to shake the feeling that that was a bad thing.

We'd arrived in New York early that afternoon and had spent the day exploring the blocks around our hotel. We were staying between Times Square and Fifth Avenue, a dozen or so blocks down from Central Park and a few blocks up from the Rockerfeller Tower. Tim and Gabi were due to fly in late afternoon so we'd arranged to meet out rather than in the hotel. What with India, Barcelona and now New York within such a short space of time my head was all over the place but I loved the fact that whereas the day before I'd been in London at my desk I was now in Times Square with my girlfriend, waiting to meet my best mate for dinner.

Hopping over the snow (yes snow!) at the side of the street I saw them from across the road. Mel jumped up shouting, 'Tim!' as I waved across the traffic. Tim grinned from beneath a deep tan and pulled Gabi close, saying something unintelligible and pointing at us from across the road. The lights took an age to change and for a little while all four of us just stood there looking at each other, not sure what to do, motioning at each other to stay put or cross the road.

We finally got permission to walk and crossed through the throng of people making their way home. Mel let go of my hand and ran towards Tim, jumping into his arms and covering his face in kisses.

'Oh my God how tanned are you????!!!!!'

I swept Gabi up in my arms and twirled her around as she squealed and put her arms tightly around my neck. Putting her down I turned towards Tim and hugged him tightly.

'Jaaaaaaaaaaaaaaay! Ha ha, how goddamn random is this!'

He slapped my back hard and squeezed my shoulder. I ruffled his hair and looked him up and down. 'My God you've got thin! Where's your belly gone?!'

He grinned. 'Food poisoning in Laos, best thing that ever happened to me! Mel,' he turned to her, 'this is Gabi, Gabi, meet Mel.'

Gabi smiled broadly and stepped towards Mel. 'So good to finally meet you!'

Mel stepped into her embrace and put her arms around her. 'Same here, what an awesome idea this was!'

'All Gabs' idea I'm afraid, nothing to do with me.' Tim held his hands up, 'You know me, I would have rather never had to see you both ever again but Gabs thought we should get you out.'

She shrugged her shoulders and grinned. 'Why the hell not hey, besides I needed a break from looking after him, he's like a child.'

She smiled and affectionately kissed Tim's cheek and then turned to me. 'Such a shame Rob couldn't make it.'

'Yeah well he can't afford to do this and go skiing next month. Anyway he sends his love.'

Tim clapped his hands together and rubbed them. 'Guys, shall we get out of the cold? We were on a beach in thirty-five degree heat yesterday, I'm frozen!'

We pushed open the door to Singapore and huddled around a small table. Standing for a few seconds we unwrapped ourselves from the layers upon layers we were wearing and pulled up the chairs. Ordering four mojitos I smiled at the table and drummed my fingers on the cloth

'I cannot believe we are doing this!'

'And I can't believe how long I've been gone. What is it, under two months?'

Mel nodded. 'Yeah, has it seemed a long time?'

Tim ran his fingers through his long curly hair and looked across the table. 'Well yes and no, I mean we've been pretty relaxed to be honest. It wasn't like India where we were moving on every other day.' He looked at Gabi. 'I think we've been taking our time a lot so I guess time has been getting away from us.'

Gabs rested her hand on Tim's. 'You know what it's like, you find a place you like and you get lost there for a week or so. When you're not in a rush you don't need to kill yourself like you guys did in India.'

Mel took a long sip from her cocktail and looked up. 'So Gabi, how long have you been away for in total?'

'Since May, wow six months, I didn't realise!'

'And have you found it hard? I've never been away for that long, I don't know if I could do it.'

She sipped her drink as she pondered her response. 'The first month or so, when I first met these guys was hard, really hard. I felt alone, it was my first time away from home, I missed my friends and my parents and I wasn't having a very good time working in the orphanage.' She chewed her lip. 'I think that was the hardest time for me.' She paused and looked at me. 'Actually tell a lie, the hardest time was when you all went back to London. Waking up that morning and having to get that train back into the mountains and the orphanage was perhaps the loneliest day of my life. I missed you all, not just Tim, so much. After four weeks of boredom in the orphanage you guys reminded me there was life outside of the village I was in!'

'And so you sent for me.'

She leant in and kissed Tim. 'And so I sent for you.'

Tim pulled away and looked at us. 'So, what news from London?'

I shrugged. 'Quite a lot has happened really, I mean you know it all from emails but yeah, Rob and I are living together, Mel and Jazz are too and …'

He looked at Mel. 'How's that working out?'

Mel nodded. 'It's OK, a little bit weird just living with one other person, but it's fine. A little bit strange but,' she looked at Gabi then back to Tim, 'well you know what I mean.'

He nodded and a brief silence descended over the table.

'How's work?'

Mel grimaced. 'Not great to be honest. My salary is less than I was promised due to NHS cutbacks and I'm working pretty much a sixty hour week. To tell you the truth I'm not enjoying it halfway as much as I thought I would.'

Gabi passed around the next set of mojitos. 'Is it something you've always wanted to do?'

'Yeah it is, ever since I was a little girl all I've ever wanted to be was a doctor, and when I got to school and realised that I was pretty good at sciences it just seemed the most logical thing to do. I loved it at uni, but I think I walked into the real world thinking it would be something different to what it actually is. It's pretty demoralising when you've spent five years of your life studying for it. I dunno, I'm hoping it's just teething problems for now. At least I'm not the only one unhappy at work!' She squeezed my hand and returned to her noodles.

'Really? Still fed up, dude?'

I nodded between a mouthful of soup. 'Yeah, but I've made the decision to look for something else as soon as I come back from the Christmas break.'

'In what though?'

I shrugged. 'That's the problem. No idea as yet but fuck it, let's not talk about it this weekend!'

Tim smiled. 'That's fine with me, I've got loads of travelling stories to bore you with instead!'

And so that's how it stayed. It was a little bit weird to be honest

427

with you. Now obviously it was amazing to see Tim and Gabi, I forgot how much I really liked her, but the whole evening had this air of falseness about it. The big fat pink elephant sitting on our table was the fact that this was the first time Tim had seen me since I started going out with his ex-girlfriend, and to be honest I wanted to talk to him about that. I think Mel probably did as well, but neither of us felt comfortable just yet doing that in front of Gabi. Who knows how much she knew about the past. It was a feeling I'd never had in London but I felt like I was fucking him over.

We left early and slowly walked the few blocks back to the hotel. We'd all been up incredibly early that morning to get our flights and were exhausted and so had decided to save the lash for the next two nights. Arranging to meet after a lie-in we said our goodnights and made our way upstairs to a welcome bed.

I sat up in bed and rested my hands underneath my head. My head fell to the left towards the open door where Mel stood in the bathroom removing her make-up. Standing just in her underwear, her golden coloured skin contrasted sharply against the bright white light and the ceramic of the bath behind her. Watching her concentrate on her reflection in the mirror I felt a surge of, of I don't know what, lust, affection, love, warmth, whatever you call it, but whatever it was it was something that made me realise how lucky I felt to be watching her right now. Yet it was also a feeling I didn't want to ruin by vocalizing it.

She leant in to splash her face with water, dried it on a towel and looked over.

'What are you looking at Camfield?'

'You.'

'And what are you thinking?'

'How lucky I am and how beautiful you look. Come to bed.'

'One sec hun.'

She brushed her teeth, turned out the light, got into bed and snuggled up to me, her body cold from the outside air. Her teeth chattered slightly as she put her arm around my chest and worked her freezing cold feet between mine. Finally, she undid her pony tail before resting her head above her hands on my chest.

'You're like a cat, you have to turn around three times before you can sit down.'

She bit my chest lightly. 'Shut up, I want to be comfortable, anyway you're my radiator, it's freezing!' She lifted her head to mine and kissed me lightly on the cheek. 'Did you have a good night?'

I nodded. 'Yeah, yeah I did, great to see them. You?'

'Yeah, definitely. Gabi's lovely, I can see why Tim did what he did.'

'She is isn't she?'

Mel smiled as I began softly stroking her back. Gently tickling my side she looked up, the whites of her eyes visible in the semi darkness.

'What's up?'

I paused. 'Did it feel weird to see Tim together?'

She sighed. 'Oh thank God! I thought it was just me that felt like that. Yes it did.'

'I feel guilty, but I don't think I should.'

She nodded. 'I know, but I think it's just time. We're used to being together now, he's never seen us together and we've never acted together in front of him.'

'You're right, I mean I believe what he told me in that email, that he is happy and not fucked off.'

'Exactly, and besides he's here with Gabi. Look, how about tomorrow I go off with Gabi for a bit. The guys working in Abercrombie & Fitch are meant to be really hot, we can go perv on them whilst spending a bit of girlie time together and you and Tim can go off and do whatever, talk about stuff. Besides Gabi and I need to bond.'

I kissed her and smiled. 'I like what you've done there, make it seem like you're being a great girlfriend by going to look at hot guys in a shop, smart.'

She kissed me back. 'I do my best. But seriously, what do you think?'

Chapter Sixty Six
November 14th 2008

WALKING INTO THE DINER I felt like I was stepping back in time three years to when I lived in Mexico. Everyone but everyone in the service industry in New York was Mexican or Puerto Rican, meaning that Spanish was constantly being spoken in the background, Mexican football was playing on TV and the radio was pumping out the latest reggaeton track from the Caribbean.

I shook my coat free from snow and slid into a booth, at which point I was immediately presented with a mug of thick black coffee. Perfect.

'OK we're not moving for at least three refills now.'

Tim drank deeply and said, 'Well why stop at three, let's make it double figures.'

I laughed. 'Yeah let's get a caffeine high for when we see the girls; we can run around being really hyperactive and having snowball fights.'

'And then have a really bad come-down and take it out on them, that'll be fun.'

I drank deeply and reminisced. 'Do you remember that caffeine party we went to when we were fifteen?'

'What at Jenny's? God yeah, nowhere would sell us alcohol would they?' He shook his head. 'Man we must have gone through a whole pot that night.'

'What was the rule? A mug every half hour or something?'

He nodded. 'Yeah I think so.'

I picked up the menu and scanned the breakfasts. I found what I was looking for and closed the card. 'It's got to be pancakes hasn't it?'

Tim chewed his lips. 'Yeah, although the fruit salad looks pretty good.'

'Tim! Man up, you don't make friends with salad remember. Have fruit with your pancakes if you want.'

'That's true, what the hell was I thinking?!' He looked around. 'I need a refill.'

Huge American Pancakes

Ingredients
- 250 grams of plain flour
- Two tablespoons of baking powder
- One tablespoon of salt
- Two tablespoons of caster sugar
- Two eggs
- One glass of milk
- Fifty grams of butter

Method
- Melt the butter and add to the milk and eggs. Whisk.
- In a separate bowl combine the flour, baking powder, sugar and salt.
- Add the milk mixture to the flour and stir to make a thick batter.
- When the batter is smooth, pour half a cupful into a hot frying pan.
- After a minute or so the mixture will start to bubble, at this point flip.
- Cook for a further minute and then remove from the heat.

Garnishes:
This is great with either bacon, ham, fried eggs, fresh strawberries or sliced bananas. All with lashings of maple syrup of course.

I was surprised our waiter didn't enlist a forklift truck to deliver our food. The plates, as big as half the table, were stacked high with four very thick pancakes and covered in fruit and bacon. The waiter also left us with half a dozen large packs of maple syrup, one obviously not being enough. Finally, just to round it off he brought out some fresh orange juice and refilled our coffees once more. All this for eight bucks.

Tim raised his coffee mug. 'Cheers dude, great to see you again.'

I raised mine and we clinked. 'Same here, great idea.'

'It's as I said last night, it was all Gabi's idea actually.'

'You guys look pretty sweet together.'

He smiled and nodded between mouthfuls of pancake. 'We are, it's going great. What I love is meeting people when we're travelling and they always ask us how long have you been together and we say, oh only six weeks, two months whatever. We then tell them the story of how I jacked it all in to be with Gabs and they look at us as if we're crazy, but the kind of crazy you know they'd love to be. It's a pretty good feeling.'

'So where you gonna be for Christmas?'

'Isla Mujeres, you been there?'

I nodded. 'Yeah and it has one of my favourite beaches in the world, ah man that makes me so jealous!'

Isla Mujeres, just north of Cancun in Mexico is a tiny island, the sort where no cars, just golf buggies, are allowed. It has the most relaxing atmosphere as most of the island life revolves around beaches. One of them, Playa Norte, faces directly into the setting sun, has warm Caribbean waters, palm trees as far as the eye can see and the odd bar with hammocks and chair hammocks that plays reggae all day long. I used to go there most weekends when I was at uni, paradise.

'Well it's not gonna be all that great as her brother is coming out for Christmas. He was meant to come out last month but she blew him off as I'd only just got out there.' He grinned. 'We barely left our hostels for the first few weeks.'

'Well as it should be, it's probably why you're looking so thin!' I shook my head,.'It's so weird sitting here with you, hearing about all of this when I've had to ask my boss for two days off to come here. I think that's what I hate most about having a job, the fact that you only get five weeks of holiday a year and you have to ask someone's permission to go away.'

'And that person could say no.'

'Exactly! And that person could say no!'

'J, you know what I'm gonna say.'

'What?'

'Change it.'

I nodded. 'I will, I will. The scheme ends next month, then I'll think about what I'm gonna do.'

'Any ideas?'

I shook my head. 'No, and I'm not worried, something will come up. It'll work out, it always does.'

A brief silence endured as we both attempted to cut into our third pancakes. It's weird, even within the space of a few weeks you could tell how much Tim had changed. He was so much calmer, chilled out, free of the London stresses where you get psychopathically angry if you have to wait a whole four minutes for a tube. I guess when you get out of that circle, you realise what an insulated society we all live in but when you get out of it, does it make it harder to return? Does it make you not want to return to it at all? But then you can't spend your whole life travelling and as much as I hate the phrase, at some point you do have to settle down, take responsibilities, ensure you have regular money coming in etc., but how do you decide when and where? And with whom?

'I don't know if I can do this, my stomach has shrunk.'

'Yeah me too, this is gonna keep me going till dinner.'

'How do Americans do it? Imagine living here, you'd be the size of a wardrobe. So, we've talked about me and Gabi, you and London, job etc.' He looked up and smiled. 'Anything else you want to talk about?'

'You're gonna make this as awkward as you can, aren't you?'

He grinned. 'Yup!' He stuffed another quarter of pancake into his mouth. 'No relax, I'm winding you up. It's just 'cause it was so hysterical last night, you both weren't yourselves at all.'

'Well we did feel a bit weird; also we don't know how much Gabi knows about you and Mel, so I thought it better to speak to you alone.'

'Nah she knows it all; over the last six weeks we've spent so much

time together that everything has come out. So remember she probably felt a bit weird about meeting Mel.'

'Well even more credit to her for inviting us out then.'

'Exactly, great girl.'

I picked up a bit of pancake and used it to mop up some syrup. 'So
… What you thinking?'

'That you guys need to chill out and not worry. Was Mel thinking the same thing?'

I nodded. 'It's a weird feeling, we both feel like we're fucking you
over.'

'Dude you're not, you're really not. Had you done this six months
ago yes, but a lot's happened, we've both moved on. I'm with Gabi,
she makes me happy, you obviously both make each other happy.
What kind of friend would I be if I wasn't happy about it? Shall I say
the word happy again? Happy.'

I sighed with relief. 'Well that makes me feel a hell of a lot
better.'

He laughed and finished off the last of his coffee. 'So it's going
well then?'

I nodded. 'Yeah, more than well, it's incredible. She's all I can
think about at the moment, I feel completely consumed by her.'

'And Jazz?'

I shook my head. 'Pretty much forgot she existed until you just
mentioned her name.'

'Good, keep it that way.'

We met the girls a few hours later on the edge of Central Park and
the top of Fifth Avenue. They were still in shock from the guys in
Abercrombie, in fact Mel had actually gone a few shades lighter and
was finding it hard to walk in a straight line. Even though everywhere
was covered in a light dusting of snow, New York was still bathed in
amazing sunlight so we decided to spend a few hours walking around
the park, bringing each other up to date with what had been going
on in each other's lives over the last few months. Central Park was
buzzing and being slap bang in the city and a Friday afternoon it was

rammed. An ice skating competition was underway at the ice rink so we paused there for a while before running around amongst the trees playing stuck in the mud and 'it'.

Suffering from withdrawal symptoms the girls needed to go shopping again and so we all caught the subway down to Greenwich Village where there are a lot more bohemian arty shops compared to the huge flagship stores on Fifth. Mel was as happy as a primary school teacher on ecstasy as she spent dollar after dollar after dollar, grinning about how awesome her winter wardrobe was going to be. Tim and Gabi didn't buy much as they needed to fit everything they owned into two rucksacks, and big hoodies weren't going to be that useful in the Caribbean.

Under strict orders from the girls we dressed up as smart as we could that evening. They'd refused to tell us where we were going; apparently they'd planned it this morning and wanted it to be a surprise. Tim and I had splashed out on two new smart jackets and Mel and Gabi were both wearing dresses they'd bought today. Mel was looking stunning in a burgundy dress with an open back, and Gabi looked great in a racing green off the shoulder dress.

We took a cab and stopped at the Rockefeller Center. I stepped out and looked around for a bar or restaurant in sight.

'So where are we going?' asked Tim.

The girls looked at each other, smiled and pointed to the sky.

'Up there.'

I looked up. The Rockefeller Tower rose hundreds of feet up into the air. After the Empire State it was one of New York's tallest skyscrapers.

Tim looked confused. 'Isn't it all offices?'

Gabi shook her head. 'There's a restaurant on the top floor, guys can only come in if they're in jackets.'

I reached for Mel's arm. 'So that's why you wanted us to buy these jackets!'

She smiled. 'Yup, all makes sense now doesn't it?! Come on, let's go up.'

We rode the lift up to the sixty-fifth floor and emerged out into the restaurant. Huge windows covered the walls all the way around as beneath us, the lights of New York glistened in the distance. The city was gearing itself up for a Friday night and the sounds of traffic floated upwards and away. Looking out across the river, New Jersey and Coney Island winked back. The Statue of Liberty, our one tourist destination tomorrow, looked like a midget in the distance, thousands of feet below us. Taking a table by the window we sat down and grinned like kids at each other, how cool was this?

'Jonathan, I think we know what this occasion calls for.'

'Indeed Timothy.' I caught the waiter's eye. 'Bottle of Veuve Cliquot please.'

Tim nodded his approval. 'Excellent choice.'

Immediately the champagne appeared, alongside some anti-pasti and fresh strawberries that apparently came free with the champagne.

Tuna Mayonnaise Served on Celery Sticks

Ingredients

- Canned tuna
- A handful of black olives
- A few slices of white onion, diced into tiny bits
- A small slice of green chilli, diced
- At least three celery sticks per person
- Two spoonfuls of mayonnaise
- Splash of vinegar
- Black pepper

Method

- Slice up the olives into small pieces (removing the stones obviously) and add to the onion, tuna and chilli.

- Add the mayonnaise and some black pepper, and mix until it becomes all creamy. If needs be, add more mayonnaise.

- Place a spoonful of the mixture at one end of a celery stick, and arrange neatly on a plate. It looks good when you create a circle of them, all pointing out.

We were in such a good mood. After a great night's sleep and a really good day walking round New York I felt like both me and Mel had left London a long way behind us, and naturally having been travelling for months Tim and Gabi were pretty chilled out already. The champagne and wine flowed as we looked out of the window trying to pinpoint whatever buildings we thought were in front of us. To our left the Empire State Building rose parallel to us, its bright white lights shining ever upwards into the night sky. Further down towards the river the small building of the United Nations perched on the riverbank, watching out onto a world it could no longer influence.

Being around another couple had made me think about my relationship a lot. What with Barcelona and the intense month we'd both had, Mel and I were now quite used to spending a lot of time with each other. Sounds silly after we'd lived together for years but it's different in a relationship. Previously I wasn't very good at sticking around. Not in a one-night-stand go-before-she-wakes-up kinda way, but in an 'I very much need my own space' sort of way. For example if we'd been out the night before together I'd normally want to go off the next day and do something else, or chill out on my own for a bit. What with New York and Barcelona I hadn't been able to run away the next day, but more importantly, I hadn't wanted to. I'd wanted to spend all day with Mel doing silly things like going to Sainsbury's, lying in the park, watching stupid films, reading the papers without saying a word. Yes it must be because we lived with each other and so were already comfortable together but in my head I knew I was in something unlike anything I've been in before. Either that or I'd changed, or maybe she'd changed me?

We finished our dinner and headed off to "Cafe Wha?" in Greenwich Village. We'd passed it during the day and it looked pretty awesome, a live rock and roll and funk club in the basement of one of the shops we'd been in. By the time we got in it was rammed and the band had just started their second set of the evening. The track list was pretty sweet, pure crowd pleasers, first they covered Train, Counting Crows, Lenny Kravitz, Killers etc. and then the lead guitarist started playing some Santana and some proper salsa. Having round after round of cuba libres we were getting pretty drunk and dancing pretty stupid. As we all grinned at each other, shouted over the music and generally all hugged I thought to myself it was one of the best nights I'd had out in months. Like in Barcelona Mel and I danced for most of the night, not wanting each song to end, upset when it did yet loving the next one even more.

Gabi and Mel took regular toilet stops to talk about us, the two of them were really getting on, and Tim and I took that opportunity to order more drinks and tell each other how much we'd missed each other. All in all good standard drunken behaviour.

As we heard the band announce their last song for the evening (for the fourth time) Mel took my hand and pulled me back onto the narrow dance floor in front of the stage.

They finished on a deliberately cheesy song that involved everyone raising their hands to the ceiling and shouting out the chorus, which we duly obliged. In between choruses we went back to kissing like teenagers, looking forward to our hotel bed at the end of the night. I looked to my left, saw Tim and Gabi doing pretty much the same thing and smiled. I put both my arms around Mel and rested them on her neck, leaning in to kiss her on the lips once again.

She melted into me and kissed me deeply.

'I'm so pleased you talked me into this.'

I smiled. 'You didn't need too much persuading, believe me.'

'Do you know how many double shifts I have to work next week for this? I'm gonna be a nightmare.'

I kissed her again. 'Well I'll just have to spoil you when you get home won't I? Anyway it's only Friday, that Sunday feeling is a long way off.'

She laid her head on my chest and moved slowly in rhythm with me, her hand gently stroking my back. I looked down at her, all I could see was her hair and her flickering eyelashes. I suddenly had a realisation that this was all I wanted from life. All I needed was already in my arms. I felt a rush of words surge up, something I'd been meaning to say for a while but had never found the right time.

'I'm in love with you.'

She lifted her head and looked at me, a smile spread from the corners of her mouth and turned itself into a grin. 'What did you say?'

I smiled back. 'That I'm in love with you. I have been for a while I guess.'

She leant in to kiss me. 'I love you too, God I love you so much,' she grinned, 'I just wanted you to say it first!'

I mock-pushed her away. 'Ha, women! Since when?!'

She shrugged. 'Barcelona, when we were dancing in the square.' She looked embarrassed. 'It kinda felt right, know what I mean?'

I nodded. 'I know just what you mean. It's exactly how I feel, have felt since, since yeah Barcelona too.'

She smiled. 'I was hoping you'd say that. Now shut up and kiss me.'

The song ended and the lights came up. We walked towards Tim and Gabi hand in hand, stupid grins plastered across our faces. Tim and Gabs were equally happy, a combination of great food, great music, great company and lots of alcohol meant that this night was one we'd all remember for a long time. Grabbing our jackets we emerged out onto the street, hailed a cab and let it whisk us away into the New York dawn.

Chapter Sixty-Seven

November 24th 2008

THE WEEK FLEW BY. Mel was right, she had to pull a lot of double shifts to make up for New York, but I still tried to see her as often as I could, even if it was just for an hour or so after her shift and I just went over to hers to sleep. Our relationship seemed to have snowballed after that night in "Café Wha?" Everything felt that much more official. I'd even invited Mel to spend Christmas Day with Matt and my Mum next month. They knew her obviously, but never as my girlfriend and I thought it was about time that they did.

I was also getting on slightly better with Jazz now. As Mel had been working so much I'd been the one going over to theirs most evenings, not the other way round and so even though we'd only had a few brief conversations it wasn't as awkward. In fact I was going to Mel's tonight, she wasn't working (amazingly) and had volunteered to cook me dinner.

Jazz opened the door with a glass of wine in her hand.

'Hey, come in, Mel isn't back yet so we're gonna have to hold on dinner for the moment!'

I came in and slung my trenchcoat over the back of the couch.

'Oh well, did she say how long she's gonna be?' I glanced at my watch. 'She's normally back by this time isn't she?'

Jazz nodded and refilled her glass. 'Yeah but her phone's off so she's either still working or underground. I'm guessing still working as she normally texts me when she's on her way.' She walked over to the table and picked up an empty glass. 'Wine? I got some Malbec in.'

I took the glass and held up my bag. 'Bought one too, we can open it when she gets back.'

Jazz walked over to the couch and settled herself into the corner. She reached over to the stereo on the bookshelf and turned on some music. I walked over to the table, put my glass down, turned the chair to face her and sat down, the coffee table between us. I drank deeply, if only to fill the silence for the time being.

I looked at the table, at the set cutlery, plates, candles and glasses.

'Did you do this?'

She nodded. 'Yeah, got back early from work and was feeling restless. The place needed a tidy anyway so I thought why not make a bit of an effort for once.'

'Fair enough, are you cooking too?'

She shook her head. 'No, you know I can't cook. Mel's doing that. I mean the stuff's all in the fridge I just don't know what she's doing with it.'

'Is there asparagus by any chance?'

'Erm I think so, why?'

I smiled to myself. 'Doesn't matter.'

Our phones vibrated simultaneously and we reached for our pockets, *guys, I'm gonna be about an hour, sorry, make a start on the wine without me! xxx*

We looked up at each other to confirm we'd just got the same text. Jazz got up and walked towards me with the half-empty bottle. 'Might as well follow orders then.'

She filled up my glass and wandered back over to the couch. An hour, an hour with Jazz and no Mel. What the hell were we going to talk about?

'Shall we see what's on TV?'

Jazz burst out laughing. 'No we are not going to see what's on TV! Mel wanted a nice dinner tonight, and we are not gonna let her walk in to find us lounging around watching TV! Stop being so difficult.'

'I'm not being difficult,' I protested. 'I was just wondering what was on!'

'Well have a look in a newspaper then. Anyway, let's talk. Mel says you're still not happy at work, what are you thinking about doing?'

I shrugged and began talking, and you know what, it wasn't too bad. We actually had a decent conversation. Turns out like everyone else in the world Jazz wasn't happy at work either and was thinking about leaving.

'The problem I have though is that I need to have money every month. What with the bills for Mum's home I can't afford to take a pay cut or be unemployed for a month. I'm beginning to feel trapped already and I'm only twenty-four!'

'How is your Mum?'

She grimaced. 'Not great really, not much worse but she's not improving either. Much as I hate myself for even thinking it in some ways I wish it could be over, it'd just be better for both our sakes.'

Jazz walked over to the kitchen and opened the bottle I brought.

'Shall we not wait …'

'It's fine I've got loads more, we'll open another when she gets here.'

She topped my glass up and sat down with a sigh. 'I still go and see her every fortnight but I'm beginning to want a bit of my life back, financially and socially. I mean I want to buy somewhere, just like Rob did, but I can't see that happening anytime soon if I'm paying thousands a year in care home charges.'

'Can you take a loan out?'

'What to pay for Mum? I could but then that'll make it harder to get a mortgage.' She sighed and looked at me directly in the eyes. 'I dunno, it's just hard sometimes.'

I felt a flicker of admiration for Jazz, a remembrance that she'd had it pretty tough. The image of her asleep in a chair at her Mum's care home wearing a wedding dress floated around my head.

She swirled her glass around in her hand and watched the tannin cling to the side. 'I haven't spoken like this to anyone really.'

'Really? Jazz, you can't keep it all in, it's unhealthy.'

She sighed. 'I know I can't.'

I continued. 'And don't beat yourself up for thinking like that about your Mum. It would be for the best and everyone knows that, it doesn't make you a bad person or an evil daughter. Hell, most people wouldn't do what you do, and you've done it on your own without any brothers and sisters. Don't be so hard on yourself.'

She blushed slightly as she took another sip. 'I guess, I guess you're right, I can't keep it bottled up can I?'

'No you can't. What about Mel, don't you talk to her?'

'Yeah I do, but not that much. It's weird, medics, doctors, whatever you call them, they kind of change when they start working in a hospital. They become almost tougher. Mel spends her days talking to people with the same problems I have, the last thing she wants when she comes home is to have more of the same shit.'

'But you're her best friend, she'd always be there for you, you know that.'

'I know, I do, I just don't want to make her be there for me, if you see what I mean?'

I paused. 'What about Keith?'

She laughed. 'What about Keith?'

'Well when you were together, you talked to him about it yeah?'

She shook her head. 'No, he wasn't like that, I never really felt like either I could or that I wanted to talk to him. We didn't really talk that much to be honest with you.'

'Right,' I looked down.

'No no no,' she reached across the table and touched my wrist, 'I didn't mean it like that. I just meant he wasn't someone I could talk to like I could talk to …' She stopped herself and looked away.

I looked at my watch. 'It's been over an hour.'

Jazz pulled out her phone. 'Oh crap, I've got a message. From Mel, says she's got to stay another half hour or so.'

'When did she send it?'

'Just after half eight.' She looked at her watch. 'So what, ten minutes ago? That's cool, she'll be back soon.' She looked at me and smiled. 'The trials of dating a doctor I suppose!'

I half smiled. 'Yeah it's not all fun and games.'

'Things going well?'

I nodded. 'Yeah, very well.'

'Cool.' She looked at her empty glass. 'Time for bottle number three I think.'

She walked over to the kitchen as I stood up to go to the toilet. Woah, a bottle of thick red and no food and I was feeling drunk.

I came back and Jazz had already opened the wine. She sat on the couch, two full glasses on the coffee table sat in front of her. I walked over, picked up my glass and sat down in the one seater couch to her left.

'Mel said you told her you love her.'

I paused. 'Yeah I did, I do.'

'How did you know?'

'I just did, I think I always did.'

We sat in silence for a few seconds as I drank deeply

'It seems you guys are pretty set for a while.'

I nodded. 'Yeah, yeah we are.'

My leg vibrated, I pulled my phone out. *Babe I've got to work the double, I can't get out of it, I'm so sorry. How about we do this next week? xxxsorryxxx*

I sighed, I felt so bad for her, she really was working so hard since we got back from New York. I texted back telling her not to worry. 'Mel isn't coming. She's got to work another shift.'

'Poor girl, she must be exhausted.'

'Yeah, she must be.' I sighed. 'Well, she said we should do this next week instead.

Jazz giggled. 'Think we'll have to buy some more wine in that case!'

I grimaced and slowly got to my feet. 'Yeah, we have drunk quite a bit haven't we, and no food either.'

She looked up quizzically. 'Where are you going?'

'Home, Mel won't be back till the morning.'

Jazz held up the half empty bottle. 'J, stay twenty minutes and finish the wine with me, it won't kill you.'

I hesitated before putting my coat back over the couch. I sat back down. Jazz filled her glass and passed the bottle to me. I couldn't quite reach to take it from her without getting out of my seat again.

'And whilst you're at it would you just sit on this couch instead of sitting as far away as possible, I'm not going to bite.'

I half-smiled. 'OK, maybe I have been doing that a bit.'

'A bit? J, you forget how easy you are to read. Now come sit.'

I moved over, filled my glass and sat back on the couch.

'You know Keith and I never slept together. He wanted to but I never let him.'

I coughed. 'OK, why are you telling me this?'

'Because I thought you should know.'

'Why?'

She shrugged and turned to me. 'Just because.'

My head flopped back on the couch and I looked up at the ceiling. 'So it sounds like it wasn't the best relationship in the world.'

Jazz almost snorted. 'It wasn't, he was just so persistent and he had a villa in Italy and I was feeling a bit needy.' She paused. 'I wouldn't really call it a relationship either, well I'm certainly not counting it as one.'

'Well he told me he was your boyfriend.'

'Really?!'

'Yeah, bit of a shock actually.'

'That doesn't surprise me, without sounding arrogant he was always a lot more into me than I was him.'

'Yeah I kinda got that impression.'

She raised the glass to her lips and drank slowly. 'I regret it really, all of it.'

My head was spinning with all the wine and no food. I was incredibly tired all of a sudden and all I wanted to do was go to bed, but I was too tired to even get up off of the couch. I shuddered at the thought of having to bus it back to Balham tonight.

'You've gone quiet.'

'Hmm?'

'I said you've gone quiet, what you thinking?' She turned to me and rested her elbow on the back of the couch, her left hand gently toying with her hair.

'Just tired really, and drunk, yeah drunk first then tired I think. You?'

'Feeling a bit drunk.'

'So Keith was a jackass then? How about since then, anyone around?'

She shook her head. 'No, no-one at all. It's pretty depressing to be honest, especially when I have to see Mel's grin all the time. I'm just not meeting anyone and it's beginning to annoy me.' She laughed, 'Actually it's beginning to frustrate me!'

I raised an eyebrow, something that took a lot more effort than I'd expected. 'How'd you mean?'

She held my eyes. 'You were the last person I made love to.' She shrugged and drank from her glass. 'And that was March, that was eight months ago.' She filled up my glass, half-smiled and went back to toying with her hair. 'Keith could never make me cum either. Not like the way you could. It's pretty frustrating, I'm getting to the point where I just really want an intense, crazy, passionate love affair.' She paused. 'You know like the kind of sex we used to have after we argued?'

I nodded and drank. 'Yeah,' I croaked.

'That sort of sex where all you can think about is that person and what they're doing to you, over and over.' She drank deeply. 'We had great sex.'

I nodded.

'Do you still think about it?'

I raised an eyebrow. 'What, sex?'

She laughed. 'Well I meant us, but yeah,' her hand rested loosely against my knee, 'the sex.'

'I er,' I stammered, 'well I, I guess I do, a bit, but I'm with Mel now.'

She shrugged and moved closer. 'Doesn't stop you still thinking about it though, does it?'

'Jazz ...'

She looked at me full on, her big brown eyes gazed into mine and then down to my lips. She opened her mouth and bit her lower lip gently. She leant over and all of a sudden we were kissing. Her mouth opened straight away, her tongue probing into my half-closed mouth.

That split second lasted a lifetime. Everything stopped as I suddenly sobered up. Do I become that guy? Do I kiss my girlfriend's best friend whilst she works a double shift to pay back a holiday I made her take? No, of course I don't.

I pushed Jazz back. 'What the hell do you think you're doing?'

'You want me, it's written all over your face, and I want you too. I'm making the move you wanted me to make but are too chicken to say.'

I stood up. 'What the hell are you talking about? I'm with Mel!'

'So why did you kiss me back?'

I exploded. 'I did not kiss you back, you kissed me and I pushed you away!'

She flicked her hand at me. 'Whatever, I don't think you're as into Mel as you might want to be.'

I snatched up my jacket. 'Don't you even dare, you know nothing about me and Mel. This,' I motioned between us, 'is nothing, means nothing, is not worth mentioning. Don't you dare think you can ruin my relationship just because you're feeling horny.'

She stood up. 'You sure it's me you should be saying that to? Go on, get the fuck out of my flat.'

'Gone.'

I turned and slammed the door behind me. The cold London air smacked me in the face like a punch. What the hell had I just done?

Chapter Sixty-Eight
November 25th 2008

```
<u free for lunch? I need to talk to you>
<yeah sure, everything ok?>
<I'll tell you later, 12.30?>
```

ROB HAD BEEN IN bed when I'd got home last night, and he'd had to be in early this morning for a client meeting so I hadn't had a chance to talk to him.

I felt horrendous, absolutely horrendous. My head was pounding from all the red wine, I'd hardly slept a wink and I was indescribably angry with myself. What a fucking idiot. Why had I kissed her? Had I kissed her? She kissed me and I pushed her away but yeah, there was contact wasn't there? I could have pushed her away sooner, why didn't I?

We walked out of the office and down the stairs into the foyer.

'Dude slow down, what's up, is someone hurt, is it Tim?'

I slowed down remembering this wasn't earth-shattering news for everyone else.

'No sorry, everyone's fine, no-one's hurt.'

He sighed. 'Phew, you had me worried. So what's up? How was dinner? Did I hear you come in last night?'

We stopped and waited for the lights to change. I nodded. 'Yeah, Mel had to work a double so never came home in the end. It was just me and Jazz.' I looked straight at him and then down.

Rob ran and caught up with me. 'Oh J you didn't?! Please tell me you didn't?!'

I looked away and began to cross the road.

'You idiot, you goddamn idiot! Why the hell did you do that? Did

448

you sleep with her?'

I shook my head. 'No I didn't sleep with her. She kissed me and I pushed her away. We were both hammered.'

We sat down on a bench, our jackets done up tight against the biting wind.

'What happened?'

'I went to Mel's thinking it was just dinner, me and her. Then Jazz opens the door, Mel texts saying she'll be an hour late so Jazz and I wait and have a few glasses of wine.'

'Then what?'

'Mel then texts to say she's gonna be later, so we carry on drinking and talking.'

'And are you thinking you want to kiss her?'

'No! God no!'

'OK, carry on.'

'So we carry on drinking, then Mel texts saying she can't make it at all, has to work a double. I get up to leave, Jazz says stay and finish the bottle. So we do and I sit next to her.'

'So you hadn't been sitting next to her all evening?'

'No, I'd been on the chair or the other couch.'

'Right, good.'

'So then she starts telling me how she hadn't had an orgasm since we broke up, her ex-boyfriend was a jackass, how she regrets it and that she thinks about the sex we used to have and she misses it.'

Rob shook his head. 'Bitch; were you tempted?'

I paused. 'Well, kind of, a hot girl telling you she misses having sex with you, and I was drunk. God I sound like such a shit.'

'What happened?'

'She then leans over and kisses me, shoves her tongue in my mouth.'

Rob shook his head. 'Christ, what did you do?'

'I pushed her away.'

'After how long?'

'That's the thing, probably like two seconds, but I didn't recoil immediately.'

'Then what?'

'We shouted at each other and I left.'

'And Mel?'

'She only finished work a few hours ago. I got a text from her saying she was exhausted and going home to sleep.'

Rob put his head in his hands. 'Oh J, you are such an idiot. Why did you kiss her back?'

'I don't know, but what do I do now? I'll never forgive myself if I've fucked this up.'

He sat up. 'OK, I am going to ask you this one last time. Do you still like Jazz?'

I shook my head. 'Absolutely not.'

'Good. Then you have to tell Mel. You have to be honest and take the consequences.'

'Really?'

'Yes really, otherwise every time you see the both of them you're gonna be terrified that Jazz will have said something.'

'You're right, I've got to be honest and hope I don't lose her over this. Jesus, what was I thinking?!' I ran my hand through my hair, 'OK, I have to tell her.'

'And she'll respect the fact you're telling her and not lying. It's like a murder case, if you admit it the punishment is less harsh.'

I shook my head. 'I'm such an idiot. You know I didn't sleep a wink last night. Just thinking that I may have hurt her makes me feel sick.'

I turned to Rob. 'What if I've lost her?'

He put his hand on my shoulder, 'Hold up, you are an idiot but you're not a cunt, you didn't sleep with Jazz and you've been feeling like shit ever since. At the end of the day it was a tiny kiss, you've just got to hope she forgives you, even though it was with Jazz. Oh J, why can't it have been with someone else?'

'I know, I know. OK, how am I gonna do this?'

'See her tonight, don't go over there, meet mutual, somewhere out so she can storm off home if she wants to, and tell her everything.'

I nodded, psyching myself up for the evening that was to come.

'Look dude, from the sounds of it, Jazz is more at fault. She'll be upset but you're not going to lose her over this. It might just take a bit of hard work, it'll be OK.'

He leant over and squeezed my shoulder. 'But I'm still angry with you though, it was a really stupid thing to do.'

'I know, I know.'

'Look, I've got to go, I've got tonnes to do. I'll speak to you later ok?'

He rose and put his sandwich wrapper in the bin.

'Ok, thanks Rob.' I held out my hand. 'I appreciate it.'

He clasped it and shrugged. 'Hey, the way you're feeling right now is a good sign, you now know that you'll never ever do it again.' He turned and walked out of the park.

I sat back and looked into the distance. He was right, I had to tell her, and soon. I had to be honest with her and hope this wasn't the end, because if it was … well I'd never forgive myself.

My leg vibrated, it was a text from Mel

How could you?

DECEMBER

Chapter Sixty-Nine
December 2nd, 2008

WHAT THE FUCK MAN?

I mean seriously, what are you doing?

It's just as well I'm emailing this to you rather than saying this to your face as I don't think you understand quite how fucking angry with you I am.

And I had to find out from Mel?! Come on J, what's going on? Not only do you cheat on Mel, you don't even have the balls to tell her. And then you don't tell me either, what were you trying to do, pretend it never happened? And so she had to find out from Jazz, how humiliating do you think it is to find out from your housemate that her boyfriend just pulled her? Then what do you think they did J? Sat down and had some dinner? God you are so stupid. Way to go and fuck up the best thing that you have in your life.

I'm not surprised she's dumped you. If Gabi did that to me I'd kill her. I mean cheating on your girlfriend with her best friend, what are you J, a 14 year old cliché? And not just that, you cheat with the girl you used to go out with, a girl who Mel, until recently was paranoid about the fact that she thought you still fancied her. Well done.

I thought everything was going well? You told her you were in love with her and this is what you do one week later? Funny way of showing it dude.

So you are going to explain to me just what on earth you thought you'd achieve by pulling Jazz, and why the hell you couldn't man up and tell Mel yourself. The worst of it is that right now I know she's hurting and who can she turn to? Her two best friends can't keep their hands off of each other and I'm out here. Well done again J, how to make the girl you love feel like shit. Do you not understand how paranoid she must've been moving in with Jazz and starting to go out with you at the same time? Do you not think that every time you guys were alone she thought that this might be happening? Well you can bet that's what she's thinking now and that she's replaying every moment the two or the three of you ever spent together, wondering if it's her fault what happened happened.

And then, if you aren't doing this already, you are going to put all of your energy into getting her back, because I am not going to let you fuck this up. As much as you don't deserve her right now, the two of you belong together, I could see that in New York and so you are gonna go out there and promise her that what happened will never ever ever happen again. You are never going to see Jazz again (I doubt Mel will ever let that happen anyway) and even if you and Mel do get through this you should know that you have probably fucked up their friendship for good. So once more, well done.

Now give me your story

Tim

Chapter Seventy
December 4th 2008

TIM, NOTHING YOU CAN SAY can make me feel any worse than I do already. Believe me. And as to trying to sort this all out, what do you think I've been doing for the last week, skipping in the park?

Let's get some things straight.

I don't know what Mel told you, but I did not pull Jazz. Well, I mean I did kind of, but it was for a second, nothing more. Let me explain.

I went over to Mel's last week for dinner, Mel couldn't make it in the end as she had to work a double shift, so Jazz and I ended up staying in and getting drunk (I didn't know till the last minute that Mel wasn't coming home). Jazz and I are on the couch talking; to cut a long story short after telling me that she missed having sex with me, she lunges for me and kisses me. I push her away but yes I admit I pushed her away a second or two after I should have pushed her away.

So I leave the house and go home, feeling like shit. Next day I have lunch with Rob and decide to tell Mel that night. Jazz gets in there first, tells Mel as soon as she gets home from her shift and Mel goes spare. She sends me this text, I call her straight back and she starts shouting down the phone. She calls me every name in the book, says how she doesn't want to see me anymore and hangs up. That was nine days ago and she still won't answer my calls. I've tried, of course I have and of course I'll carry on trying but I don't know what to do mate. When she spoke to me on the phone she said how she couldn't believe me and Jazz had "made out" on her couch. Now help me out here, her lunging for me and me pushing her away does not constitute "making out", so I think Jazz has been telling her things that didn't happen. For all I know Jazz has been saying that I made a move on her, and even though I hope she won't believe it, if the thought enters her head who knows what she'll think? I call her constantly, I've been round to the hospital, I ring on her doorbell until the neighbours shout at me to go away; I've written her letters but for all I know she rips them up without even reading them or Jazz intercepts them before they get to her. I dunno, I just need to speak to her, explain to her what happened and pray she can find room to forgive me. But what I'm scared of is this Tim, what if she doesn't believe me? What if in some sick world Jazz planned to make a move on me so she could tell Mel and break us up, is that so foreign an idea? And now, even though Mel is undoubtedly angry with Jazz, the best friend always wins in these situations don't they? What if each night she's sitting with Jazz, being convinced to write me out of her life?

I love her Tim, I love her so fucking much that I can't even imagine walking on without her. I've realised this last week what it's been like and I've got nothing, absolutely nothing without her. I know she's hurting and the thought that I'm the one causing her that pain rips me up but I just don't know what to do. I don't know how to go about getting her back when she won't even open her door or answer her phone. Tim what am I going to do? How am I going to get through to her? Do I carry on trying until she changes her phone number, do I carry on trying in the vain hope she'll open the door one day, even if it is just to tell me to fuck off?

I know you're dicked off with me, believe me, I am as well but I need you at the moment. Help me out, please.

J

p.s. Some shitty birthday it's going to be this year.

I closed the top of my laptop and looked at my phone. No messages. I dialled Mel's number, no answer. I got up and left my room and slowly walked down the stairs, putting my weight heavily on each foot as I passed each step. Entering the kitchen I put the hood of my hoodie up and turned on the heating. Looking at myself in the bay windows before drawing the curtains I was shocked at how pale I looked. India seemed a lifetime ago.

Rob wasn't in. He was out on a date with a friend of Emma's and I was resentful, bored, depressed and moody. Living in a two definitely has its downsides as it involves a lot of being on your own and I didn't want to be on my own right now. Or did I? I was pretty piss poor company at the moment. Let's face it, there was only one person I wanted to be with at the moment and if I couldn't be with her I couldn't be arsed to pour my heart out about it to anyone else.

I opened the fridge and took out some vegetables. I had some mince I needed to eat and felt like some hot hamburger soup with crusty bread. I'll try her again when I've finished cooking.

Hamburger Soup

Ingredients
- 200 grams good quality mince
- One onion, finely sliced
- Two sticks of celery, sliced
- Two carrots, peeled and sliced
- One bay leaf (remember to remove it when finished cooking)
- Few sprigs of thyme, chopped
- A good handful of parsley, chopped
- About ten tablespoons of barley, already soaked
- Half a can of tomato soup
- Half a can of chopped tomatoes
- Two beef stock cubes

Method
- Make sure you have pre-cooked the barley. If not, boil it in cold

water, drain and boil again, then leave to simmer for an hour or so.

- Boil up the stock cubes in around a pint and a half of water.

- Add the tomatoes, soup, celery, carrots, parsley, thyme and bay leaf.

- Bring to the boil.

- Whilst you are doing this, brown the onion and mince for a few minutes.

- After draining the excess fat off of the mince, add the meat and onion to the mixture and bring to the boil again.

- Simmer for around an hour (or longer if you can). Add some black pepper.

- When the barley is cooked, add to the pot.

- Remember to spoon off the excess fat produced by the mince every ten minutes or so.

- When ready, grate each portion with cheese, parmesan works best.

- Serve with crusty bread and loads of butter.

I sat down at the table and mechanically spooned the soup into my mouth. I flipped up my phone again; no messages. I sighed and slammed my phone down hard on the wooden table, the loud bang resonating around the empty flat. I was so angry with myself. Being the cheater was a pretty weird experience, one I'd never had before and one I vowed I would never have again. You realise what a feeling of power you have over someone, and what they have over you. But then again that's what love is isn't it? Letting someone in, giving someone that power in the hope they won't abuse it but instead make you stronger. Well I fucked that one up didn't I? Being drunk was no excuse. Sure I'd had a bottle and a half of red wine and no food but unless you've just downed a litre of sambuca, you always know what you're doing, don't you? For one stupid second I thought it was a good idea to kiss Jasmine, for one stupid second I let it happen and now here I am one week later looking at having lost Mel. It was all too easy to just lay the blame at Jazz's feet. I kissed her back and I've got to acknowledge that.

I did however feel positively sick when I thought about the sort of stuff Jazz may have been saying to Mel, and the sort of stuff she may have believed. We "made out"?! I mean seriously, she wouldn't have believed that would she? Is Jazz fucked up enough to make stuff up like that to hurt Mel? What is she trying to achieve, make us both unhappy? Break us up so she can make a move on me or so that she can just have Mel back to herself? But this surely fucks up their friendship doesn't it? How can Mel trust Jazz after this; this can't be what Jazz wanted can it, to just hurt me and more importantly hurt Mel? God what a mess, this literally fucks up everything.

I looked out through the chink in the curtains at the pitch black sky and tried not to think about the one thing I hadn't stopped thinking about. Jazz thought I wanted her, Jazz thought I wasn't being honest with myself about Mel. Her words cut straight through me and on some level I think she may be right. I hate her for saying it but I think she may be right. Not that I want Jazz over Mel, that's not true at all, but in that it feels safe and right with Mel, and that scares me. It feels like this could be it with Mel (if she takes me back obviously) and I don't know if I'm ready for this to be it. Jazz embodies something exotic, foreign, tantalising and forbidden, and that intrigues me. But then I'm so happy when I'm with Mel and this hurt I'm feeling now, well that's got to mean something, doesn't it? I'm continually running, never putting down roots, giving the impression I'm everybody's friend, constantly flitting around, but the truth of it is that I'm scared. I'm scared of people getting to know me too well; if I continually run they can't get too close. Mel was there, after years of friendship and months as lovers she knew me pretty much better than anyone else. Did I subconsciously push her away? The fact that I did it a week after telling her I was in love with her speaks volumes surely. But then again I was saying before how with her I don't want to run away anymore, I want to stick around in the morning, I want her to know me inside out, hell I'm amazed that after knowing me inside out she still wants to stick around. Or did at least. Did I just have one slip?

The sound of my phone vibrating on the large pine table shook me from my musings.

OK "The Mitre", one hour if you want to talk

I grabbed my keys and left my flat. The half-eaten soup lay sprawled out around the bowl.

I placed my bottle of Corona opposite a small glass of dry white and waited. I felt nervous, ridiculously nervous. I glanced to the door, but found I had to move right round to see it so I swapped places, swapping the glasses on the table as well.

Opening the door to the pub she swept up the two steps to the table and undid her jacket.

I rose to great her. 'Hey! How are you doing?'

She turned and removed her jacket as I went towards her, removing any chance I had of any contact.

'How do you think I am?' She sat down and looked at the wine in front of her. 'I'm driving, I don't want to drink.' She rose again and headed off to the bar.

'Let me, what do you want?' She ignored me and carried on walking. I felt pathetic.

Mel returned with a half-pint of Coke and put it down hard in the middle of the table. She refused to catch my eyes.

'So, you pulled Jazz and then didn't bother telling me. Care to explain?'

'I should have told you, I was going to tell you that evening. Look Mel, I don't know what Jazz has said but it was for a second, no more then I pushed her away I promise you.'

'Because that makes it alright.'

'No, no it doesn't.' I dropped my head and placed my hands on the table reaching for hers. She sat back. 'Mel, I am so so sorry, we were talking and then all of a sudden Jazz kisses me and I push her off me but we'd already kissed and …' I tailed off.

Now she looked up at me, her eyes full of tears about to fall. 'How could you?'

I fell silent.

'How could you do that to me with Jazz?'

'I—'

'You know how I feel about you both and you just threw it all in my face.'

'But—'

She held her hands up and raised her voice. 'How do you think it feels living with Jazz? How do you think it feels getting upset and hiding in my bedroom because I don't want her to know I'm upset, because she's part of the reason I'm upset.'

'I don't know what she told you but—'

'Oh does it matter what she told me?' she snapped. 'Does it change anything? Is this how you treat people you're in love with?'

I shook my head.

'Good, because if you do you're in for a very lonely life, I can tell you.'

I looked down at the table, there was nothing I could say to that.

'Look,' she looked at her watch, 'I've got to go in a few minutes, I just wanted to let you say your piece so you'd stop calling me. So do it.'

I was lost for words, '... Stop calling you? What are you saying?'

She snapped. 'What do you think I'm saying? We're over, we have been since you pulled my housemate on my couch. When I walk out that door J, I don't want to see you again. I don't want you calling me, I don't want you stalking me at the hospital and I sure as hell don't want you turning up at my flat. That's it, go off and do what you like with who you like, although,' she raised her finger, 'if you have any decency left in you, you will never see Jazz again. Sleep with the world I don't care, but don't go near her.'

My heart was pounding in my chest; I felt like I was fighting for my future, as if there was an egg timer placed between us on the table, and that time was rapidly running out. 'Mel, I don't want anyone else, I love you. I'm not going to stop calling because I'm not going to give up on you. We are made to be together, I know that and deep down you know that too.'

A few tears began to roll down Mel's face. 'So why did you do it J? Why did you have to fuck it up? I wanted this to be it for me, I thought it would be.'

I reached for her hands which she moved back and rested in her lap. 'It is! Mel, I want this to be it for me too! I fucked up, I fucked up big time but don't let that be it. Hate me, take some time if you need but please don't write me out of your life.' My eyes began to fill. 'I couldn't take it.' For a few seconds we held each other's watery gaze. I could see her soften slightly.

The wall went up, she shook her head. 'No J. It was it, but now it isn't anymore.'

'But Mel, it was a second, literally a second and then I pushed her away. Listen, I don't know what she told you but I promise—'

'J, that doesn't matter!' she said exasperatedly. 'I don't care if it was a second or an hour, you still did it! How can I ever trust you again? How can I be with someone who obviously has such little respect for me that he'd do that with my best friend? Someone who has such little respect for me that he can't even tell me himself.'

'I was going to that night.'

'Course you were.'

'I was! I was with Rob when I got your text and we had just been talking about me telling you that night! Ask him!'

She sat back. 'What did you say?'

'Ask Rob! I was going to tell you.'

'You and Rob were talking about it before you told me?'

Ah fuck.

'Well, I told him but I—'

'Laughing about me I suppose? Was he telling you to have an affair, use us both?'

'No! He was the one that told me to tell you!'

Her eyes widened. 'So you weren't even going to tell me?! Rob had to tell you to tell me?'

She pushed her chair back and rose to her feet. Any softness, any chance I had was now lying in tatters before me.

'You've said your piece. We're done, J.'

She walked towards the door. I picked up my jacket and phone, 'Wait, don't go!'

She wheeled around, her ice cold stare stopped me dead in my tracks. 'Do not try and follow me!' she said through gritted teeth.

I held up my hands. 'OK.'

'I mean it J, stop calling.'

She pushed the door open and disappeared out into the cold night.

Chapter Seventy-One
December 11th 2008

'HOW MANY GLASSES MATE?'

I looked confused and looked around me, 'Er none.'

The barman nodded his head slowly and handed over the bottle. I gripped the wine tightly by the neck and pushed open the doors that led down to the dock. It was freezing cold and I was only wearing a shirt so I dug my remaining hand deep into my jeans pocket for warmth. I picked a spot to the side of the entrance and sat on the steps leading up to the door. I looked up at the sky; dark clouds tinged with the yellow reflections of a London evening hung low and heavy.

I didn't want to admit it but I was beginning to lose hope. She still wasn't returning my calls and although I had stopped going to the hospital she still wasn't opening her door at home. I'd never seen such a stubborn side of her before. There was literally silence, no angry calls, no accusing texts and no screaming matches, she had just completely cut me out of her life. It was awful, worse than awful. At least arguments give you something to go on, a hold somewhere; this silence made me feel like I was freefalling down a waterfall.

I didn't try and follow her after the pub because in my head I didn't believe that she'd leave my life completely, that she'd be so set in her decision. Maybe it was arrogant or just stupid of me, I dunno, but now I was having doubts. I still thought I'd see her again, but each day that passed where she didn't see me, was a day where she moved on that little bit further from me. Apart from India I'd pretty much seen Mel every day for the last few years and to have her remove herself from my life was such an abysmal feeling. I still don't know what to do, I don't know how to get her to talk to me but I know I can't stop, I mustn't stop.

I felt a rush of heat on my back as the door opened and out walked Freya with a bottle of wine in her hand and a smile on her face.

'Rob and I have been looking all over the place for you! What are you doing out here? It's freezing!'

She parked herself down next to me and placed her wine next to my almost empty bottle.

'I couldn't take listening to another Abba song,' I said into the cold night air. 'I would've slit my wrists, or someone else's at least.'

She laughed. 'Considering we're an events company you would have thought we could have organised a better Christmas party than this.'

I half smiled. 'I know; trying to dance to "Dancing Queen" and "Waterloo" is pretty much my idea of hell at the best of times.'

I picked up the bottle and drank deeply. 'Anyway, how come you were both looking for me?'

Freya shrugged. ''Cause you and Rob are pretty much the only people I can be arsed to talk to in the office. Besides,' she put her arm on my shoulder, 'we're worried about you.'

'Really?'

'Yeah really. I know he'd never say it but Rob is, you can see it in his face. And I care about you too. It's plain obvious when you're upset and right now the whole world can see you are; I just want to know if there's anything either of us can do?'

I shook my head. 'Nah, I know I'm pretty poor company at the moment but there's really nothing anyone can do, I've just got to deal with it, whatever "it" is going to be.'

She lifted the bottle to her lips and then passed it to me. 'Still not heard from her?'

I shook my head. 'Nup.'

'How long are you going to keep trying for?'

'As long as it takes.'

'But J this is what I'm worried about, as long as it takes for what?'

'For me to get her back obviously.'

Freya paused. 'Bite my head off if you want, but hasn't she said she doesn't want to come back?'

'Yeah, but I must be able to change her mind, that can't be it.'

Freya closed her mouth and turned back to look out at the Thames.

'J, you can't force it OK.' She paused. 'Maybe, maybe you are gonna have to accept it that she doesn't want to see you. Maybe you should stop calling.'

I shook my head. 'No, I'm not giving up.'

'Maybe that's not your decision to make.'

I fell silent.

'Look I didn't mean to …'

'It's OK, you're right, I just feel like I can't stop yet. It's only been two weeks and I know, I know that this can't be it. So just let me do this for a little while longer OK, because I need your support.'

She squeezed my shoulder. 'OK.'

I changed the subject. 'How's stuff going with Christian?'

She smiled. 'Probably not what you want to hear at the moment but really good, great actually.'

'Don't be silly, just because I'm not happy doesn't mean I don't want anyone else to be. That's great news, how long has it been now?'

She chewed her lip. 'Erm a month, six weeks or so. But it's really tough when you start seeing someone around this time of year I think.'

'How do you mean?'

'Well for a start there are so many parties going on, everyone's so busy but also, well I'm going home for a week at Christmas and he lives quite near me but …'

I passed the bottle back to Freya. 'But what?'

'Well I don't want to do the whole meet the family thing just yet, it's still too new.' She paused. 'But yeah, it's going pretty well.'

I turned to her. 'Look at that grin, this is serious!'

She slapped my hand. 'Oh shush, anyway what are you doing for Christmas?'

I sighed. 'Well Mel was meant to be coming to stay at my Mum's but now,' I shrugged, 'I dunno what's happening, and if she doesn't come I'm gonna have to tell my family why and then listen to their lectures. God I really can't be arsed.' I felt myself killing the mood again. 'Anyway, New Year, new starts and everything.'

'J, can you keep a secret?'

I turned to her. 'Course I can.'

'I'm handing in my notice on Monday.'

'No way! I thought you were happy? Have you got somewhere else lined up?'

She shook her head. 'No, it's Christmas, no-one's hiring at the moment.'

'So what are you gonna do?'

She shrugged. 'Dunno but I don't want to stay in this job, and not knowing what you want to do isn't a big enough reason for carrying on doing something you know you don't want to do.'

I nodded. 'Makes sense, but what are you going to do about money?'

'Well I've got four weeks' notice and I reckon I can go a month or so without earning so I'm just gonna give myself that time to work out what I want to do and apply for that.'

'Well, I can see you starting the ball rolling to be honest.'

She took another swig. 'How do you mean?'

'I'm gonna do the same thing in January and I don't think Rob is going to be that far behind me. Don't tell anyone this, obviously.'

Freya waved her hand. 'Obviously, what are you both gonna do?'

'I dunno, it depends on the whole Mel thing as well I guess, but something similar to your idea. Now that I've worked out what I don't want to do I need to work out what I do want to do. And if me and Mel don't work out,' I shrugged, 'Dunno, I've been thinking about going away again, take some time out.'

'And see Tim?'

I shook my head. 'No, not alone with Tim and Gabi, I'd feel like a clinger-on. Besides ...'

'What?'

'Well this whole Mel thing. He's really pissed off with me and hasn't been answering any emails. It's all fucked to be honest.'

Freya tilted her head back and finished the last of the wine. She got to her feet and extended her hand down. 'Come on, Mr Grumpy, I can hear them playing "Grease" and I want to dance with you. Try and forget about it for the rest of the night, let's go and dance stupidly.'

I took hold of her outstretched hand and followed her back inside.

Chapter Seventy-Two
December 18th 2008

I CHECKED MY PHONE, nothing from Mel. I checked my inbox, still nothing from Tim. I walked over to the window and gazed out. I felt completely isolated, pretty much alone. It had sunk in now, she still wasn't returning my calls and I was beginning to think she never would.

Rob was making a noise in the kitchen downstairs. He'd been good recently, especially when you consider how awful I must've been to live with since Mel and I broke up.

I heard the doorbell over my music and listened for Jess's voice. Rob's date the other night had gone really well and I knew she was coming over later to watch a DVD. She seemed nice, very very laid back which was perfect for Rob and perfect for the relationship as neither one was rushing into anything at the moment. As Rob had told me before. 'Being with her at the moment is more fun than not being with her so why question it any further?'

Rob's voice boomed up the stairs. 'J? Can you come down here please?' I turned my music off and went down to say hi to Jess.

'Hi.'

I stopped dead on the stairs. 'What the hell are you doing here?'

She looked up at me from the hallway, her long dark hair, soaked from the rain covered most of her face. 'I've come to set a few things straight, to, to apologise really. Is there somewhere we can talk?'

'J, dinner will be ready in fifteen, make it quick. Jazz, you're not welcome for dinner.'

Rob walked back into the kitchen leaving us facing each other.

'Well?'

She looked around. 'Is there somewhere we can go rather than standing in the hall?'

I nodded over to the lounge. 'In there.'

We walked through and sat down at the table.

'So what do you want?'

Jazz swallowed. She looked nervous, a look I'd never seen before and as she lifted her head to match mine I saw a flash of pain behind her eyes.

'I fucked up. J, I'm sorry. So very very sorry.'

I was stunned, she was apologising?

'For what, jumping me or lying to Mel about it after?'

'Everything, I don't know, I wanted to hurt you both, really hurt you.'

'Why?' I said tersely

'I don't quite know why. It all got far too out of hand.'

I raised my voice. 'Too out of hand?! So you planned it all?'

She sighed. 'Look I never meant for all of this to happen.' She looked up at me. 'I promise you.'

I leant back and folded my arms. 'You are aware of how little your promises mean to me, right?'

She nodded.

'So what did you mean to happen?'

'I wanted to kiss you,' she said softly. 'I knew how you'd react, I knew you'd push me away, then I wanted to tell Mel, make it sound as if you'd kissed me.'

I waved my hand exasperatedly. 'But why? Jazz, I don't understand!'

'I wanted to break you guys up,' she said simply.

'Well congratufuckinglations, mission accomplished. Now why are you here, to gloat?'

She paused. 'I saw how much I'd hurt Mel. I'm not here for you J, I'm here for her. She's been a mess, a complete mess these last few weeks and much as I hate to admit it, she's crazy about you and I've just got to take a step back.'

So, Your Girlfriend's a Vegetarian?

I ran my fingers through my hair. 'I'm still confused, "take a step back" from what exactly? Are you talking about me and you because if you think we could ever get back—'

She grimaced. 'No, believe it or not this has nothing to do with me and you. I don't want to get back with you, I think we'd be a disastrous couple.'

I felt a slight wave of rejection. 'You really are going to have to help me out here, why on earth did you do it then?'

Now she raised her voice. 'Because I'm sick of being the only one on my own, OK. Everyone else has it so fucking easy, you have this perfect relationship with Mel, Tim is travelling the world with his girlfriend, Andy and Laura have just got engaged and what have I got? Nothing. Who have I got? No-one. An absent father and a half-dead mother.'

'You've got Mel, well at least you did until recently.'

'That's the point! I don't have her anymore because she's with you all the time! You guys can't spend more than a second apart.'

I snapped back. 'So you tried to break us up because you thought I'd taken her away from you.' I shook my head. 'You're meant to be happy for your friends if they're happy. What does that say about you, Jazz?'

She calmed down. 'Well that's just it, I've realised what I did was wrong and so I've come to apologise.'

'Well that's just great, although you're three weeks too late as Mel isn't even answering my calls. Thanks, you've ruined the best thing in my life.'

A flash of anger raced through her eyes. 'You're not completely blameless in this either, you know.'

'You lied about it! Fine, I shouldn't have kissed you back, I know that, God knows I know that, but when you started lying to Mel about it, what hope was I left with?' I sighed. 'Anyway, have you told Mel all of this?'

She nodded. 'Yeah, I told her everything last night.'

My heart began to thud. 'What did you say to her?'

'The truth. That I'd kissed you, that after the slightest of pauses you'd pushed me back and told me you were in love with her.'

'And what did she say?'

Jazz shrugged. 'I don't know, she's confused.'

'What did you tell her after that evening?'

'That you'd kissed me. That you'd kissed me, I was drunk so kissed you back, then pushed you away, then we had an argument, you left and told me not to tell Mel.'

I shook my head. 'Jesus Jazz. And she believed you?'

Jazz looked down and nodded. 'Yeah, she did.'

'Which would explain why she isn't answering my calls.'

'Yeah, but now she knows that isn't true.'

I felt the blood rush around my head. 'Do you think she'll forgive me?'

'I don't know. She's gone to her parents for a few days, after that who knows. She's not exactly going to confide in me about it.'

'How long were you planning to do this?'

She shook her head. 'I only thought about it when we were waiting for Mel to come home. I dunno, maybe the wine went straight to my head but when I saw the disappointment on your face that Mel was going to be an hour late and you were going to have to talk to me, something in me snapped. I had this sudden feeling that all I was ever going to be was a time-filler, a starter, an insignificance.' She began to get upset. 'That no-one would ever want to be with me, just me.'

I felt a wave of sorrow go through my body and I softened. 'Jazz, you've got to stop comparing everything back to your Dad. Not everyone is going to leave you and the longer you act like this the worse you're going to become and the more you'll push people away.'

She sniffed and looked down. 'I know, I just wanted you both to feel like it feels to be me, miserable and lonely.'

I got up and walked around the lounge. I couldn't believe I was about to say this.

'Jazz you need to sort yourself out, you need to get rid of your past as it's ruining your future.'

Her eyes followed me around the room.

'You need to talk to someone, professionally, because you do have a lot to give, believe me you really do.' I paused and looked straight at her. 'I should know better than most but it's just that you're a little bit lost right now.'

She nodded quickly, holding back the tears. 'After everything I've done to you this year, thank you for saying that.'

I shrugged. 'It's the truth. I've hated you at points over the last few months but I've never forgotten what you've had to deal with on your own. It explains a lot.'

She half smiled through the tears that now ran down her cheeks. 'Anyway, this wasn't meant to be about me, it was meant to be about Mel.' She looked up. 'Go get her, she's in pain and she shouldn't be.'

'You said she's at her parents right?'

She nodded. 'Yeah, she's confused, she's gone probably because she thought I may do something like this. I don't think she's ready to talk about it.'

I got to my feet, 'When is she back?'

'I don't know, she's not exactly talking to me at the moment.'

I felt a pang of pain for Mel. I desperately wanted to see her, to hold her, to make her feel better. Was there now a chance? I prayed she believed Jazz, now all I needed was to talk to her.

Jazz got to her feet. 'You guys are perfect for each other, I can see that now and I'm just sorry that my jealousy got in the way of it. I really really am sorry.' She gulped. 'I hope at some point you can forgive me, both of you.'

I followed Jazz through to the door. 'Let's just see, OK. But I mean it about speaking to a professional, I think it's the best thing to do.'

She nodded. 'I know.' She opened the door and turned to look at me. 'I'm going away for a bit, only to Bristol until after Christmas. I'm sorry J, I really am.' She smiled. 'I hope it works out.'

She disappeared out into the night, closing the door softly behind her.

I turned from the door and immediately pulled out my phone. Dialling Mel's number I willed her to answer. It rang, and rang. She didn't pick up.

Rob stuck his head out from the kitchen. 'Food's ready, Jess will be here in ten, come tell me what the hell that was about!'

Rosemary and Lamb Kebabs with Vegetable Rice

Ingredients

- About 200g lamb steak per person, cut into cubes
- One pack of rosemary
- Two cloves of garlic
- Olive oil
- Three red onions cut into chunks
- One large field mushroom, diced
- Rice for two people
- One vegetable stock cube
- One diced carrot
- Two cloves
- Handful of peas
- Yoghurt (to serve)
- Mint (to serve)

Method

- Dice the lamb and rosemary, slice the garlic and mix with olive oil.
- Leave to chill in the fridge for a few hours.
- Arrange the lamb onto skewers, interspersed by the chunks of mushrooms and onion.
- Boil up some water and start cooking the rice.
- Dice the carrots and add to the boiling water.
- Add a stock cube and the two cloves to the pan.
- Grill the lamb for approximately ten minutes, making sure to turn the skewers every few minutes.
- Drain the rice when cooked, and place the skewers on top.
- Garnish with a dollop of yoghurt and some torn pieces of mint.

Rob shook his head. 'Poor girl, poor poor girl.'

I nodded and dipped a piece of lamb in some yoghurt. 'I know, I really felt sorry for her just now.'

'I didn't realise she was so messed up, I just thought she was a bitch.'

I smiled at Rob's abruptness. 'No, with the right person she can be great, she just needs to get some confidence in herself.'

'And stop screwing over her friends and potential boyfriends.'

'Well that's what she does, she pushes people away and leaves them before they get the chance to leave her, that way she won't get hurt like she did when her Dad left.'

Rob nodded slowly as if understanding Jazz for the first time. 'I can see why you guys would never have worked, you're exactly the same as each other.'

I sat back. 'What?! I would never have done something like that!'

'No, but you run away too. Jesus you'd never both be in the same room, it'd be a nightmare.'

I started to laugh. 'It never ceases to amaze me how you find the funny side of everything.'

He shrugged. 'Nothing is ever as serious as we think it is. Have you spoken to Mel?'

I shook my head. 'No, she's still not picking up. Do you think it's too late?'

Rob chewed his lip. 'I dunno, I honestly don't know. It's been over three weeks, that's quite a long time y'know. But then again this is you and her, I don't think normal rules apply.'

Chapter Seventy-Four
December 20th 2008

'HELLO?'

'Mel, you picked up!'

'Yeah I did.'

'Where are you? Are you in London?'

'Yes I'm in London, why wouldn't I be?'

'I just thought that you may have …'

'Why, did you speak to Jazz?'

I fell silent for a second.

'Yes.'

'Right, I thought she would've told you.'

'So, can I see you? I'd love to see you Mel.'

I could tell she was shaking her head, 'No J, no you can't'.

I didn't push it. 'OK, well is it OK if we talk for a bit now?'

'Yeah, that's OK.'

'How are you?'

'OK, I've been at home for a bit, spending some time with Alexia, catching up with old friends.'

'When did you get back?'

'Yesterday, it's quite nice having the place to myself. I think I need it. Besides, I'm working loads up until Christmas which is good, it keeps my mind off of things.'

I felt sick with nerves, I was struggling to hold the phone as my hands were shaking so much. 'Mel, I am so so sorry. You were right when you said whatever Jazz told you doesn't matter, I should never have done it and I should have told you right away. I love you, I love you so much and the thought that I've been causing you pain over the last few weeks has killed me.'

I paused, she said nothing back.

I carried on. 'And, and if you could find it in your heart to forgive me I would never ever do anything like this ever again.' I heard her sniff. 'I would always be completely honest with you, and I would treat you like you deserve to be treated.'

I stopped and hoped she'd say something.

She took a deep breath. 'I'm so confused right now. I don't think you'll ever know how much you hurt me, most of all because it was with Jazz, but now I find out that she was lying all the time and ...' She sighed. 'I don't know what to believe, part of me just wants to chuck it all in and start afresh somewhere else where I don't have to see either of you ...'

'Mel don't do that, don't do that. We are meant to be together, you know that.' I heard her breathe heavily. 'Remember New York? Remember dancing together in "Café Wha?" I want to have that feeling with you for the rest of my life. Don't let this stupid mistake ruin that, please.'

'I need some time J. I need to work out what I want.'

'That's fine, take as long as you need, I'm not going anywhere.'

She regained her composure. 'I'm not promising anything, far from it.'

'Look, I promise I'll respect your decision, I'll stop calling if that's what you want. But, just don't forget how the last few months have felt, OK?'

I felt anger surge inside her. 'J, you can't say that, you ruined it, all of it! I can't think of New York or Barcelona without thinking of you and Jazz ...'

'But she told you that—'

'Yes, she told me that you didn't start it, but you still kissed her back knowing full well how paranoid I was. That's what you still don't get J, you don't respect me!'

'Mel, please believe me I really do. Love is respect isn't it? I love you, I respect you.'

'I don't believe you, you can't do that to someone you love.'

I sighed deeply. 'I do love you, more than I have anyone I've ever met. And you're right, I should have pushed her away immediately but I didn't, and I'm truly sorry but please don't let that ruin everything.'

'J I'm gonna go, I need some space. I'll call you after Christmas so please don't call me before.'

'OK I won't. You know I'd love for you to still come to my Mum's.'

'That's not gonna happen.'

'OK.' I paused. 'Are you going home for Christmas?'

'Yeah I think so, I'll call you soon.'

'OK, I'll speak to you soon then.'

'Yeah, oh and J?'

'Yeah?'

'Happy Birthday.'

She hung up.

Chapter Seventy-Five
December 25th 2008

IT **WAS WITH A** strange feeling that I sped down the motorway towards St Albans. I felt like it was all hanging in the balance and I wasn't really in control of any of it. I didn't know if I should be optimistic about Mel or if I was just deluding myself and come next week I'd come crashing down to earth, single and soon to be jobless.

Matt and I had been in charge of Christmas lunch for the last four or five years. Each year we followed the same ritual where Mum would make scrambled eggs and smoked salmon for breakfast, with the odd glass of champagne or white wine, and then Matt and I would take over in the kitchen. It was something we both loved doing, and a real bonding moment each year. This year we were trying goose with a spicy citrus rub. It would be accompanied by sweet potatoes and King Edward roast potatoes, honeyed carrots, Brussels sprouts, bacon and chestnuts, a joint of beef, pigs in blankets and thick gravy.

Citrus Spiced Goose

Ingredients
- One very very large goose
- Four large oranges
- Two large lemons
- One spoonful of Chinese 5 spice
- Two spoonfuls of olive oil
- Grated nutmeg
- Two pinches of rock salt

Method

- Grate the oranges and lemons into a bowl and combine with the nutmeg, salt and Chinese 5 spice.

- Add the olive oil and mix so it becomes a paste.

- Score the goose, making sure to cut quite deep as it's coated in fat.

- Rub the spices into the goose, massaging them in and ensuring everything is coated.

- Cut the leftover oranges and lemons into quarters and place inside the goose.

- Cover and refrigerate overnight if possible, if not then at least for a few hours.

- When it's time to cook, heat the oven to 180 degrees and roast for fifteen minutes per 450 grams, plus an extra twenty minutes.

- Geese produce a lot of fat so frequently drain it off, but keep it for cooking the potatoes.

- When it's ready remove from the oven, wrap in foil and leave to rest for ten minutes before carving.

Roast Sweet and King Edward Potatoes

Ingredients

- Roughly two potatoes per person, peeled and cut into irregular sized chunks
- Two cloves of garlic
- Clear blossom honey
- A few sprigs of fresh rosemary
- Black pepper
- Goose fat

Method

- Boil the potatoes for around ten minutes then coat the King Edward Potatoes in goose fat and cook in the oven for ten minutes.

- After ten minutes coat the sweet potatoes and add to the King Edwards, adding the rosemary, black pepper and garlic, cook for another half an hour.

- Remove and cover with honey, put back into the oven and cook for another twenty minutes.

Honeyed Carrots

Ingredients
- Several carrots, at least three per person, peeled and sliced into long thick strips.
- Clear blossom honey.

Method
- Add two spoonfuls of honey to boiling water, and boil the carrots for ten minutes.
- Drain, drizzle with more honey and serve.

Of course, we'd started drinking with breakfast at eleven, which meant we were a little bit tipsy when we started cooking lunch, but that just made it more fun especially when it came to stuffing the goose.

Matt is scared of raw meat so I was in charge of disposing of the innards whilst he peeled the potatoes and carrots. Mum was in the lounge reading a travel book on Vietnam I'd bought her (she was off in February) so it gave me and Matt time to catch up. I speak to him most weeks but we had been a bit slack recently and hadn't seen each other for a few months so he was a bit clueless as to what had been happening. As much as he was trying to put on a brave face, even he was wondering about whether Mel and I had a future.

'The way I see it is that before Jazz owned up to everything, you were out, you had no chance but now, well maybe there is a chance.' He paused. 'Thing is, I know you'll hate me for saying this but don't you think you're better off making a clean break?'

I looked up from the orange I was trying to grate without cutting myself. 'Why on earth would you say that?'

'Well think about it, this will never be over. Knowing Mel like I do there is no way she is going to give up on Jazz. Instead it'll be the opposite, she'll be there to support her even more and will probably even end up feeling guilty herself about the whole thing.'

'You're probably right.'

'Yeah, so my question is do you want to get caught up in that? Do you want to have the burden of being one of two people responsible for looking after Jazz and helping her get back on her feet?'

I shook my head, 'No, but there is no way I'm walking away.'

'Look I'm your brother, I have to look out for you or no-one else will; I'm just saying I've been with damaged people whilst they're getting help and it's pretty hard.'

'But I won't be with her, I'll hopefully be with Mel.'

'But she will be with Jazz constantly, and you know she will,' Matt insisted. 'Just be aware of what you're walking into OK?'

I nodded. 'I will, but I'd do anything to get her back, I don't care if that means helping out with Jazz. Anyway, who knows if I'll even have that chance?'

Matt looked up from the carrots. 'What do you mean?'

I shrugged. 'Well it's been almost a month and I've seen her once and spoken to her once. I have this horrible sickly feeling that she's moving on from me and there's nothing I can do about it.'

'I think you've done all you can and now you have to wait. I mean she said she'd call you next week didn't she?'

'Yeah, but I hate just waiting for my phone to ring, it's paralysing. Every time I take a shower I'm scared I'm gonna miss her call.'

'How do you think you'd be if she didn't want to get back together?'

'Ruined.'

'No you wouldn't.'

I looked at him straight on. 'Matt you haven't seen me as much since we've been going out. She's become everything.'

'You sure?'

'Yes.'

'She'll call. C'mon, it's Christmas, let's go wind up Mum.'

Matt left the kitchen to go next door. I pulled out my phone and quickly sent a text.

So, Your Girlfriend's a Vegetarian?

Hey, I know I'm not meant to contact you but I just wanted to say Merry Christmas. Lots of love, J x

I put the goose in the oven, giving us a good hour before we needed to start cooking everything else, and went into the lounge. The room was as Christmassy as it could be. Every year Mum gets excited at having 'ma boys' home for a few days and so stocks the fridge with every food imaginable, has boxes of chocolates lying around everywhere and buys a ridiculously large Christmas tree. This year it stood proud in the corner by the window, its arms draped in tinsel, chocolate and flashing fluorescent lights.

At the table Mum had already set out the Scrabble board and was picking her letters. I sat down and pulled out a handful and started rearranging them in front of me. 'You are all gonna kick my arse, I haven't played this in ages.'

Matt looked at me from underneath a bright orange paper hat. 'You're the youngest, you're not supposed to win.'

'Well who is?' Mum looked up. 'Not you I hope?'

Matt flexed his muscles. 'Course it's me, your brain cells are dying off, he doesn't have any, whereas I'm in peak condition, now let's start.'

We started playing as a relaxed silence flooded over us. We talked a bit about our lives, about work and about relationships. Both Mum and Matt had broken up with their respective partners over the last few months, both citing a lack of either banter in Matt's case or maturity in Mum's case and now both were happy on their own. I guess I'd been living in quite a bubble recently, what with India, getting together with Mel, saying goodbye to Tim, moving house, Barcelona, New York and then breaking up with Mel. I hadn't taken much time to properly find out what was going on with my family and that made me feel bad. It also reassured me that life does go on. Just as Rob said a few days ago, nothing is ever as serious as people think it is. Yeah, I will be devastated if Mel and I never get back together but I'll get over it at some point. I looked at my Mum and brother, heads lowered, brows furrowed, concentrating on the letters in front of them and I felt a wave of familiarity and protectiveness. Whatever had happened over the last year, all the heartbreaks or feelings of joy, I was here with my family playing Scrabble just as I had been last year, and fingers crossed, just as I would be next year. There is no place I'd rather be. Sure I want to have Mel sitting at my side next year, and I'm sure both Matt and Mum want people there too, but if that doesn't happen it doesn't happen and we move on with our lives. January was just around the corner, and if I was facing it on my own, then so be it, at least I'd be facing it knowing I had the support of my family in whatever I did.

I looked up and smiled at my Mum, who smiled back, but mainly because she'd just laid down an eight-letter word.

Matt came last, which made me laugh out loud, lots. Mum ended up winning, meaning Matt made a very quiet retreat to the kitchen to put the potatoes on.

As soon as he left, my Mum reached for my hand. 'You OK?'

I nodded. 'Yeah I am, I really am. Whatever happens I'll deal with it, I know I can.' I grimaced. ' I just wish I had a bit of control over things y'know.'

She smiled and put her hand to my cheek. 'Mel is an amazing girl darling. If she takes you back you make sure you never give her any reason to do this again. If you have lost her, well you'll get through it; you've got all of us. It won't be as bad as you may think. Remember J, whatever happens it always happens for the best even if you can't quite see it yet.'

'I know Mum, I know.'

The goose was awesome, definitely never going back to turkey. As predicted we got absolutely stuffed and couldn't even finish our plates let alone the cheesecake sitting in the fridge. As is another tradition in our family, on Christmas Day we spent the afternoon and evening watching back-to-back films we'd hired. Not coming from a big family we'd never had the sort of Christmas where you have twenty people sitting around a room pretending to like each other. Instead we locked ourselves away, didn't see anyone for two days, ate and watched TV, I loved it.

Mum fell asleep shortly into the second film and was out for the count. Matt and I sprawled out on the two couches, ridiculously content and munching our way through obscene amounts of Quality Street chocolates. I was right, this was just what I needed. Conversation was sporadic and unnecessary as we both began to doze off; the half-empty glass of red wine in my hand added to my meat-induced sleepiness.

Suddenly my phone vibrated to life and shook me from my half-sleep.

Open the door

A momentary confusion and I sprang up immediately. She couldn't be, could she? My Mum and Matt sat up as I leapt over their outstretched legs and ran down the stairs. I heard my Mum shout after me as I fumbled with the keys and yanked open the door. I ran out into the cold evening and looked down the street. There she was. She stood on the other side of the road, half bathed in the glow of a nearby streetlight. Shaking, I ran towards her, the freezing cold night jarring my warm limbs and sending chills up through my shoeless feet. She held out her hands and I took them, squeezing them hard.

'I can't believe you're here.'

She smiled coyly. 'I had to see you, I can't explain it, but I just had to see you.'

I opened my mouth to speak but she raised a finger to my lips. 'When you sent me that text this morning I suddenly realised that it was all up to me, that if I only said yes I could get that feeling back and J, I want that feeling back.'

I took her in my arms and kissed her deeply. I felt tears run down her cheeks and mix in with mine. Pulling apart I looked at her before kissing her again. 'I want that back too, I have missed you so much.' I squeezed her hands tightly. 'I promise I will never ever fuck up like that again.'

She shook her head and for a brief second I saw a toughness in her watery eyes. 'No you won't, consider this your second chance. As much as I wish it wasn't so at times, I'm in love with you, stupidly in love with you and I always want to be in love with you. So,' she shrugged, 'here I am.'

I hugged her tightly and kissed her again. 'Come inside, it's freezing.'

She took my hand and we walked across the road. 'I'm starving, got any food?'

Epilogue
December 31st 2008

THERE IS DEFINITELY SOMETHING to be said for having a naked picnic in bed on New Year's Eve. Obviously if you have your girlfriend with you as well then that is even better.

Me and Mel, well we were going to be OK, more than OK actually. Since Christmas Day we'd spent every second together. At my Mum's that evening, her parents' on Boxing Day (they were a little annoyed that their daughter had run out of the house as soon as lunch was finished on Christmas Day) and then in my flat since the day after Boxing Day. I had of course apologised so many times, she'd cried a lot and got a bit angry again, wanting to know exactly what happened and how it happened. I'd told her every minute detail, and now it was something we just wanted to put behind us. I fucked up, I fucked up big time and Mel forgave me. End of.

Tim had finally emailed me from Mexico over Christmas. I guess Rob must have filled him in on what happened in the lead-up to the holidays and that even though I had been a dick, it hadn't been as bad as Tim first thought. He wasn't exactly apologetic, I think he was still pretty angry with me, but at least we were talking again.

As far as Jazz was concerned, Mel really didn't know what to do. She'd hurt her so much and considering they were best friends, that was something Mel had found really hard to digest. In fact it had taken a while for Mel to see that it really wasn't about Jazz hating her or being jealous of her relationship with me, it was Jazz hating herself and not letting herself be happy. Mel was gonna forgive her, that was never really in doubt, and I know she will support her through counselling, I just hope that it won't intrude on our relationship and put that under strain.

A lot has happened over the last few months, I feel like I've hit the ground running since India and not really stopped since. It's weird how it all works out though; I might have woken up this year in bed with Jazz but I'm putting this year to bed with Mel, something I never imagined I would do but now that it's a reality I can't imagine next year without her. I guess Mum was right when she said everything always works out for the best.

I can't help thinking about what's around the corner though. I'm gearing up to leave my job, something that worries me as I don't know what I want to do but I also feel it's about time that I manned up and worked out what it is I do want to do. But is that settling? I hope not.

I opened the next bottle of champagne and refilled Mel's glass. She dipped some pitta bread in hummus and placed it in my mouth before leaning in and kissing my nose.

'You look deep in thought,' she said.

'I'm always deep in thought!'

'Only about things like crisps though, what's up?'

I shrugged. 'Dunno, just letting the last twelve months go round in my head.'

She smiled. 'Quite eventful really, for all of us.'

'Yeah. Yeah they have been.'

She went quiet for a moment. 'Are you going to quit on Monday?'

I nodded. 'Why?'

'I think I'm going to do the same.'

I raised my eyebrow. 'Really?'

She nodded. 'I'm desperately unhappy at work; it's not what I thought it would be like at all and I don't think I want to do it anymore.'

I picked up some smoked salmon and dangled it in her mouth. 'So what instead?'

'That's the problem, no idea.' I stroked her hair as her head rested on my chest. She continued. 'But I do feel like we're growing up.'

'I know what you mean, it's like we need to start making those decisions about what we actually want to do with our lives.'

She sat up. 'Well, what do you want to do?'

'I don't know. At this moment in time all I know is that I want to be with you. If I had to guess I'd say I want to do something where I use my languages but I don't know what.'

She thought for a minute. 'OK, ask me.'

'What do you want to do?'

'I want to be a doctor, use the skills I've got but I don't want to do it here.'

'Well, where do you want to do it?'

'I don't know yet. Why, where do you want to find a job?'

I shrugged. 'I don't know yet either.'

She paused and then looked at me straight in the eyes. 'Why don't we go find a place?'

My brow furrowed. 'What, do a Gabi and Tim?'

She nodded and sat up excitedly. 'Sort of. I want to see the world again, I want to feel like there's life outside of this city. That London isn't the be-all and end-all. J let's do it. We're both quitting, we both can't afford to stay in London unemployed, hell we don't even think that we want to work here anyway.'

Her excitement was infectious. 'Go on.'

'Well, you just said that you feel we need to start making decisions.' She grabbed my hands. 'This is one of those times. We've got each other, we don't need anyone else. Let's put a bag on our shoulders and go out and see the world, spend a few months here, a few months there.' She smiled broadly. 'You're thinking about it, I can tell you are.'

I smiled back. 'Leaving the country with you, not knowing where we're going, what we'll do or where we'll end up …'

She nodded. 'But knowing we'll be together.'

'But knowing we'll be together.'

She sat astride me and rested her arms on my shoulders. 'What do you say?'

I grinned and pulled her towards me. 'That I can't think of anything else I'd rather do.'

The End

Coming soon:

So, Your Girlfriend Wants to go Travelling?

Prologue

I WAS TRAPPED.

To my left was a thin wall of metal and glass and to my right was my comatose girlfriend. She hadn't so much as moved in six hours and I was almost at breaking point. I tried to climb over her but that didn't work, I tried to climb out from behind me but I was blocked in by the wall so instead I slumped back down in my seat and looked out of the window. We should be landing in a couple of hours anyway, I guess I can hold on until then.

We were apparently flying over the Amazon, although it was pitch black outside and all I could see was the blinking light of the wing and my pale reflection in the plastic window cover. I shuffled around and tried to get comfortable but what with my knees being up by my ears and the baby crying two rows in front I resigned myself to another sleepless flight. Jealously looking at Mel I half considered pinging her eye mask back onto her face but thought she probably wouldn't find it funny to be woken up like that. At least that way I'd be able to go to the toilet.

Cranning my neck to see the screen showing the inflight movie a dozen rows in front, I plugged my headphones in and watched, through the afro of the guy in front of me, a very bad dubbing of James Bond into French. Contemplating suicide I flicked through the radio channels in an attempt to encounter just a smidge of distraction from the humming of the aircraft. Finding the Air France relaxation channel I settled back and let the music flow over me. Feeling a surge of tiredness I allowed myself to become enveloped by my seat, which all of a sudden felt like an armchair. Maybe I would be able to sleep for a little bit.....

I opened my eyes all of two minutes later as the sound of an explosion from the film through everyone else's headphones shook me awake. My body thanked me for the nap and began to start up again, pushing all images and feelings of sleep as far away as possible. I lifted my window shutter fully and was just in time for dawn. The sky was a multitude of dark and light blues and fierce yellows as in the distance a shimmer of light began to make itself known. The new sun illuminated the sea of clouds beneath us and began to fill the cabin with light. Today was the start of our travels. Today was the beginning of a new life for me and Mel for whilst we had passports and boarding cards in our pockets, we had no return tickets. Whilst we had ideas about where we wanted this next stage to take us, we couldnt be sure for certain where it would. And I loved that uncertainty.

Soon enough we'd be landing and all the plans we'd made over the last few weeks would suddenly become real. Even though we were at 50,000 feet I felt the warmth of the rising sun on my face. At this moment we had no place in the world, we were merely hovering above it and this moment, this calm before the storm was a moment to be cherished.

A severe looking air hostess reached across and slammed the window shutter shut, blocking out the dawn.

'Sir the other passengers are still asleep, keep the light out.'

I sighed and turned back to the mute film.

XXXXXXXXXXXXXXXXXXXXXXXXXXXXXXXXXXXXXXXXXXXXXXXXXXXX

I looked up at the rain smashing down hard above me and breathed deeply. The storm, which had been threatening for hours was now upon us as thick grey clouds swamped the sky and took out the sun. A crack of thunder immediately followed a flash of lightning as the rain poured down heavier, as if the previous half an hour had merely been a practice round, a warm up for the main act.

Luckily I was thirty metres underwater and it was seventy degrees

I turned from looking up at the surface and swam down to join the rest of the group. Pattie, my instructor motioned at me to look into the reef we were currently hovering above and I half somersaulted and kicked down, head first. A small black cave, no wider than a football opened up in front of me and deep in the blackness I could just about make out a moray eel opening and closing its mouth in warning. Two rows of sharp teeth glistened in the gloom as its dead black eyes flickered from my face to Pattie's. Using one hand and my chin I opened the viewfinder of my Christmas present and aimed it into the hole. Knowing full well it would never come out I took aim and snapped at the eel.

Reversing out from the reef I flipped onto my back and looked up at the sky. The rain still beat down but the surface of the ocean acted like a windscreen. Above me there was such power crashing down to earth but here, a little way below it, all was tranquil, everything moved in that slow lullaby way, back and forth, back and forth.

Feeling a hand wriggle its way into mine I looked up and smiled at Gabi. Obviously, smiling with a regulator in your mouth underwater is a pretty stupid thing to do and as I coughed a lungful of saltwater hard into my mouthpiece I made a note not to do that again. Day four of dive school tiger, you're not Jacques Costeau yet. Gabi swam down to me and using her eyes to smile, gave my little finger a squeeze to check I was ok. Her loose hair waved in front of her mask like branches in the wind, making it hard to catch her eyes so I opted for a reciprocated finger squeeze, how could anything not be fine?

Pattie twanged the bungee cord wrapped around her oxygen tank, sending soundwaves reverberating around us. She looked at all of us and raised her thumb, dive talk for time's up. Looking up at the surface we began to kick slowly up, spiralling as we went. At five metres below the surface we paused for a safety stop to let the nitrogen in our blood escape. Hovering between the two worlds I felt magical, as if I was flying, and well looking at the ocean floor deep beneath me, I guess I was. Gently kicking up I made my final ascent, the sounds of the world we'd left behind came rushing to my ears as I got nearer and ever nearer, until I broke the surface and emerged back into life. I inflated my life jacket and lay on my back, allowing myself to be gently rocked by the waves. Gabi broke through just to my right and after doing the same, allowed me a cheeky grin

'Tim, I'm going to make a pledge right now to spend every New Year's Day doing this!'

I kicked my legs gently and floated over to her. 'I guess we should never go to Iceland for Christmas then?'

She shook her head. 'Nup, I think we've stumbled upon the key to a happy life, sun in winter. Race you back.'

Gabi swam off back to the boat where the other divers were beginning to make their way out of the water. I waited a few seconds before swimming after her, resisting the urge to pull at her ankles and get in front.

Recipes

Breakfast

Starters, Sides, Snacks and Tapas

Main Courses

Desserts

Drinks